HELLBOY AND THE BUREAU FOR PARANORMAL RESEARCH AND DEFENSE

1955

Created by MIKE MIGNOLA

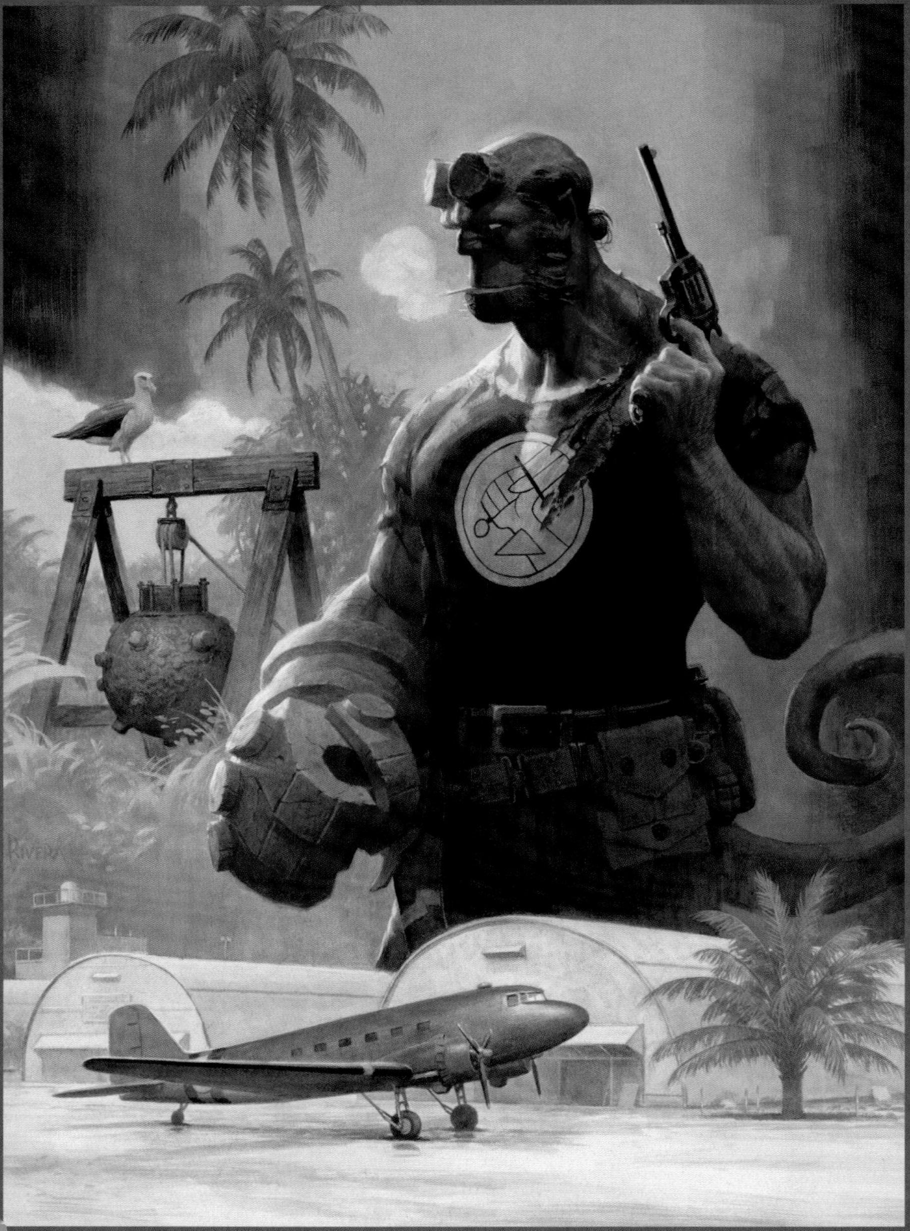

MIKE MIGNOLA'S

HELLBOY
AND THE B.P.R.D. 1955

Stories by
MIKE MIGNOLA & CHRIS ROBERSON

SECRET NATURE
Art by SHAWN MARTINBROUGH

✠

OCCULT INTELLIGENCE
Art by BRIAN CHURILLA

✠

BURNING SEASON
Pencils by PAOLO RIVERA
Inks by JOE RIVERA

✠

Colors by DAVE STEWART
Letters by CLEM ROBINS
Cover art by PAOLO RIVERA
Chapter break art by
PAOLO RIVERA, SHAWN MARTINBROUGH,
& DAVE STEWART

Publisher MIKE RICHARDSON ✠ *Editors* SCOTT ALLIE *and* KATII O'BRIEN
Collection Designer PATRICK SATTERFIELD ✠ *Digital Art Technician* CHRISTINA McKENZIE

DARK HORSE BOOKS

Special thanks to Sanjay Dharawat

Published by Dark Horse Books
A division of Dark Horse Comics, Inc.
10956 SE Main Street • Milwaukie, OR 97222

DarkHorse.com
International Licensing (503) 905-2377
Comic Shop Locator Service ComicShopLocator.com

First edition: June 2018
ISBN 978-1-50670-531-6

1 3 5 7 9 10 8 6 4 2
Printed in China

Hellboy and the B.P.R.D.: 1955

This book collects Hellboy and the B.P.R.D.: 1955—Secret Nature, Hellboy and the B.P.R.D.: 1955—Occult Intelligence #1–#3, and Hellboy and the B.P.R.D.: 1955—Burning Season.

Library of Congress Cataloging-in-Publication Data

Names: Mignola, Michael, author. | Roberson, Chris, author. | Martinbrough, Shawn, artist. | Churilla, Brian, artist. | Rivera, Paolo, 1981- penciller, artist. | Rivera, Joe, inker. | Stewart, Dave, colourist, artist. | Robins, Clem, 1955- letterer.
Title: Hellboy and the B.P.R.D., 1955 / stories by Mike Mignola and Chris Roberson ; Secret Nature art by Shawn Martinbrough, Occult Intelligence art by Brian Churilla, Burning Season pencils by Paolo Rivera, inks by Joe Rivera ; colors by Dave Stewart ; letters by Clem Robins ; cover art by Paolo Rivera ; chapter break art by Paolo Rivera, Shawn Martinbrough, and Dave Stewart.
Other titles: B.P.R.D. 1955 | 1955 | At head of title: Mike Mignola's
Description: First edition. | Milwaukie, OR : Dark Horse Books, 2018. | "This book collects Hellboy and the B.P.R.D.: 1955-Secret Nature, Hellboy and the B.P.R.D.: 1955-Occult Intelligence #1-#3, and Hellboy and the B.P.R.D.: 1955-Burning Season."
Identifiers: LCCN 2017058401 | ISBN 9781506705316 (paperback)
Subjects: LCSH: Comic books, strips, etc. | BISAC: COMICS & GRAPHIC NOVELS / Horror. | COMICS & GRAPHIC NOVELS / Fantasy. | FICTION / Occult & Supernatural.
Classification: LCC PN6727.M53 H376 2018 | DDC 741.5/973--dc23
LC record available at https://lccn.loc.gov/2017058401

SECRET NATURE

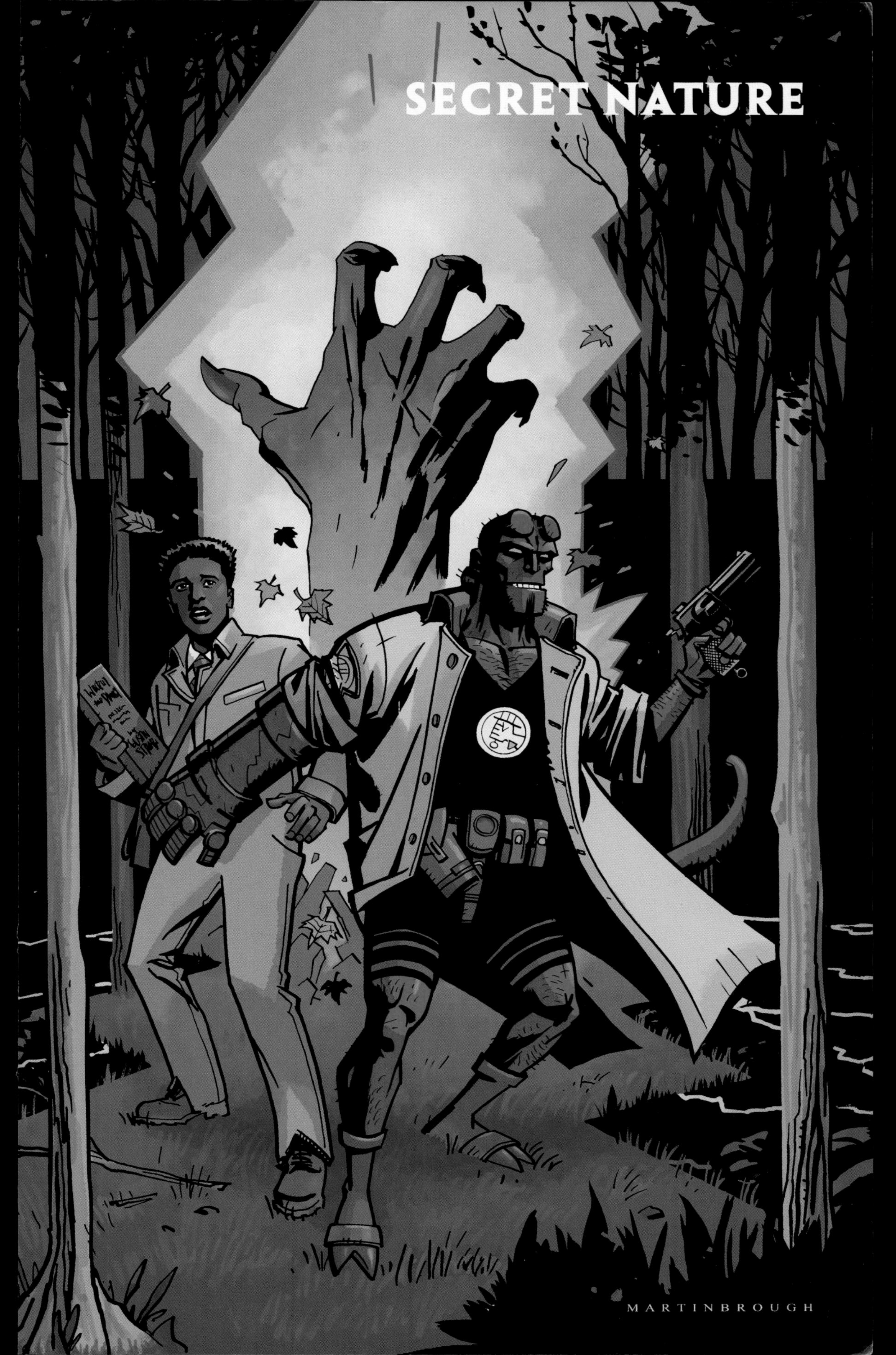
MARTINBROUGH

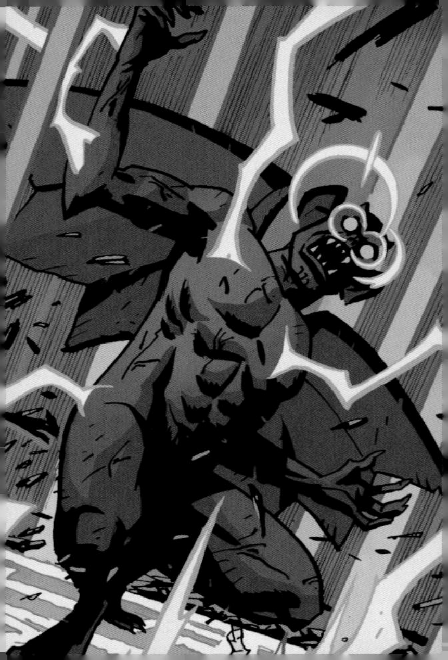

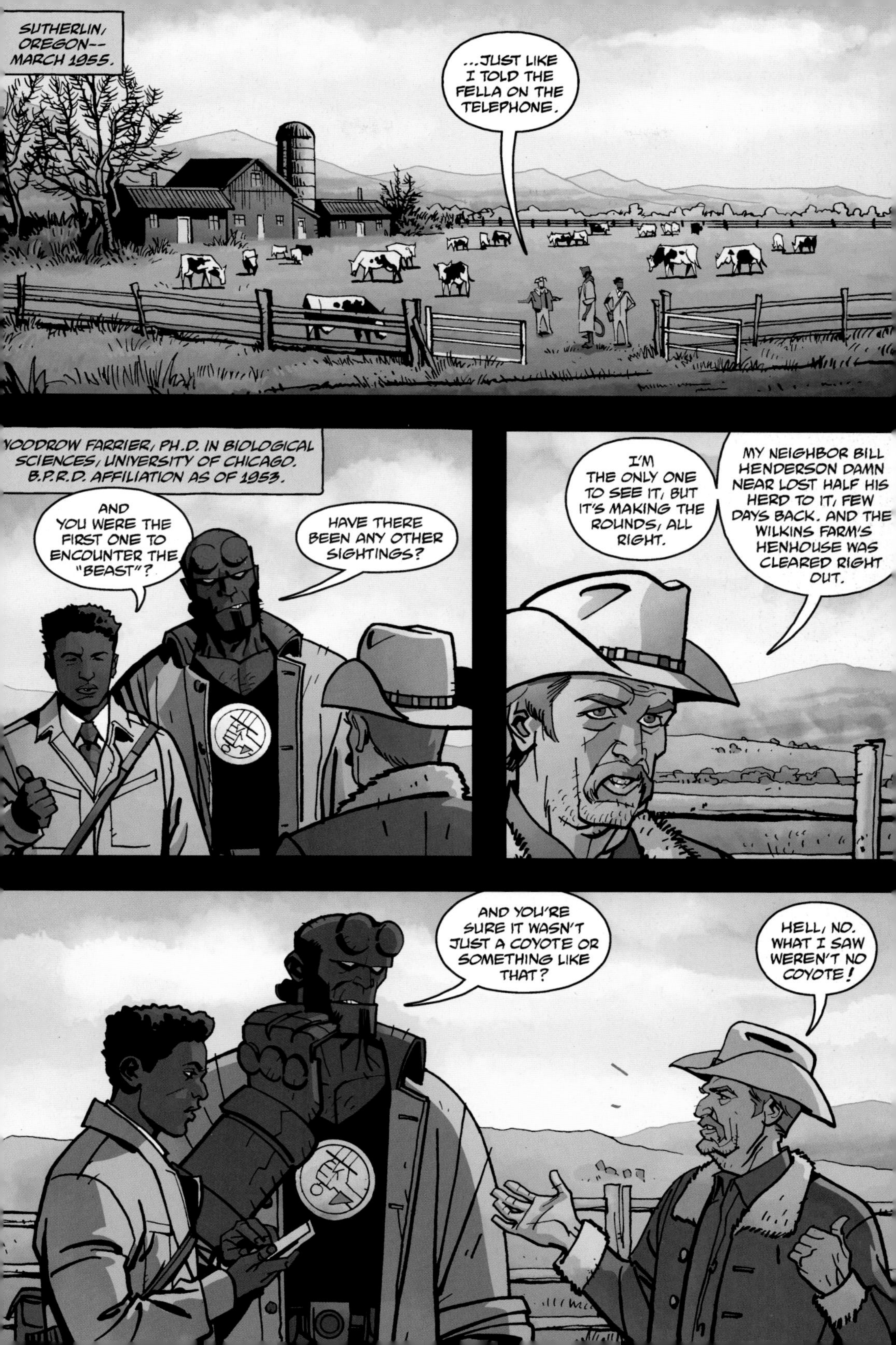
SUTHERLIN, OREGON-- MARCH 1955.
...JUST LIKE I TOLD THE FELLA ON THE TELEPHONE.
WOODROW FARRIER, PH.D. IN BIOLOGICAL SCIENCES, UNIVERSITY OF CHICAGO. B.P.R.D. AFFILIATION AS OF 1953.
AND YOU WERE THE FIRST ONE TO ENCOUNTER THE "BEAST"?
HAVE THERE BEEN ANY OTHER SIGHTINGS?
I'M THE ONLY ONE TO SEE IT, BUT IT'S MAKING THE ROUNDS, ALL RIGHT.
MY NEIGHBOR BILL HENDERSON DAMN NEAR LOST HALF HIS HERD TO IT, FEW DAYS BACK. AND THE WILKINS FARM'S HENHOUSE WAS CLEARED RIGHT OUT.
AND YOU'RE SURE IT WASN'T JUST A COYOTE OR SOMETHING LIKE THAT?
HELL, NO. WHAT I SAW WEREN'T NO COYOTE!

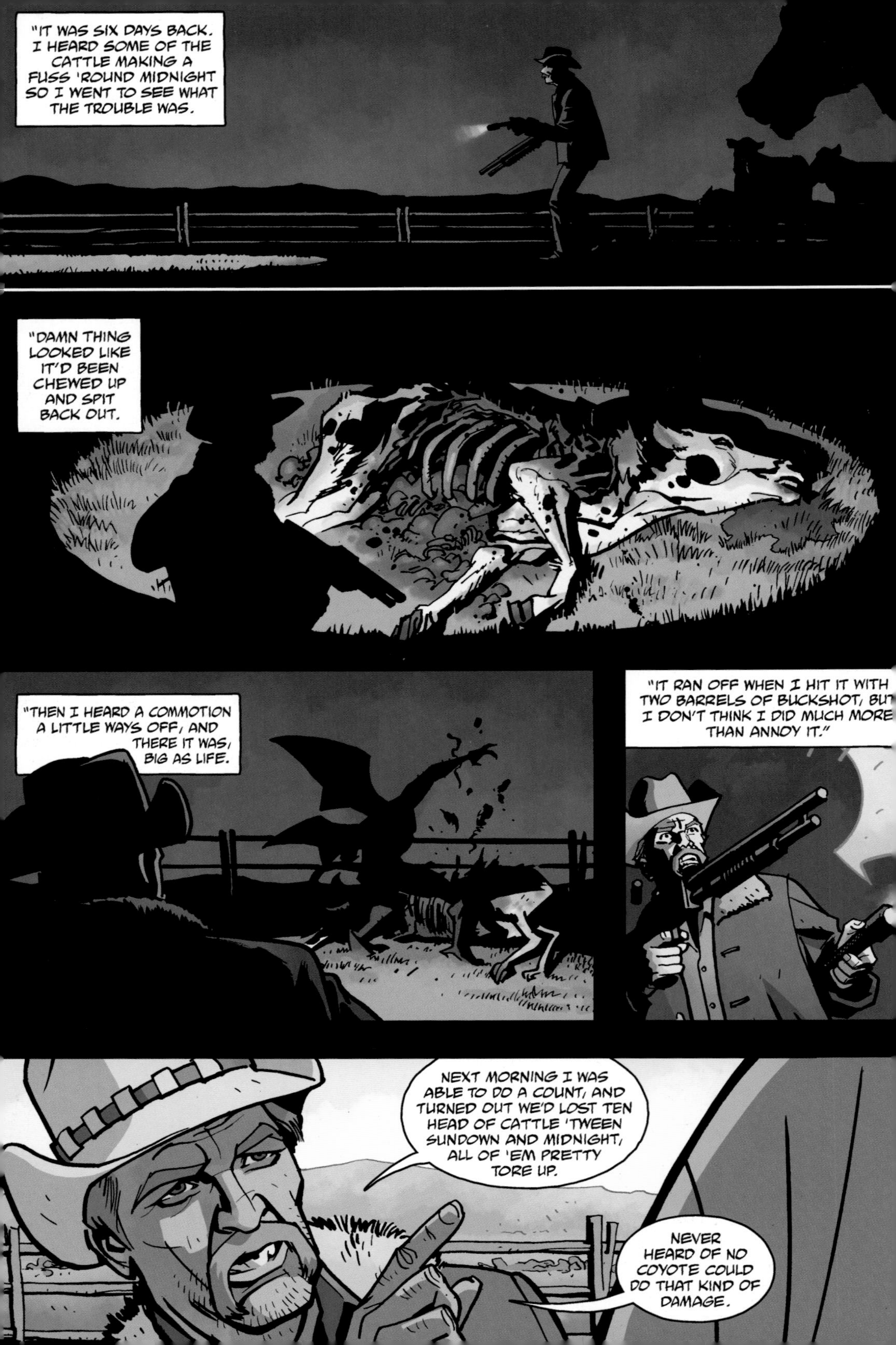
"IT WAS SIX DAYS BACK. I HEARD SOME OF THE CATTLE MAKING A FUSS 'ROUND MIDNIGHT SO I WENT TO SEE WHAT THE TROUBLE WAS.
"DAMN THING LOOKED LIKE IT'D BEEN CHEWED UP AND SPIT BACK OUT.
"THEN I HEARD A COMMOTION A LITTLE WAYS OFF, AND THERE IT WAS, BIG AS LIFE.
"IT RAN OFF WHEN I HIT IT WITH TWO BARRELS OF BUCKSHOT, BUT I DON'T THINK I DID MUCH MORE THAN ANNOY IT."
NEXT MORNING I WAS ABLE TO DO A COUNT, AND TURNED OUT WE'D LOST TEN HEAD OF CATTLE 'TWEEN SUNDOWN AND MIDNIGHT, ALL OF 'EM PRETTY TORE UP.
NEVER HEARD OF NO COYOTE COULD DO THAT KIND OF DAMAGE.

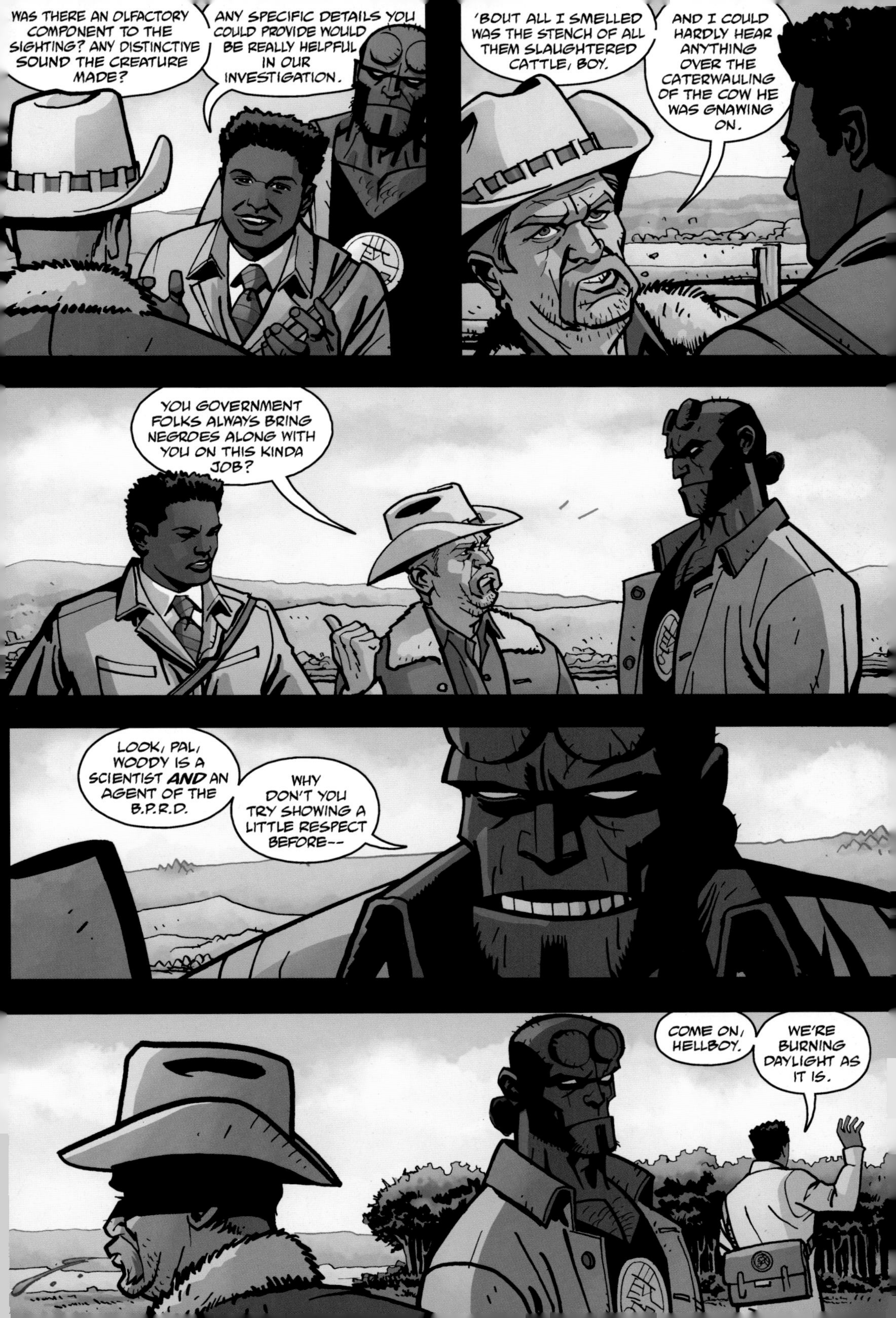
WAS THERE AN OLFACTORY COMPONENT TO THE SIGHTING? ANY DISTINCTIVE SOUND THE CREATURE MADE?
ANY SPECIFIC DETAILS YOU COULD PROVIDE WOULD BE REALLY HELPFUL IN OUR INVESTIGATION.
'BOUT ALL I SMELLED WAS THE STENCH OF ALL THEM SLAUGHTERED CATTLE, BOY.
AND I COULD HARDLY HEAR ANYTHING OVER THE CATERWAULING OF THE COW HE WAS GNAWING ON.
YOU GOVERNMENT FOLKS ALWAYS BRING NEGROES ALONG WITH YOU ON THIS KINDA JOB?
LOOK, PAL, WOODY IS A SCIENTIST **AND** AN AGENT OF THE B.P.R.D.
WHY DON'T YOU TRY SHOWING A LITTLE RESPECT BEFORE--
COME ON, HELLBOY.
WE'RE BURNING DAYLIGHT AS IT IS.

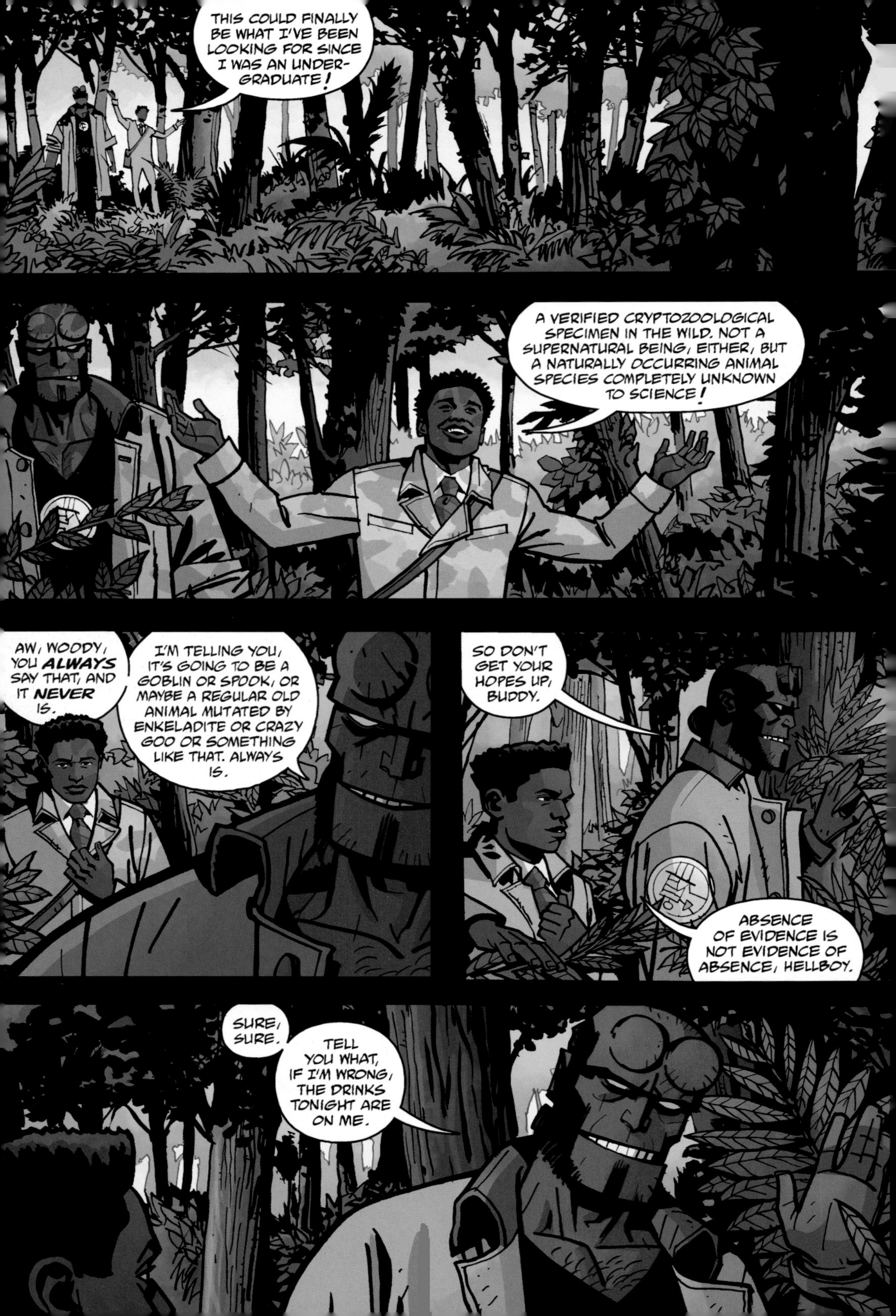
THIS COULD FINALLY BE WHAT I'VE BEEN LOOKING FOR SINCE I WAS AN UNDER-GRADUATE!
A VERIFIED CRYPTOZOOLOGICAL SPECIMEN IN THE WILD. NOT A SUPERNATURAL BEING, EITHER, BUT A NATURALLY OCCURRING ANIMAL SPECIES COMPLETELY UNKNOWN TO SCIENCE!
AW, WOODY, YOU **ALWAYS** SAY THAT, AND IT **NEVER** IS.
I'M TELLING YOU, IT'S GOING TO BE A GOBLIN OR SPOOK, OR MAYBE A REGULAR OLD ANIMAL MUTATED BY ENKELADITE OR CRAZY GOO OR SOMETHING LIKE THAT. ALWAYS IS.
SO DON'T GET YOUR HOPES UP, BUDDY.
ABSENCE OF EVIDENCE IS NOT EVIDENCE OF ABSENCE, HELLBOY.
SURE, SURE.
TELL YOU WHAT, IF I'M WRONG, THE DRINKS TONIGHT ARE ON ME.

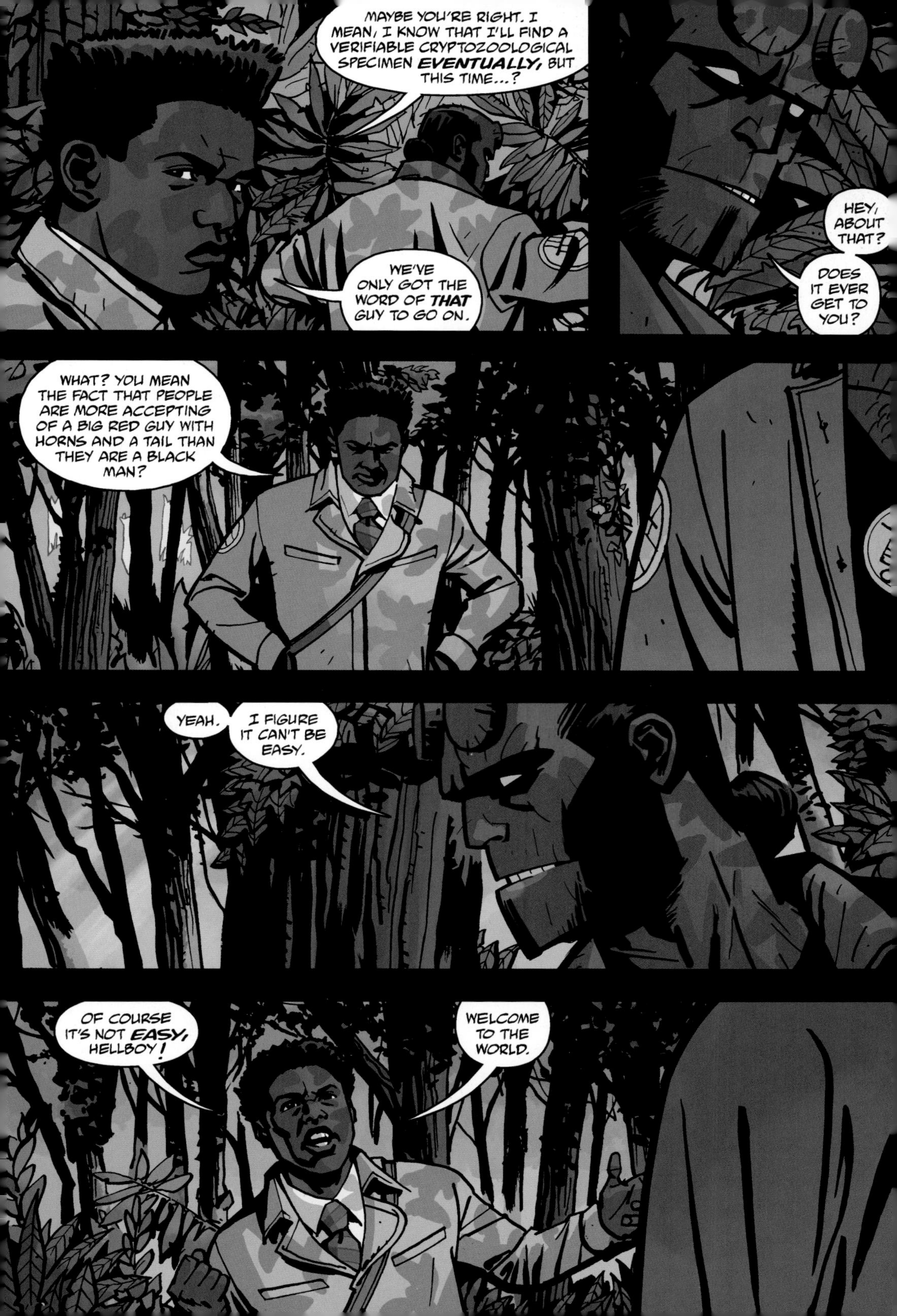
MAYBE YOU'RE RIGHT. I MEAN, I KNOW THAT I'LL FIND A VERIFIABLE CRYPTOZOOLOGICAL SPECIMEN EVENTUALLY, BUT THIS TIME...?
WE'VE ONLY GOT THE WORD OF THAT GUY TO GO ON.
HEY, ABOUT THAT?
DOES IT EVER GET TO YOU?
WHAT? YOU MEAN THE FACT THAT PEOPLE ARE MORE ACCEPTING OF A BIG RED GUY WITH HORNS AND A TAIL THAN THEY ARE A BLACK MAN?
YEAH.
I FIGURE IT CAN'T BE EASY.
OF COURSE IT'S NOT EASY, HELLBOY!
WELCOME TO THE WORLD.

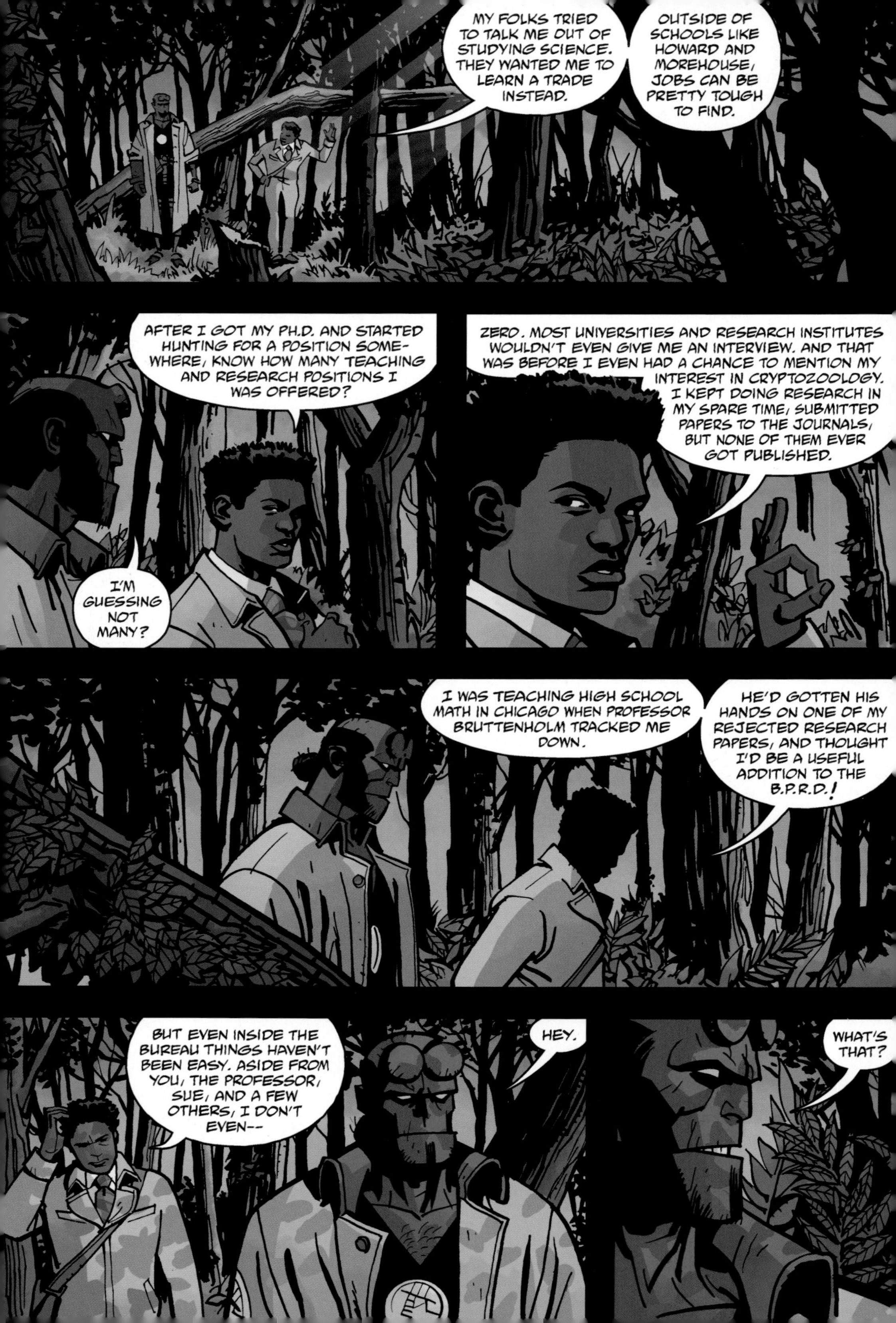
MY FOLKS TRIED TO TALK ME OUT OF STUDYING SCIENCE. THEY WANTED ME TO LEARN A TRADE INSTEAD.
OUTSIDE OF SCHOOLS LIKE HOWARD AND MOREHOUSE, JOBS CAN BE PRETTY TOUGH TO FIND.
AFTER I GOT MY PH.D. AND STARTED HUNTING FOR A POSITION SOME-WHERE, KNOW HOW MANY TEACHING AND RESEARCH POSITIONS I WAS OFFERED?
I'M GUESSING NOT MANY?
ZERO. MOST UNIVERSITIES AND RESEARCH INSTITUTES WOULDN'T EVEN GIVE ME AN INTERVIEW. AND THAT WAS BEFORE I EVEN HAD A CHANCE TO MENTION MY INTEREST IN CRYPTOZOOLOGY. I KEPT DOING RESEARCH IN MY SPARE TIME, SUBMITTED PAPERS TO THE JOURNALS, BUT NONE OF THEM EVER GOT PUBLISHED.
I WAS TEACHING HIGH SCHOOL MATH IN CHICAGO WHEN PROFESSOR BRUTTENHOLM TRACKED ME DOWN.
HE'D GOTTEN HIS HANDS ON ONE OF MY REJECTED RESEARCH PAPERS, AND THOUGHT I'D BE A USEFUL ADDITION TO THE B.P.R.D.!
BUT EVEN INSIDE THE BUREAU THINGS HAVEN'T BEEN EASY. ASIDE FROM YOU, THE PROFESSOR, SUE, AND A FEW OTHERS, I DON'T EVEN--
HEY.
WHAT'S THAT?

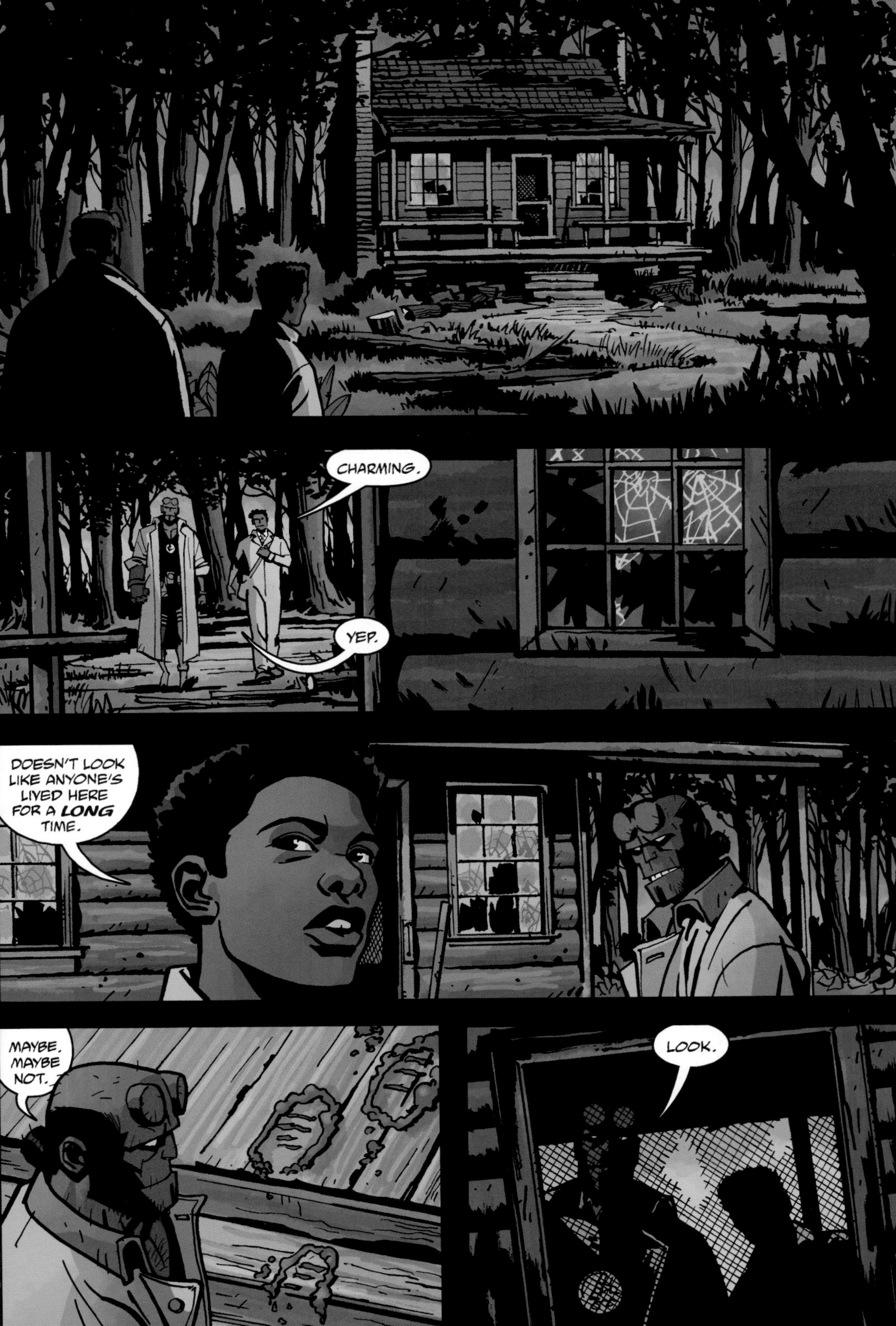
CHARMING.
YEP.
DOESN'T LOOK LIKE ANYONE'S LIVED HERE FOR A **LONG** TIME.
MAYBE. MAYBE NOT.
LOOK.

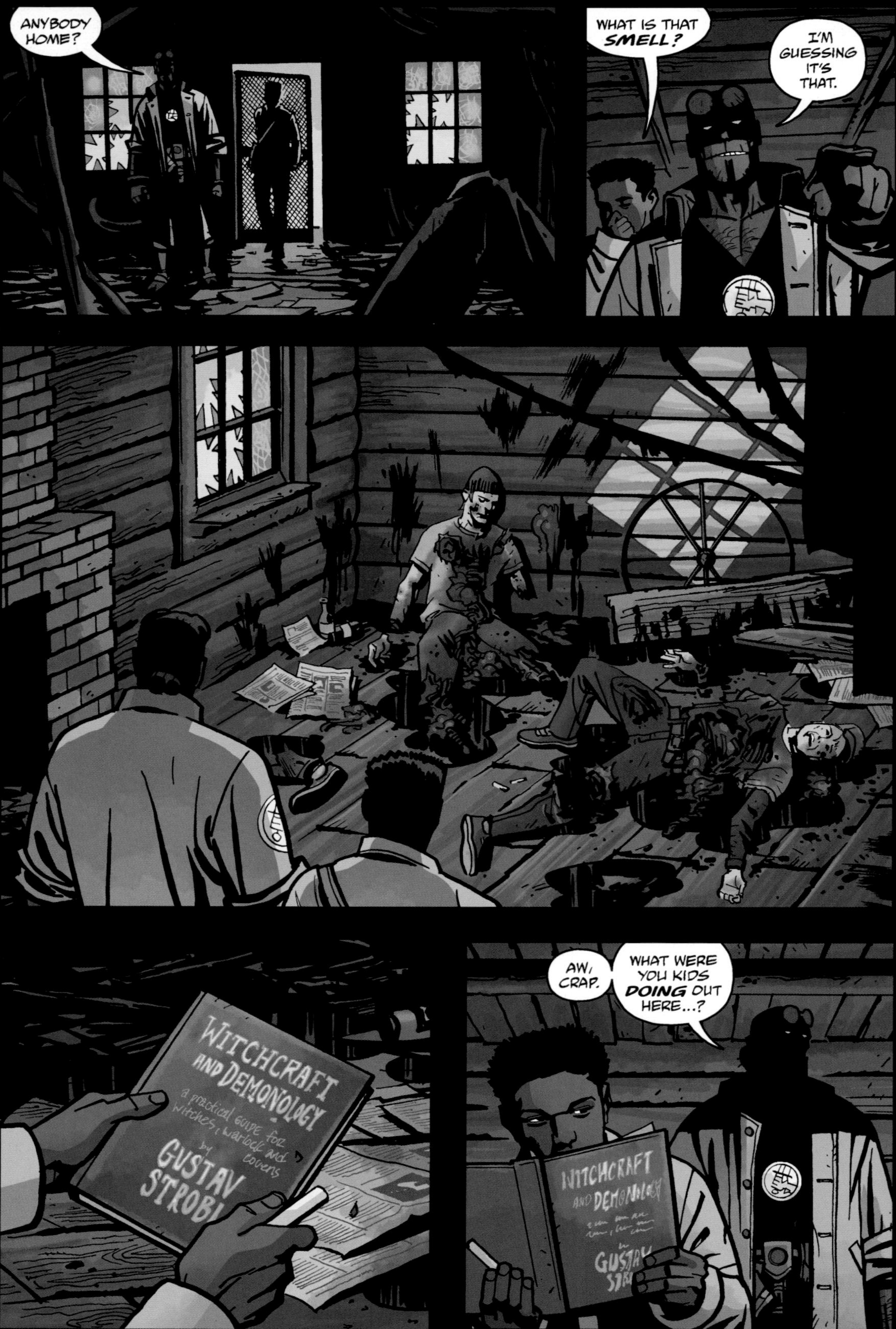
ANYBODY HOME?
WHAT IS THAT SMELL?
I'M GUESSING IT'S THAT.
WITCHCRAFT AND DEMONOLOGY
a practical guide for witches, warlock and covens
by
GUSTAV
AW, CRAP.
WHAT WERE YOU KIDS DOING OUT HERE...?
WITCHCRAFT AND DEMONOLOGY

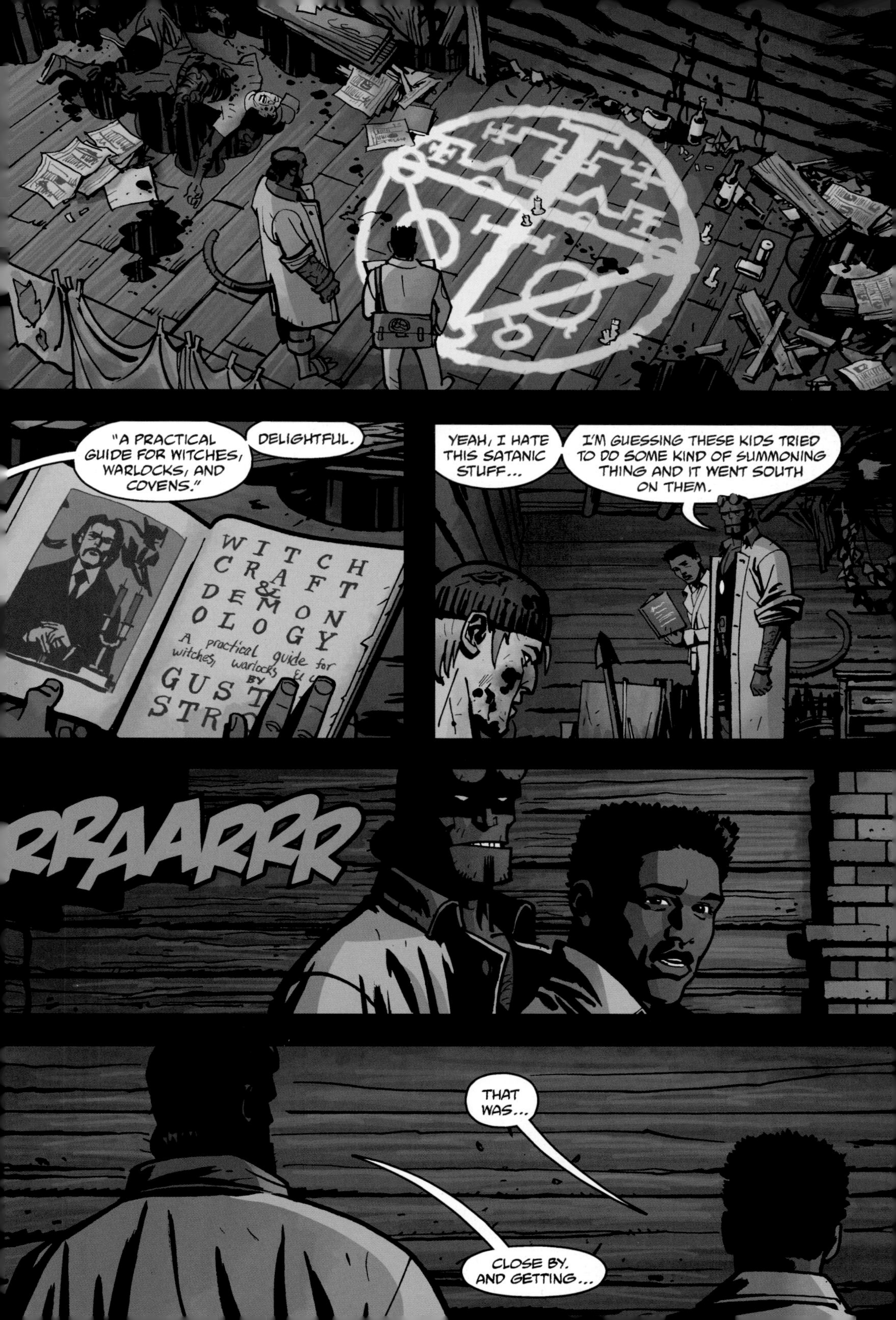
"A PRACTICAL GUIDE FOR WITCHES, WARLOCKS, AND COVENS."
DELIGHTFUL.
WITCH CRAFT & DEMON OLOGY
A practical guide for witches, warlocks
BY
GUST
STR
YEAH, I HATE THIS SATANIC STUFF...
I'M GUESSING THESE KIDS TRIED TO DO SOME KIND OF SUMMONING THING AND IT WENT SOUTH ON THEM.
RRAARRR
THAT WAS...
CLOSE BY. AND GETTING...

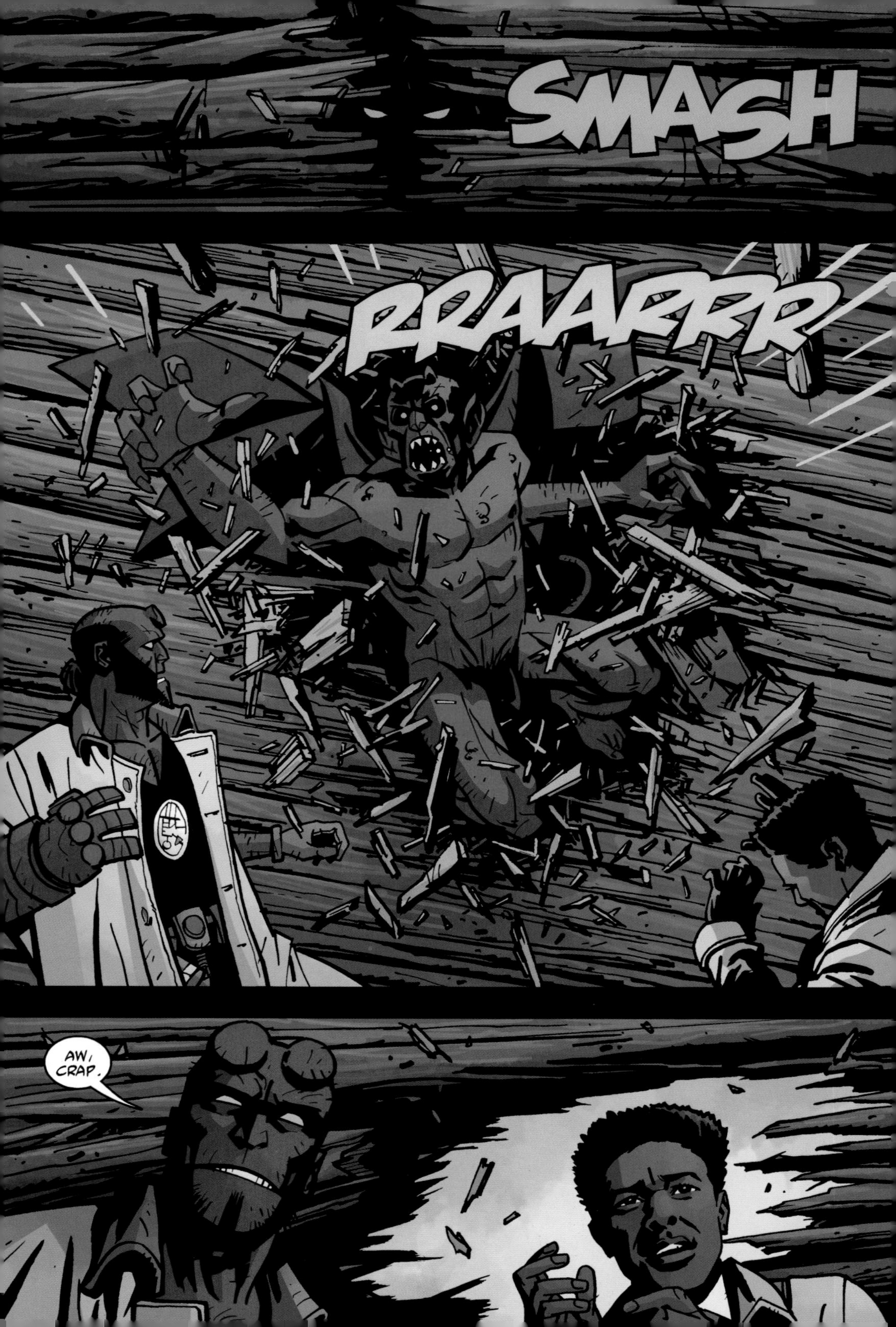
SMASH
RRAARRR
AW, CRAP.

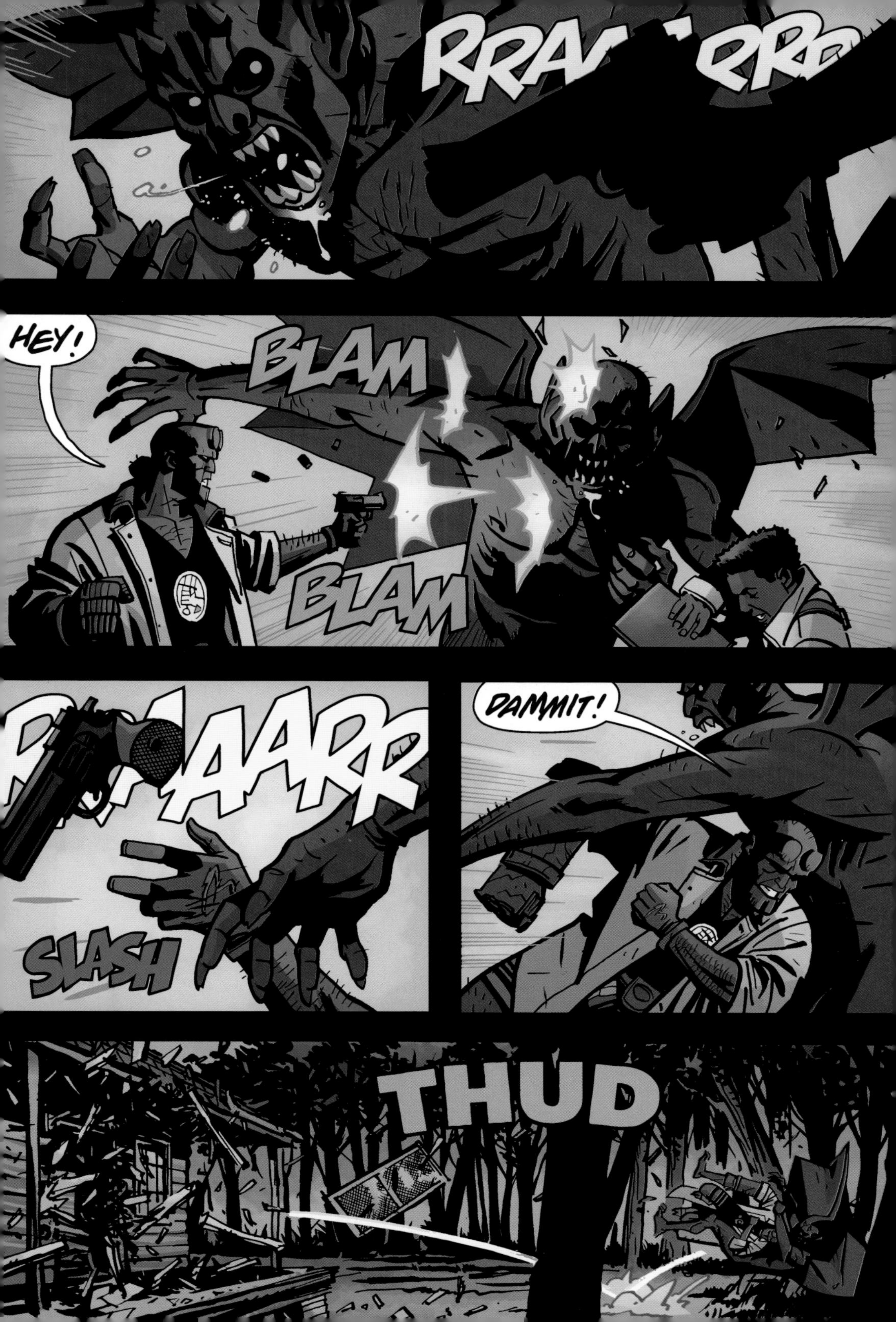

HEY!
BLAM
BLAM
SLASH
DAMMIT!
THUD

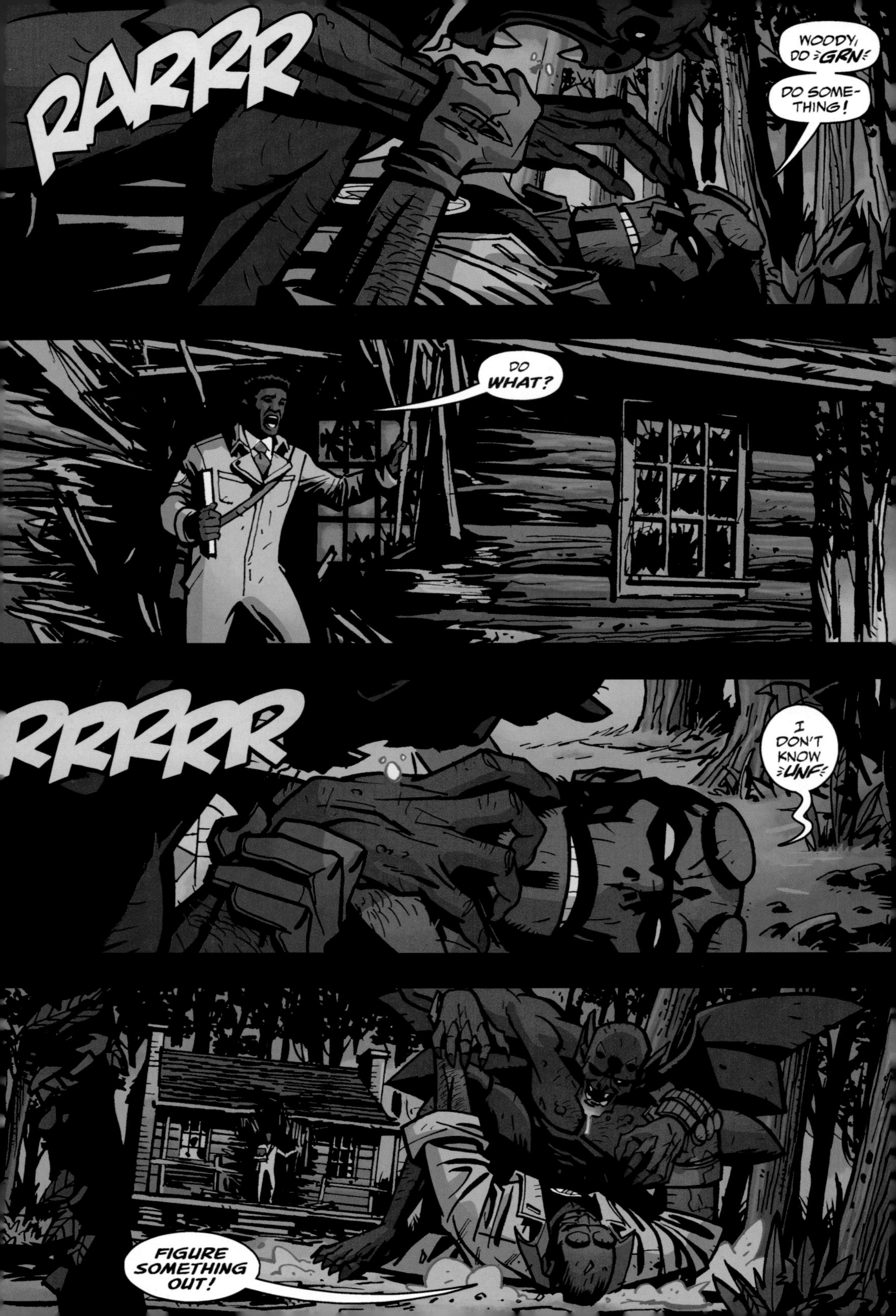
RARRR
WOODY, DO GRN
DO SOME-THING!
DO WHAT?
RRRRR
I DON'T KNOW UNF
FIGURE SOMETHING OUT!

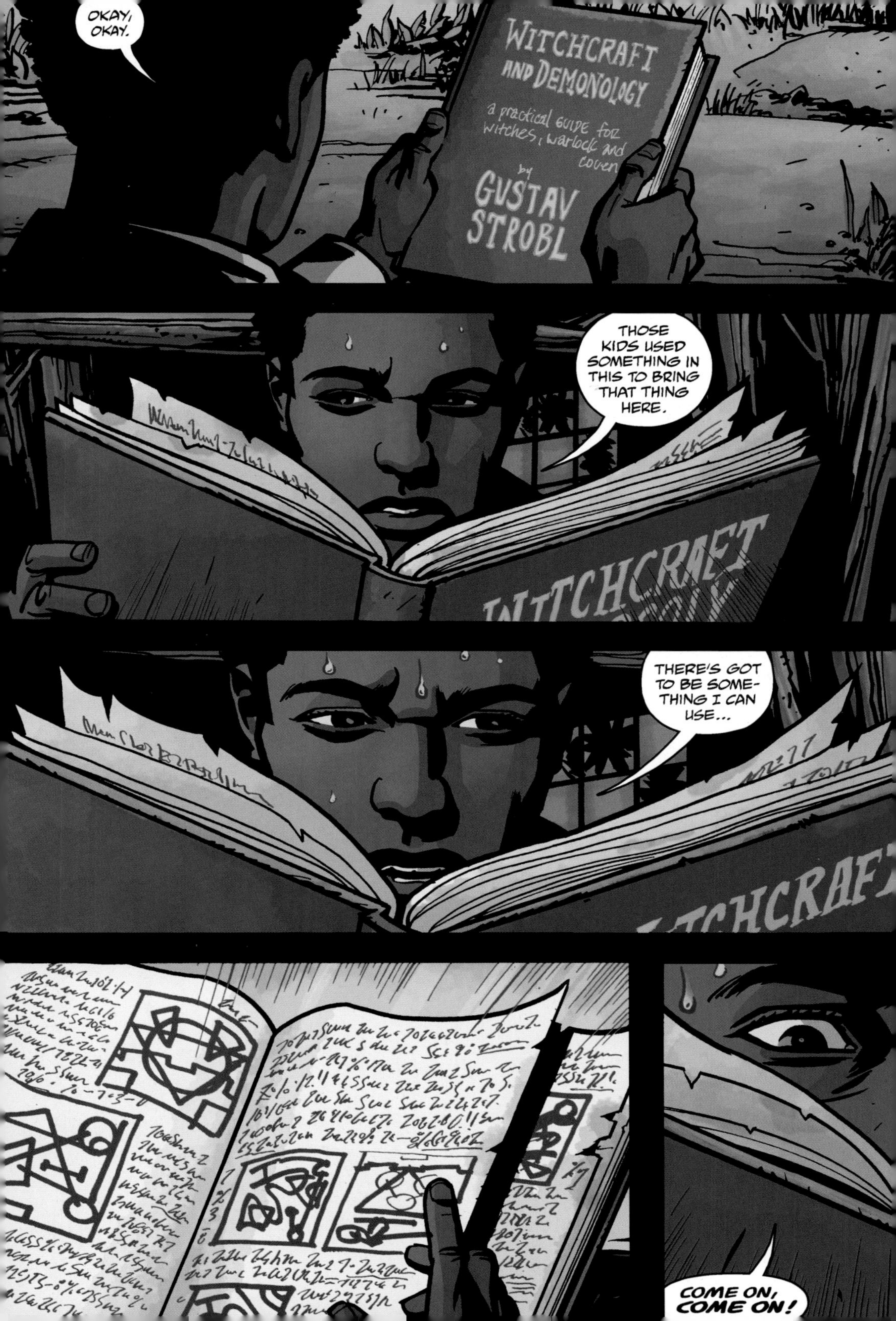
OKAY, OKAY.
WITCHCRAFT AND DEMONOLOGY
a practical GUIDE for witches, warlock and coven
by GUSTAV STROBL
THOSE KIDS USED SOMETHING IN THIS TO BRING THAT THING HERE.
WITCHCRAFT
THERE'S GOT TO BE SOME-THING I CAN USE...
COME ON, COME ON!

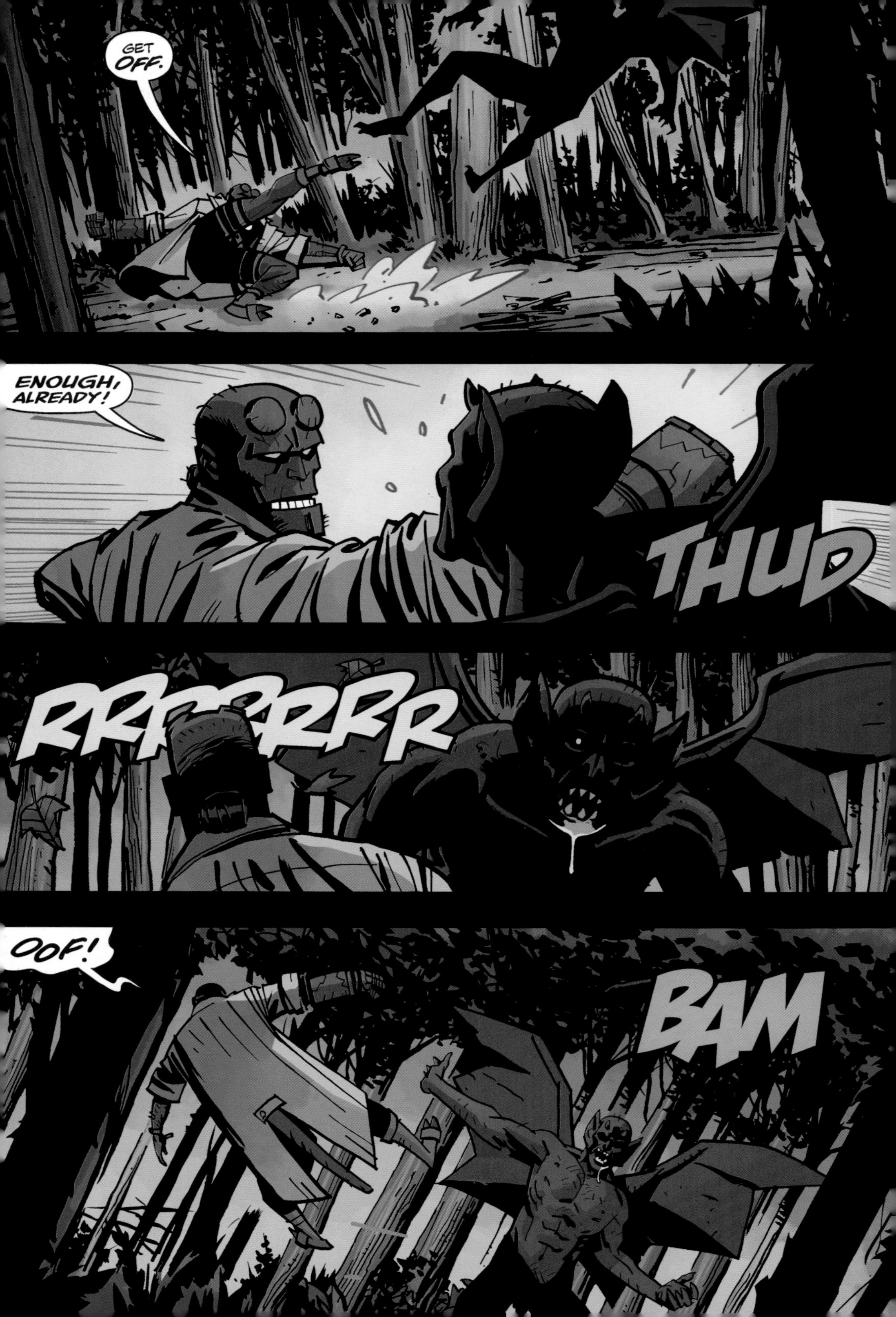
GET OFF.
ENOUGH, ALREADY!
THUD
RRRRRRRR
OOF!
BAM

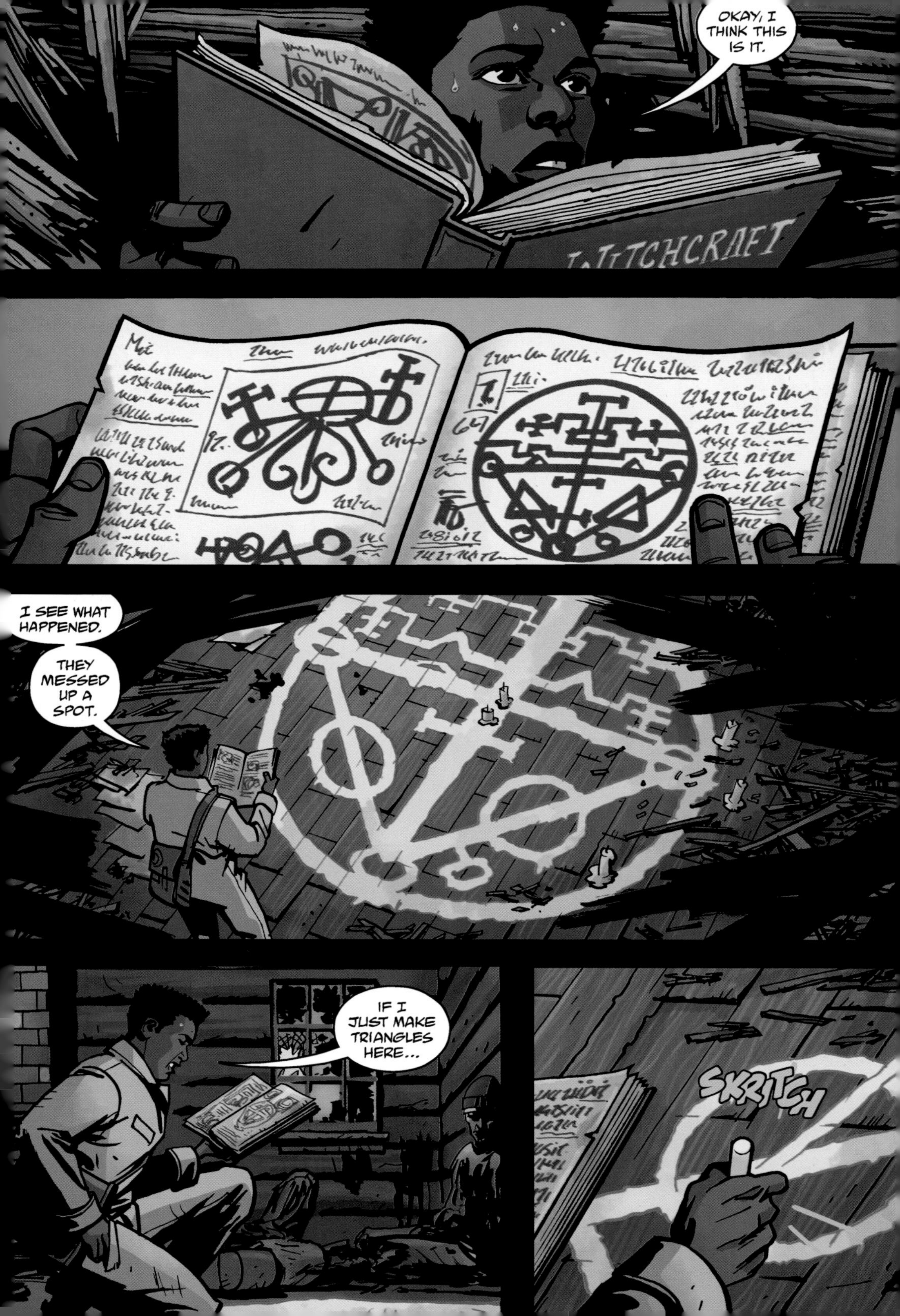
OKAY, I THINK THIS IS IT.
WITCHCRAFT
I SEE WHAT HAPPENED.
THEY MESSED UP A SPOT.
IF I JUST MAKE TRIANGLES HERE...
SKRITCH

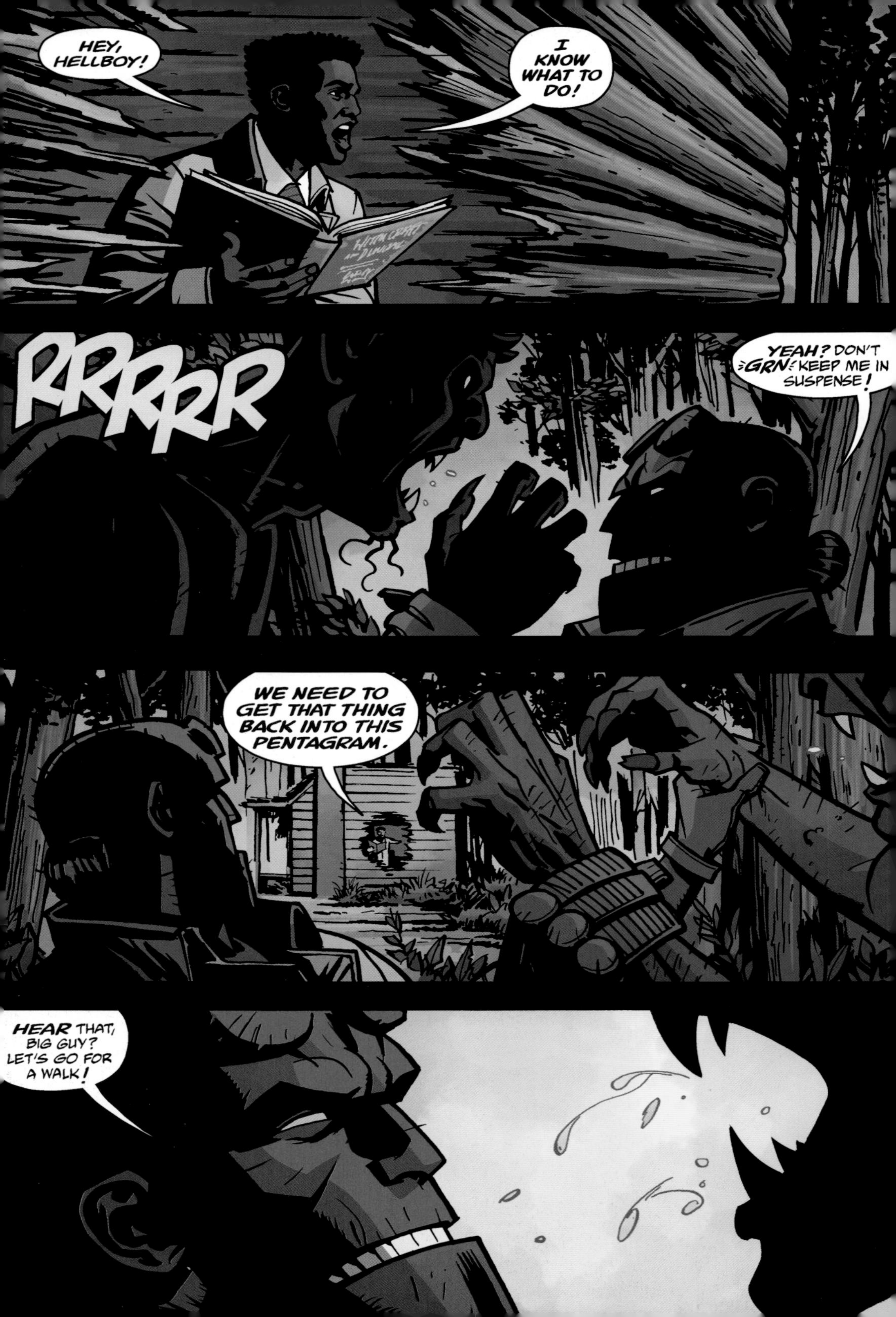
HEY, HELLBOY!
I KNOW WHAT TO DO!
RRRRR
YEAH? DON'T GRN KEEP ME IN SUSPENSE!
WE NEED TO GET THAT THING BACK INTO THIS PENTAGRAM.
HEAR THAT, BIG GUY? LET'S GO FOR A WALK!

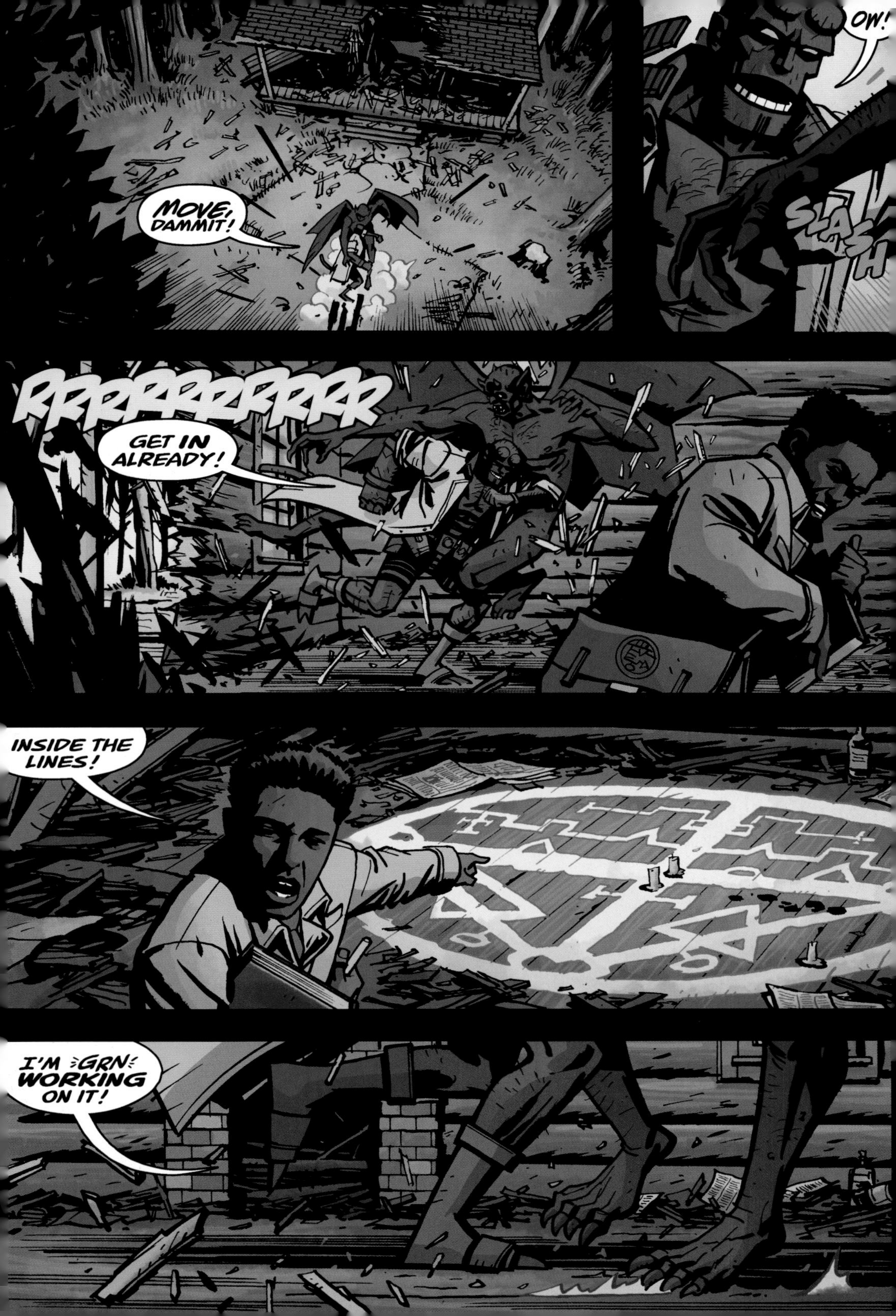
MOVE, DAMMIT!
OW!
SLASH
RRRRRRRRRRR
GET IN ALREADY!
INSIDE THE LINES!
I'M GRN WORKING ON IT!

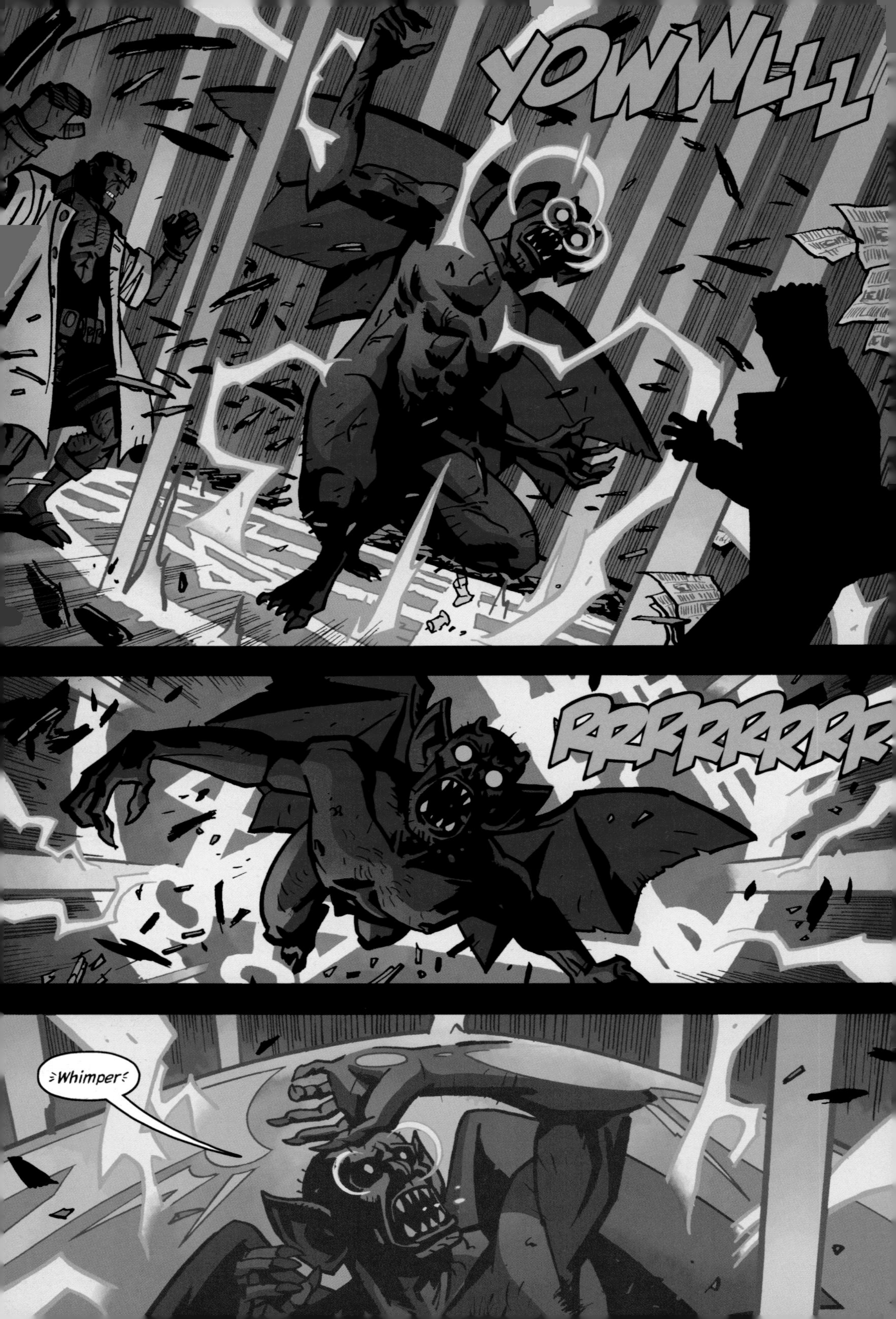
YOWWLLL
RRRRRRRRR
Whimper

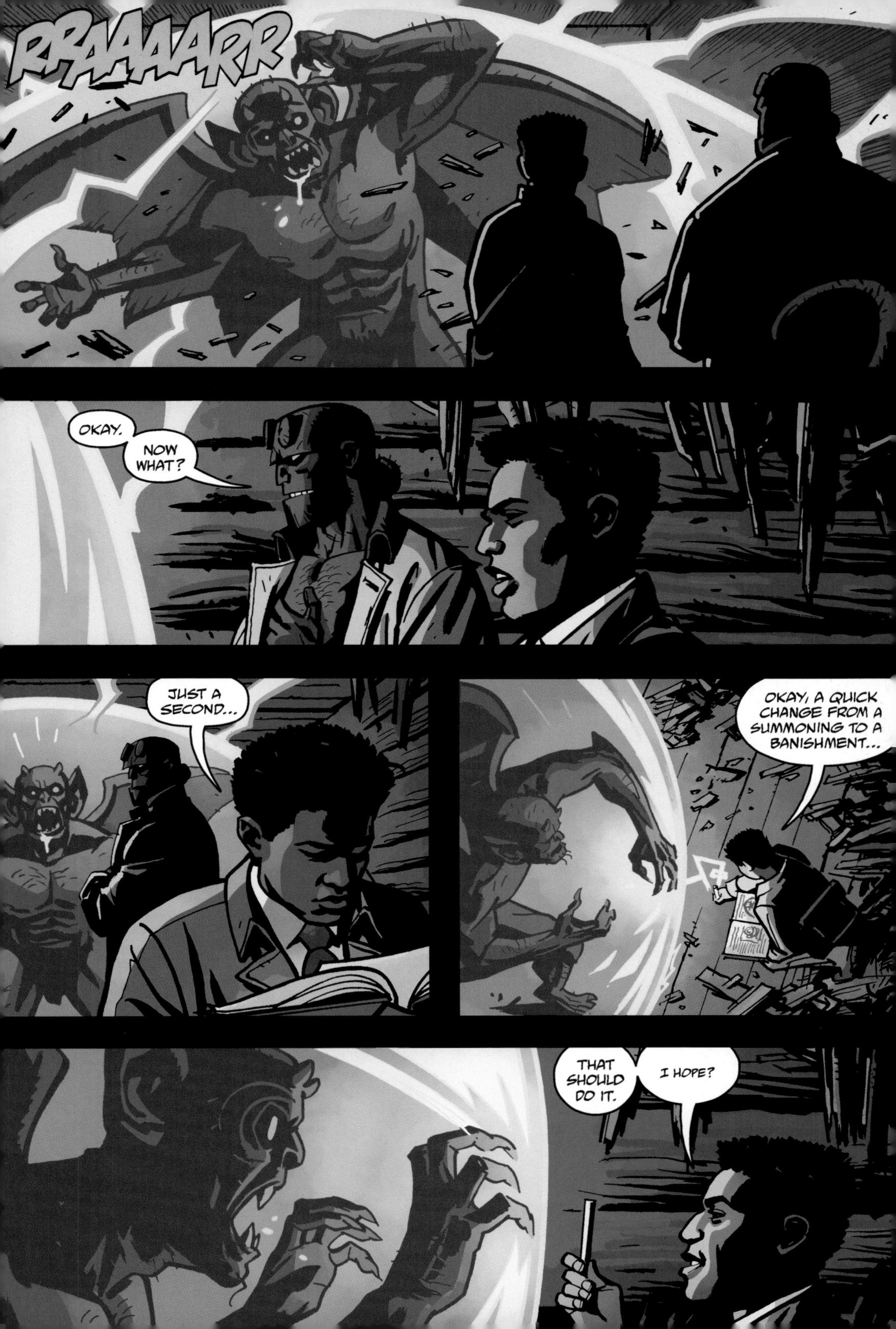
RRAAAARR
OKAY.
NOW WHAT?
JUST A SECOND...
OKAY, A QUICK CHANGE FROM A SUMMONING TO A BANISHMENT...
THAT SHOULD DO IT.
I HOPE?

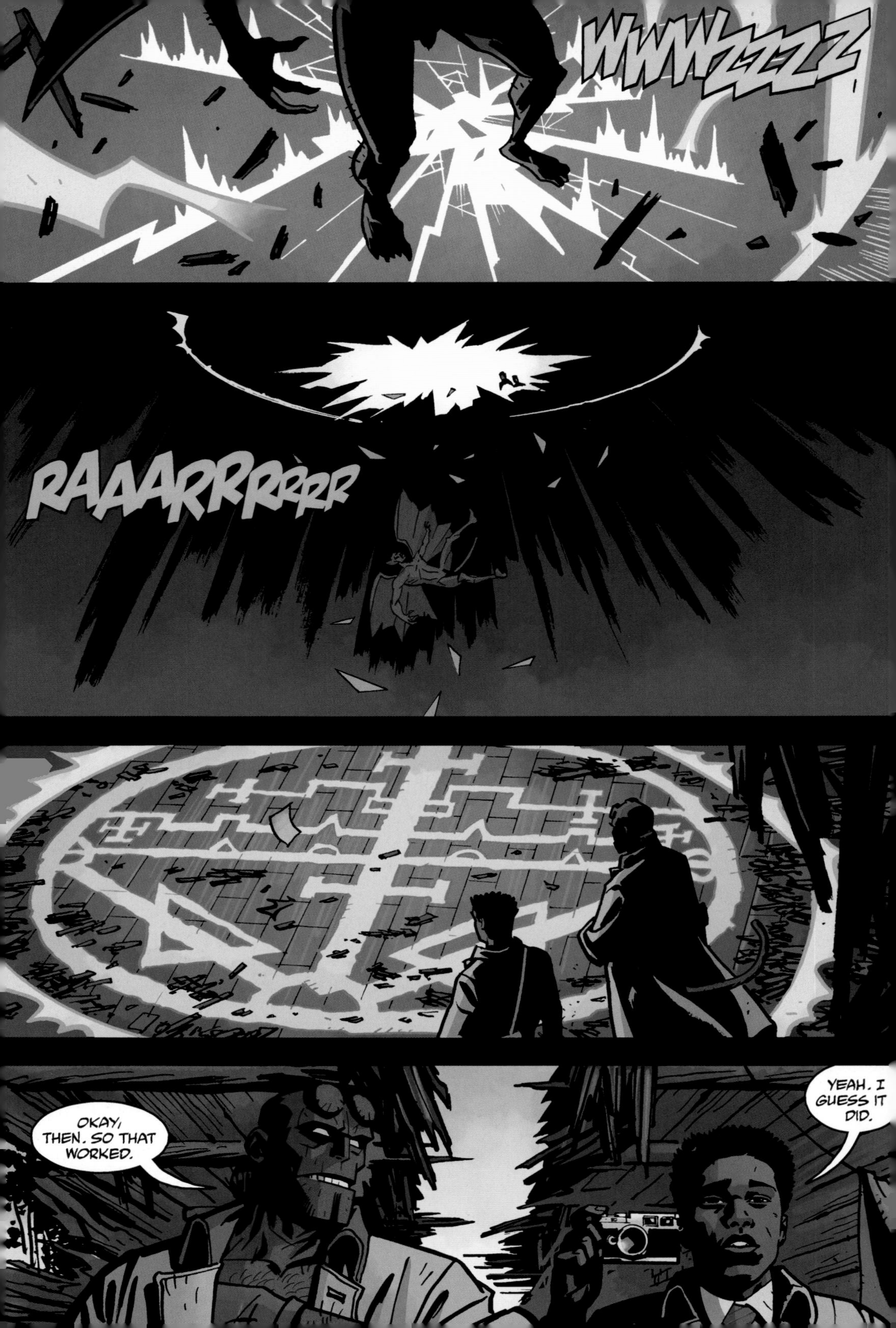
WWWZZZZZ
RAAARRRRRR
OKAY, THEN. SO THAT WORKED.
YEAH. I GUESS IT DID.

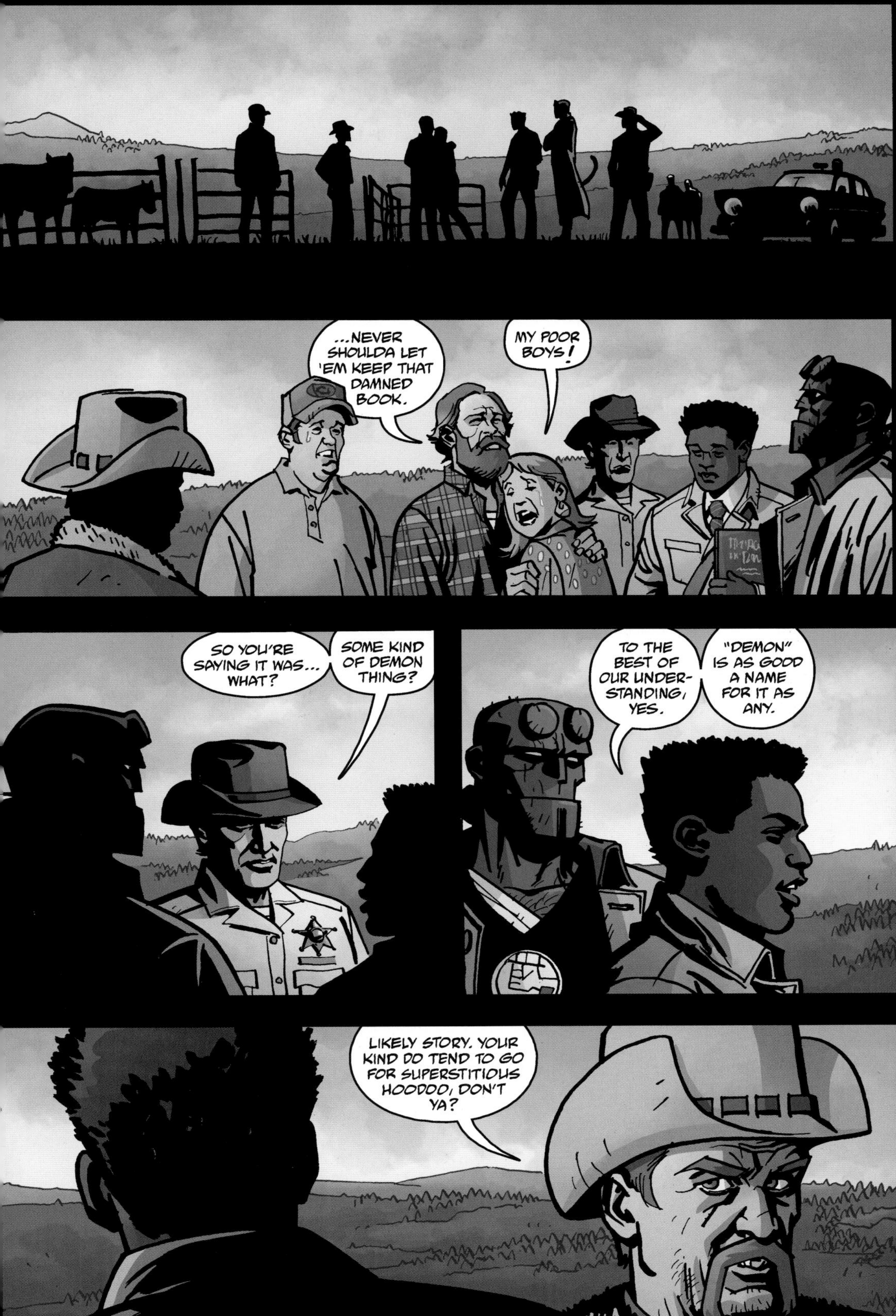
...NEVER SHOULDA LET 'EM KEEP THAT DAMNED BOOK.
MY POOR BOYS!
SO YOU'RE SAYING IT WAS... WHAT?
SOME KIND OF DEMON THING?
TO THE BEST OF OUR UNDER-STANDING, YES.
"DEMON" IS AS GOOD A NAME FOR IT AS ANY.
LIKELY STORY. YOUR KIND DO TEND TO GO FOR SUPERSTITIOUS HOODOO, DON'T YA?

LOOK, MAC, I TOLD YOU BEFORE!

SHOW A LITTLE RESPECT OR I'M LIABLE TO--

LEAVE IT, HELLBOY.

THE PROFESSOR'S EXPECTING OUR REPORT. LET'S NOT KEEP HIM WAITING.

YEAH, YEAH, ALL RIGHT.

BUT YOU KNOW, YOU WERE WRONG ABOUT IT BEING A MUTATED ANIMAL.

WE WERE BOTH WRONG, THIS TIME, BUT A BET'S A BET. DRINKS ARE ON ME.

NEXT TIME I HOPE IT IS A CRYPTO-WHATEVER THING, THOUGH. I'VE HAD MY FILL OF ALL THIS DEMON NONSENSE.

WITCHCRAFT AND DEMONO

a practical guide witches, warlock covens

THE END

OCCULT INTELLIGENCE

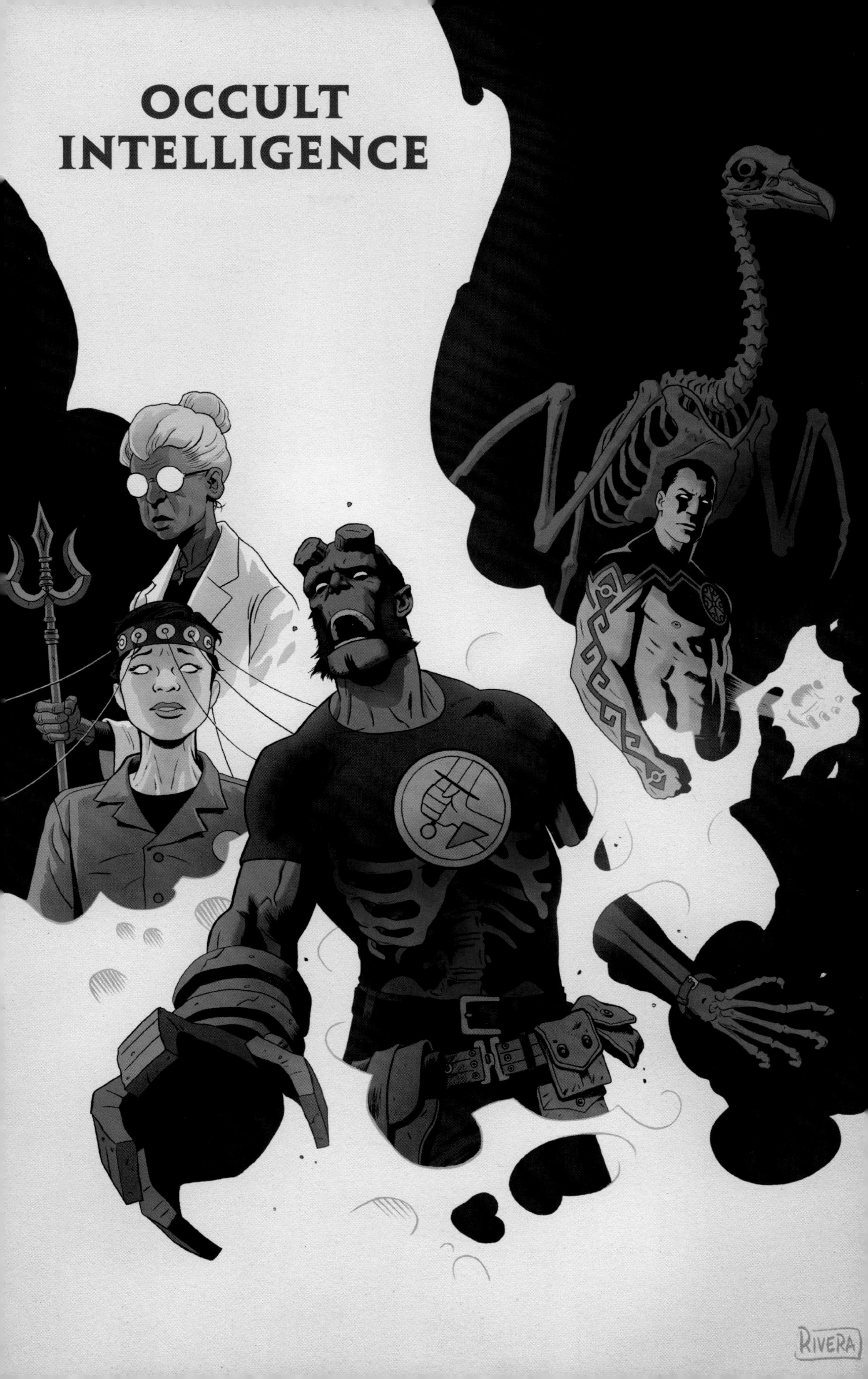
RIVERA

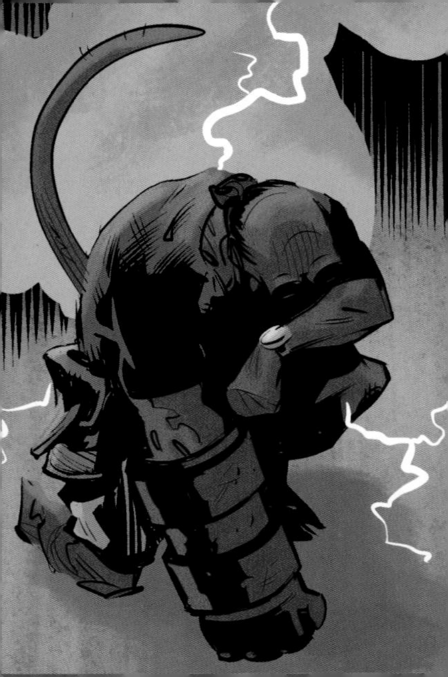

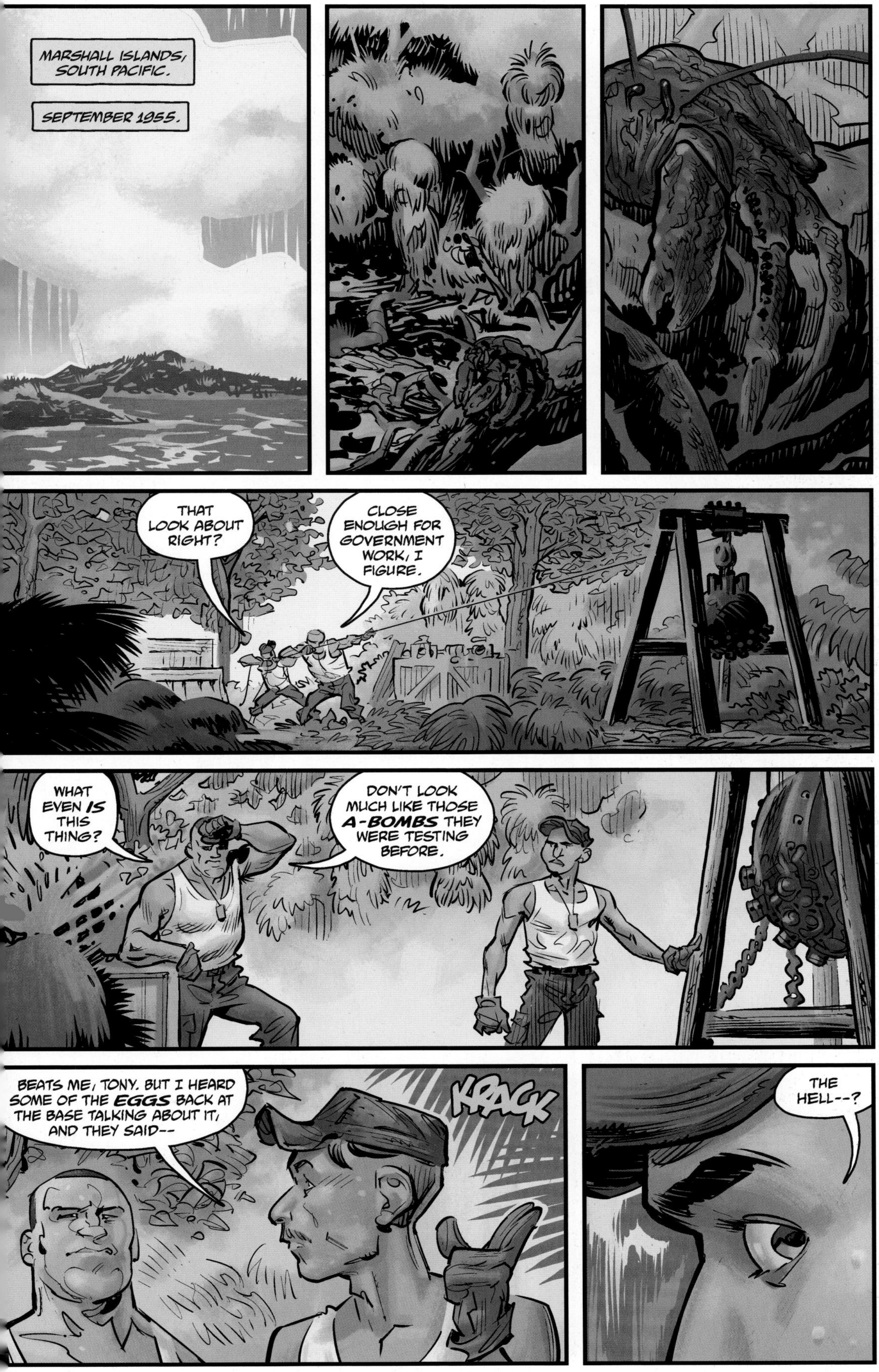
MARSHALL ISLANDS, SOUTH PACIFIC.
SEPTEMBER 1955.
THAT LOOK ABOUT RIGHT?
CLOSE ENOUGH FOR GOVERNMENT WORK, I FIGURE.
WHAT EVEN IS THIS THING?
DON'T LOOK MUCH LIKE THOSE A-BOMBS THEY WERE TESTING BEFORE.
BEATS ME, TONY. BUT I HEARD SOME OF THE EGGS BACK AT THE BASE TALKING ABOUT IT, AND THEY SAID--
KRACK
THE HELL--?

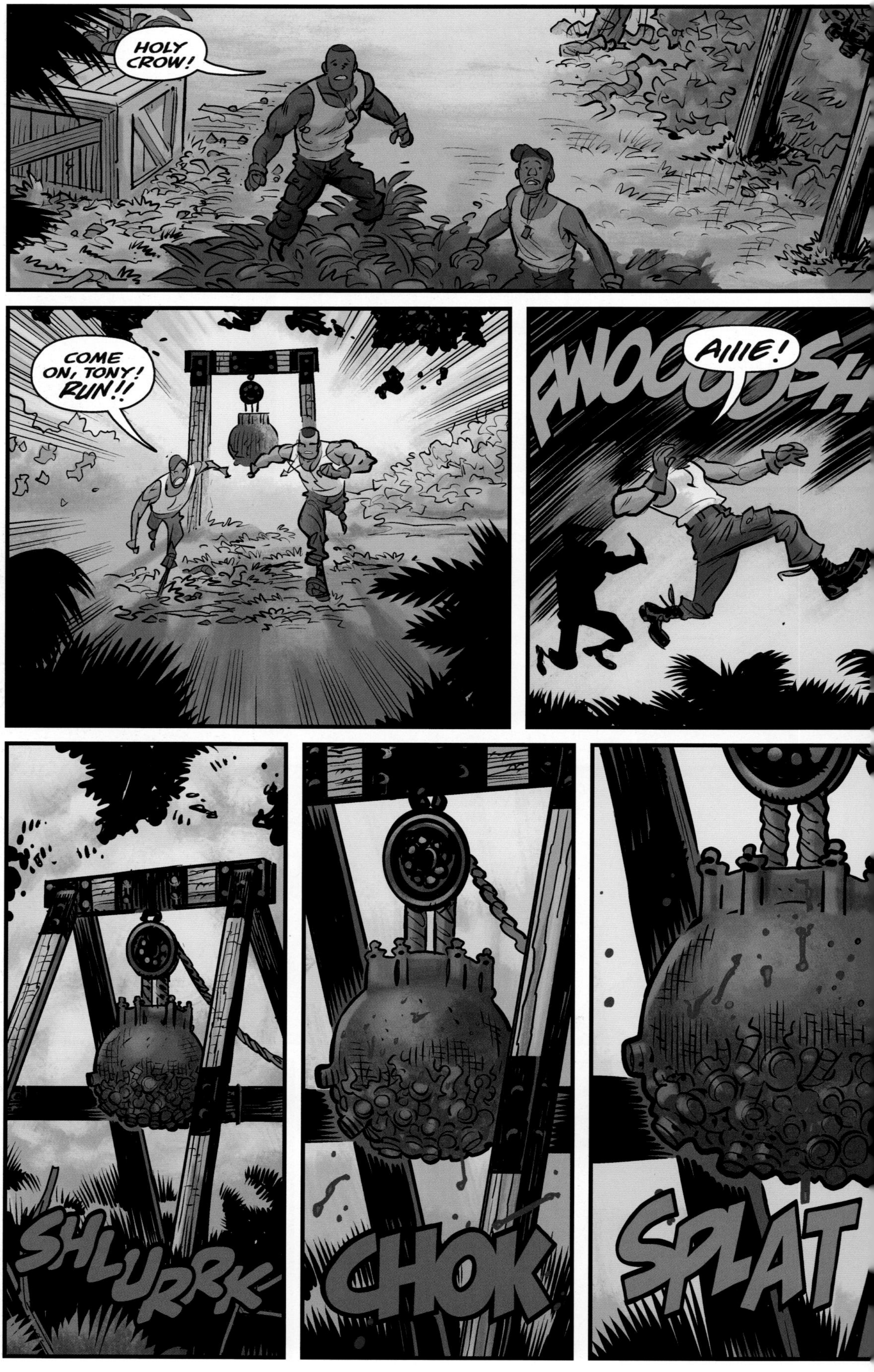
HOLY CROW!
COME ON, TONY! RUN!!
FWOOOOSH
AIIIE!
SHLURRK
CHOK
SPLAT

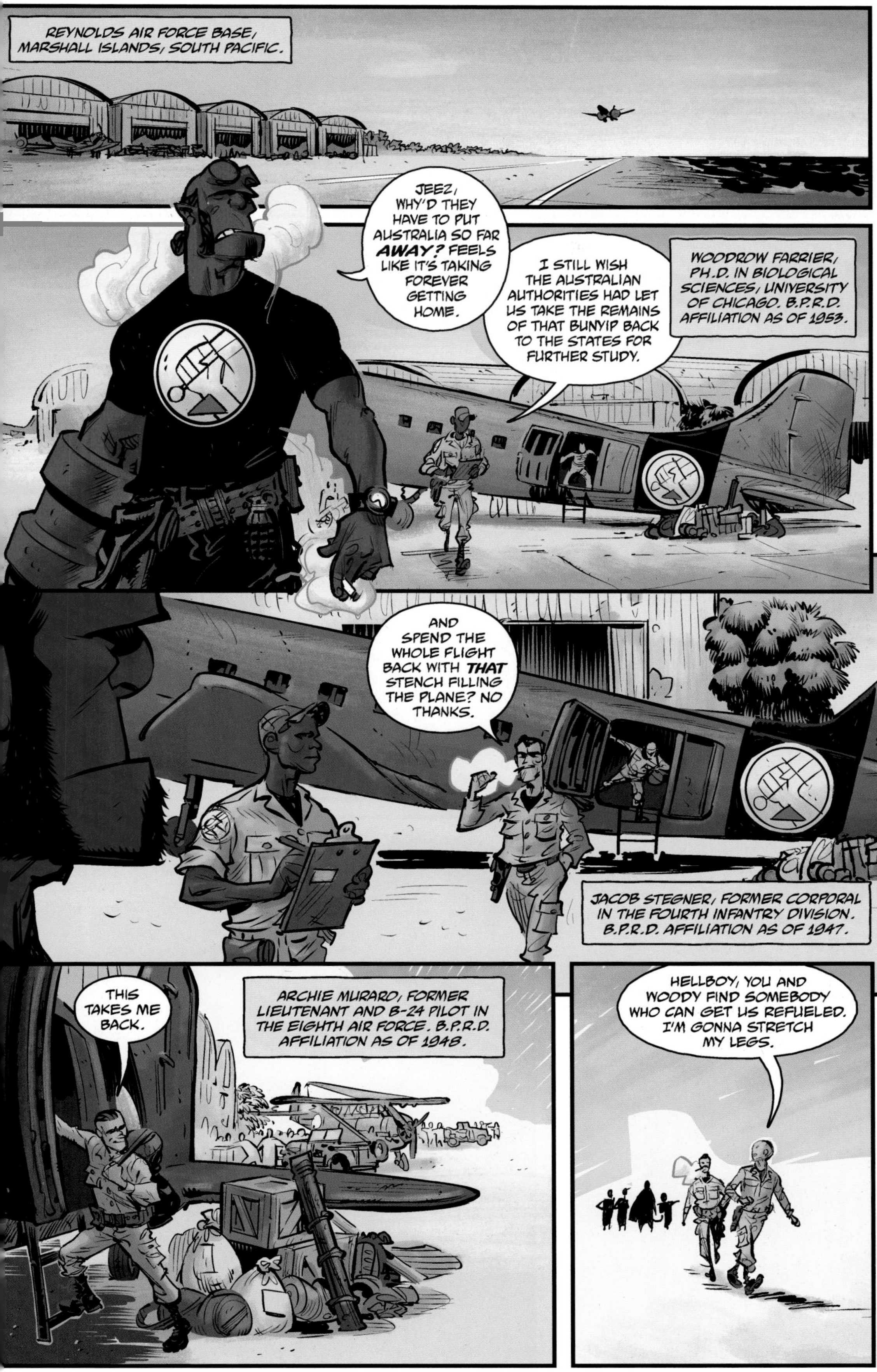
REYNOLDS AIR FORCE BASE, MARSHALL ISLANDS, SOUTH PACIFIC.
JEEZ, WHY'D THEY HAVE TO PUT AUSTRALIA SO FAR **AWAY?** FEELS LIKE IT'S TAKING FOREVER GETTING HOME.
I STILL WISH THE AUSTRALIAN AUTHORITIES HAD LET US TAKE THE REMAINS OF THAT BUNYIP BACK TO THE STATES FOR FURTHER STUDY.
WOODROW FARRIER, PH.D. IN BIOLOGICAL SCIENCES, UNIVERSITY OF CHICAGO. B.P.R.D. AFFILIATION AS OF 1953.
AND SPEND THE WHOLE FLIGHT BACK WITH **THAT** STENCH FILLING THE PLANE? NO THANKS.
JACOB STEGNER, FORMER CORPORAL IN THE FOURTH INFANTRY DIVISION. B.P.R.D. AFFILIATION AS OF 1947.
THIS TAKES ME BACK.
ARCHIE MURARO, FORMER LIEUTENANT AND B-24 PILOT IN THE EIGHTH AIR FORCE. B.P.R.D. AFFILIATION AS OF 1948.
HELLBOY, YOU AND WOODY FIND SOMEBODY WHO CAN GET US REFUELED. I'M GONNA STRETCH MY LEGS.

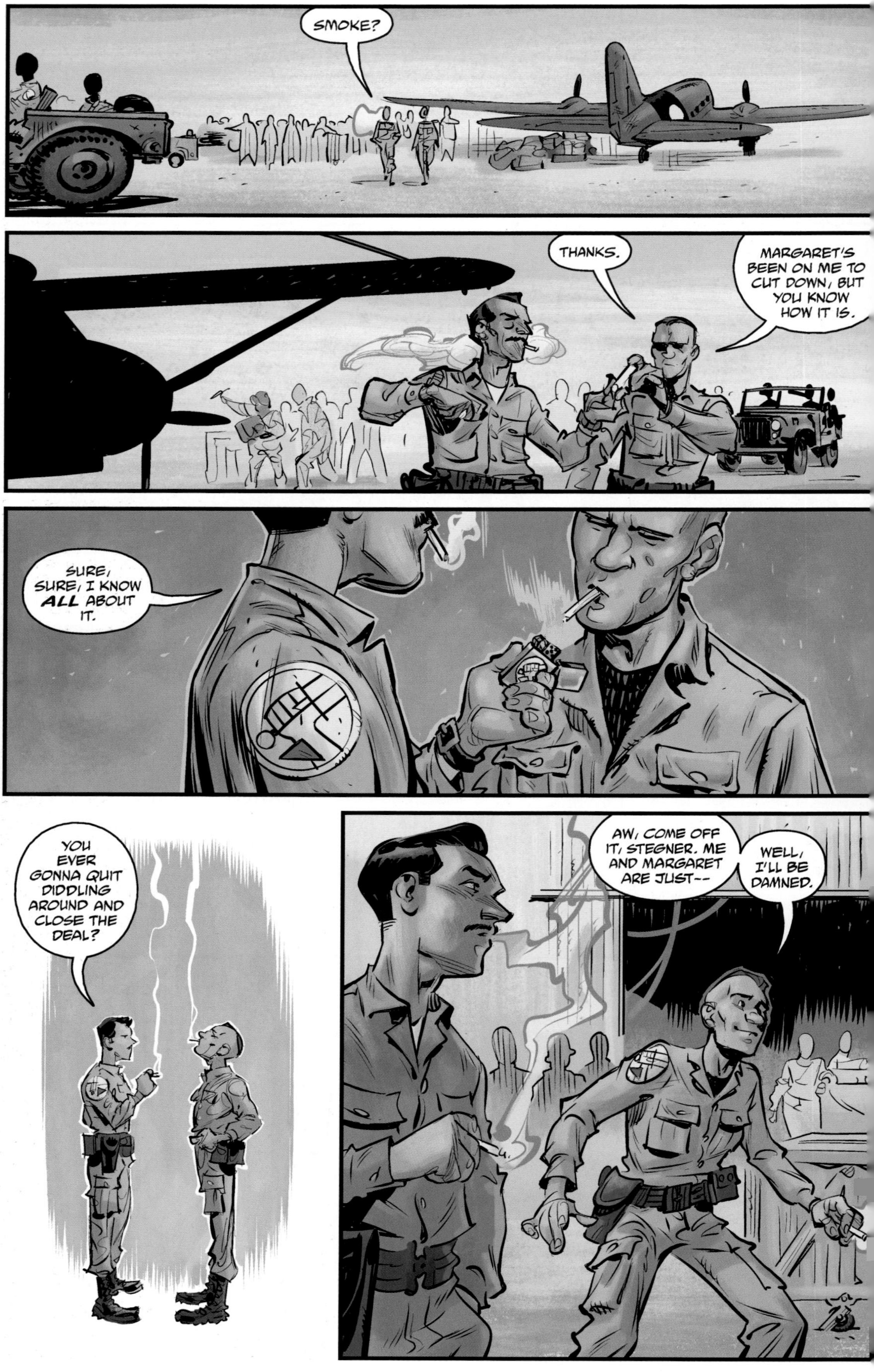
SMOKE?
THANKS.
MARGARET'S BEEN ON ME TO CUT DOWN, BUT YOU KNOW HOW IT IS.
SURE, SURE, I KNOW ALL ABOUT IT.
YOU EVER GONNA QUIT DIDDLING AROUND AND CLOSE THE DEAL?
AW, COME OFF IT, STEGNER. ME AND MARGARET ARE JUST--
WELL, I'LL BE DAMNED.

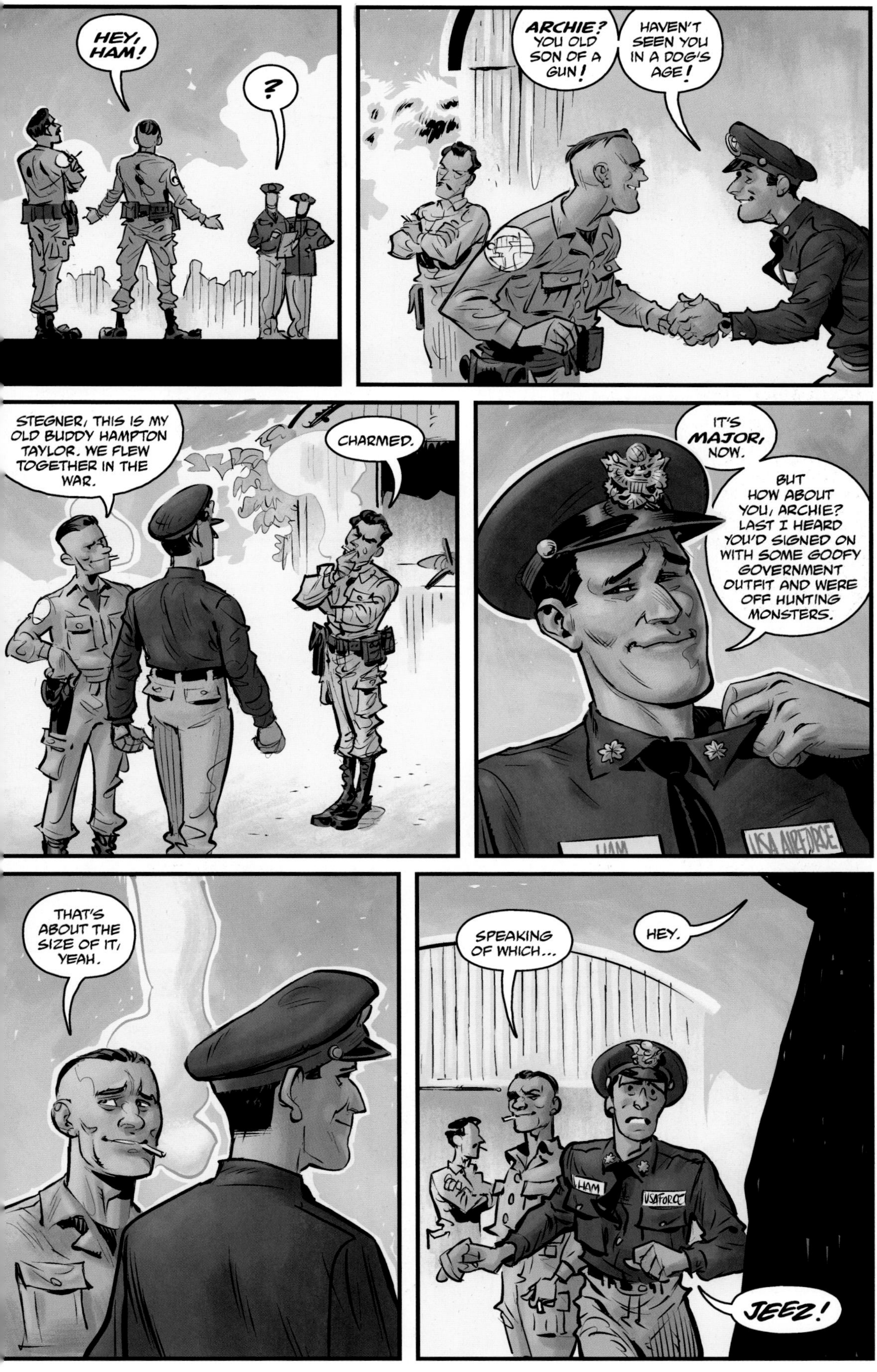
HEY, HAM!
?
ARCHIE? YOU OLD SON OF A GUN!
HAVEN'T SEEN YOU IN A DOG'S AGE!
STEGNER, THIS IS MY OLD BUDDY HAMPTON TAYLOR. WE FLEW TOGETHER IN THE WAR.
CHARMED.
IT'S MAJOR, NOW.
BUT HOW ABOUT YOU, ARCHIE? LAST I HEARD YOU'D SIGNED ON WITH SOME GOOFY GOVERNMENT OUTFIT AND WERE OFF HUNTING MONSTERS.
USA AIRFORCE
THAT'S ABOUT THE SIZE OF IT, YEAH.
SPEAKING OF WHICH...
HEY.
HAM
USAFORCE
JEEZ!

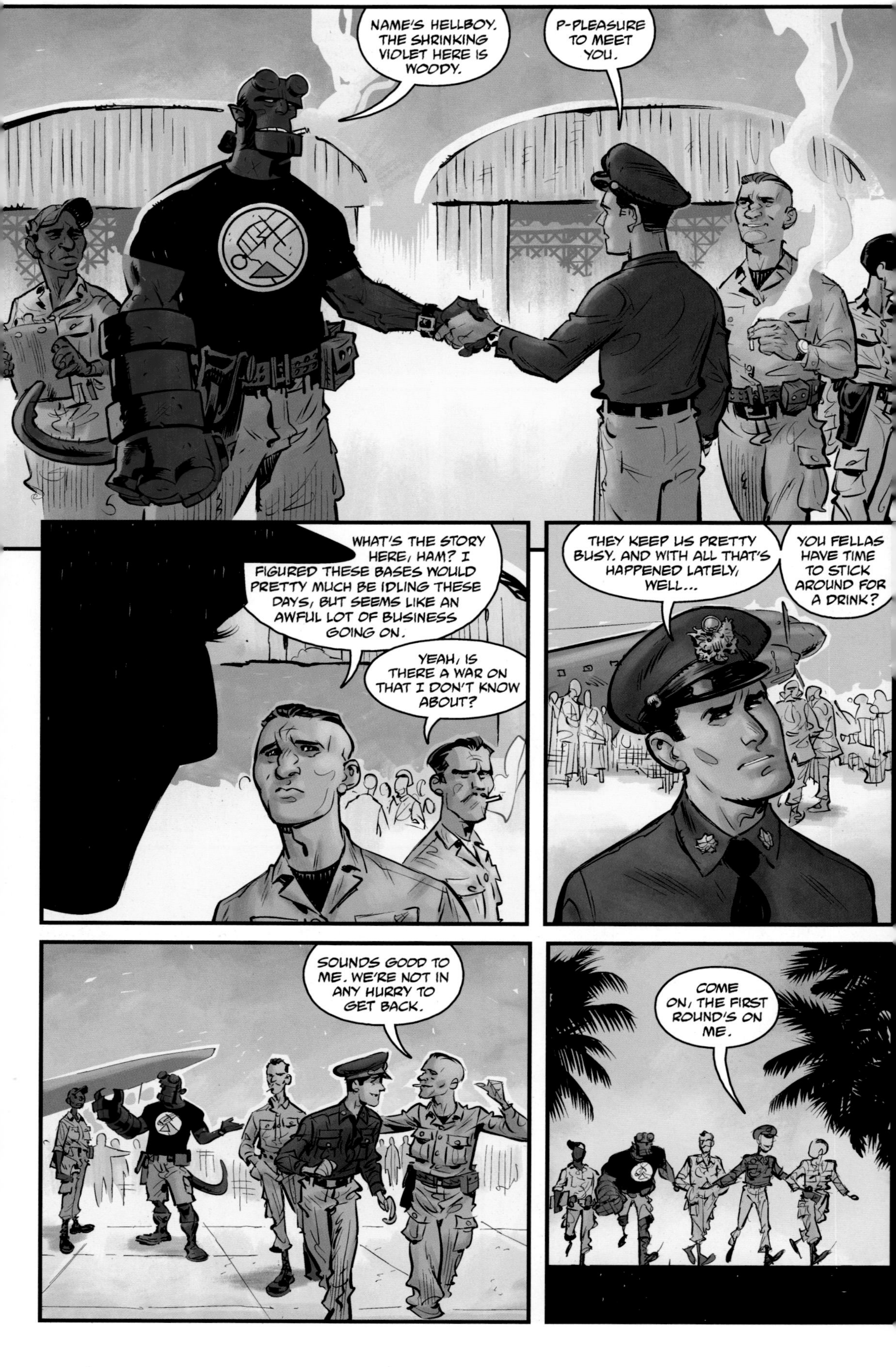
NAME'S HELLBOY. THE SHRINKING VIOLET HERE IS WOODY.
P-PLEASURE TO MEET YOU.
WHAT'S THE STORY HERE, HAM? I FIGURED THESE BASES WOULD PRETTY MUCH BE IDLING THESE DAYS, BUT SEEMS LIKE AN AWFUL LOT OF BUSINESS GOING ON.
YEAH, IS THERE A WAR ON THAT I DON'T KNOW ABOUT?
THEY KEEP US PRETTY BUSY. AND WITH ALL THAT'S HAPPENED LATELY, WELL...
YOU FELLAS HAVE TIME TO STICK AROUND FOR A DRINK?
SOUNDS GOOD TO ME. WE'RE NOT IN ANY HURRY TO GET BACK.
COME ON, THE FIRST ROUND'S ON ME.

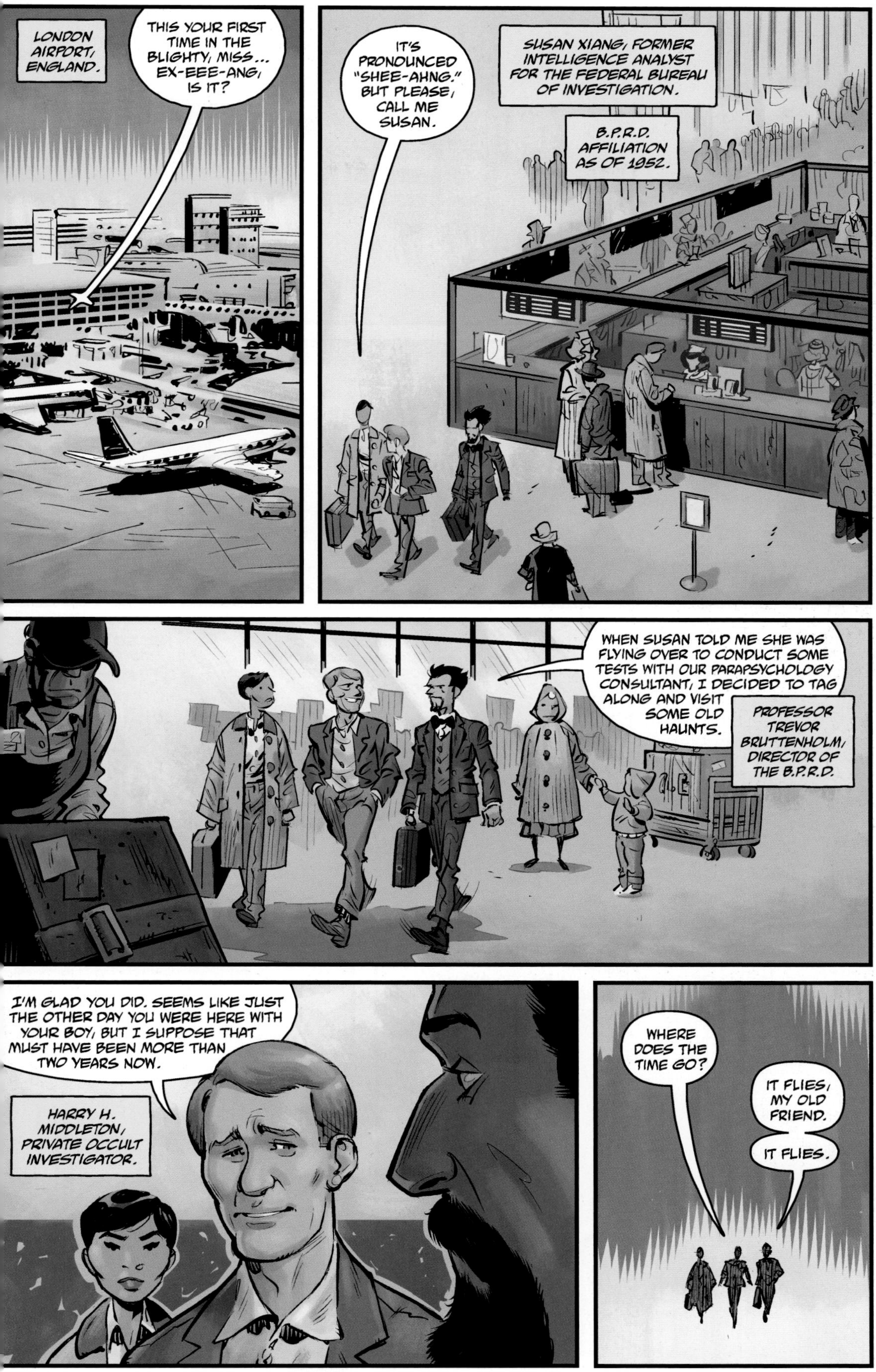

LONDON AIRPORT, ENGLAND.
THIS YOUR FIRST TIME IN THE BLIGHTY, MISS... EX-EEE-ANG, IS IT?
IT'S PRONOUNCED "SHEE-AHNG." BUT PLEASE, CALL ME SUSAN.
SUSAN XIANG, FORMER INTELLIGENCE ANALYST FOR THE FEDERAL BUREAU OF INVESTIGATION.
B.P.R.D. AFFILIATION AS OF 1952.
WHEN SUSAN TOLD ME SHE WAS FLYING OVER TO CONDUCT SOME TESTS WITH OUR PARAPSYCHOLOGY CONSULTANT, I DECIDED TO TAG ALONG AND VISIT SOME OLD HAUNTS.
PROFESSOR TREVOR BRUTTENHOLM, DIRECTOR OF THE B.P.R.D.
I'M GLAD YOU DID. SEEMS LIKE JUST THE OTHER DAY YOU WERE HERE WITH YOUR BOY, BUT I SUPPOSE THAT MUST HAVE BEEN MORE THAN TWO YEARS NOW.
HARRY H. MIDDLETON, PRIVATE OCCULT INVESTIGATOR.
WHERE DOES THE TIME GO?
IT FLIES, MY OLD FRIEND.
IT FLIES.

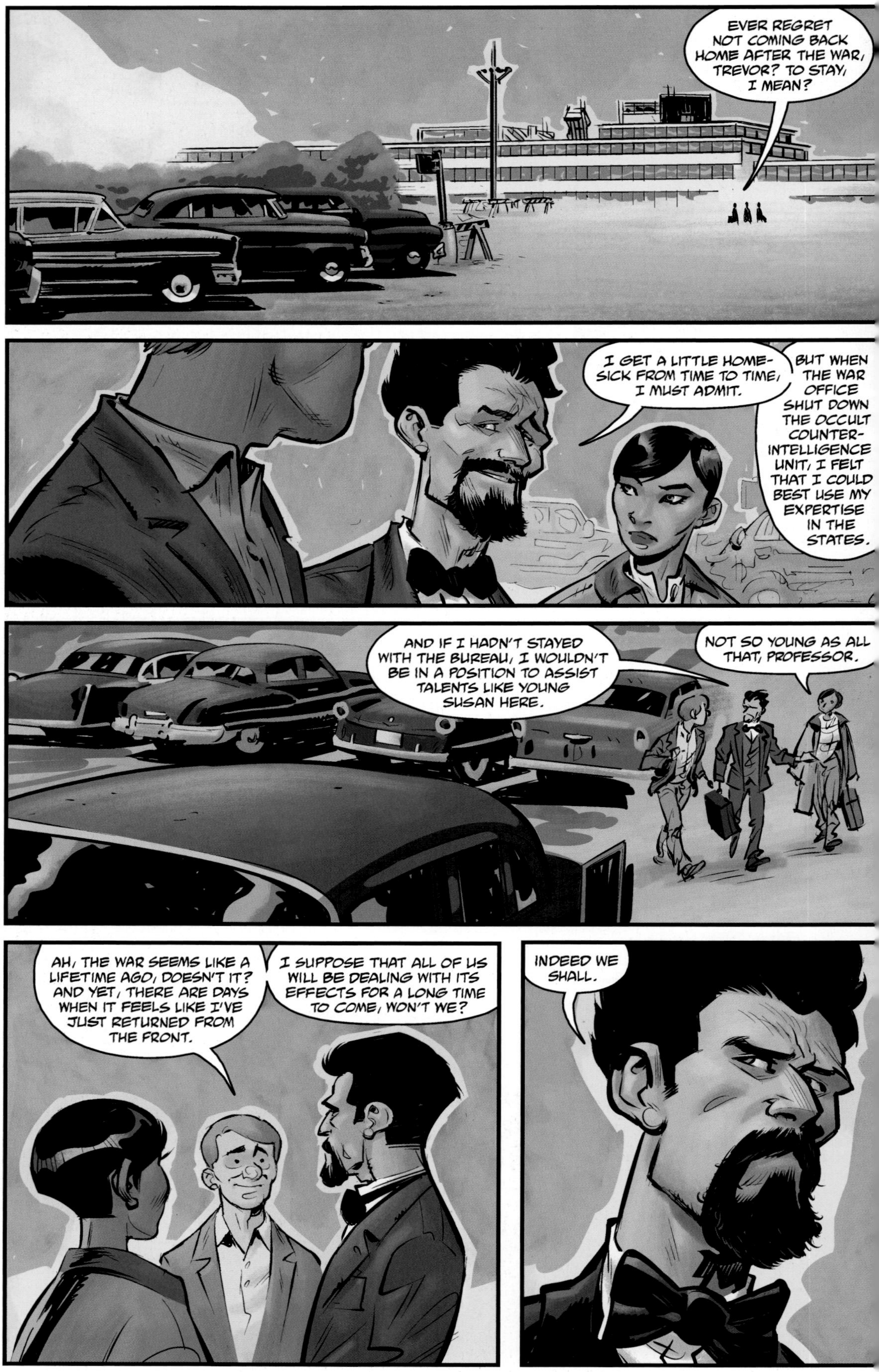
EVER REGRET NOT COMING BACK HOME AFTER THE WAR, TREVOR? TO STAY, I MEAN?
I GET A LITTLE HOME-SICK FROM TIME TO TIME, I MUST ADMIT.
BUT WHEN THE WAR OFFICE SHUT DOWN THE OCCULT COUNTER-INTELLIGENCE UNIT, I FELT THAT I COULD BEST USE MY EXPERTISE IN THE STATES.
AND IF I HADN'T STAYED WITH THE BUREAU, I WOULDN'T BE IN A POSITION TO ASSIST TALENTS LIKE YOUNG SUSAN HERE.
NOT SO YOUNG AS ALL THAT, PROFESSOR.
AH, THE WAR SEEMS LIKE A LIFETIME AGO, DOESN'T IT? AND YET, THERE ARE DAYS WHEN IT FEELS LIKE I'VE JUST RETURNED FROM THE FRONT.
I SUPPOSE THAT ALL OF US WILL BE DEALING WITH ITS EFFECTS FOR A LONG TIME TO COME, WON'T WE?
INDEED WE SHALL.

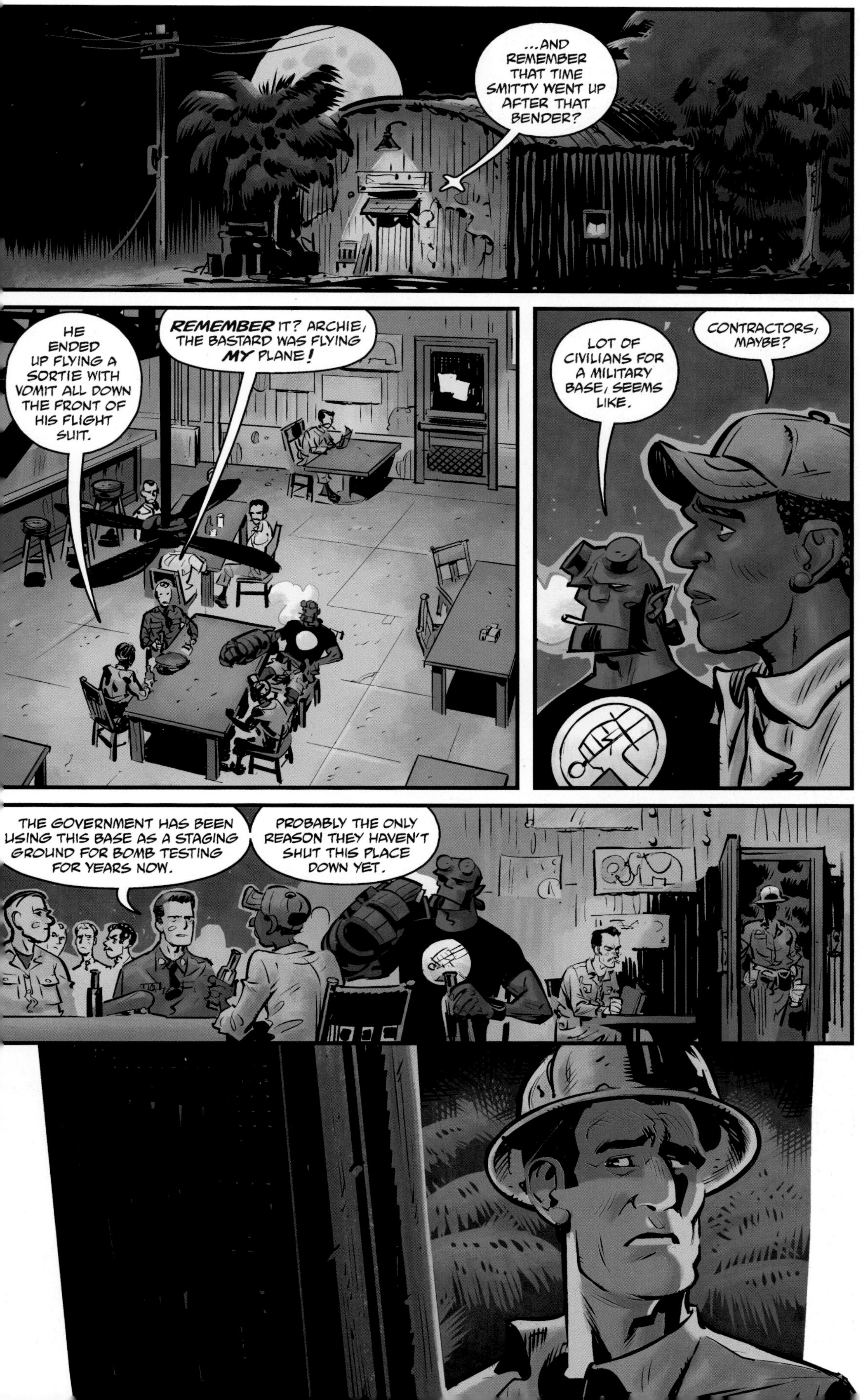
...AND REMEMBER THAT TIME SMITTY WENT UP AFTER THAT BENDER?
HE ENDED UP FLYING A SORTIE WITH VOMIT ALL DOWN THE FRONT OF HIS FLIGHT SUIT.
REMEMBER IT? ARCHIE, THE BASTARD WAS FLYING MY PLANE!
LOT OF CIVILIANS FOR A MILITARY BASE, SEEMS LIKE.
CONTRACTORS, MAYBE?
THE GOVERNMENT HAS BEEN USING THIS BASE AS A STAGING GROUND FOR BOMB TESTING FOR YEARS NOW.
PROBABLY THE ONLY REASON THEY HAVEN'T SHUT THIS PLACE DOWN YET.

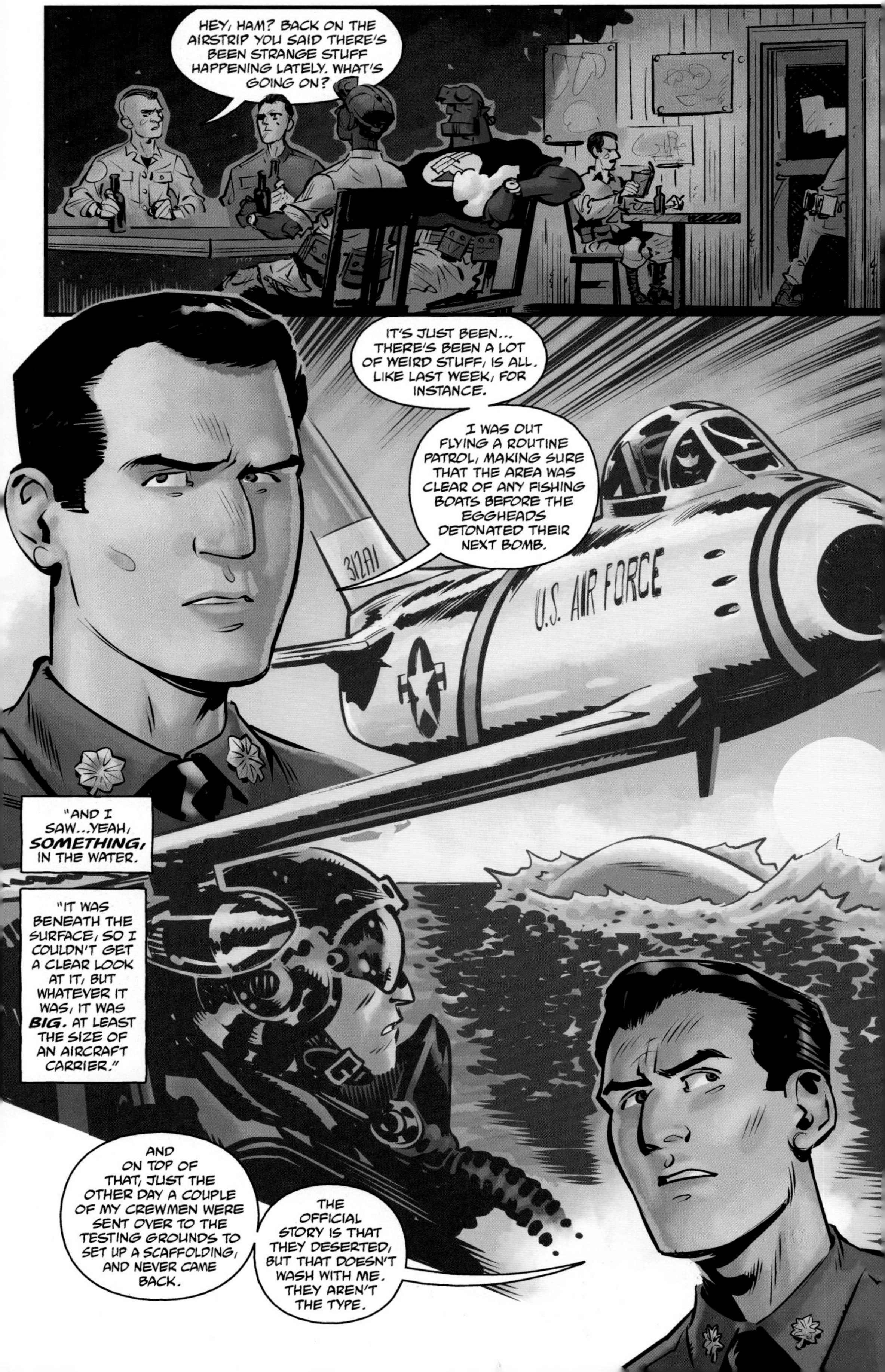
HEY, HAM? BACK ON THE AIRSTRIP YOU SAID THERE'S BEEN STRANGE STUFF HAPPENING LATELY. WHAT'S GOING ON?
IT'S JUST BEEN... THERE'S BEEN A LOT OF WEIRD STUFF, IS ALL. LIKE LAST WEEK, FOR INSTANCE.
I WAS OUT FLYING A ROUTINE PATROL, MAKING SURE THAT THE AREA WAS CLEAR OF ANY FISHING BOATS BEFORE THE EGGHEADS DETONATED THEIR NEXT BOMB.
312A1
U.S. AIR FORCE
"AND I SAW...YEAH, **SOMETHING,** IN THE WATER.
"IT WAS BENEATH THE SURFACE, SO I COULDN'T GET A CLEAR LOOK AT IT, BUT WHATEVER IT WAS, IT WAS **BIG.** AT LEAST THE SIZE OF AN AIRCRAFT CARRIER."
AND ON TOP OF THAT, JUST THE OTHER DAY A COUPLE OF MY CREWMEN WERE SENT OVER TO THE TESTING GROUNDS TO SET UP A SCAFFOLDING, AND NEVER CAME BACK.
THE OFFICIAL STORY IS THAT THEY DESERTED, BUT THAT DOESN'T WASH WITH ME. THEY AREN'T THE TYPE.

THE CREW THAT REPLACED THEM SAID THAT THE SCAFFOLDING HAD BEEN COMPLETELY DEMOLISHED-- LIKE A TORNADO HIT IT.

THE *E-BOMB* WAS JUST SITTING THERE, SCRATCHED ALL OVER.

WHAT'S AN "*E-BOMB*"?

OH. UM...WELL, NOT SURE, REALLY. THE LAST FEW YEARS THE GOVERNMENT HAS BEEN TESTING ATOMIC BOMBS ALL OVER THESE ISLANDS.

BUT THE GUYS WHO WERE DOING THE *A-BOMB* TESTING CLEARED OUT LATE LAST YEAR, AND A WHOLE NEW GROUP OF EGGHEADS CAME IN.

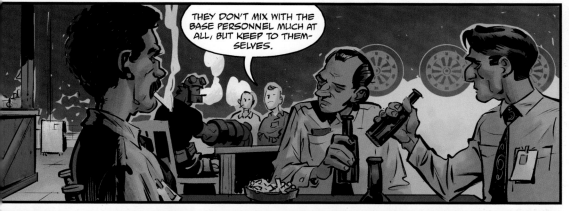

THEY DON'T MIX WITH THE BASE PERSONNEL MUCH AT ALL, BUT KEEP TO THEM- SELVES.

Hmmm.

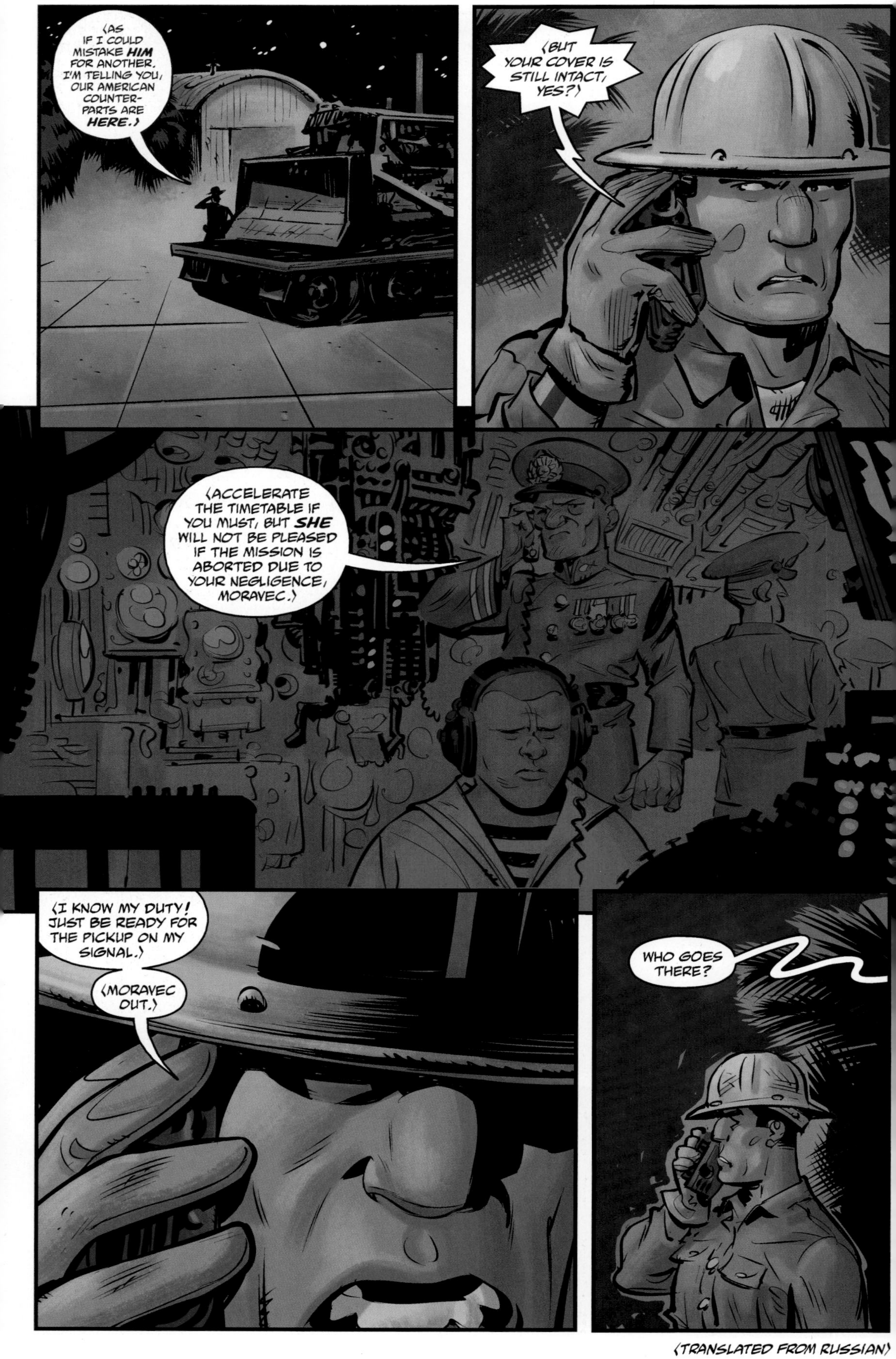
⟨AS IF I COULD MISTAKE HIM FOR ANOTHER. I'M TELLING YOU, OUR AMERICAN COUNTER-PARTS ARE HERE.⟩
⟨BUT YOUR COVER IS STILL INTACT, YES?⟩
⟨ACCELERATE THE TIMETABLE IF YOU MUST, BUT SHE WILL NOT BE PLEASED IF THE MISSION IS ABORTED DUE TO YOUR NEGLIGENCE, MORAVEC.⟩
⟨I KNOW MY DUTY! JUST BE READY FOR THE PICKUP ON MY SIGNAL.⟩
⟨MORAVEC OUT.⟩
WHO GOES THERE?

⟨TRANSLATED FROM RUSSIAN⟩

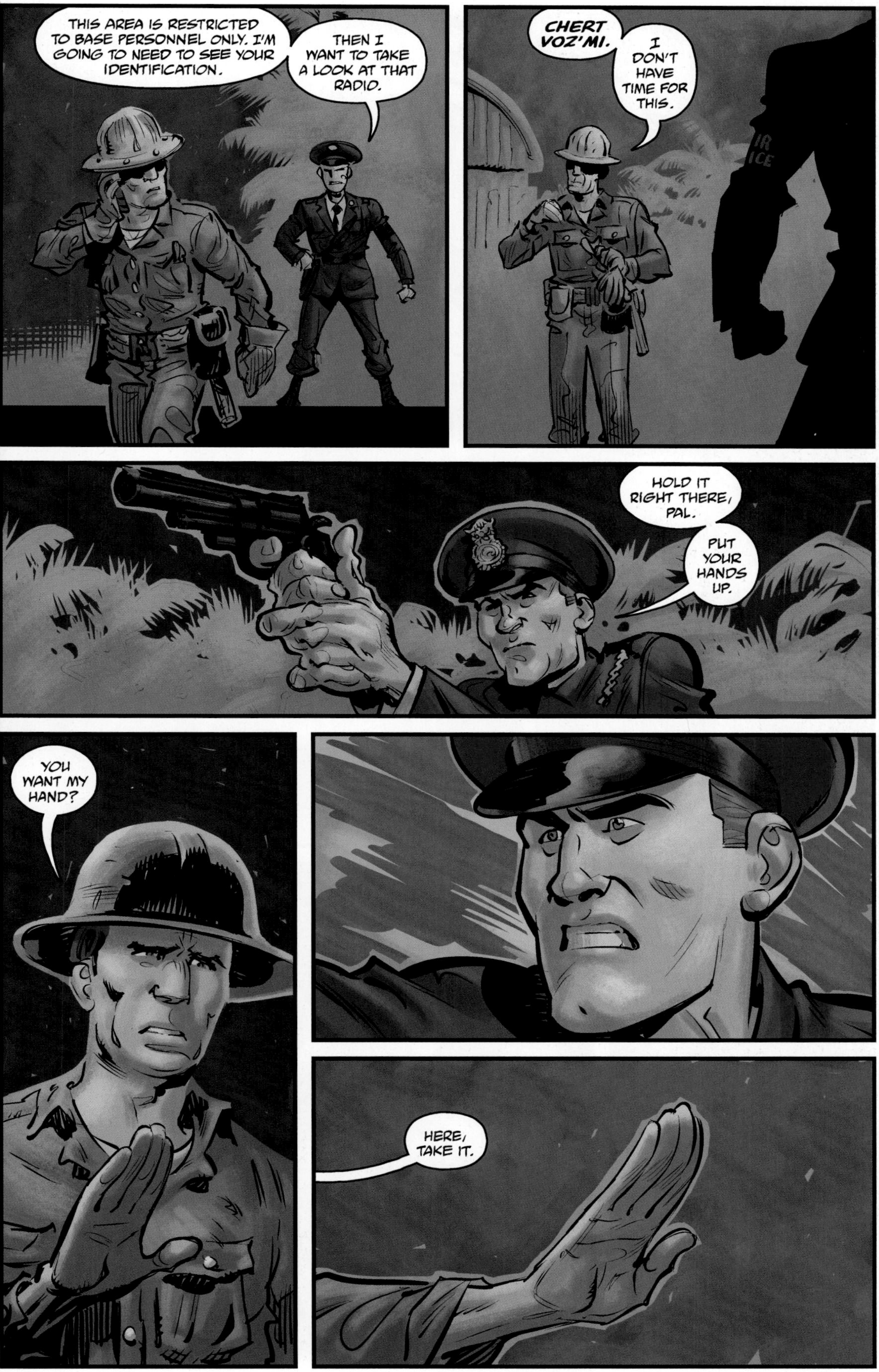
THIS AREA IS RESTRICTED TO BASE PERSONNEL ONLY. I'M GOING TO NEED TO SEE YOUR IDENTIFICATION.
THEN I WANT TO TAKE A LOOK AT THAT RADIO.
CHERT VOZ'MI.
I DON'T HAVE TIME FOR THIS.
HOLD IT RIGHT THERE, PAL.
PUT YOUR HANDS UP.
YOU WANT MY HAND?
HERE, TAKE IT.

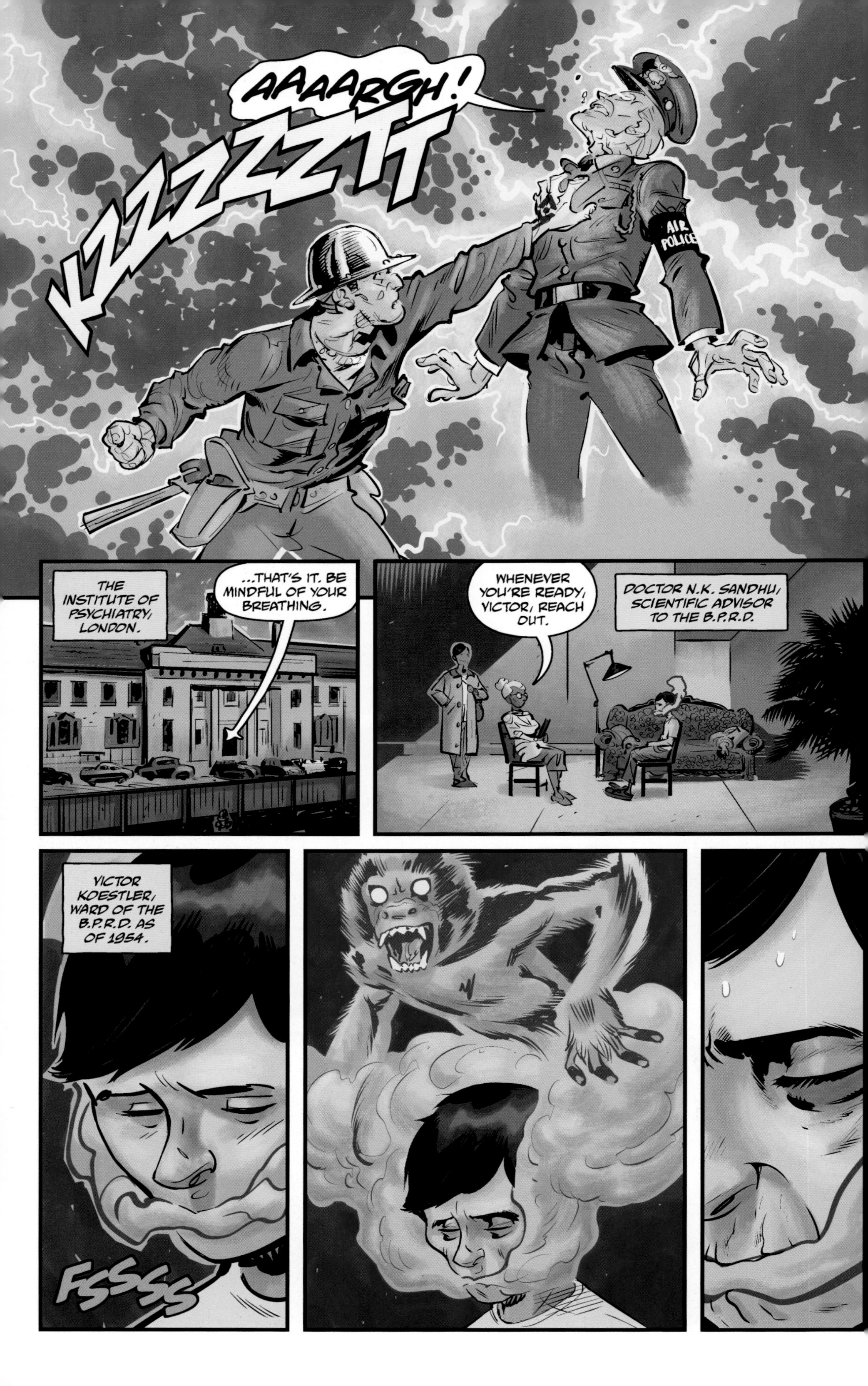
AAAARGH!
KZZZZZTT
THE INSTITUTE OF PSYCHIATRY, LONDON.
...THAT'S IT. BE MINDFUL OF YOUR BREATHING.
WHENEVER YOU'RE READY, VICTOR, REACH OUT.
DOCTOR N.K. SANDHU, SCIENTIFIC ADVISOR TO THE B.P.R.D.
VICTOR KOESTLER, WARD OF THE B.P.R.D. AS OF 1954.
FSSSS

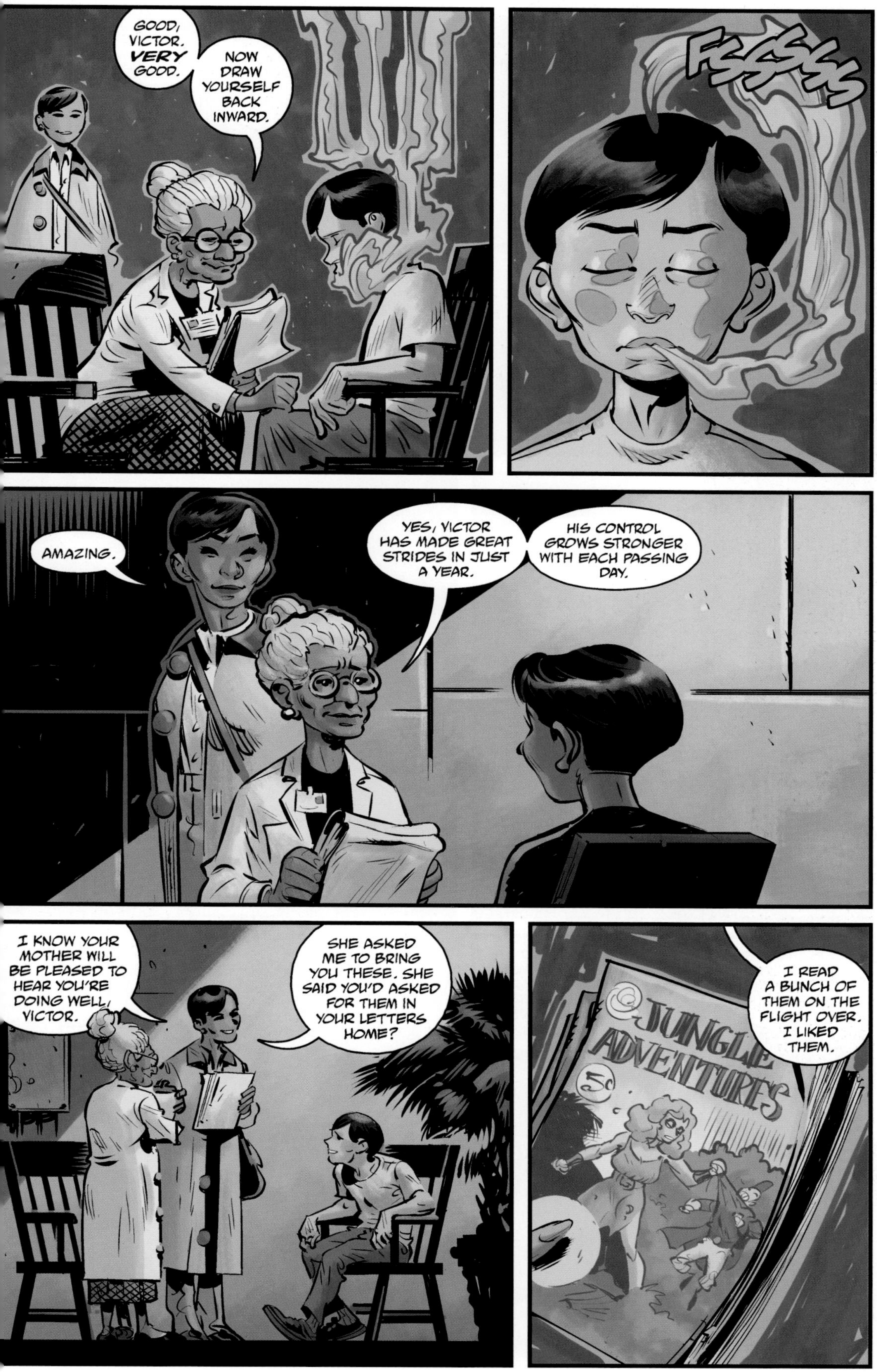
GOOD, VICTOR. VERY GOOD.
NOW DRAW YOURSELF BACK INWARD.
FSSSSS
AMAZING.
YES, VICTOR HAS MADE GREAT STRIDES IN JUST A YEAR.
HIS CONTROL GROWS STRONGER WITH EACH PASSING DAY.
I KNOW YOUR MOTHER WILL BE PLEASED TO HEAR YOU'RE DOING WELL, VICTOR.
SHE ASKED ME TO BRING YOU THESE. SHE SAID YOU'D ASKED FOR THEM IN YOUR LETTERS HOME?
JUNGLE ADVENTURES
5¢
I READ A BUNCH OF THEM ON THE FLIGHT OVER. I LIKED THEM.

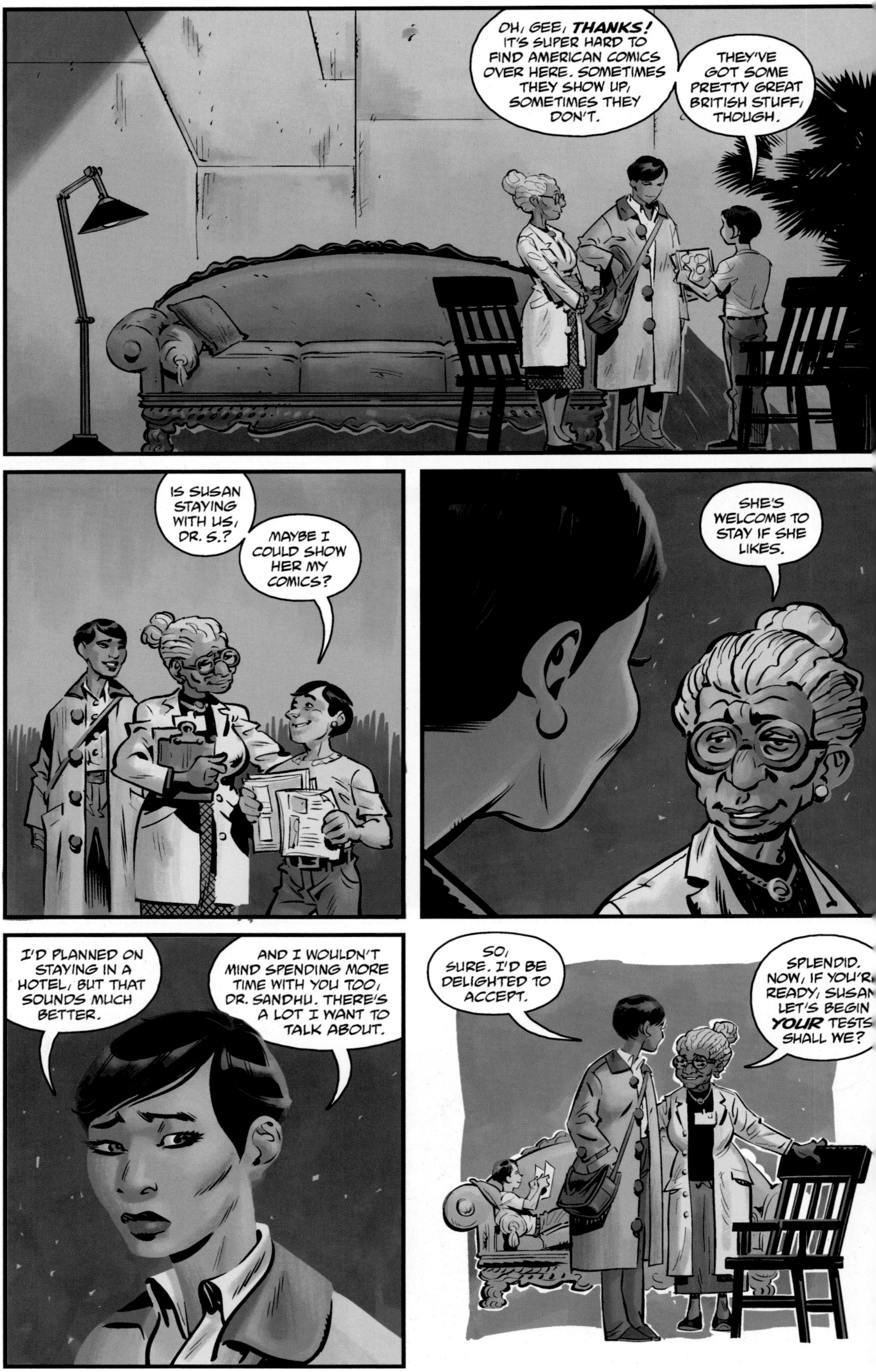
OH, GEE, **THANKS!** IT'S SUPER HARD TO FIND AMERICAN COMICS OVER HERE. SOMETIMES THEY SHOW UP, SOMETIMES THEY DON'T.
THEY'VE GOT SOME PRETTY GREAT BRITISH STUFF, THOUGH.
IS SUSAN STAYING WITH US, DR. S.?
MAYBE I COULD SHOW HER MY COMICS?
SHE'S WELCOME TO STAY IF SHE LIKES.
I'D PLANNED ON STAYING IN A HOTEL, BUT THAT SOUNDS MUCH BETTER.
AND I WOULDN'T MIND SPENDING MORE TIME WITH YOU TOO, DR. SANDHU. THERE'S A LOT I WANT TO TALK ABOUT.
SO, SURE. I'D BE DELIGHTED TO ACCEPT.
SPLENDID. NOW, IF YOU'R READY, SUSAN LET'S BEGIN ***YOUR*** TESTS SHALL WE?

YOU DIDN'T REALLY COME ALL THIS WAY JUST TO HANG ABOUT A BIT, DID YOU, TREVOR?

WHAT ARE YOU *REALLY* HERE FOR? SOME B.P.R.D. BUSINESS?

TELL ME, HARRY, DO YOU SEE MUCH OF THE OLD CROWD THESE DAYS? ARE YOU STILL IN CONTACT WITH OUR COLLEAGUES FROM THE BRITISH PARANORMAL SOCIETY, FOR EXAMPLE?

MOST OF THEM SEEM TO HAVE GONE TO GROUND. BUT IT SEEMS LIKE *SOMEONE* ELSE IS STILL INVESTIGATING OUT THERE.

NO, NOTHING OFFICIAL. JUST FOLLOWING UP ON A HUNCH, I SUPPOSE YOU COULD SAY.

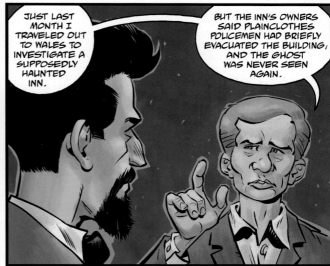

JUST LAST MONTH I TRAVELED OUT TO WALES TO INVESTIGATE A SUPPOSEDLY HAUNTED INN.

BUT THE INN'S OWNERS SAID PLAINCLOTHES POLICEMEN HAD BRIEFLY EVACUATED THE BUILDING, AND THE GHOST WAS NEVER SEEN AGAIN.

"WHEN I SPOKE TO THE POLICE, THOUGH, THEY DENIED ALL KNOWLEDGE OF ANY SUCH INVESTIGATION, OR INDEED OF THE MEN THAT THE OWNERS DESCRIBED."

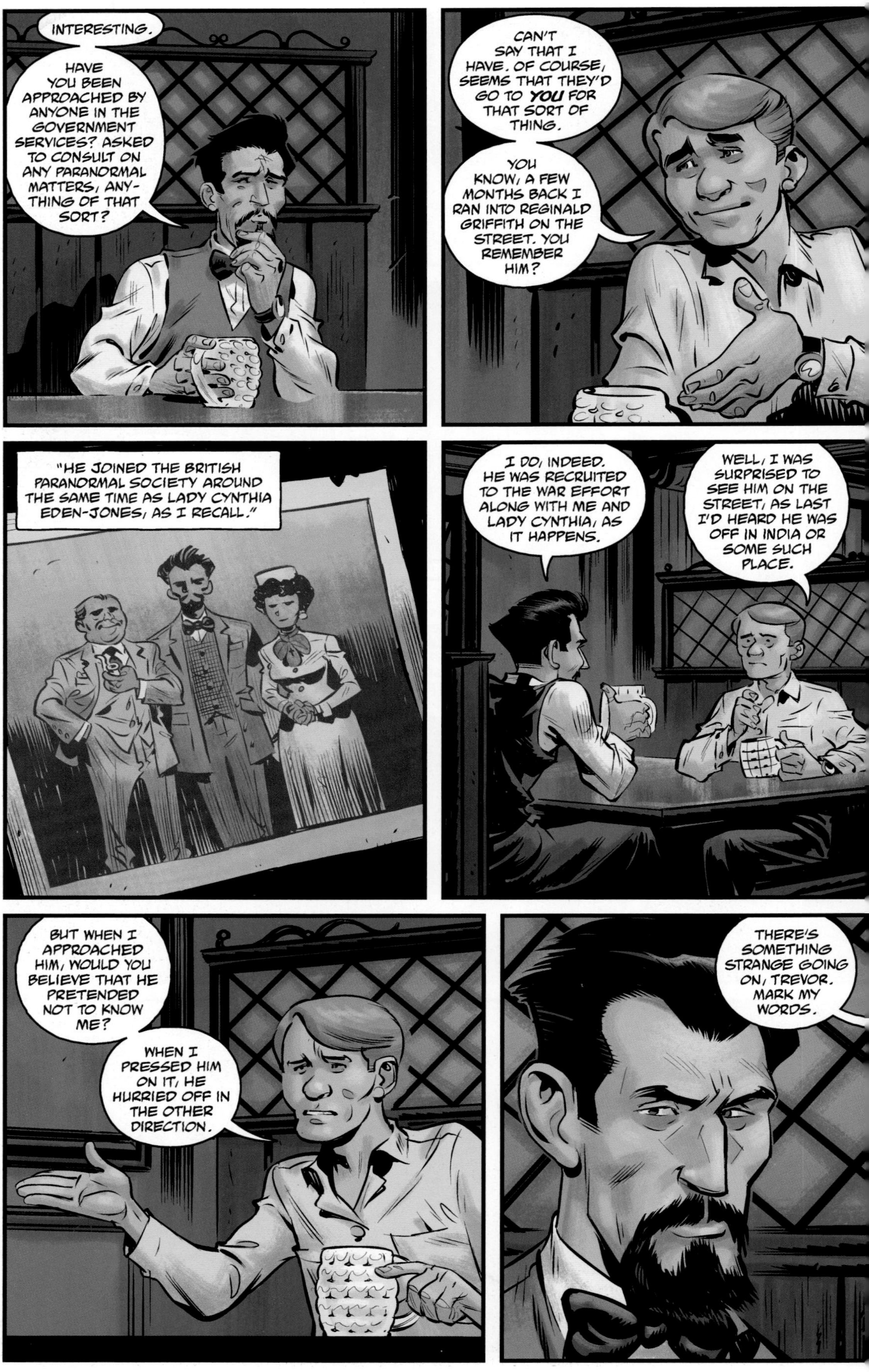
INTERESTING.
HAVE YOU BEEN APPROACHED BY ANYONE IN THE GOVERNMENT SERVICES? ASKED TO CONSULT ON ANY PARANORMAL MATTERS, ANY-THING OF THAT SORT?
CAN'T SAY THAT I HAVE. OF COURSE, SEEMS THAT THEY'D GO TO **YOU** FOR THAT SORT OF THING.
YOU KNOW, A FEW MONTHS BACK I RAN INTO REGINALD GRIFFITH ON THE STREET. YOU REMEMBER HIM?
"HE JOINED THE BRITISH PARANORMAL SOCIETY AROUND THE SAME TIME AS LADY CYNTHIA EDEN-JONES, AS I RECALL."
I DO, INDEED. HE WAS RECRUITED TO THE WAR EFFORT ALONG WITH ME AND LADY CYNTHIA, AS IT HAPPENS.
WELL, I WAS SURPRISED TO SEE HIM ON THE STREET, AS LAST I'D HEARD HE WAS OFF IN INDIA OR SOME SUCH PLACE.
BUT WHEN I APPROACHED HIM, WOULD YOU BELIEVE THAT HE PRETENDED NOT TO KNOW ME?
WHEN I PRESSED HIM ON IT, HE HURRIED OFF IN THE OTHER DIRECTION.
THERE'S SOMETHING STRANGE GOING ON, TREVOR. MARK MY WORDS.

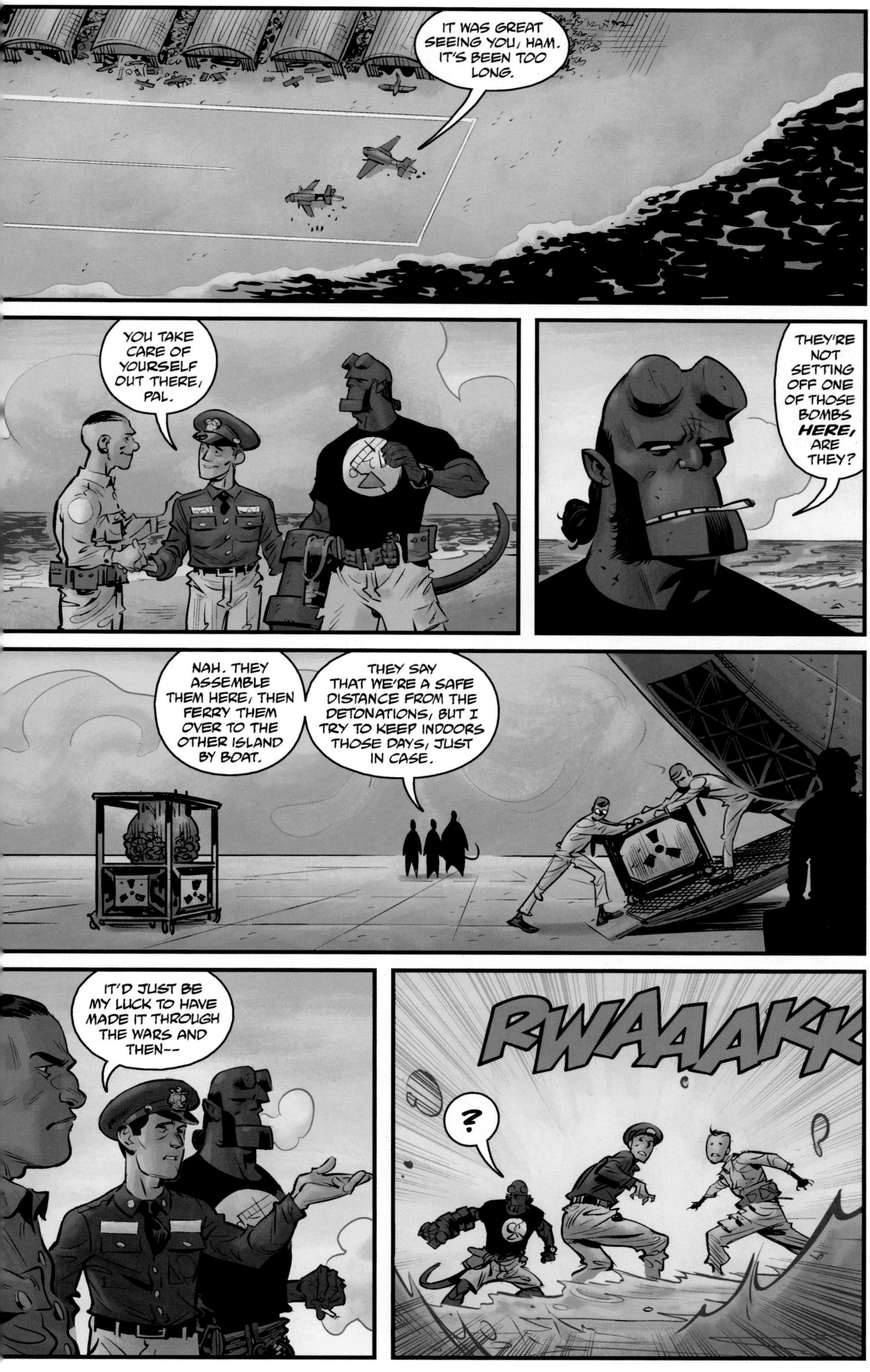
IT WAS GREAT SEEING YOU, HAM. IT'S BEEN TOO LONG.
YOU TAKE CARE OF YOURSELF OUT THERE, PAL.
THEY'RE NOT SETTING OFF ONE OF THOSE BOMBS HERE, ARE THEY?
NAH. THEY ASSEMBLE THEM HERE, THEN FERRY THEM OVER TO THE OTHER ISLAND BY BOAT.
THEY SAY THAT WE'RE A SAFE DISTANCE FROM THE DETONATIONS, BUT I TRY TO KEEP INDOORS THOSE DAYS, JUST IN CASE.
IT'D JUST BE MY LUCK TO HAVE MADE IT THROUGH THE WARS AND THEN--
RWAAAKK
?

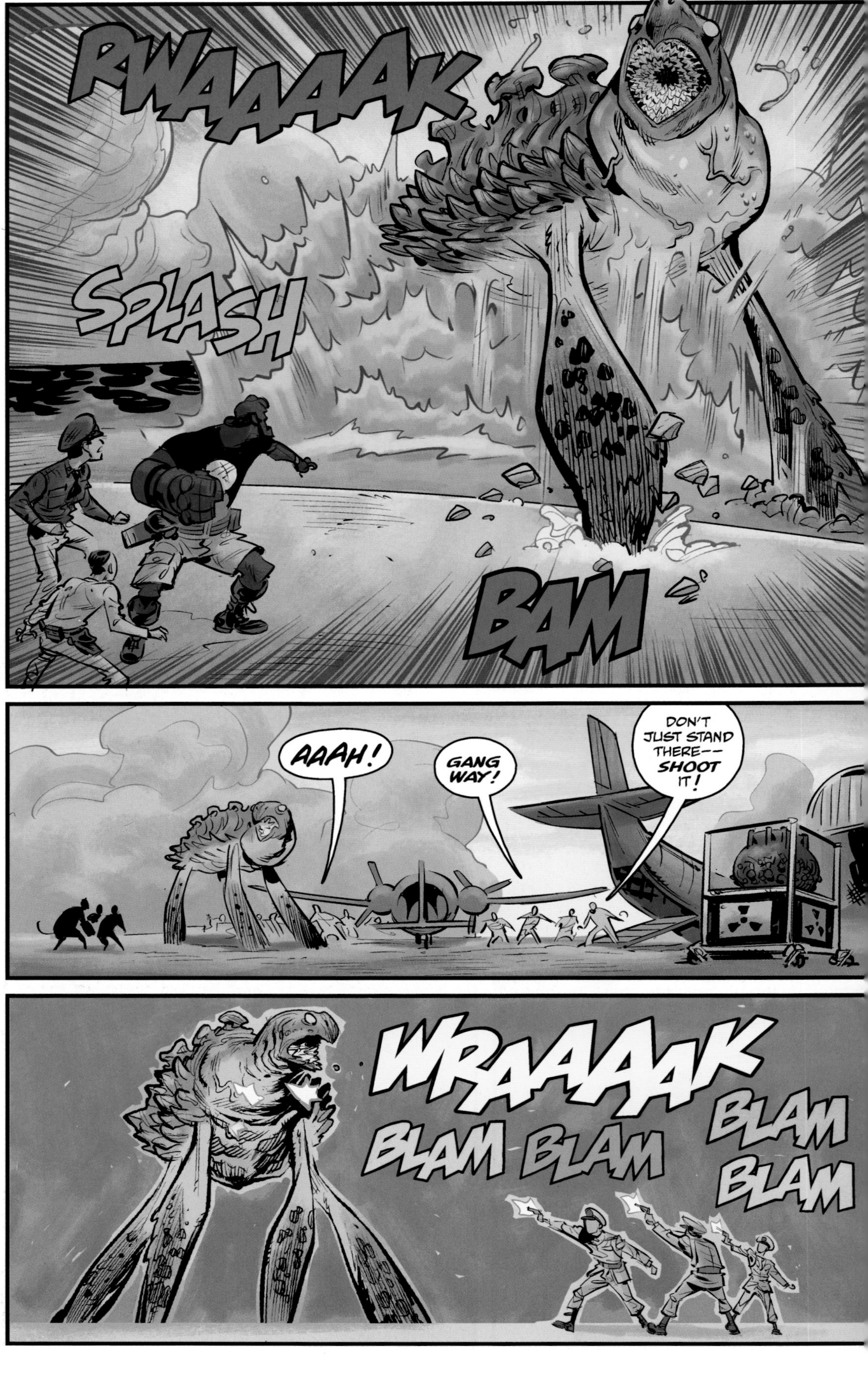
RWAAAAK
SPLASH
BAM
AAAH!
GANG WAY!
DON'T JUST STAND THERE-- SHOOT IT!
WRAAAAK
BLAM BLAM BLAM
BLAM BLAM

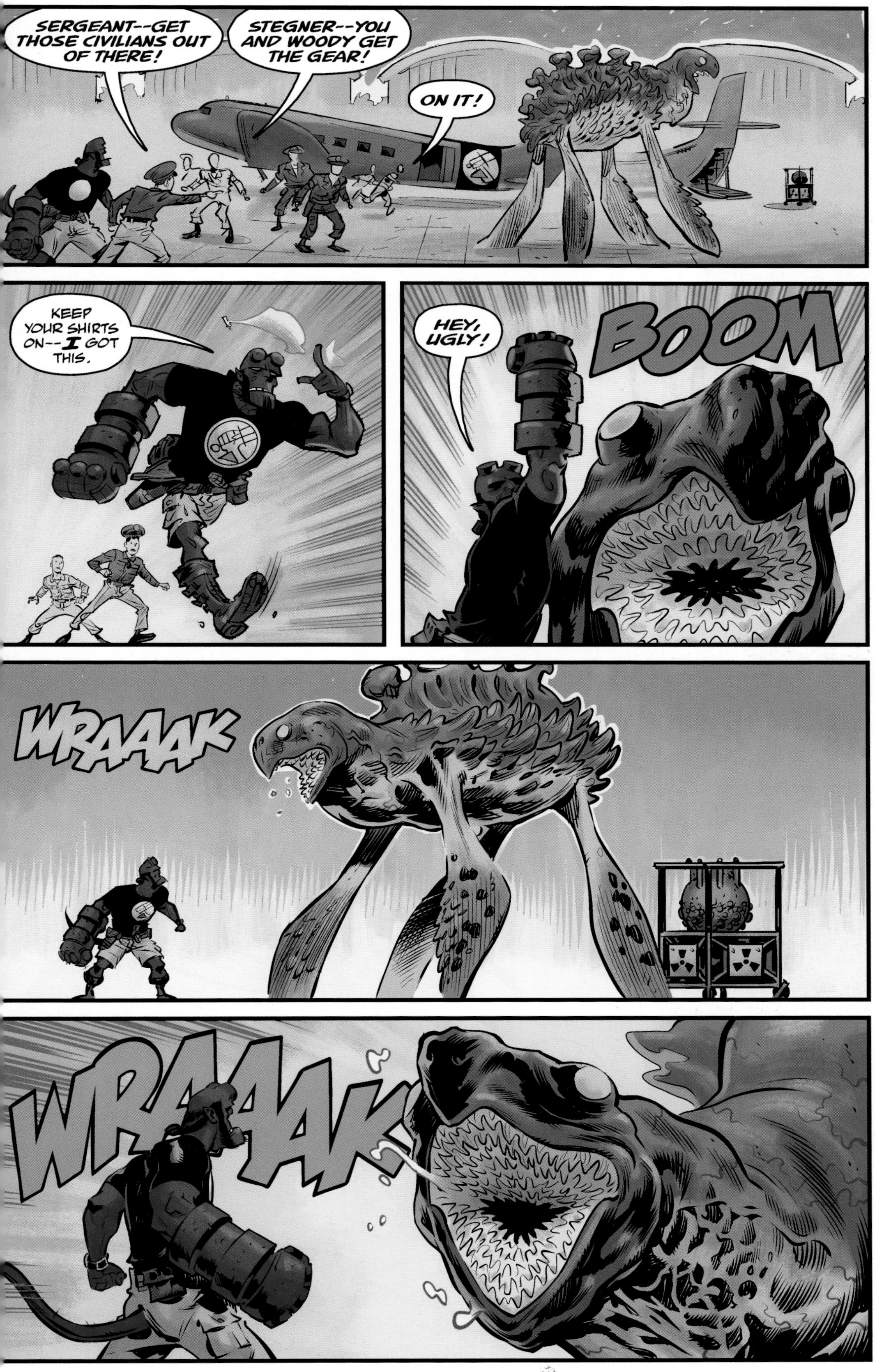
SERGEANT--GET THOSE CIVILIANS OUT OF THERE!
STEGNER--YOU AND WOODY GET THE GEAR!
ON IT!
KEEP YOUR SHIRTS ON--I GOT THIS.
HEY, UGLY!
BOOM
WRAAAK
WRAAAK

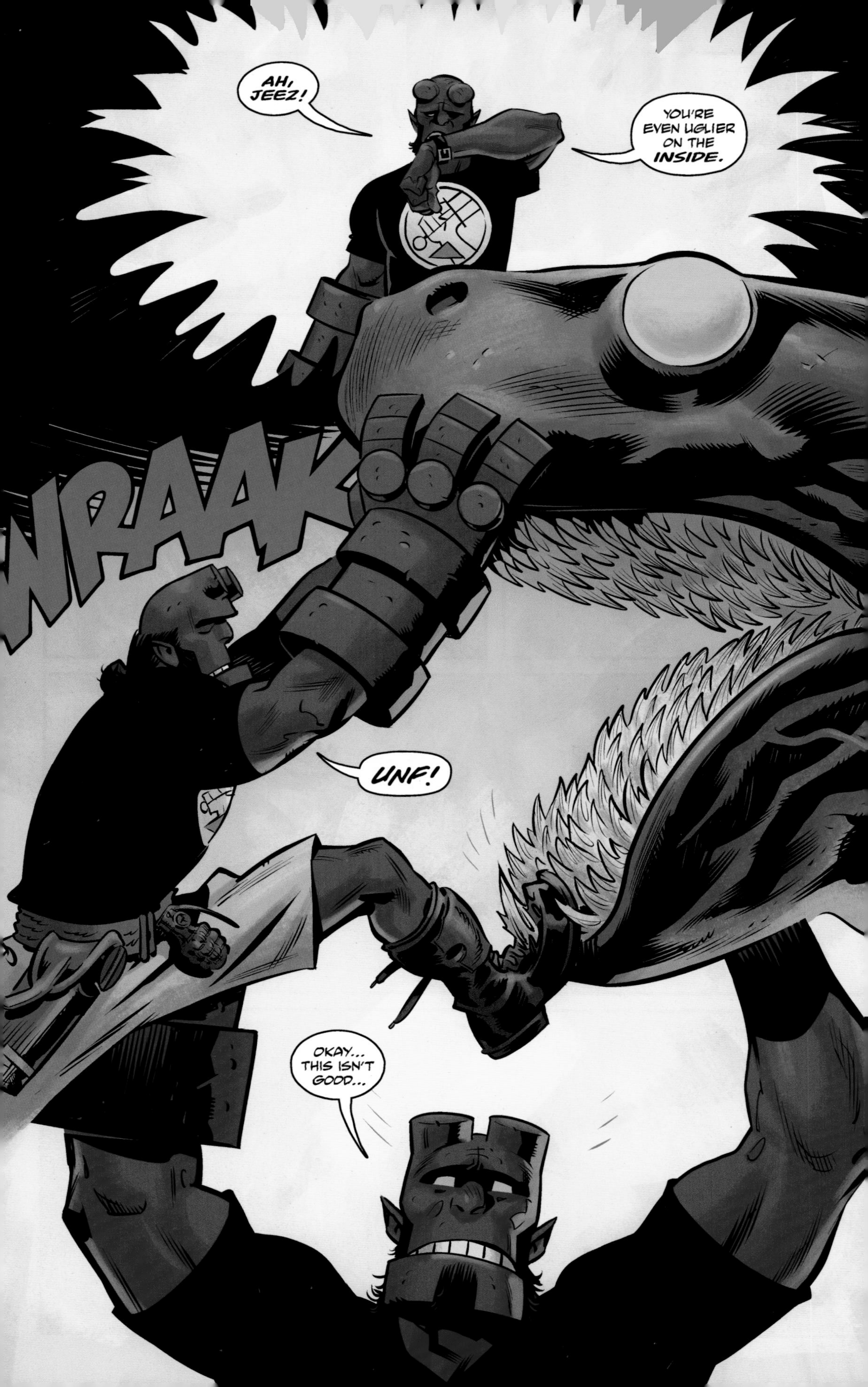
AH, JEEZ!
YOU'RE EVEN UGLIER ON THE INSIDE.
WRAAK
UNF!
OKAY... THIS ISN'T GOOD...

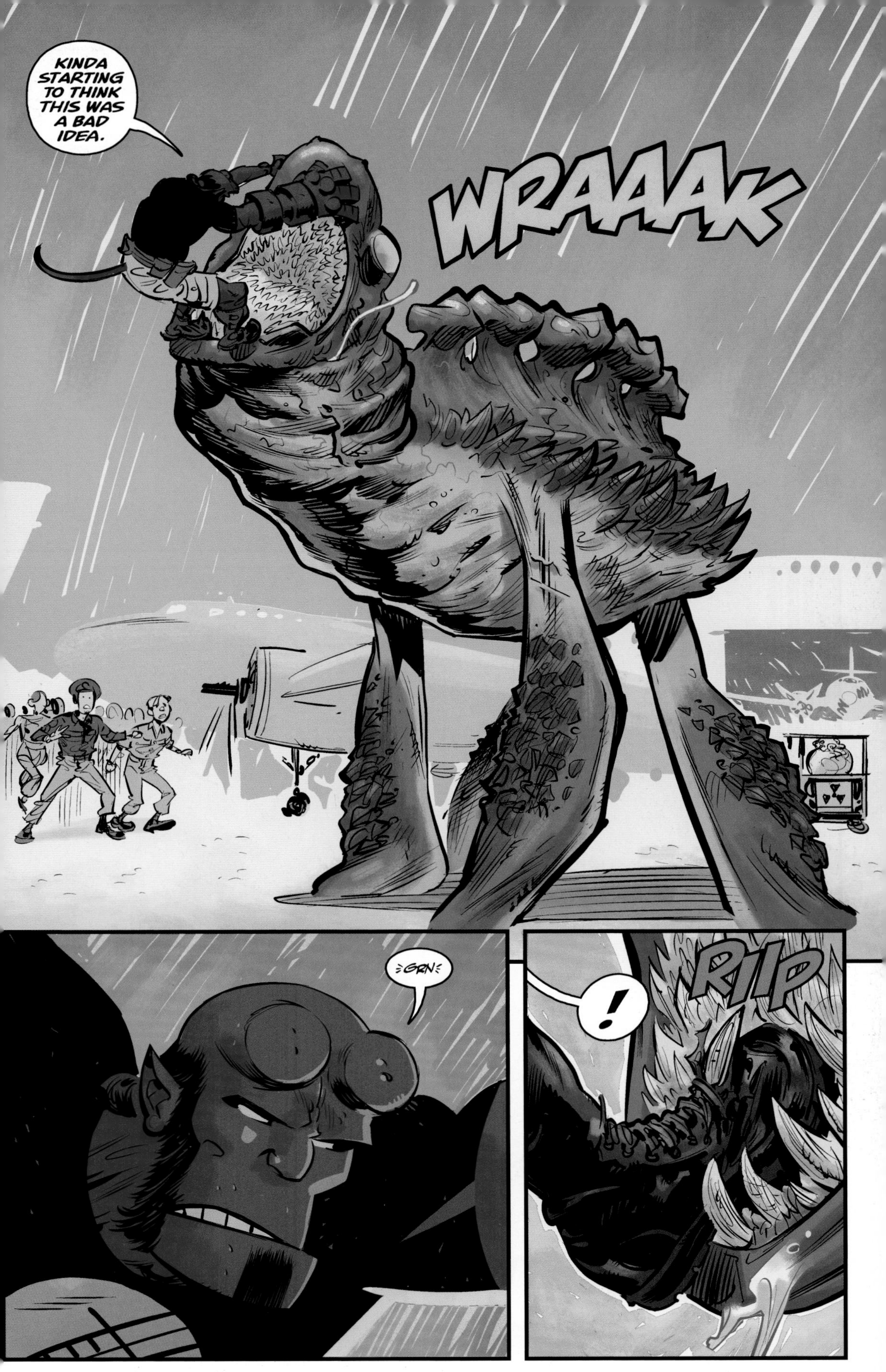
KINDA STARTING TO THINK THIS WAS A BAD IDEA.
WRAAAK
GRN
!
RIP

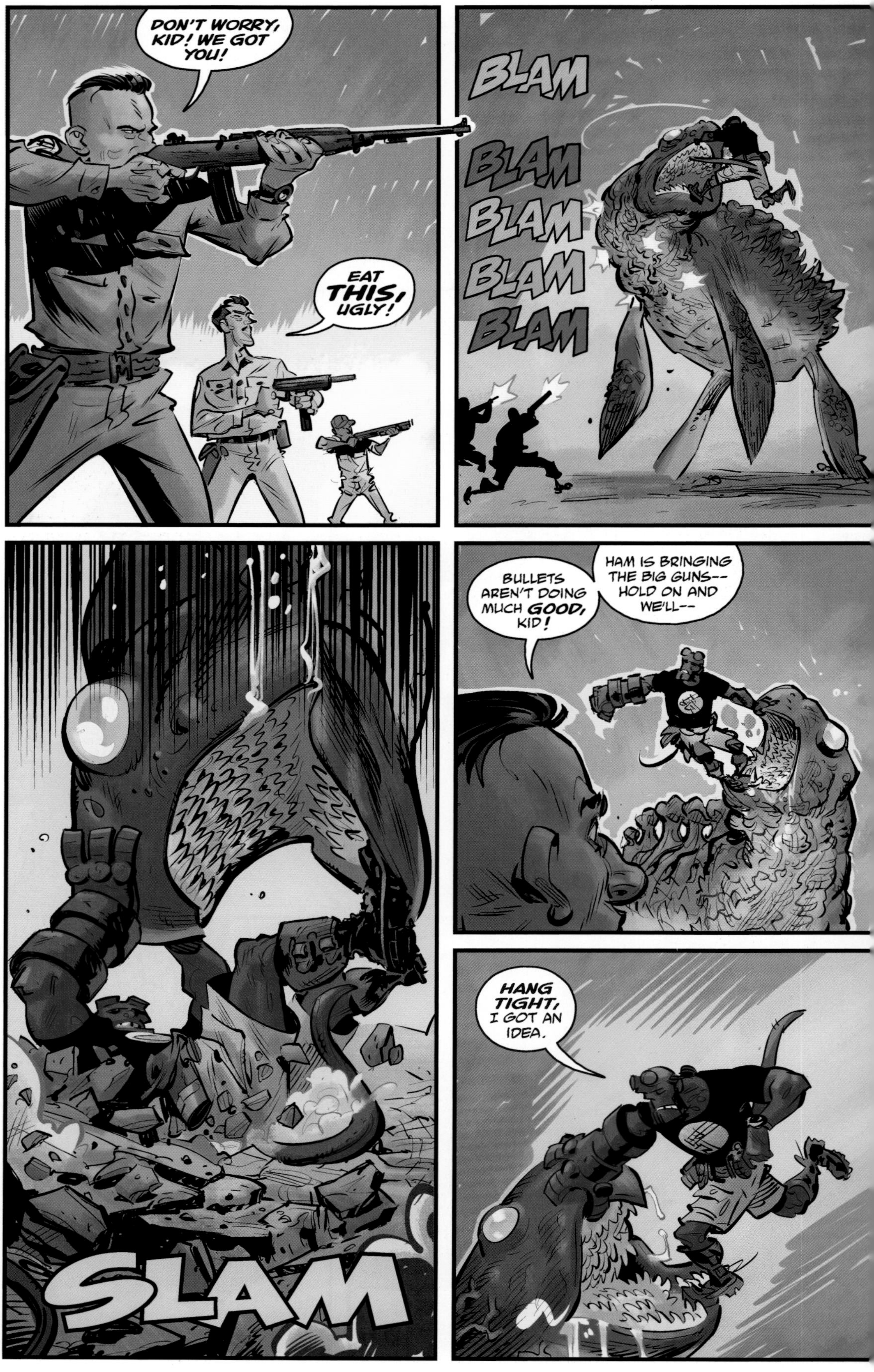
DON'T WORRY, KID! WE GOT YOU!
EAT THIS, UGLY!
BLAM
BLAM
BLAM
BLAM
BLAM
SLAM
BULLETS AREN'T DOING MUCH GOOD, KID!
HAM IS BRINGING THE BIG GUNS-- HOLD ON AND WE'LL--
HANG TIGHT, I GOT AN IDEA.

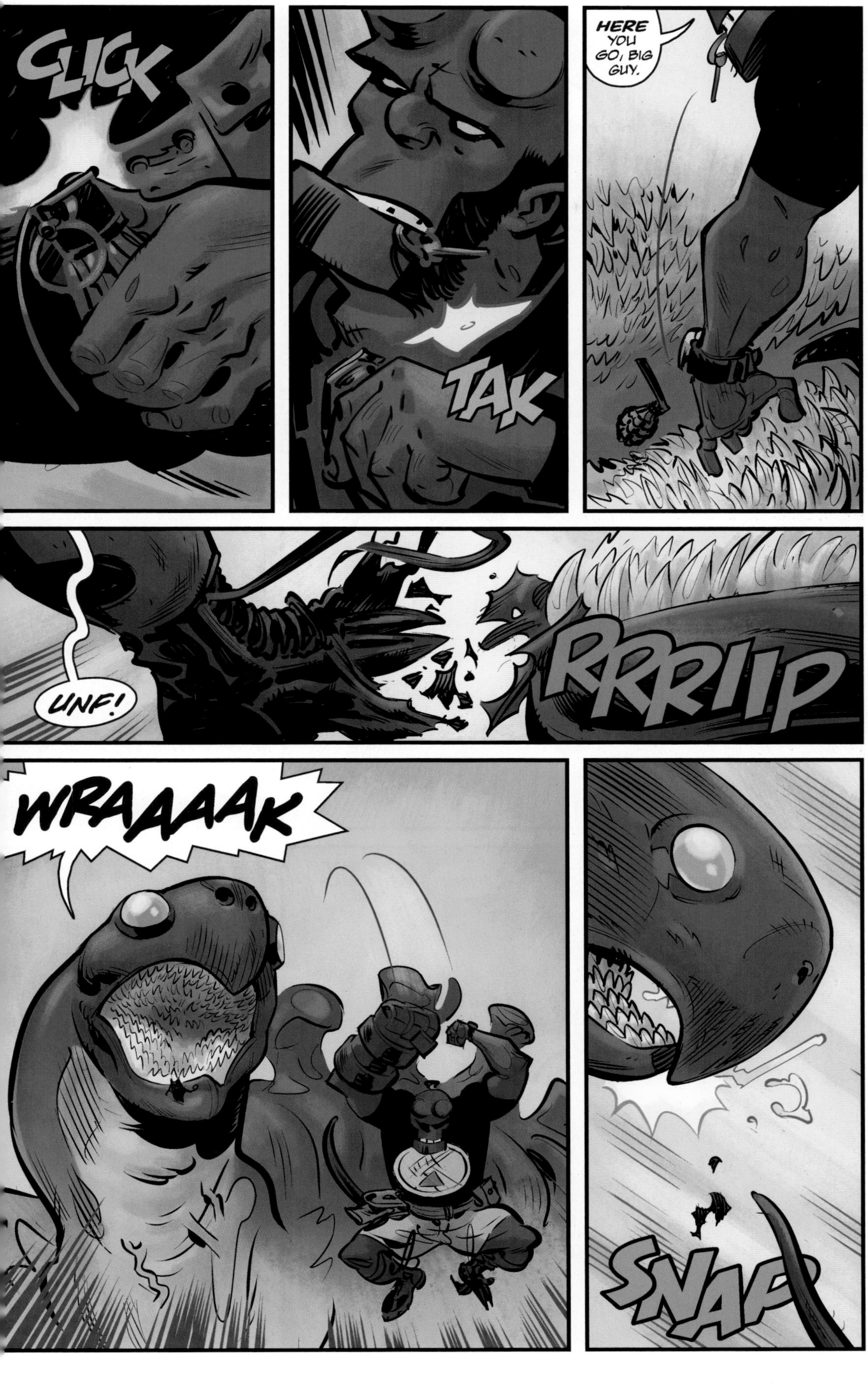
CLICK
TAK
HERE YOU GO, BIG GUY.
UNF!
RRRIIP
WRAAAAK
SNAP

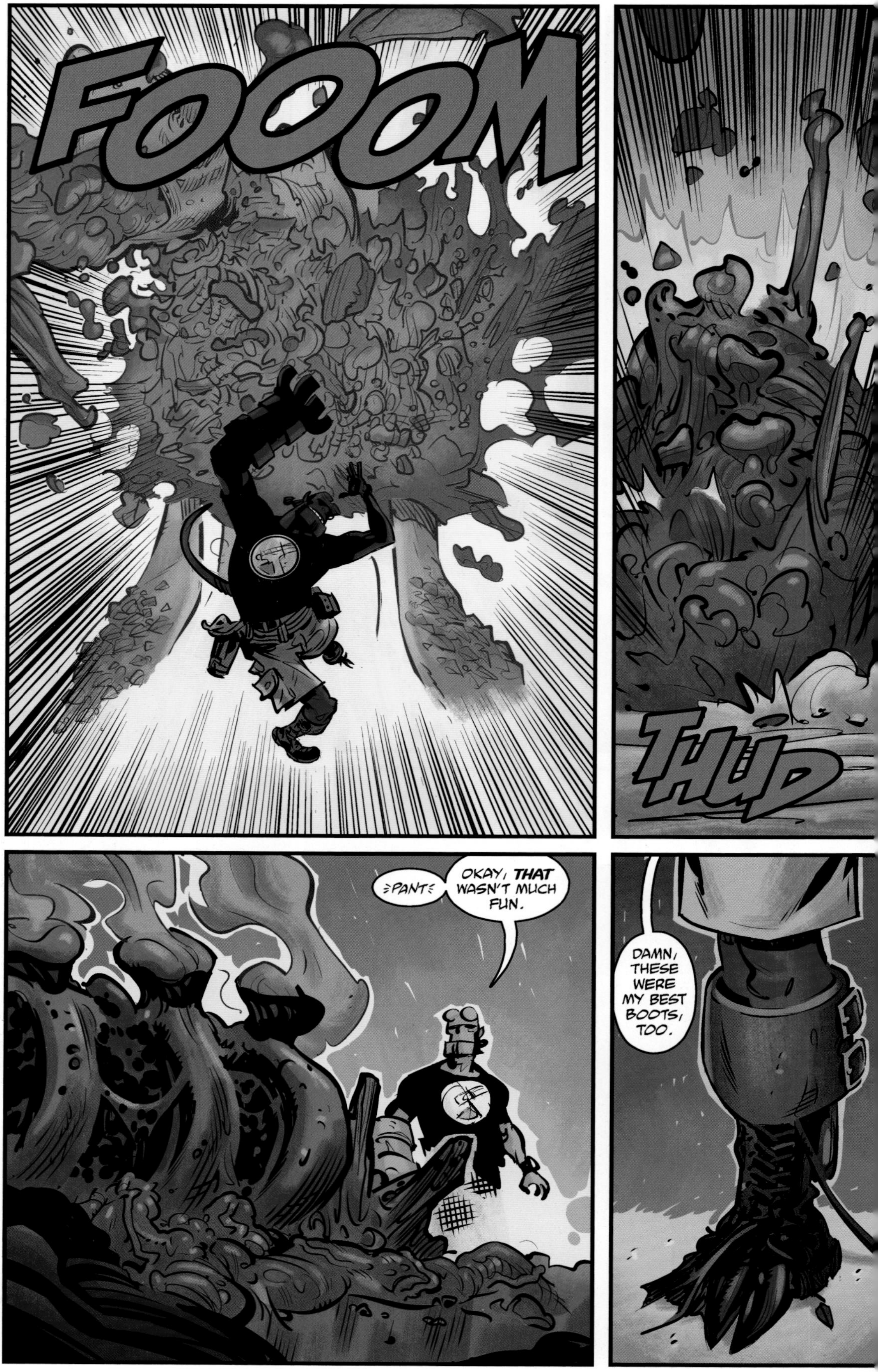
FOOOM
THUD
PANT
OKAY, THAT WASN'T MUCH FUN.
DAMN, THESE WERE MY BEST BOOTS, TOO.

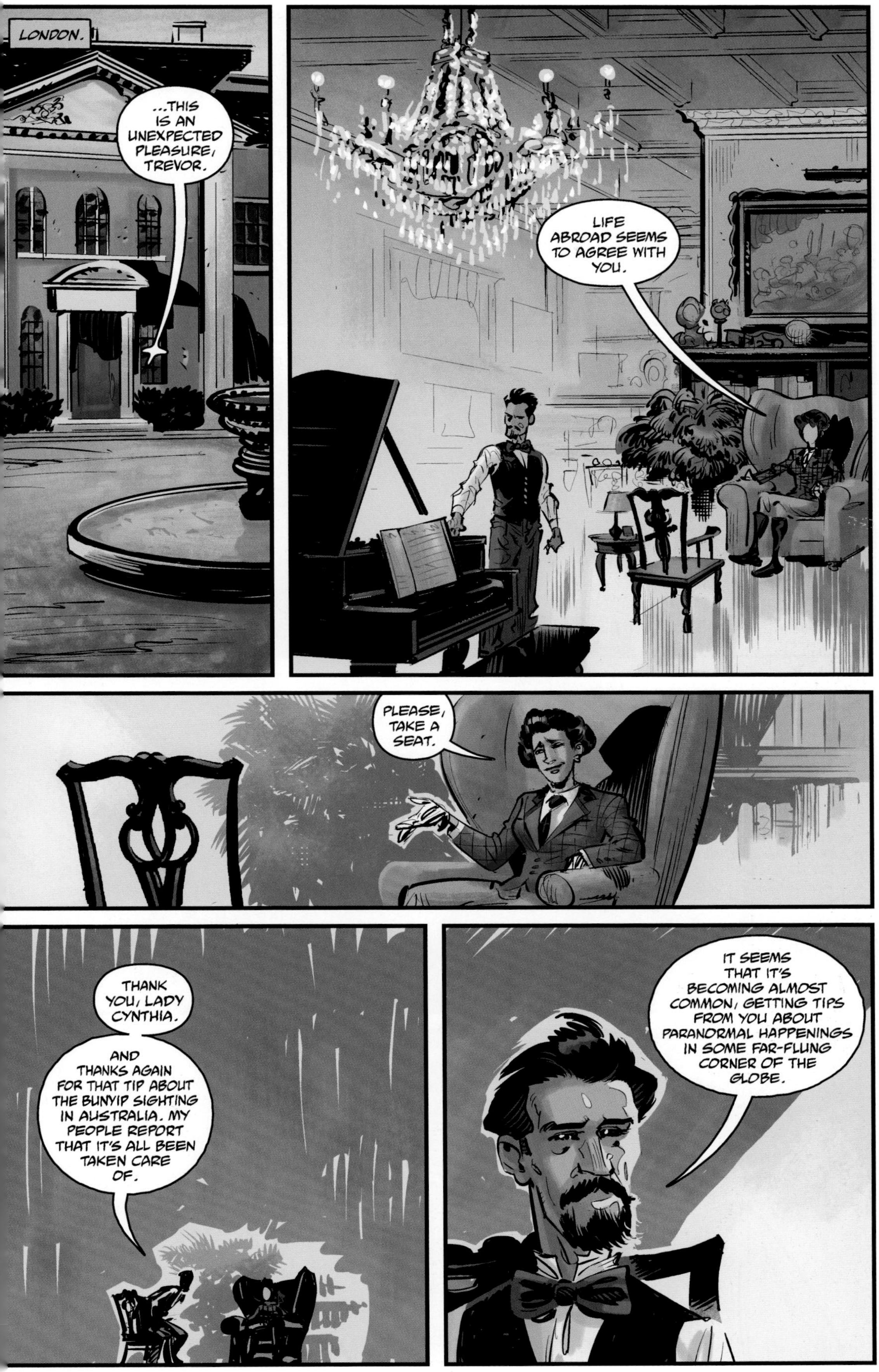
LONDON.
...THIS IS AN UNEXPECTED PLEASURE, TREVOR.
LIFE ABROAD SEEMS TO AGREE WITH YOU.
PLEASE, TAKE A SEAT.
THANK YOU, LADY CYNTHIA.
AND THANKS AGAIN FOR THAT TIP ABOUT THE BUNYIP SIGHTING IN AUSTRALIA. MY PEOPLE REPORT THAT IT'S ALL BEEN TAKEN CARE OF.
IT SEEMS THAT IT'S BECOMING ALMOST COMMON, GETTING TIPS FROM YOU ABOUT PARANORMAL HAPPENINGS IN SOME FAR-FLUNG CORNER OF THE GLOBE.

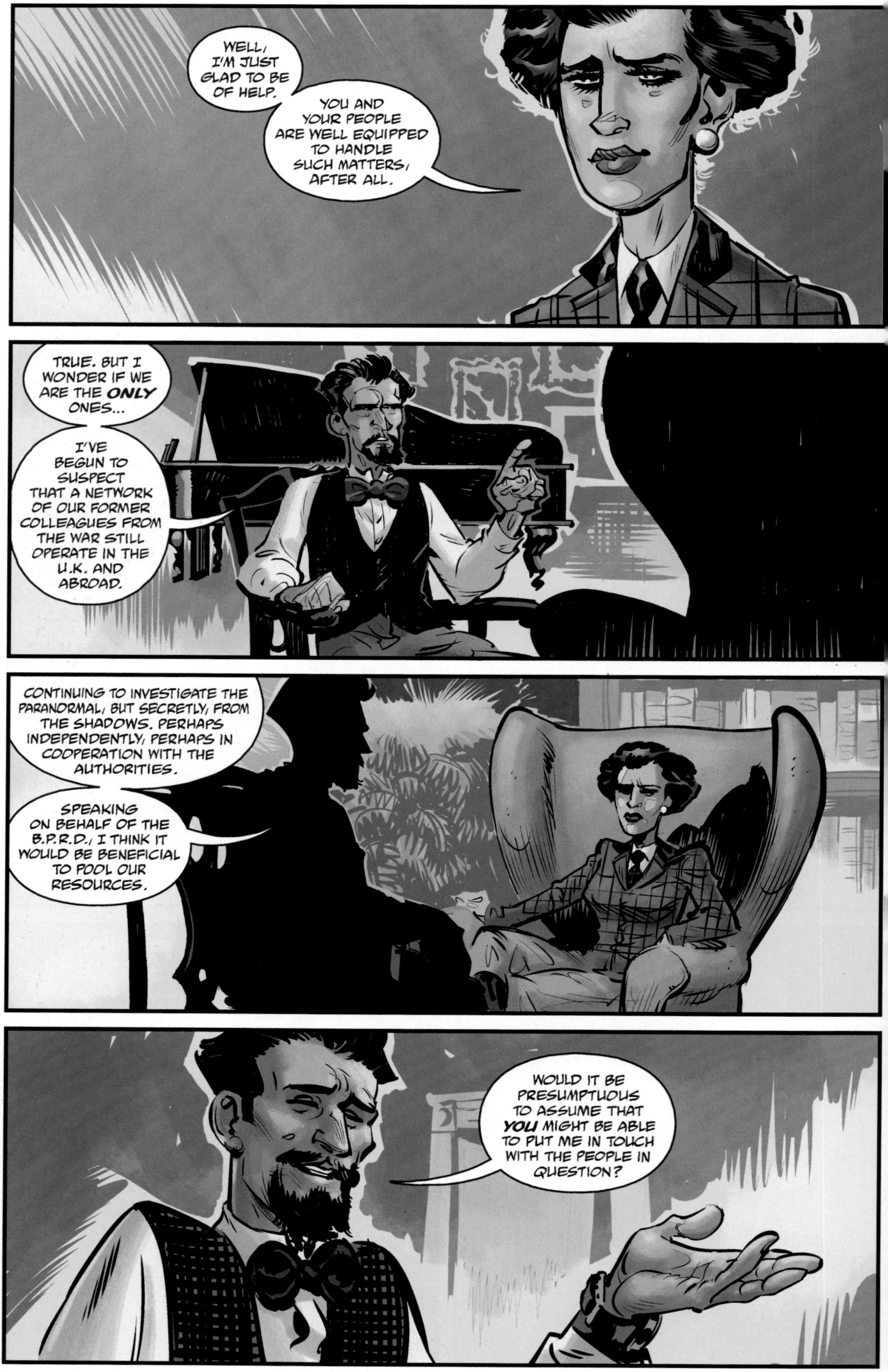
WELL, I'M JUST GLAD TO BE OF HELP.
YOU AND YOUR PEOPLE ARE WELL EQUIPPED TO HANDLE SUCH MATTERS, AFTER ALL.
TRUE. BUT I WONDER IF WE ARE THE ONLY ONES...
I'VE BEGUN TO SUSPECT THAT A NETWORK OF OUR FORMER COLLEAGUES FROM THE WAR STILL OPERATE IN THE U.K. AND ABROAD.
CONTINUING TO INVESTIGATE THE PARANORMAL, BUT SECRETLY, FROM THE SHADOWS. PERHAPS INDEPENDENTLY, PERHAPS IN COOPERATION WITH THE AUTHORITIES.
SPEAKING ON BEHALF OF THE B.P.R.D., I THINK IT WOULD BE BENEFICIAL TO POOL OUR RESOURCES.
WOULD IT BE PRESUMPTUOUS TO ASSUME THAT YOU MIGHT BE ABLE TO PUT ME IN TOUCH WITH THE PEOPLE IN QUESTION?

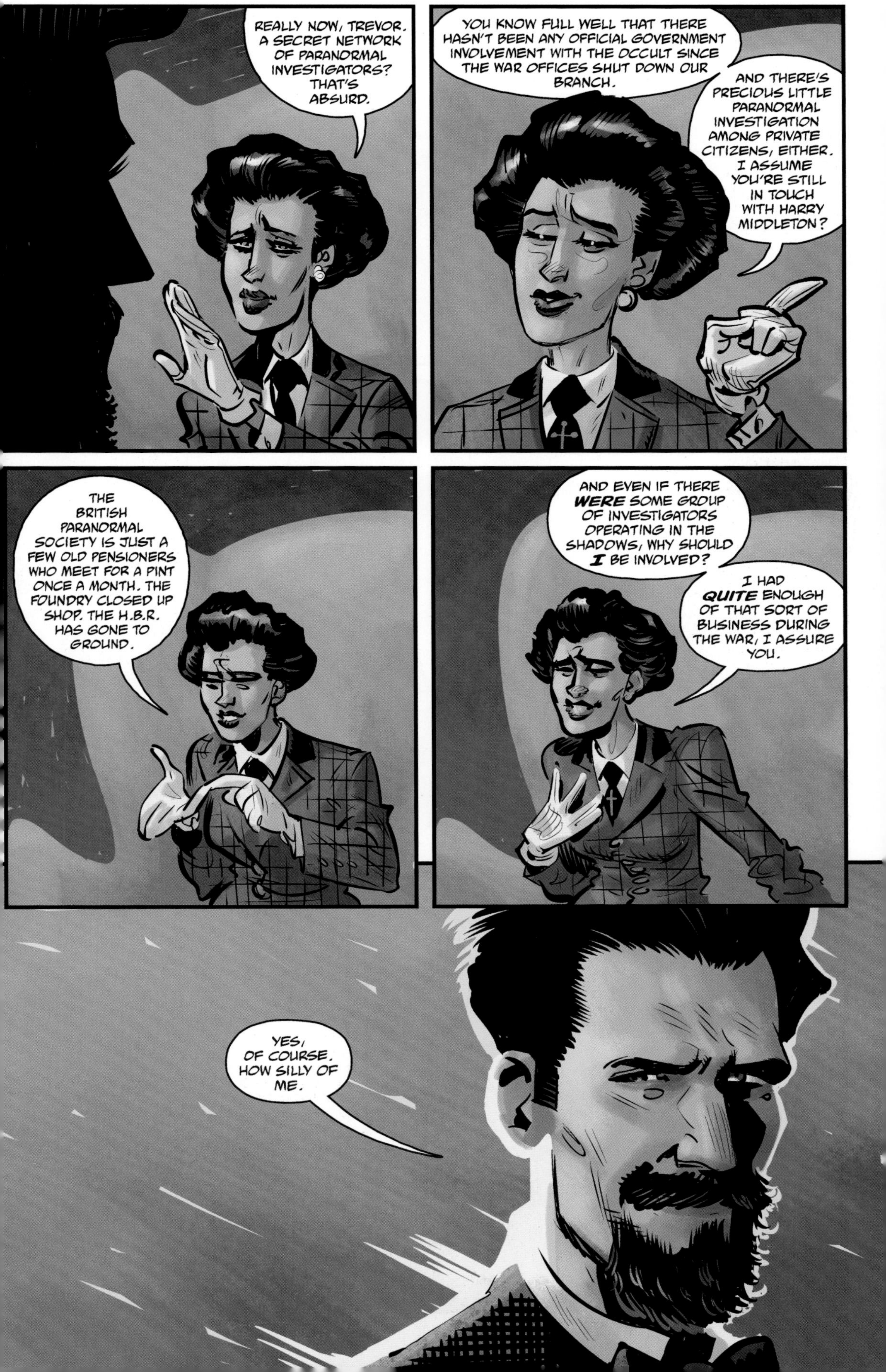
REALLY NOW, TREVOR. A SECRET NETWORK OF PARANORMAL INVESTIGATORS? THAT'S ABSURD.
YOU KNOW FULL WELL THAT THERE HASN'T BEEN ANY OFFICIAL GOVERNMENT INVOLVEMENT WITH THE OCCULT SINCE THE WAR OFFICES SHUT DOWN OUR BRANCH.
AND THERE'S PRECIOUS LITTLE PARANORMAL INVESTIGATION AMONG PRIVATE CITIZENS, EITHER. I ASSUME YOU'RE STILL IN TOUCH WITH HARRY MIDDLETON?
THE BRITISH PARANORMAL SOCIETY IS JUST A FEW OLD PENSIONERS WHO MEET FOR A PINT ONCE A MONTH. THE FOUNDRY CLOSED UP SHOP. THE H.B.R. HAS GONE TO GROUND.
AND EVEN IF THERE **WERE** SOME GROUP OF INVESTIGATORS OPERATING IN THE SHADOWS, WHY SHOULD **I** BE INVOLVED?
I HAD **QUITE** ENOUGH OF THAT SORT OF BUSINESS DURING THE WAR, I ASSURE YOU.
YES, OF COURSE. HOW SILLY OF ME.

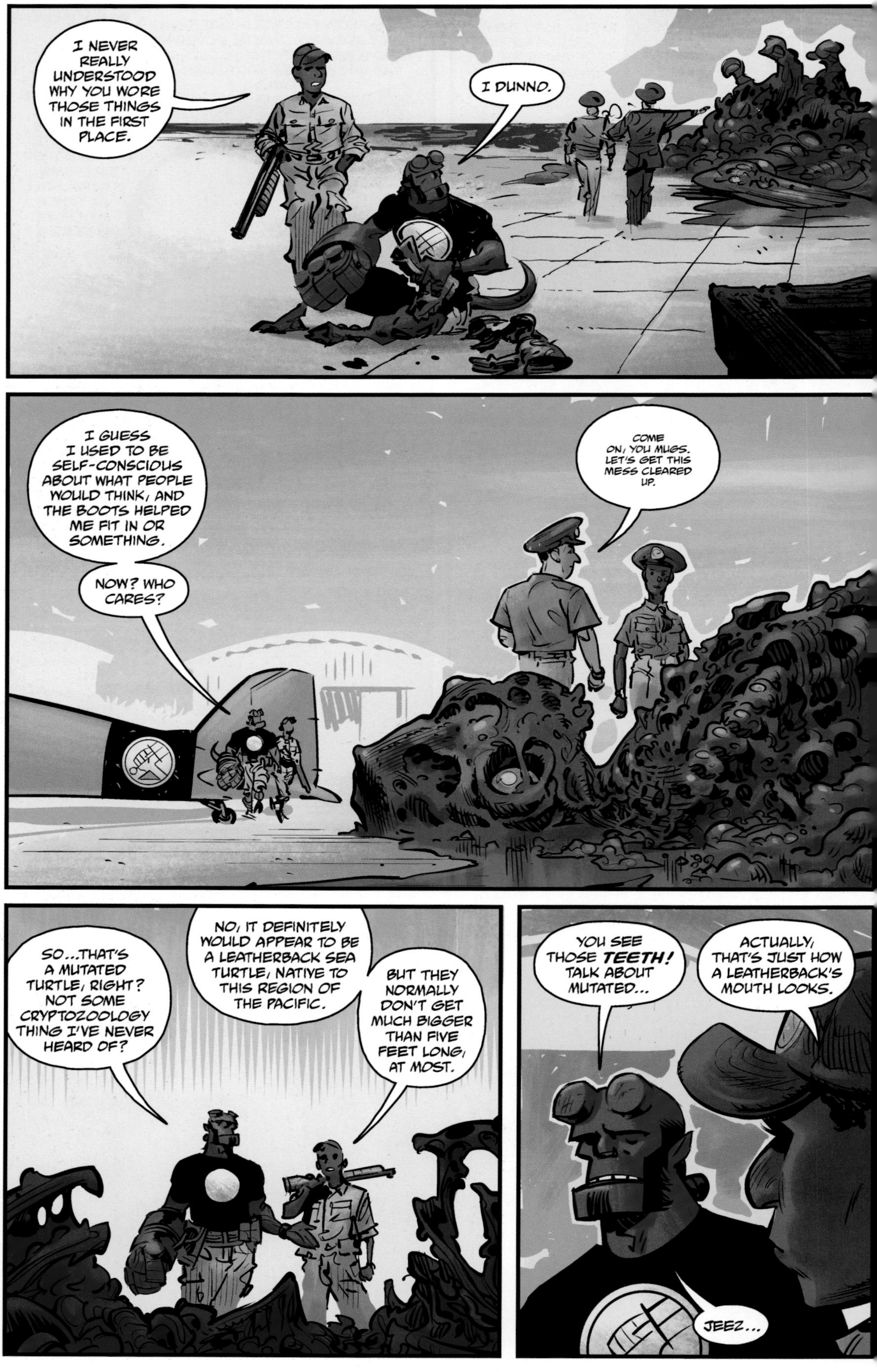
I NEVER REALLY UNDERSTOOD WHY YOU WORE THOSE THINGS IN THE FIRST PLACE.
I DUNNO.
I GUESS I USED TO BE SELF-CONSCIOUS ABOUT WHAT PEOPLE WOULD THINK, AND THE BOOTS HELPED ME FIT IN OR SOMETHING.
NOW? WHO CARES?
COME ON, YOU MUGS. LET'S GET THIS MESS CLEARED UP.
SO...THAT'S A MUTATED TURTLE, RIGHT? NOT SOME CRYPTOZOOLOGY THING I'VE NEVER HEARD OF?
NO, IT DEFINITELY WOULD APPEAR TO BE A LEATHERBACK SEA TURTLE, NATIVE TO THIS REGION OF THE PACIFIC.
BUT THEY NORMALLY DON'T GET MUCH BIGGER THAN FIVE FEET LONG, AT MOST.
YOU SEE THOSE **TEETH!** TALK ABOUT MUTATED...
ACTUALLY, THAT'S JUST HOW A LEATHERBACK'S MOUTH LOOKS.
JEEZ...

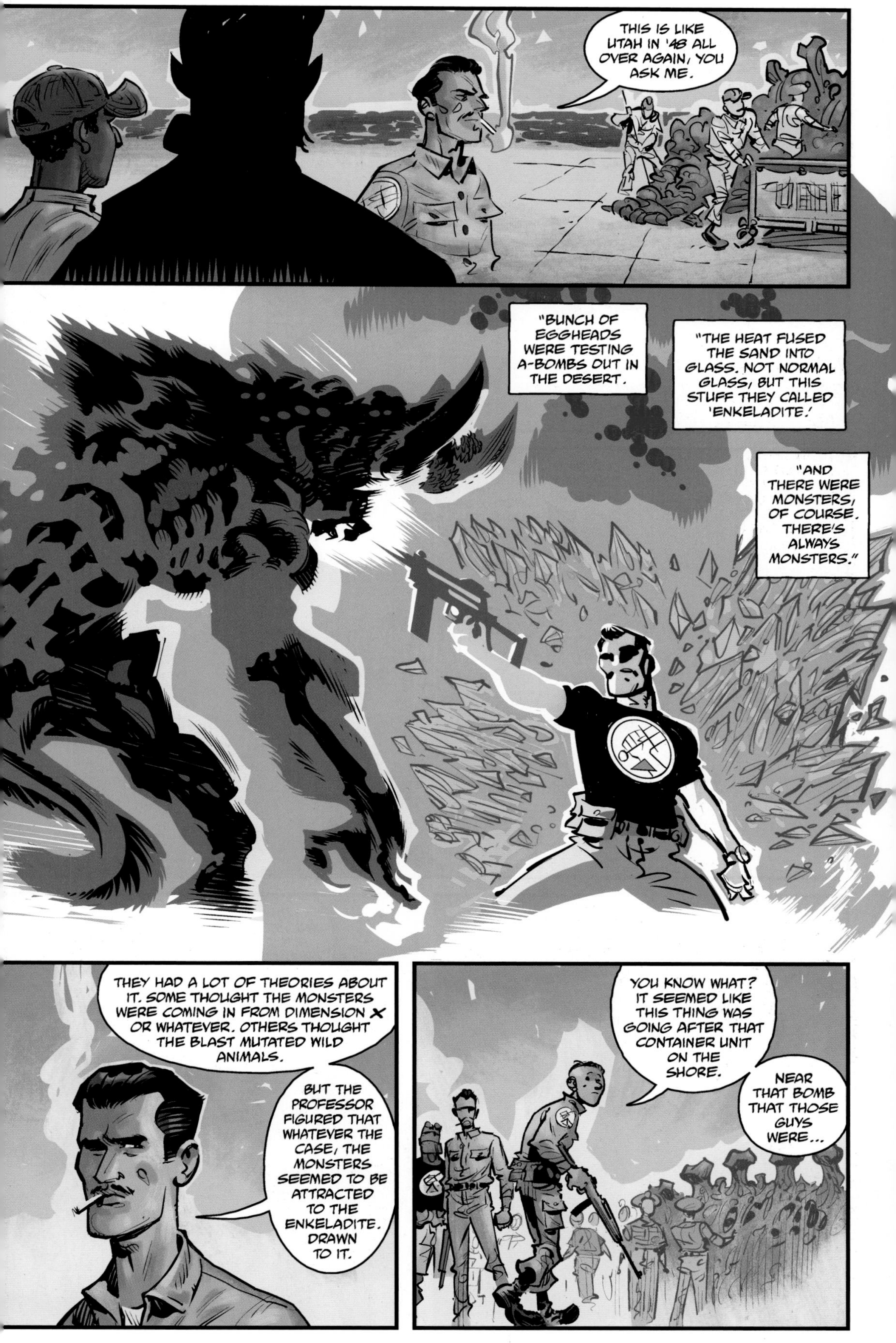
THIS IS LIKE UTAH IN '48 ALL OVER AGAIN, YOU ASK ME.
"BUNCH OF EGGHEADS WERE TESTING A-BOMBS OUT IN THE DESERT.
"THE HEAT FUSED THE SAND INTO GLASS. NOT NORMAL GLASS, BUT THIS STUFF THEY CALLED 'ENKELADITE.'
"AND THERE WERE MONSTERS, OF COURSE. THERE'S ALWAYS MONSTERS."
THEY HAD A LOT OF THEORIES ABOUT IT. SOME THOUGHT THE MONSTERS WERE COMING IN FROM DIMENSION X OR WHATEVER. OTHERS THOUGHT THE BLAST MUTATED WILD ANIMALS.
BUT THE PROFESSOR FIGURED THAT WHATEVER THE CASE, THE MONSTERS SEEMED TO BE ATTRACTED TO THE ENKELADITE. DRAWN TO IT.
YOU KNOW WHAT? IT SEEMED LIKE THIS THING WAS GOING AFTER THAT CONTAINER UNIT ON THE SHORE.
NEAR THAT BOMB THAT THOSE GUYS WERE...

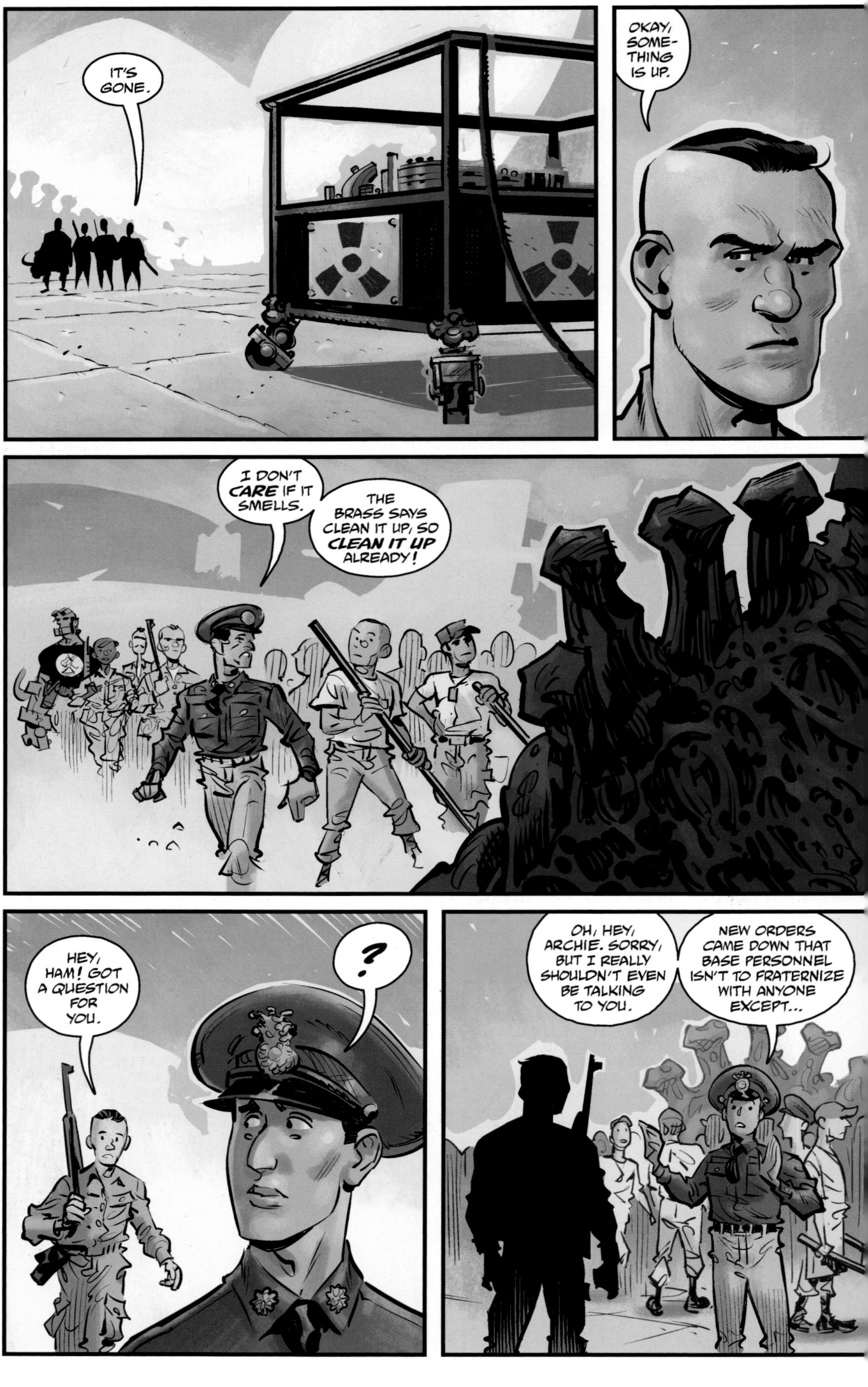
IT'S GONE.
OKAY, SOME-THING IS UP.
I DON'T CARE IF IT SMELLS.
THE BRASS SAYS CLEAN IT UP, SO CLEAN IT UP ALREADY!
HEY, HAM! GOT A QUESTION FOR YOU.
?
OH, HEY, ARCHIE. SORRY, BUT I REALLY SHOULDN'T EVEN BE TALKING TO YOU.
NEW ORDERS CAME DOWN THAT BASE PERSONNEL ISN'T TO FRATERNIZE WITH ANYONE EXCEPT...

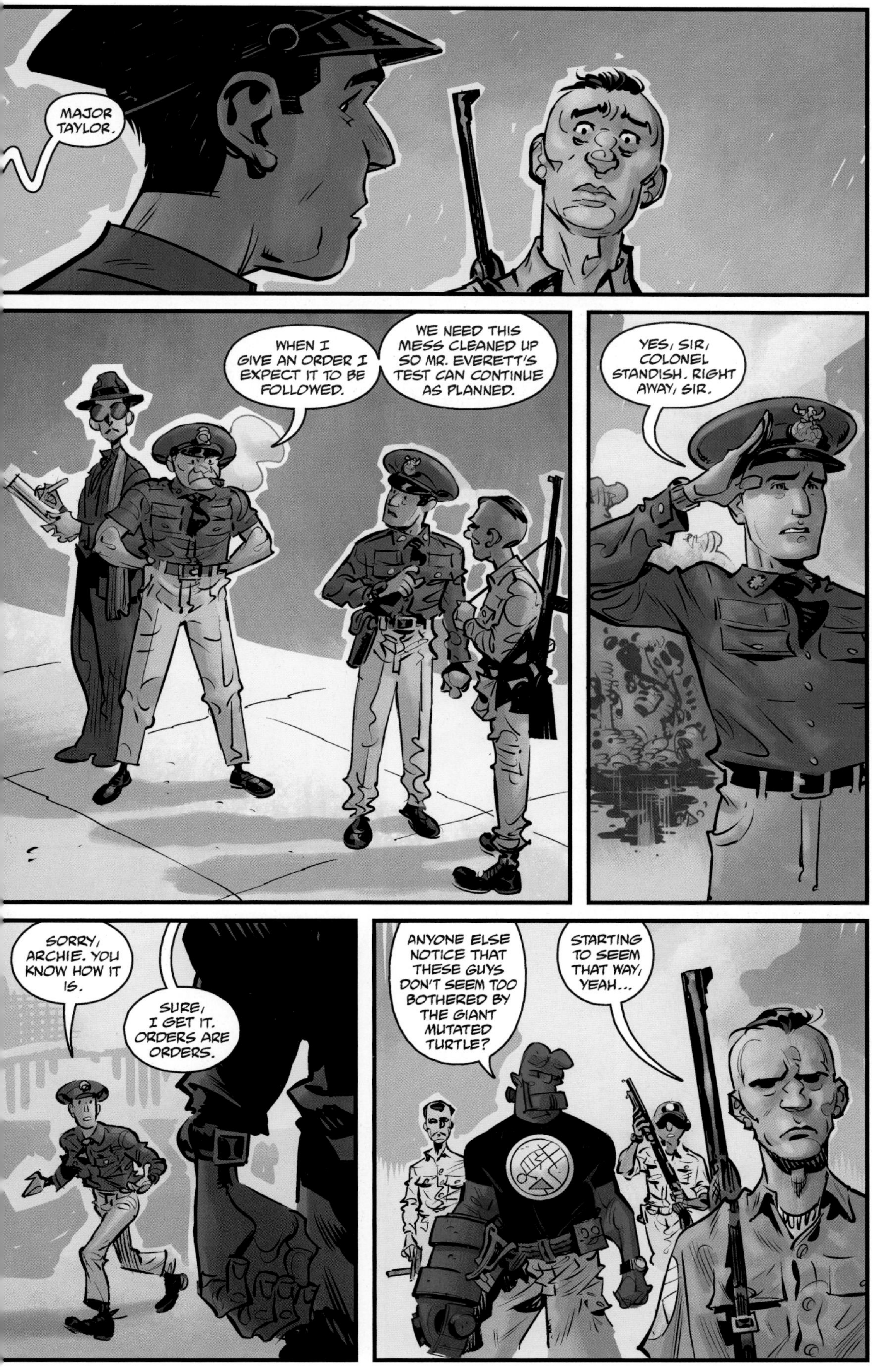
MAJOR TAYLOR.
WHEN I GIVE AN ORDER I EXPECT IT TO BE FOLLOWED.
WE NEED THIS MESS CLEANED UP SO MR. EVERETT'S TEST CAN CONTINUE AS PLANNED.
YES, SIR, COLONEL STANDISH. RIGHT AWAY, SIR.
SORRY, ARCHIE. YOU KNOW HOW IT IS.
SURE, I GET IT. ORDERS ARE ORDERS.
ANYONE ELSE NOTICE THAT THESE GUYS DON'T SEEM TOO BOTHERED BY THE GIANT MUTATED TURTLE?
STARTING TO SEEM THAT WAY, YEAH...

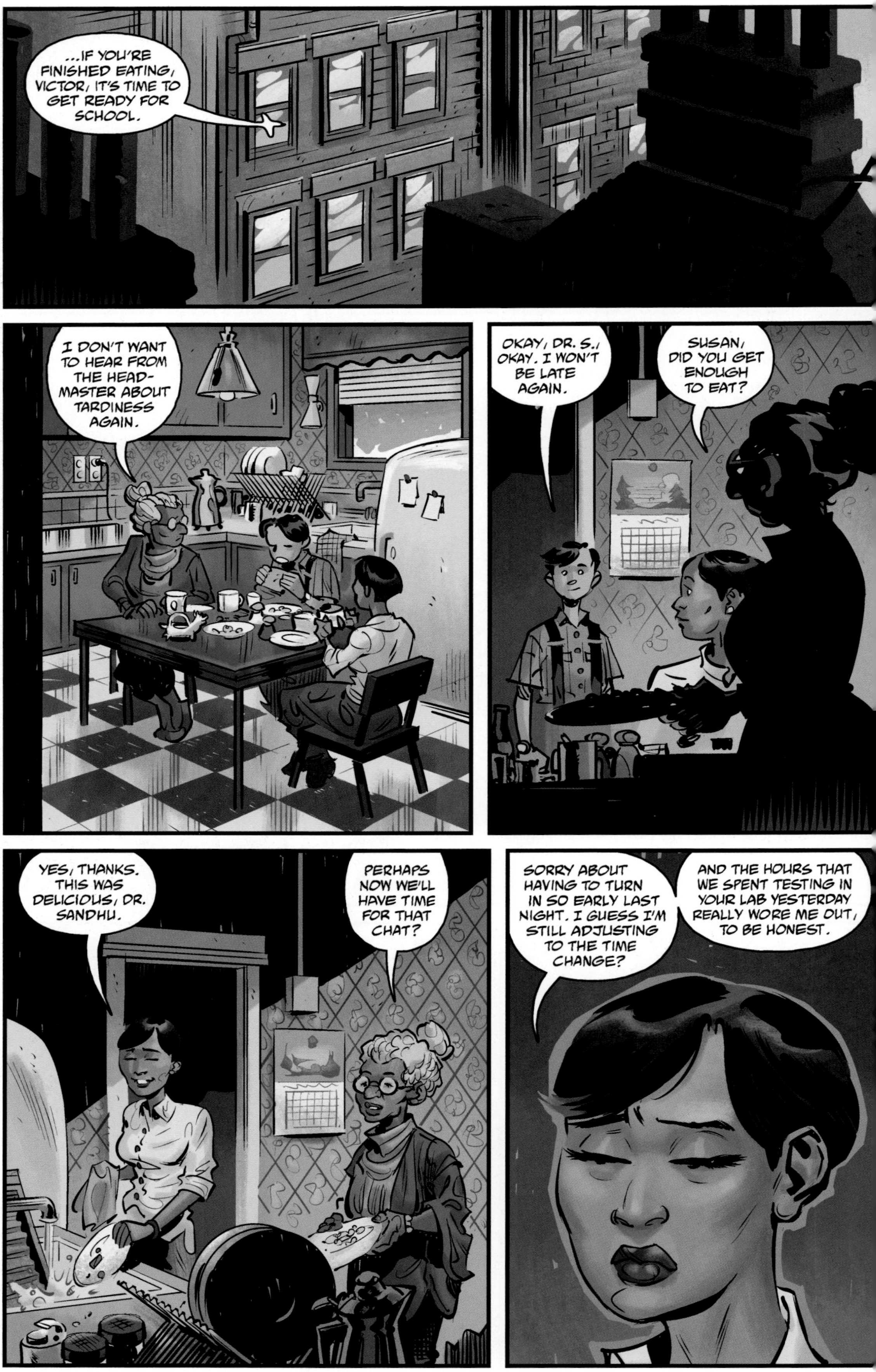
...IF YOU'RE FINISHED EATING, VICTOR, IT'S TIME TO GET READY FOR SCHOOL.
I DON'T WANT TO HEAR FROM THE HEAD-MASTER ABOUT TARDINESS AGAIN.
OKAY, DR. S., OKAY. I WON'T BE LATE AGAIN.
SUSAN, DID YOU GET ENOUGH TO EAT?
YES, THANKS. THIS WAS DELICIOUS, DR. SANDHU.
PERHAPS NOW WE'LL HAVE TIME FOR THAT CHAT?
SORRY ABOUT HAVING TO TURN IN SO EARLY LAST NIGHT. I GUESS I'M STILL ADJUSTING TO THE TIME CHANGE?
AND THE HOURS THAT WE SPENT TESTING IN YOUR LAB YESTERDAY REALLY WORE ME OUT, TO BE HONEST.

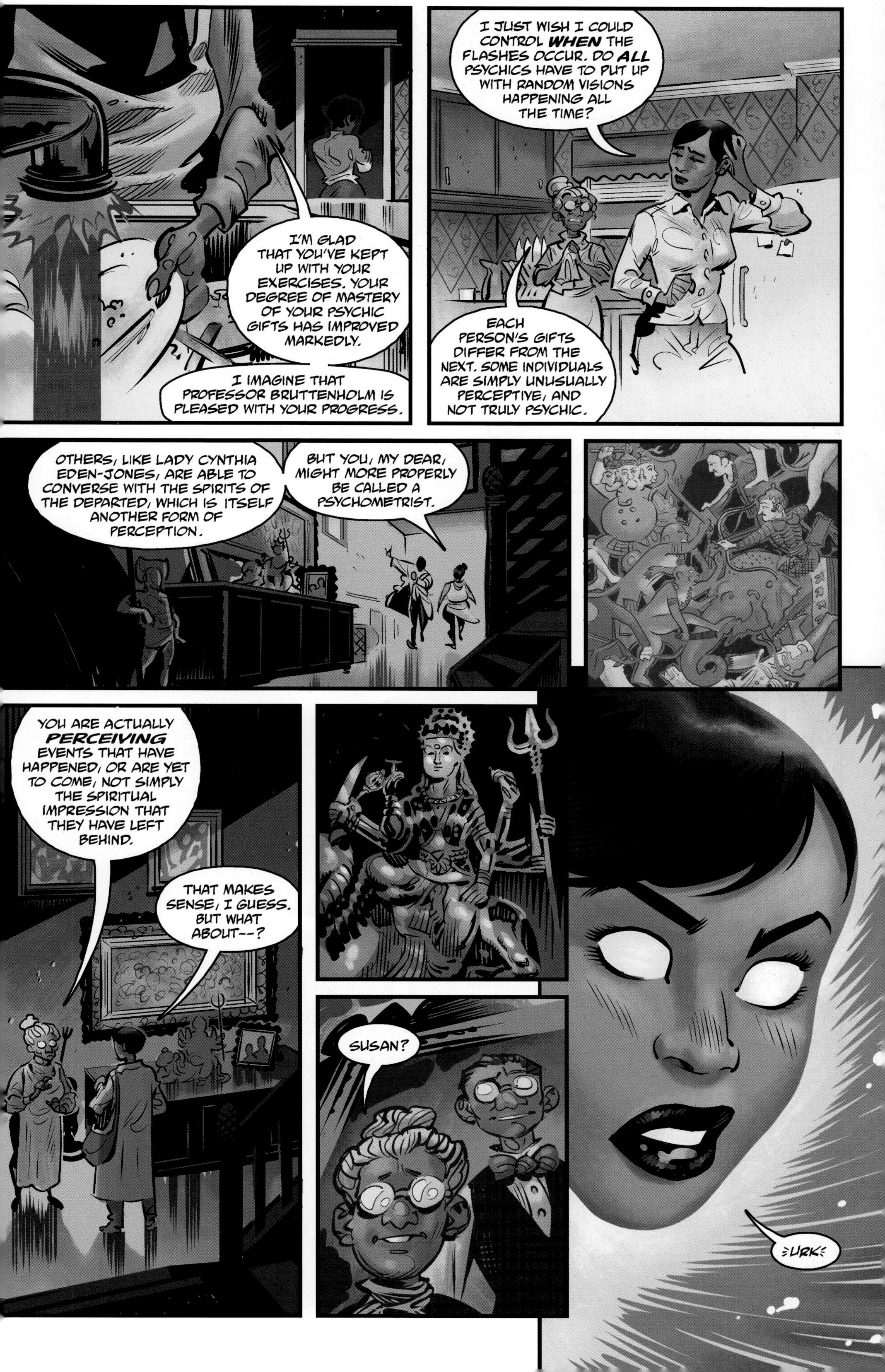
I'M GLAD THAT YOU'VE KEPT UP WITH YOUR EXERCISES. YOUR DEGREE OF MASTERY OF YOUR PSYCHIC GIFTS HAS IMPROVED MARKEDLY.
I IMAGINE THAT PROFESSOR BRUTTENHOLM IS PLEASED WITH YOUR PROGRESS.
I JUST WISH I COULD CONTROL **WHEN** THE FLASHES OCCUR. DO **ALL** PSYCHICS HAVE TO PUT UP WITH RANDOM VISIONS HAPPENING ALL THE TIME?
EACH PERSON'S GIFTS DIFFER FROM THE NEXT. SOME INDIVIDUALS ARE SIMPLY UNUSUALLY PERCEPTIVE, AND NOT TRULY PSYCHIC.
OTHERS, LIKE LADY CYNTHIA EDEN-JONES, ARE ABLE TO CONVERSE WITH THE SPIRITS OF THE DEPARTED, WHICH IS ITSELF ANOTHER FORM OF PERCEPTION.
BUT YOU, MY DEAR, MIGHT MORE PROPERLY BE CALLED A PSYCHOMETRIST.
YOU ARE ACTUALLY ***PERCEIVING*** EVENTS THAT HAVE HAPPENED, OR ARE YET TO COME, NOT SIMPLY THE SPIRITUAL IMPRESSION THAT THEY HAVE LEFT BEHIND.
THAT MAKES SENSE, I GUESS. BUT WHAT ABOUT--?
SUSAN?
URK

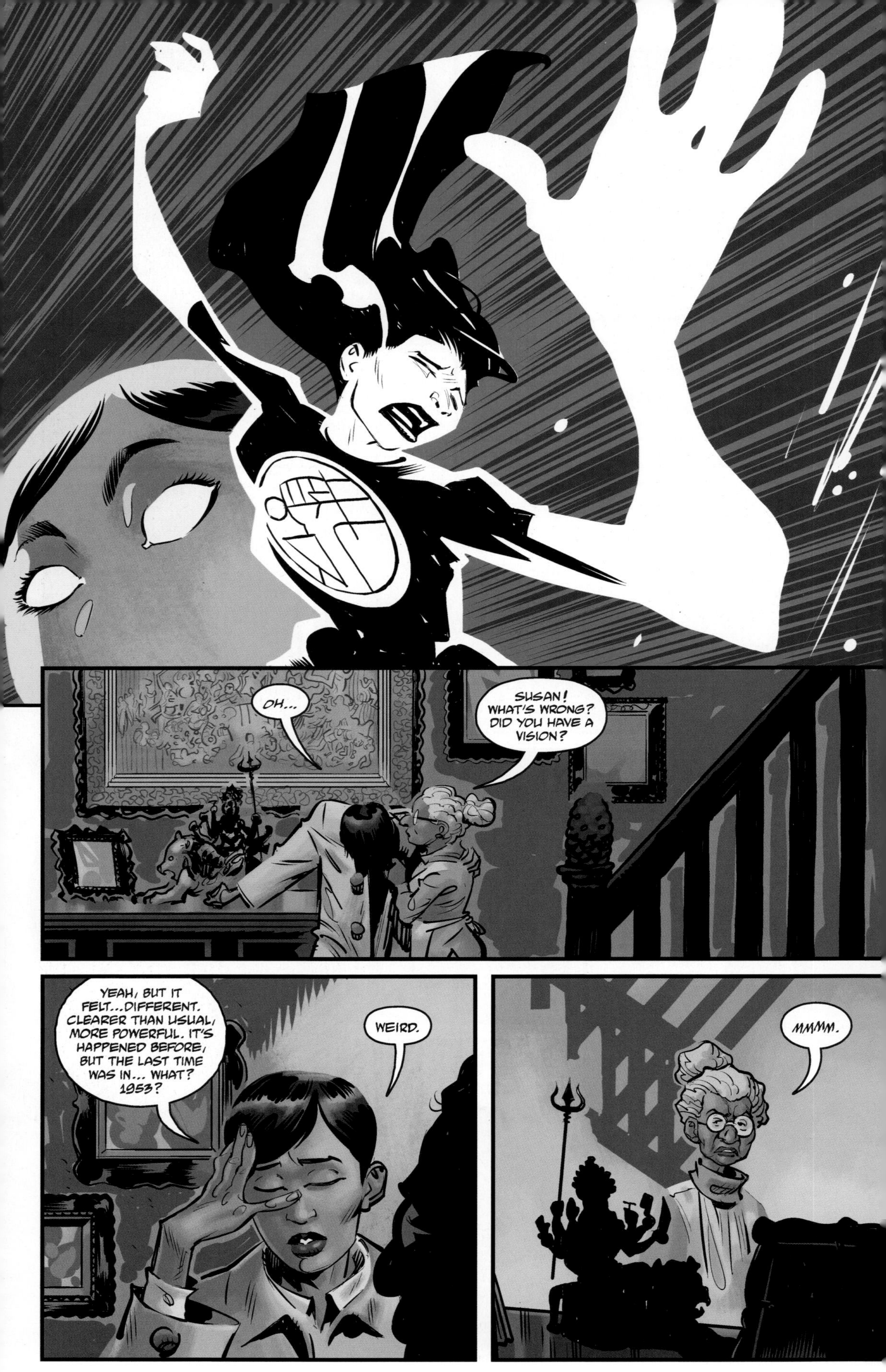
OH...
SUSAN! WHAT'S WRONG? DID YOU HAVE A VISION?
YEAH, BUT IT FELT...DIFFERENT. CLEARER THAN USUAL, MORE POWERFUL. IT'S HAPPENED BEFORE, BUT THE LAST TIME WAS IN... WHAT? 1953?
WEIRD.
MMMM.

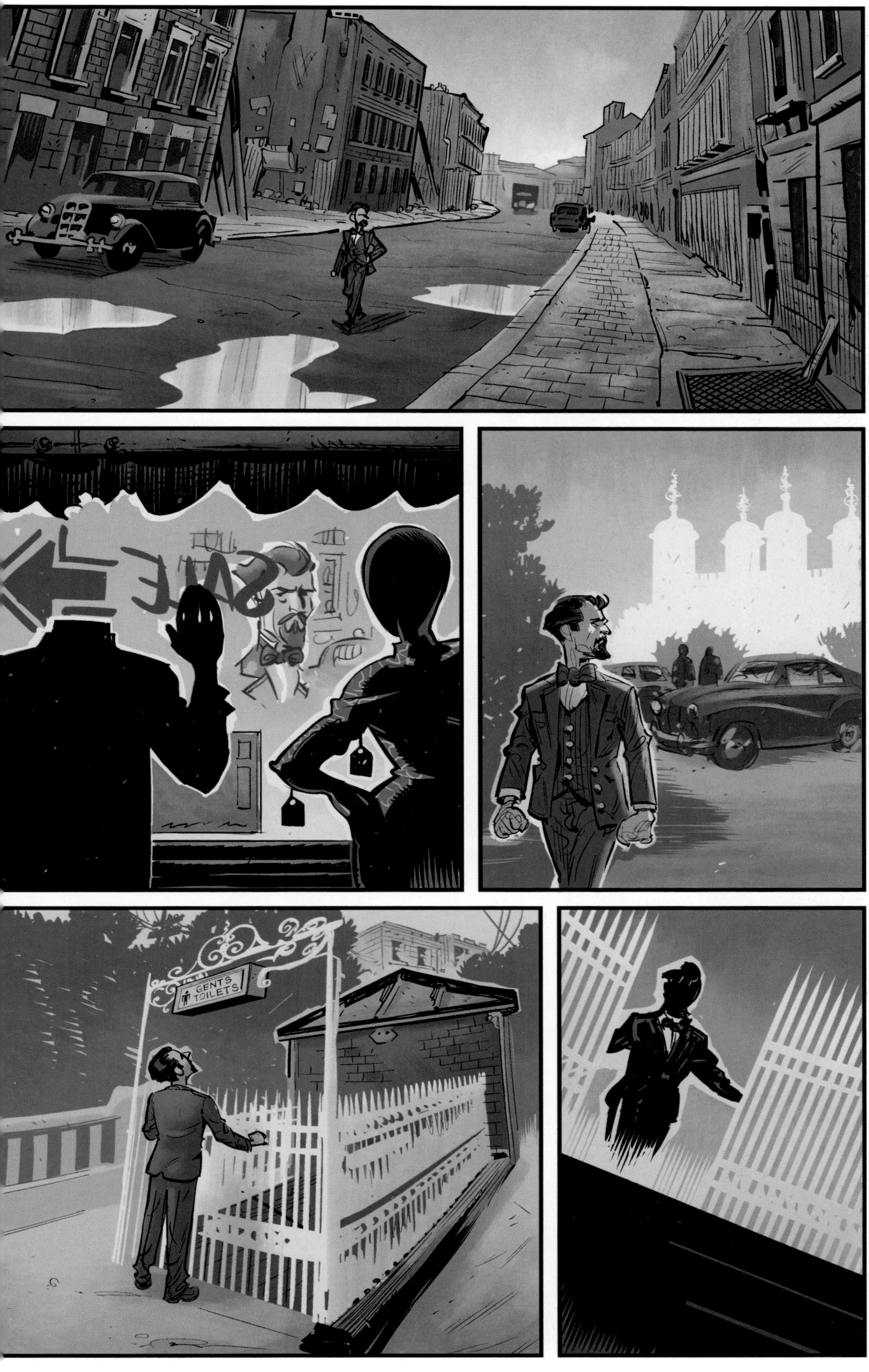
GENTS
TOILETS

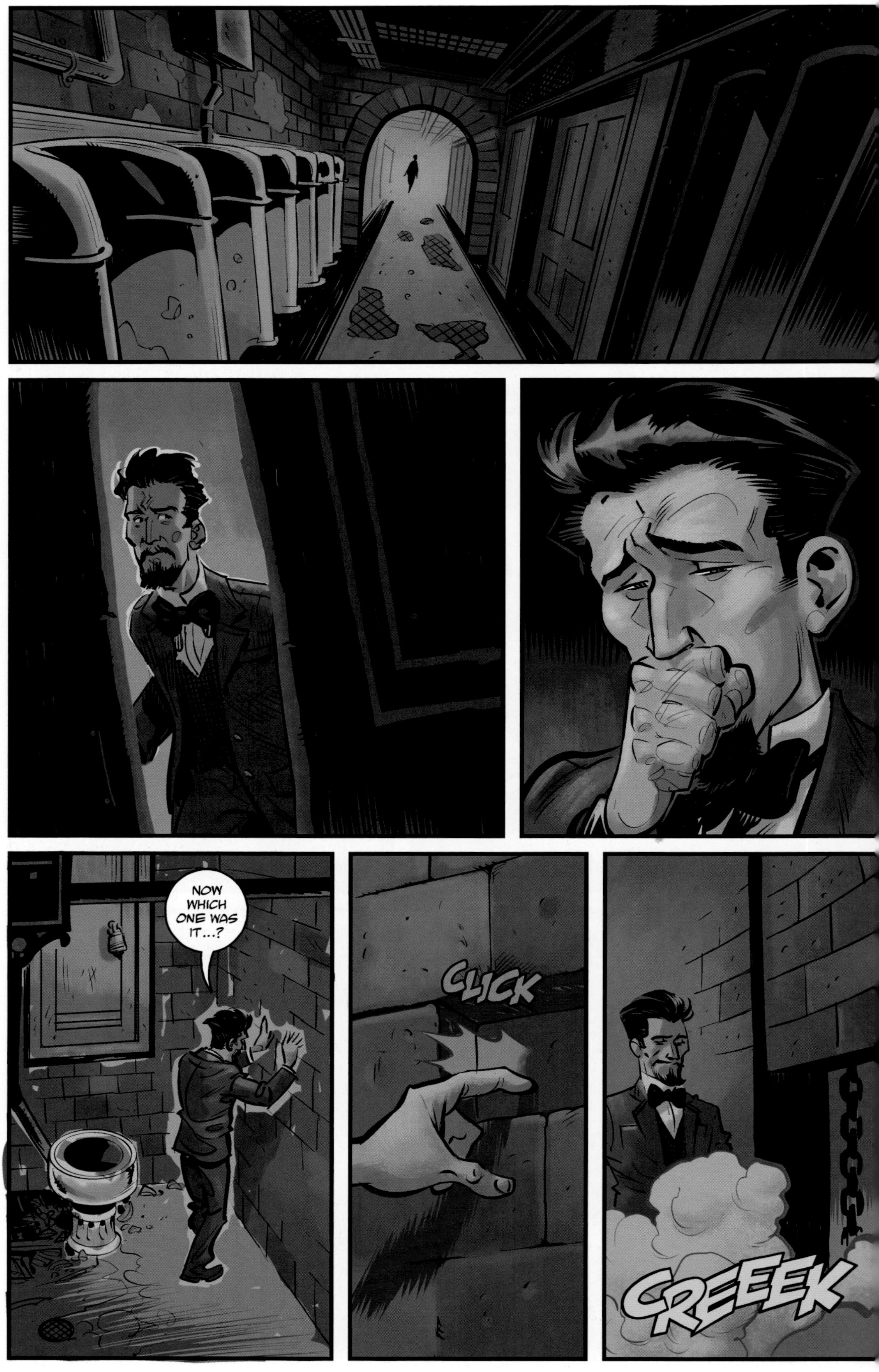
NOW WHICH ONE WAS IT...?
CLICK
CREEEK

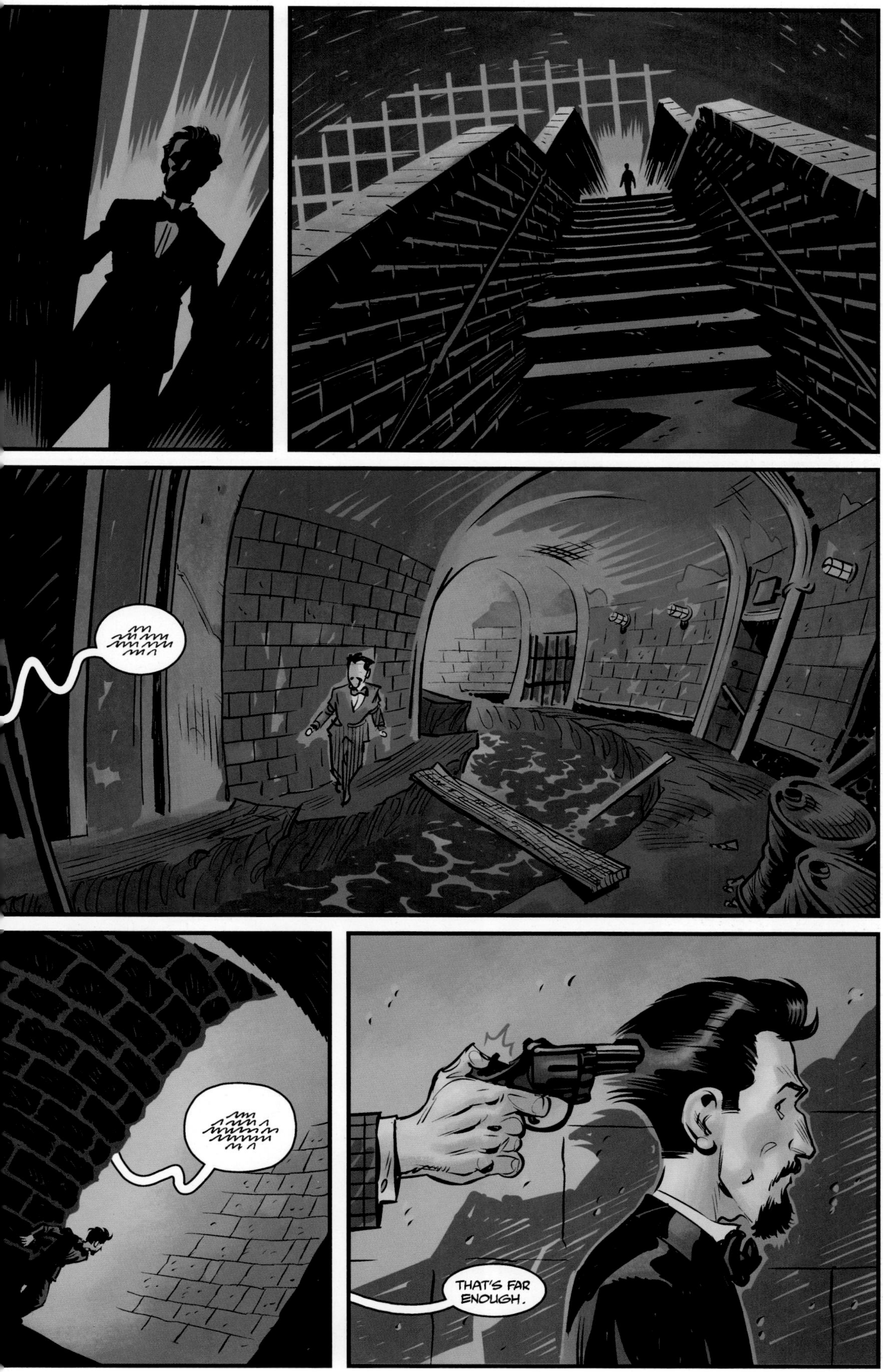
THAT'S FAR ENOUGH.

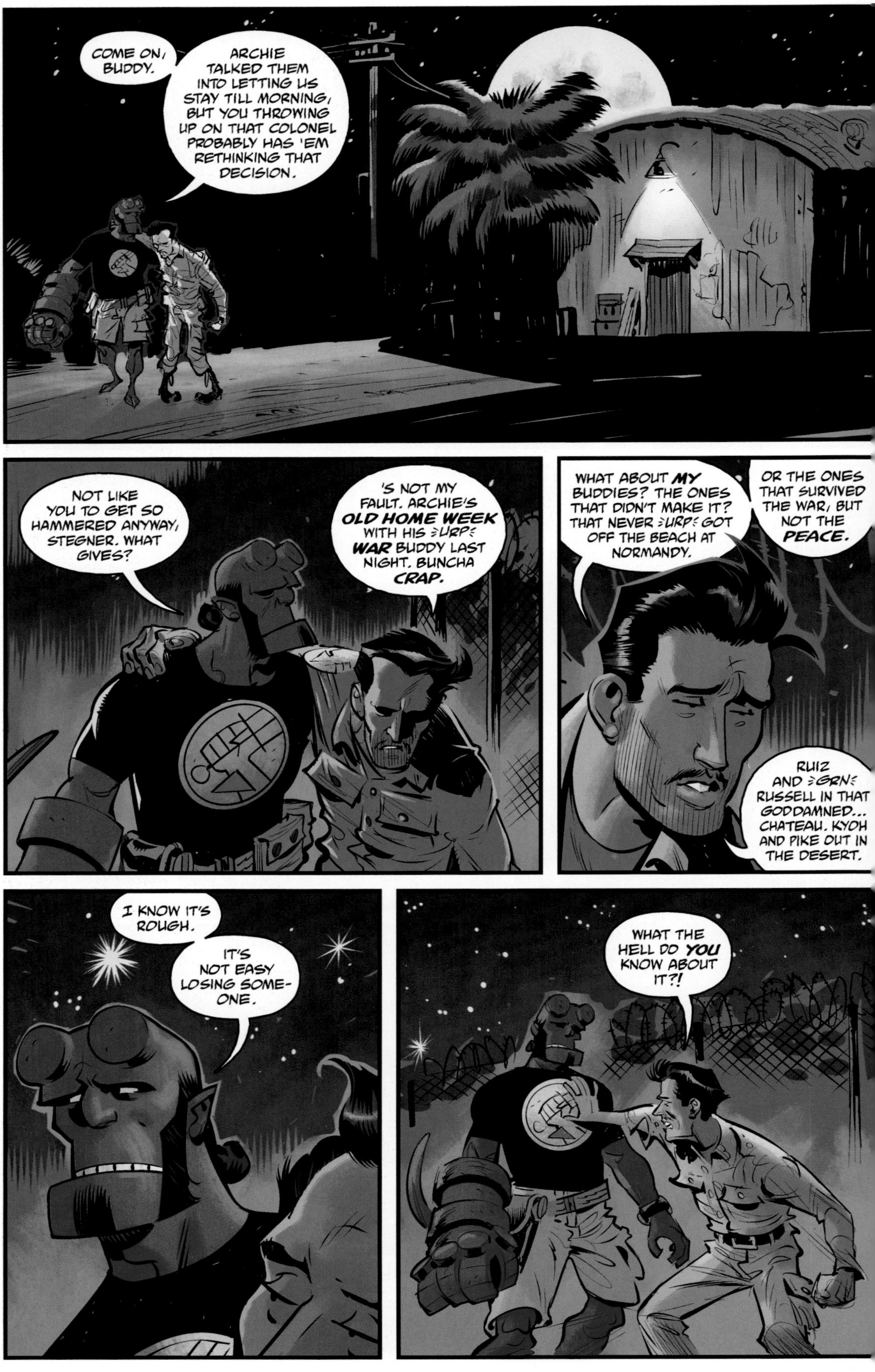
COME ON, BUDDY.
ARCHIE TALKED THEM INTO LETTING US STAY TILL MORNING, BUT YOU THROWING UP ON THAT COLONEL PROBABLY HAS 'EM RETHINKING THAT DECISION.
NOT LIKE YOU TO GET SO HAMMERED ANYWAY, STEGNER. WHAT GIVES?
'S NOT MY FAULT. ARCHIE'S OLD HOME WEEK WITH HIS URP WAR BUDDY LAST NIGHT. BUNCHA CRAP.
WHAT ABOUT MY BUDDIES? THE ONES THAT DIDN'T MAKE IT? THAT NEVER URP GOT OFF THE BEACH AT NORMANDY.
OR THE ONES THAT SURVIVED THE WAR, BUT NOT THE PEACE.
RUIZ AND GRN RUSSELL IN THAT GODDAMNED... CHATEAU. KYOH AND PIKE OUT IN THE DESERT.
I KNOW IT'S ROUGH.
IT'S NOT EASY LOSING SOME-ONE.
WHAT THE HELL DO YOU KNOW ABOUT IT?!

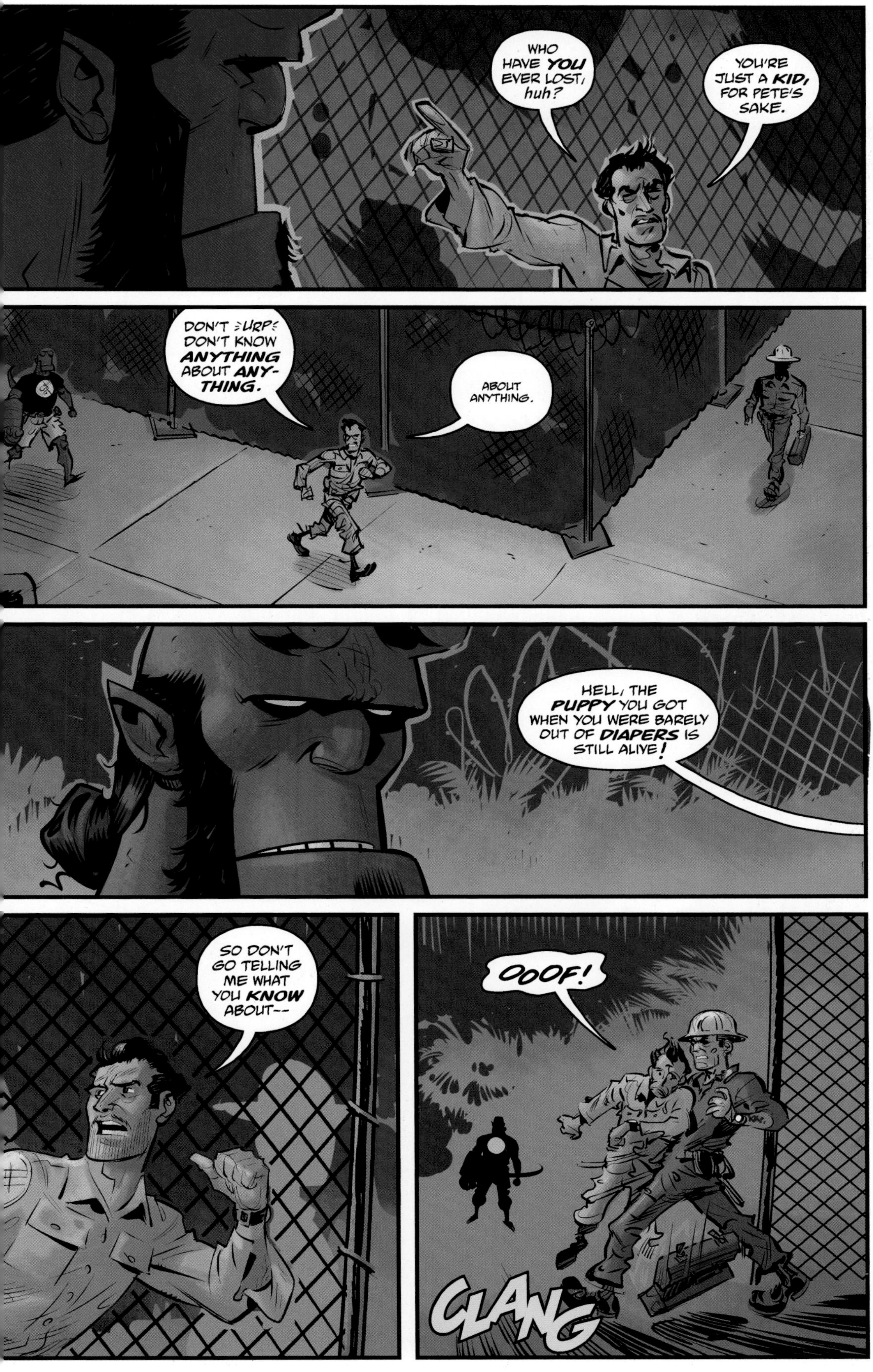
WHO HAVE YOU EVER LOST, huh?
YOU'RE JUST A KID, FOR PETE'S SAKE.
DON'T URP DON'T KNOW ANYTHING ABOUT ANY-THING.
ABOUT ANYTHING.
HELL, THE PUPPY YOU GOT WHEN YOU WERE BARELY OUT OF DIAPERS IS STILL ALIVE!
SO DON'T GO TELLING ME WHAT YOU KNOW ABOUT--
OOOF!
CLANG

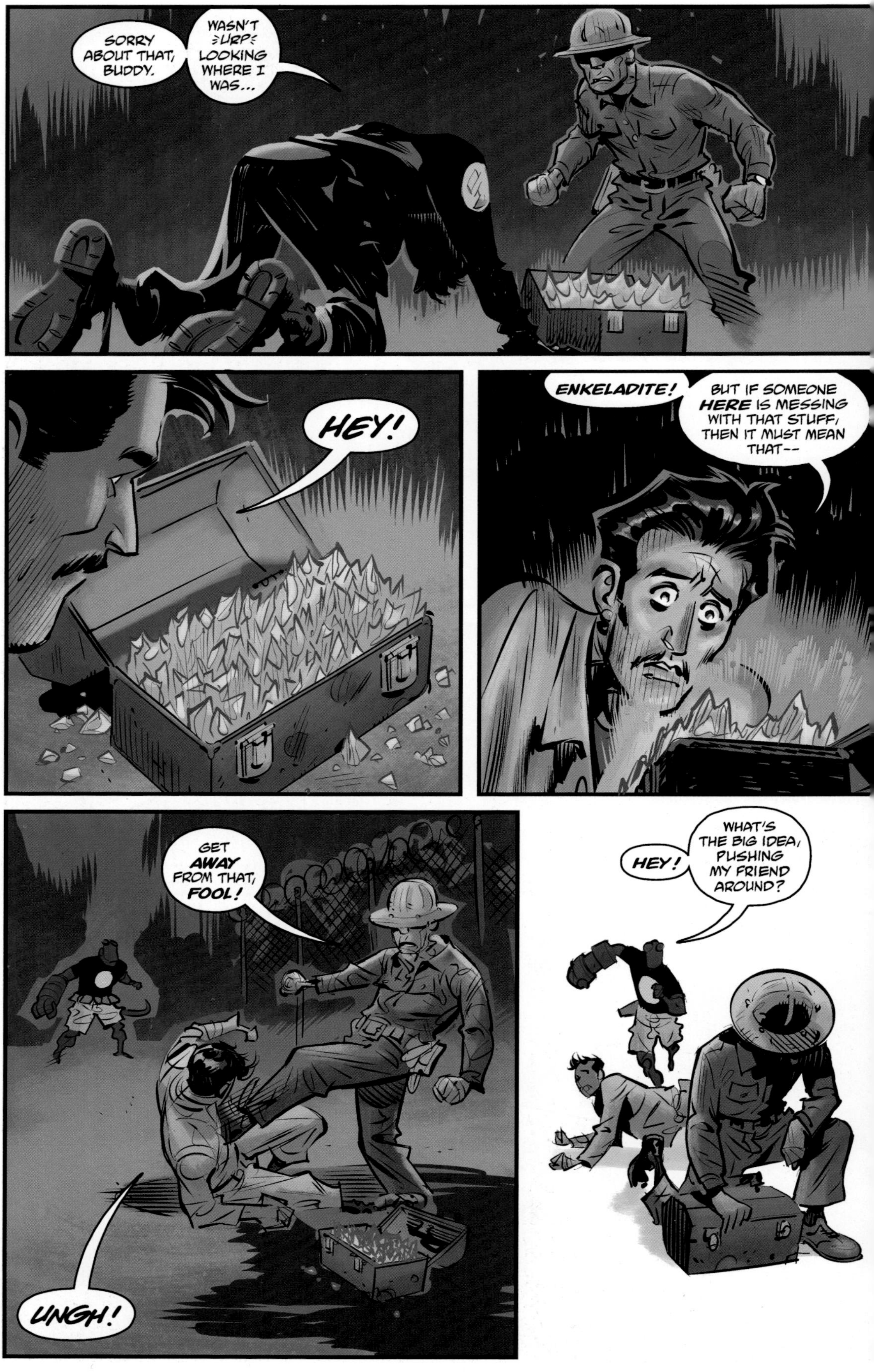
SORRY ABOUT THAT, BUDDY.
WASN'T =URP= LOOKING WHERE I WAS...
HEY!
ENKELADITE!
BUT IF SOMEONE **HERE** IS MESSING WITH THAT STUFF, THEN IT MUST MEAN THAT--
GET **AWAY** FROM THAT, **FOOL!**
UNGH!
HEY!
WHAT'S THE BIG IDEA, PUSHING MY FRIEND AROUND?

YOU! ALWAYS IT IS YOU!

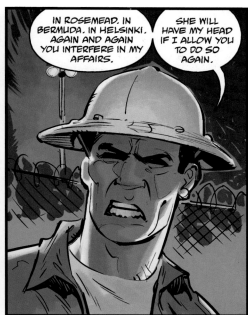

IN ROSEMEAD. IN BERMUDA. IN HELSINKI. AGAIN AND AGAIN YOU INTERFERE IN MY AFFAIRS.

SHE WILL HAVE MY HEAD IF I ALLOW YOU TO DO SO AGAIN.

HEY, SETTLE DOWN. I'VE BEEN TO THOSE PLACES, SURE, BUT I DON'T EVEN **KNOW** YOU, PAL.

IF YOUR GIRLFRIEND OR WHOEVER HAS SOME BEEF WITH YOU, IT'S NOTHING TO DO WITH ME.

ENOUGH!

Heh.

YOU'RE PUNCHING OUTSIDE OF YOUR WEIGHT-CLASS, IF YOU THINK--

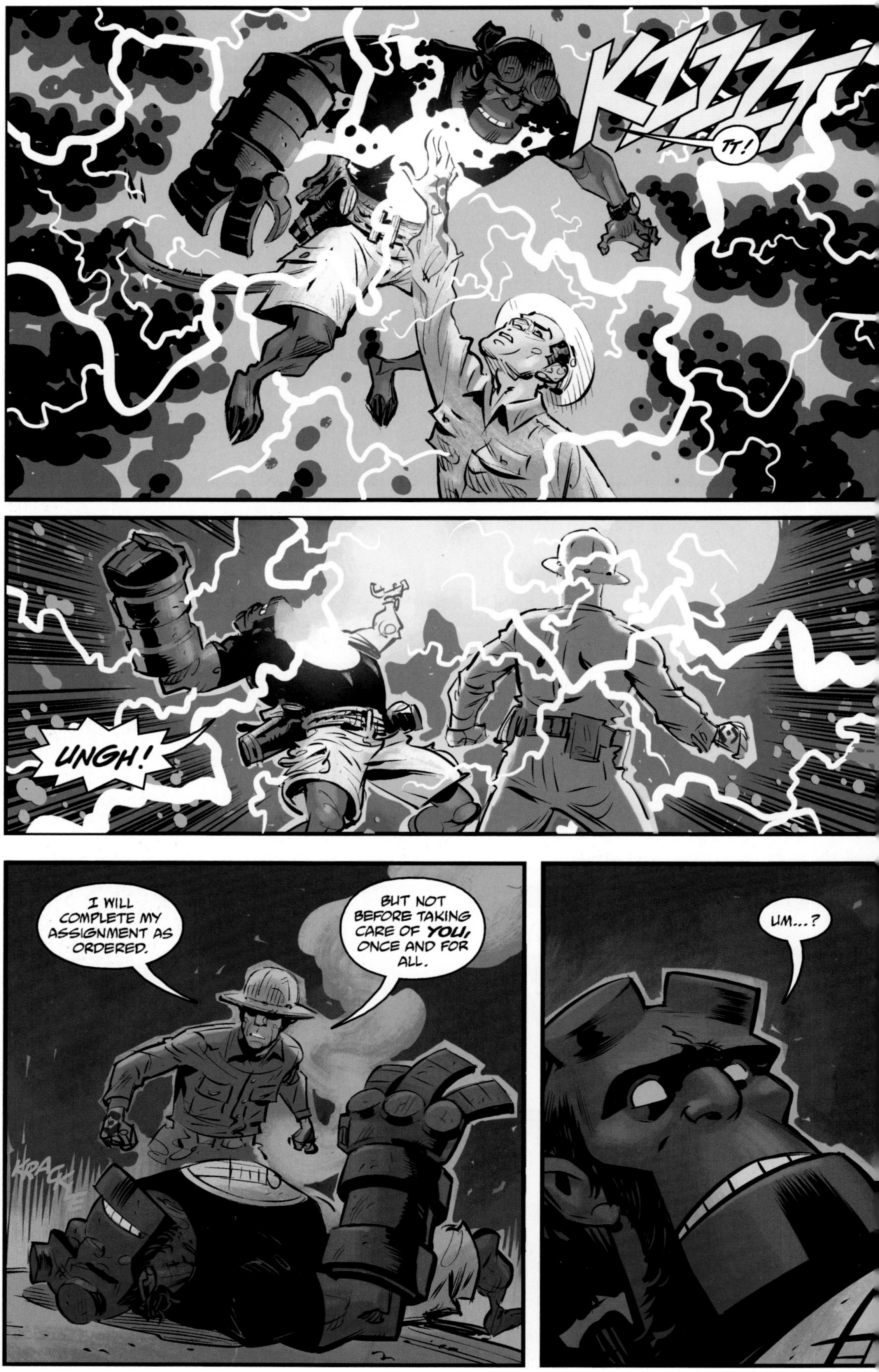
KZZZT
TT!
UNGH!
I WILL COMPLETE MY ASSIGNMENT AS ORDERED.
BUT NOT BEFORE TAKING CARE OF YOU, ONCE AND FOR ALL.
KRACKLE
UM...?

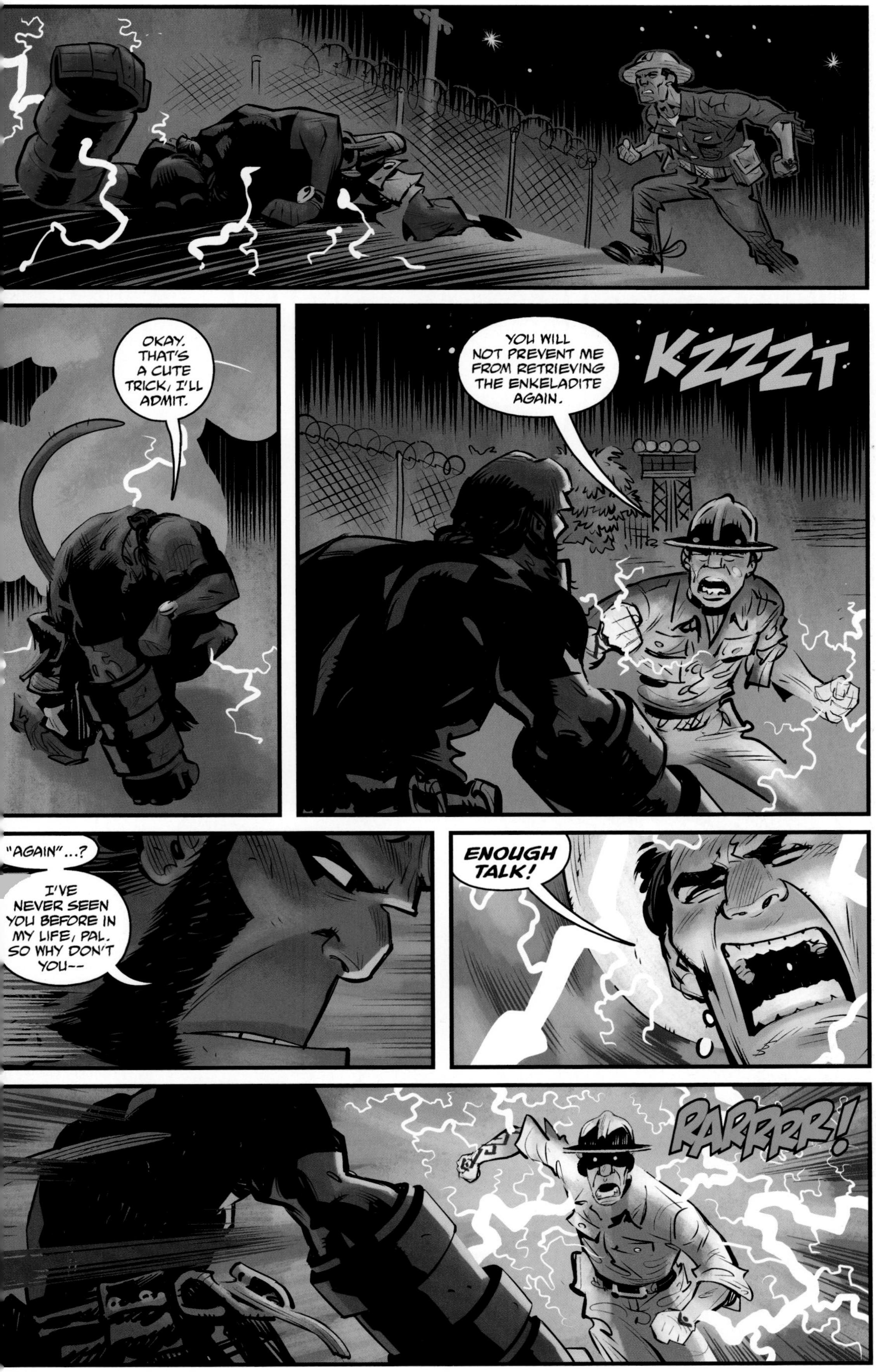

OKAY. THAT'S A CUTE TRICK, I'LL ADMIT.
YOU WILL NOT PREVENT ME FROM RETRIEVING THE ENKELADITE AGAIN.
KZZZT
"AGAIN"...?
I'VE NEVER SEEN YOU BEFORE IN MY LIFE, PAL. SO WHY DON'T YOU--
ENOUGH TALK!
RARRRR!

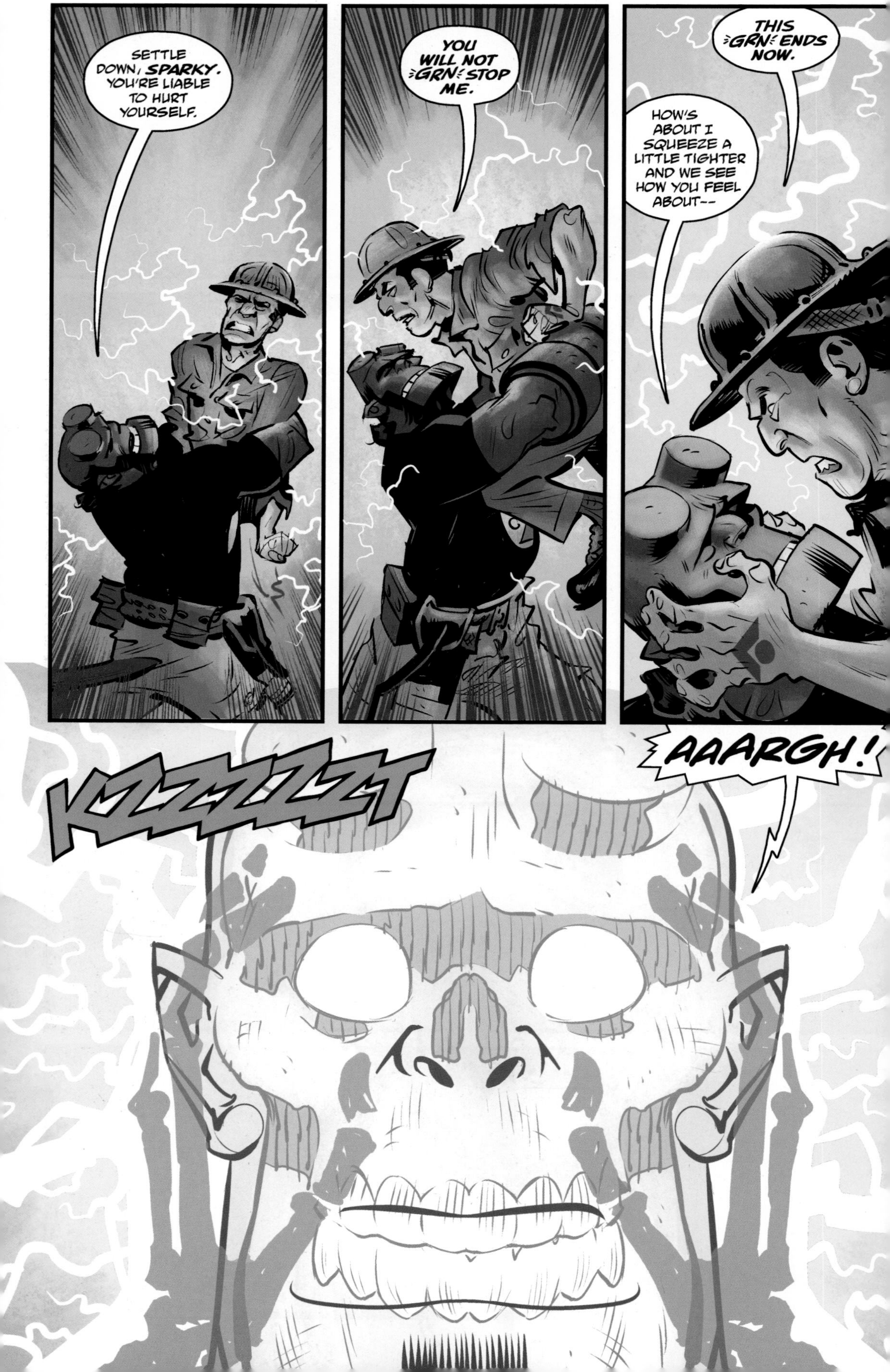
SETTLE DOWN, SPARKY. YOU'RE LIABLE TO HURT YOURSELF.
YOU WILL NOT GRN STOP ME.
THIS GRN ENDS NOW.
HOW'S ABOUT I SQUEEZE A LITTLE TIGHTER AND WE SEE HOW YOU FEEL ABOUT--
KZZZZZT
AAARGH!

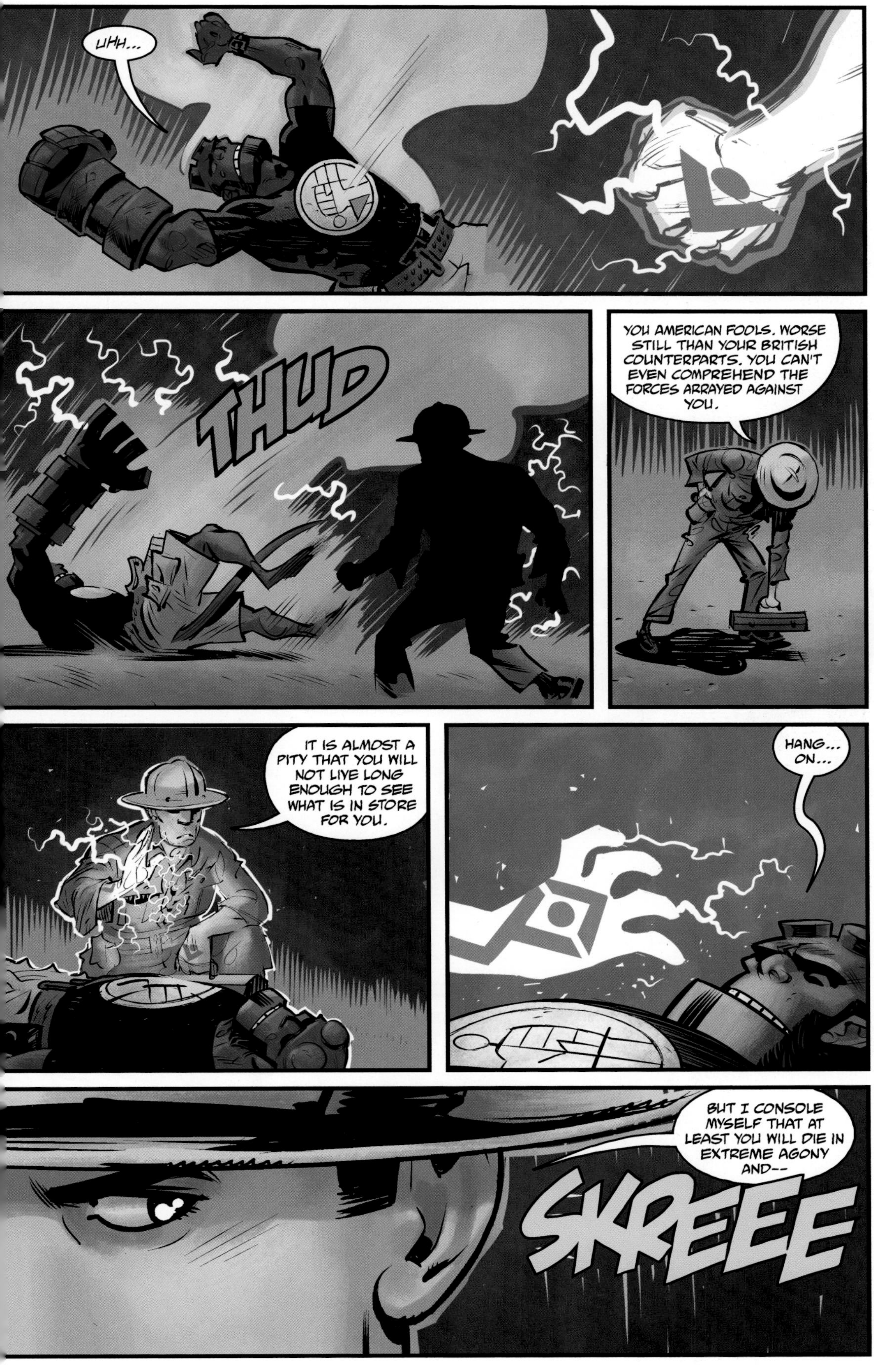
UHH...
THUD
YOU AMERICAN FOOLS. WORSE STILL THAN YOUR BRITISH COUNTERPARTS. YOU CAN'T EVEN COMPREHEND THE FORCES ARRAYED AGAINST YOU.
IT IS ALMOST A PITY THAT YOU WILL NOT LIVE LONG ENOUGH TO SEE WHAT IS IN STORE FOR YOU.
HANG... ON...
BUT I CONSOLE MYSELF THAT AT LEAST YOU WILL DIE IN EXTREME AGONY AND--
SKREEEE

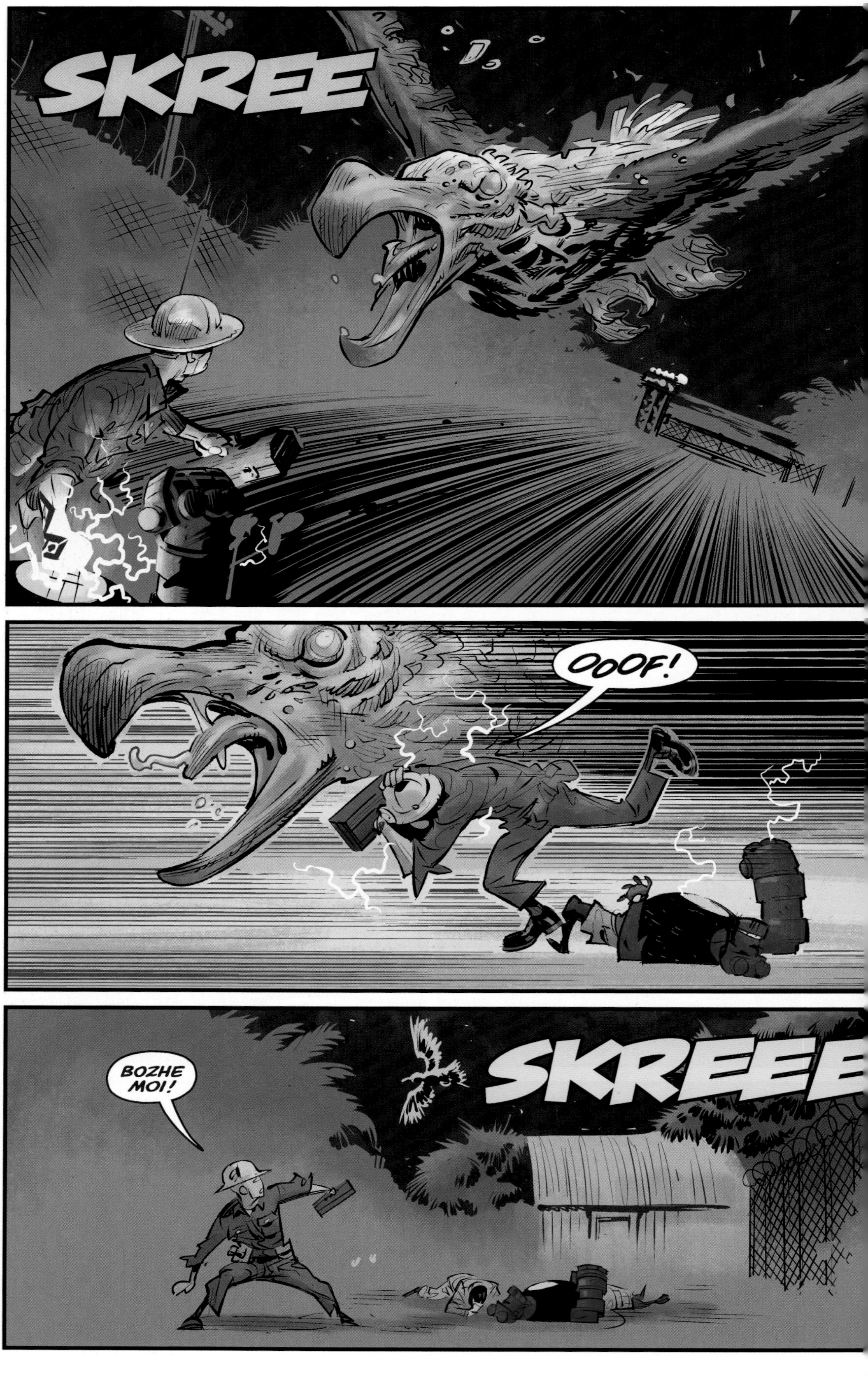
SKREE
OOOF!
BOZHE MOI!
SKREEE

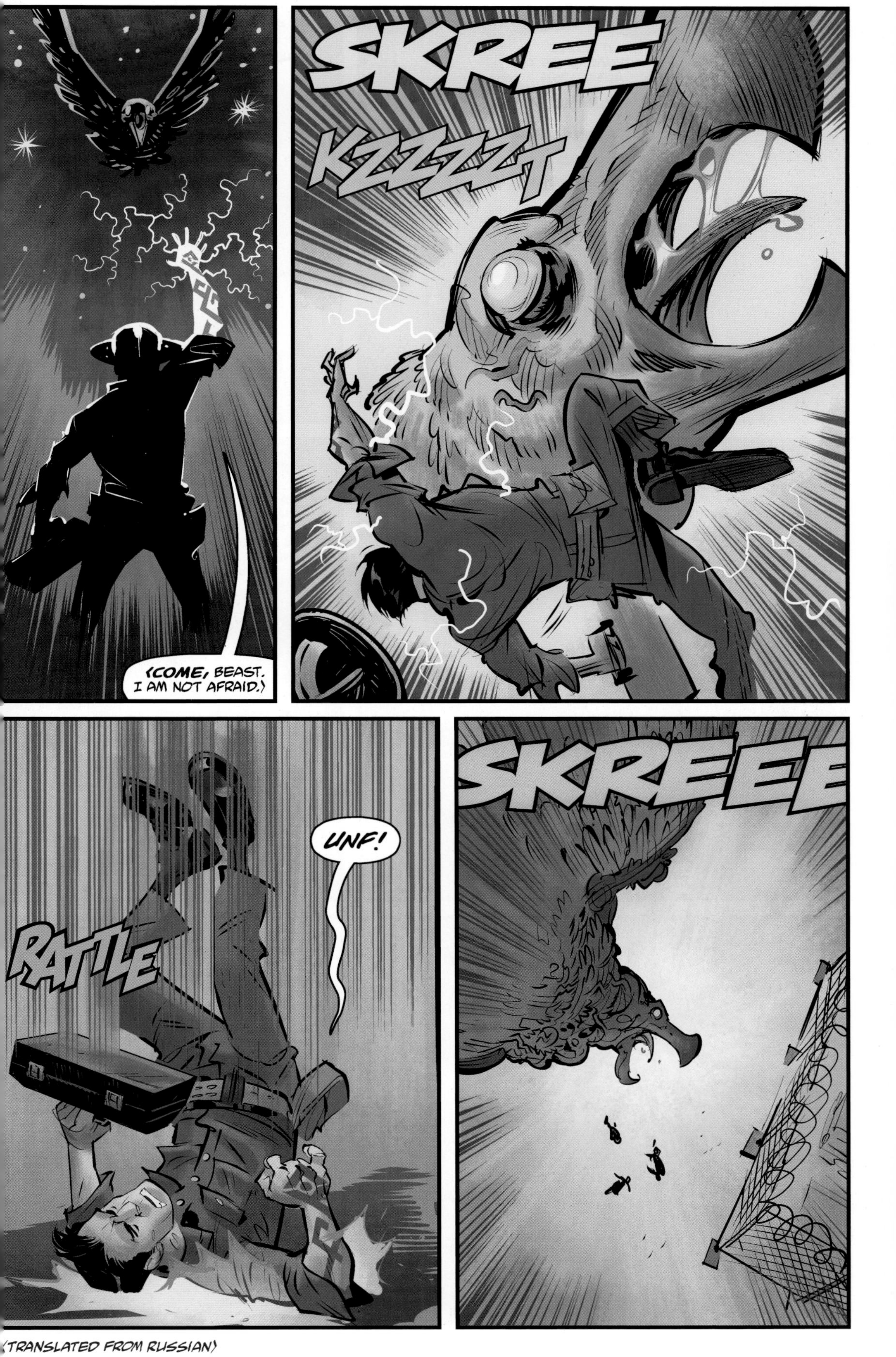
(COME, BEAST. I AM NOT AFRAID.)
SKREE
KZZZZZT
RATTLE
UNF!
SKREEE

(TRANSLATED FROM RUSSIAN)

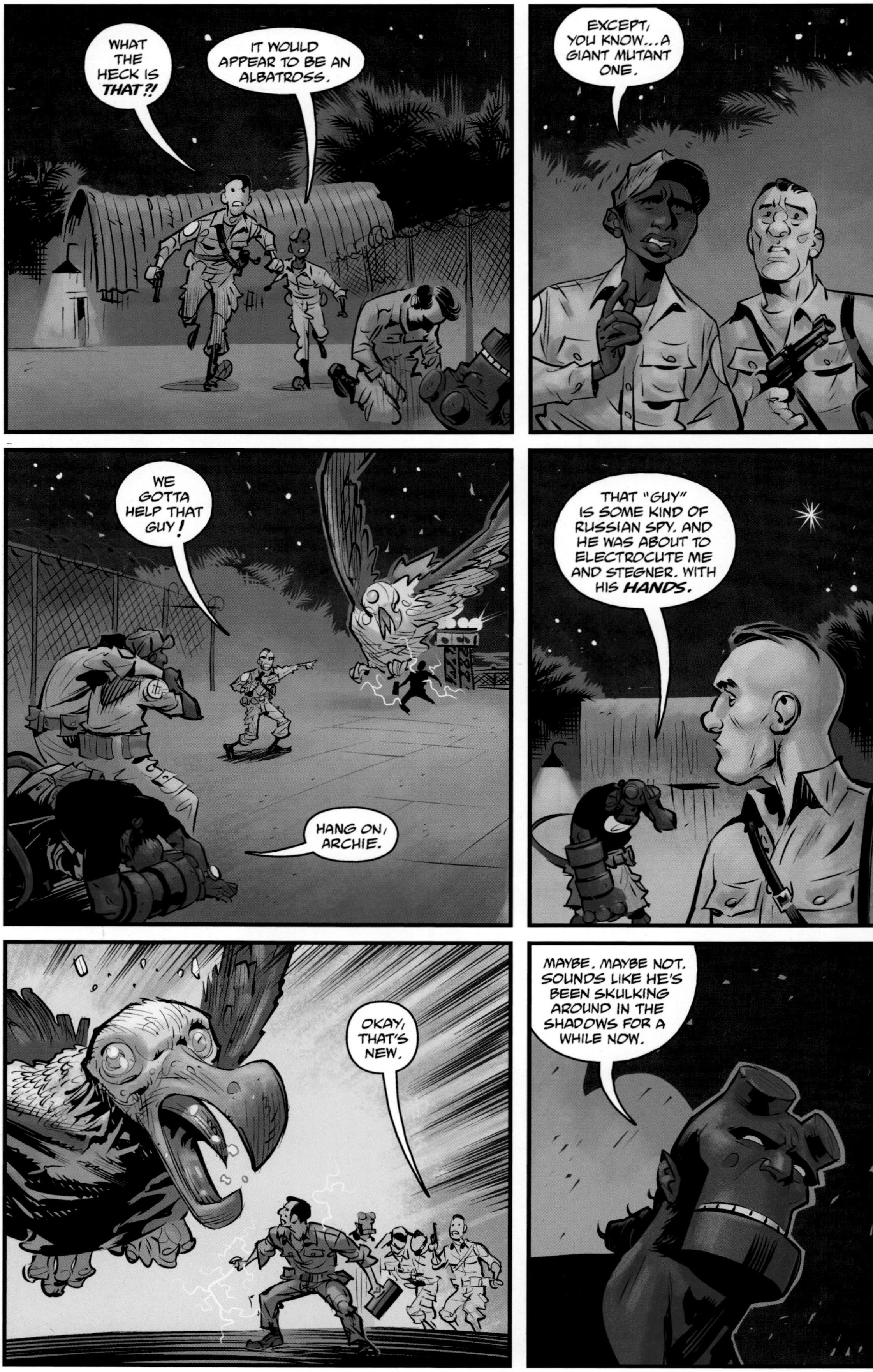
WHAT THE HECK IS THAT?!
IT WOULD APPEAR TO BE AN ALBATROSS.
EXCEPT, YOU KNOW... A GIANT MUTANT ONE.
WE GOTTA HELP THAT GUY!
HANG ON, ARCHIE.
THAT "GUY" IS SOME KIND OF RUSSIAN SPY. AND HE WAS ABOUT TO ELECTROCUTE ME AND STEGNER. WITH HIS HANDS.
OKAY, THAT'S NEW.
MAYBE. MAYBE NOT. SOUNDS LIKE HE'S BEEN SKULKING AROUND IN THE SHADOWS FOR A WHILE NOW.

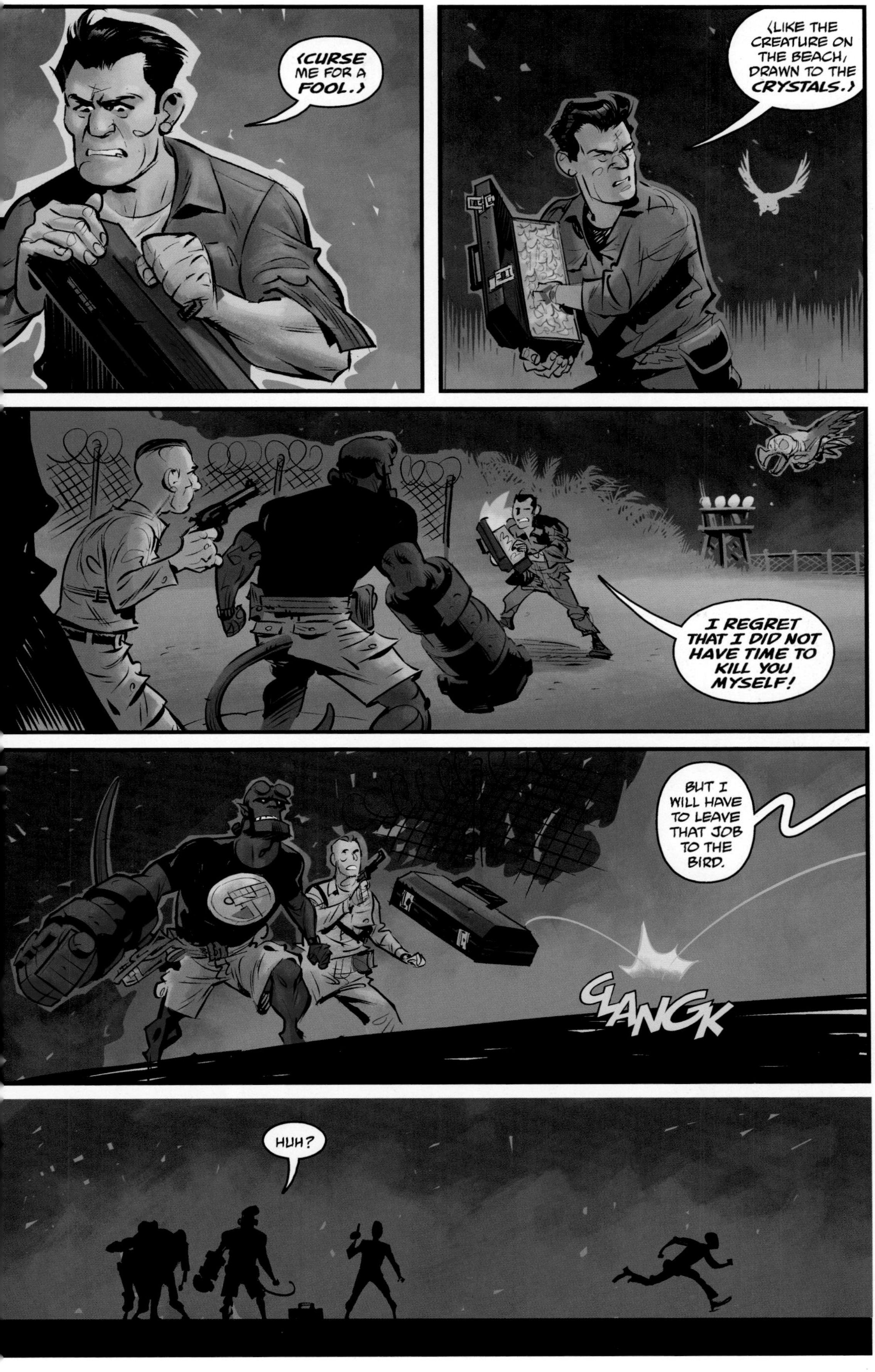
⟨CURSE ME FOR A FOOL.⟩
⟨LIKE THE CREATURE ON THE BEACH, DRAWN TO THE CRYSTALS.⟩
I REGRET THAT I DID NOT HAVE TIME TO KILL YOU MYSELF!
BUT I WILL HAVE TO LEAVE THAT JOB TO THE BIRD.
CLANGK
HUH?

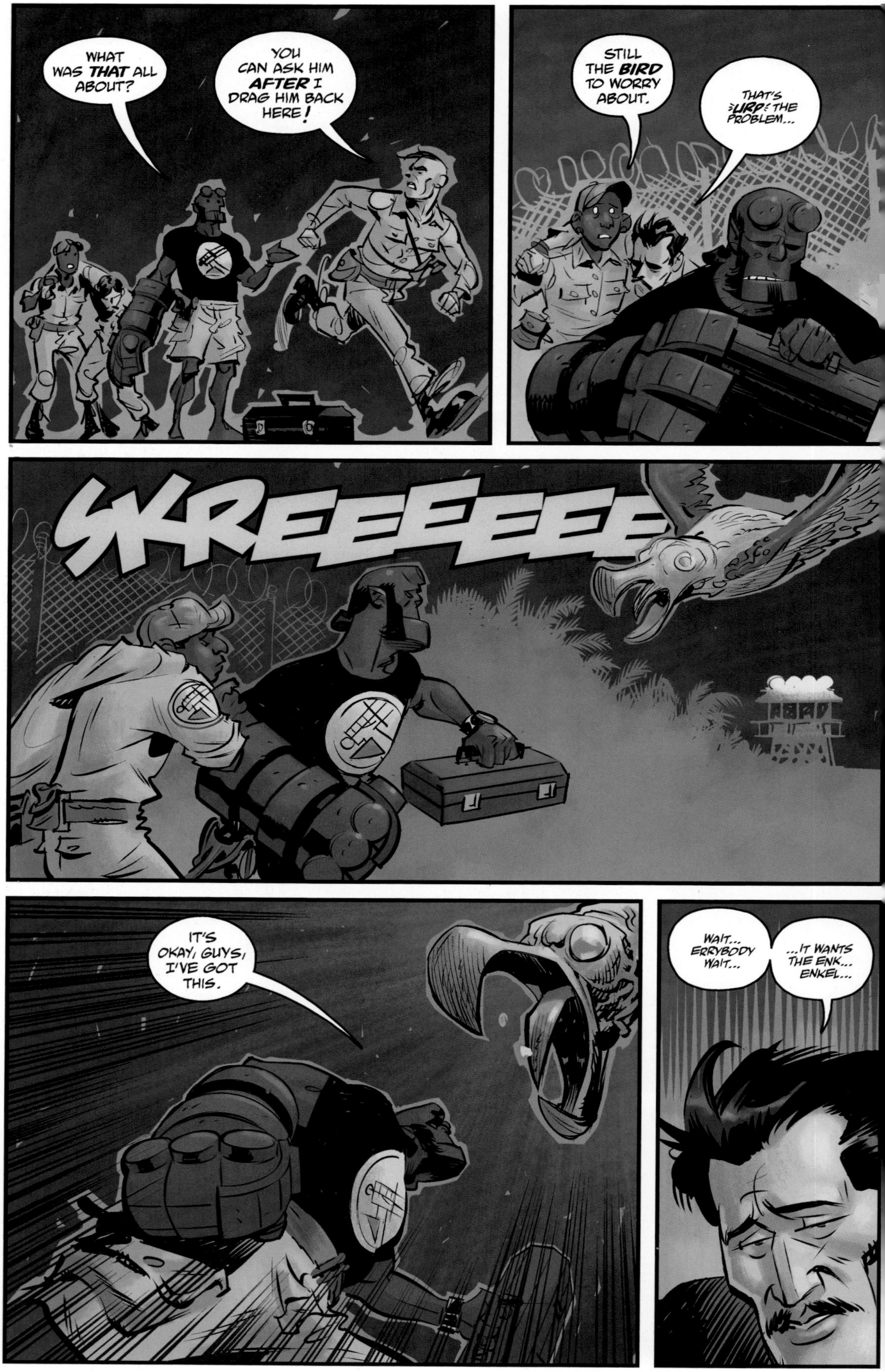
WHAT WAS THAT ALL ABOUT?
YOU CAN ASK HIM AFTER I DRAG HIM BACK HERE!
STILL THE BIRD TO WORRY ABOUT.
THAT'S URP THE PROBLEM...
SKREEEEEEE
IT'S OKAY, GUYS, I'VE GOT THIS.
WAIT... ERRYBODY WAIT...
...IT WANTS THE ENK... ENKEL...

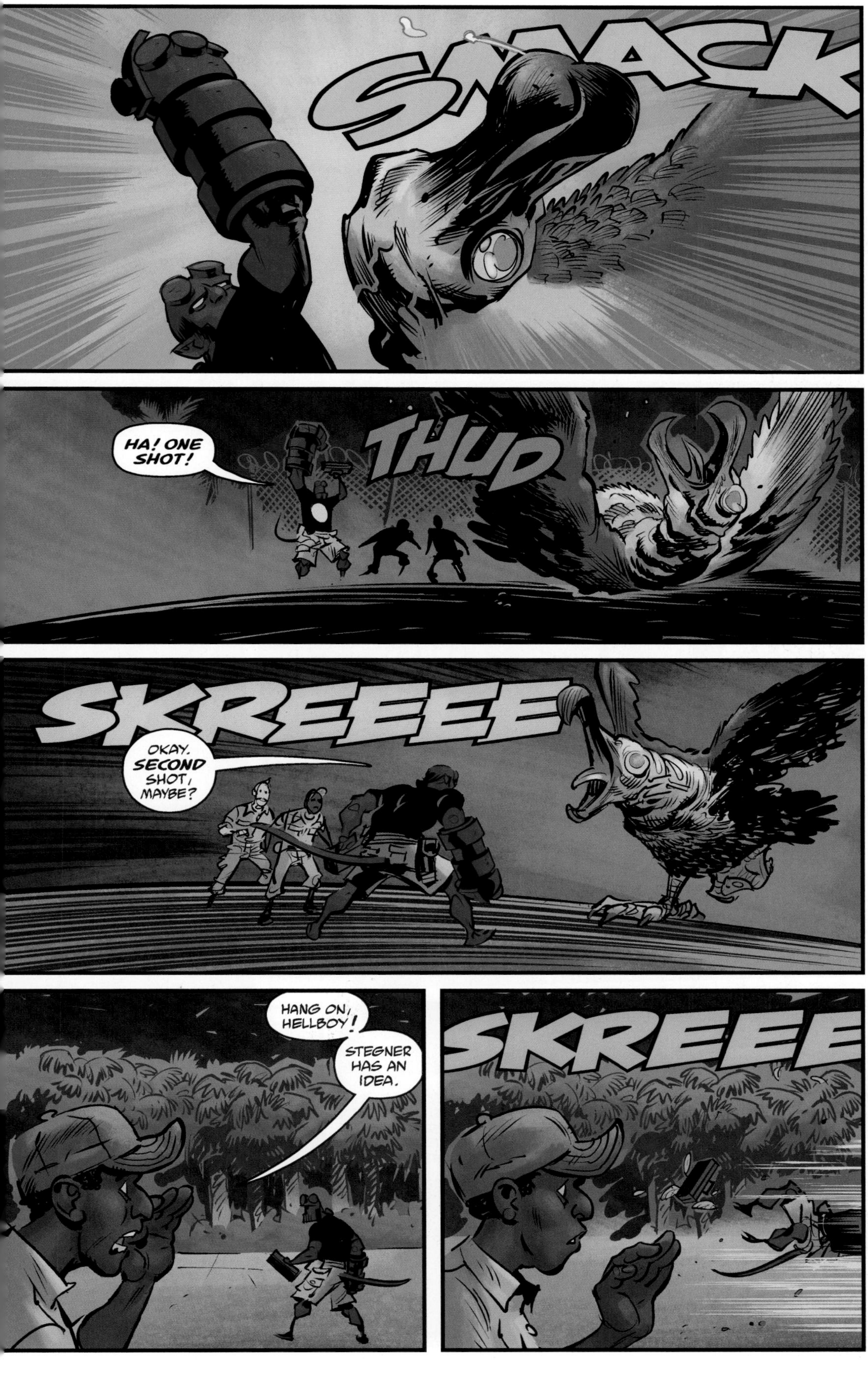
SMACK
THUD
HA! ONE SHOT!
SKREEEE
OKAY. SECOND SHOT, MAYBE?
HANG ON, HELLBOY!
STEGNER HAS AN IDEA.
SKREEE

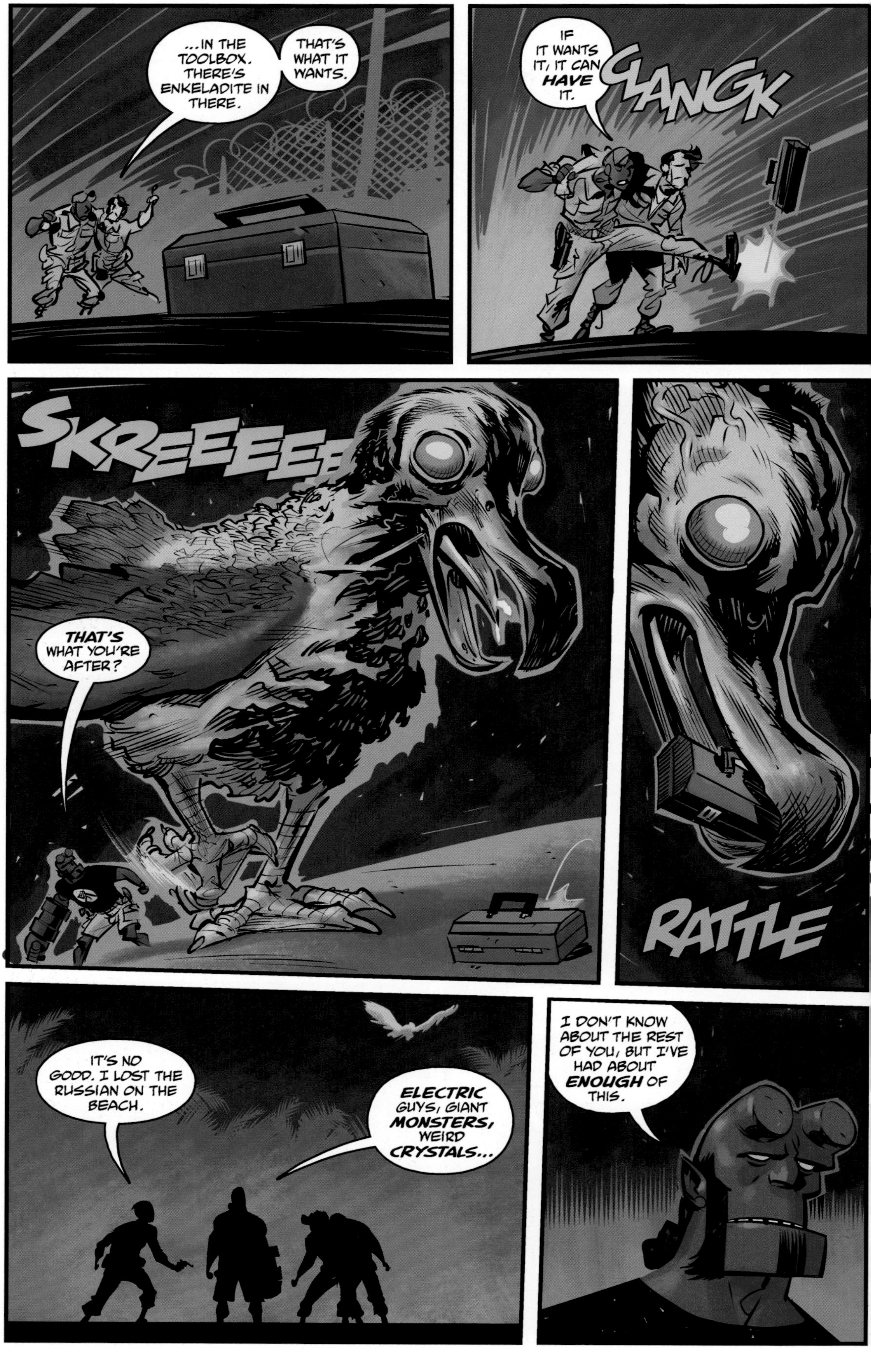
...IN THE TOOLBOX. THERE'S ENKELADITE IN THERE.
THAT'S WHAT IT WANTS.
IF IT WANTS IT, IT CAN HAVE IT.
CLANGK
SKREEEEEE
THAT'S WHAT YOU'RE AFTER?
RATTLE
IT'S NO GOOD. I LOST THE RUSSIAN ON THE BEACH.
ELECTRIC GUYS, GIANT MONSTERS, WEIRD CRYSTALS...
I DON'T KNOW ABOUT THE REST OF YOU, BUT I'VE HAD ABOUT ENOUGH OF THIS.

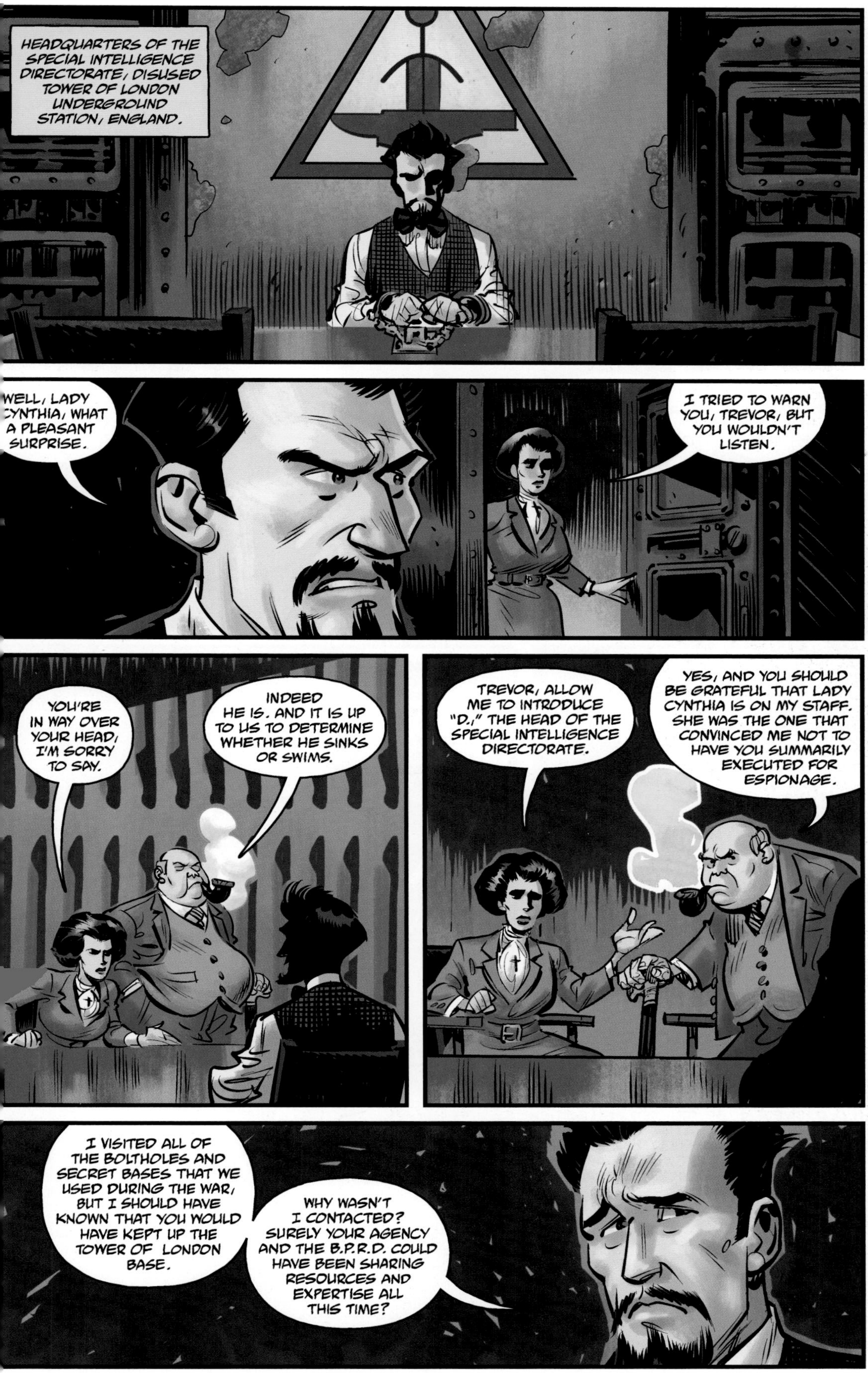
HEADQUARTERS OF THE SPECIAL INTELLIGENCE DIRECTORATE, DISUSED TOWER OF LONDON UNDERGROUND STATION, ENGLAND.
WELL, LADY CYNTHIA, WHAT A PLEASANT SURPRISE.
I TRIED TO WARN YOU, TREVOR, BUT YOU WOULDN'T LISTEN.
YOU'RE IN WAY OVER YOUR HEAD, I'M SORRY TO SAY.
INDEED HE IS. AND IT IS UP TO US TO DETERMINE WHETHER HE SINKS OR SWIMS.
TREVOR, ALLOW ME TO INTRODUCE "D.," THE HEAD OF THE SPECIAL INTELLIGENCE DIRECTORATE.
YES, AND YOU SHOULD BE GRATEFUL THAT LADY CYNTHIA IS ON MY STAFF. SHE WAS THE ONE THAT CONVINCED ME NOT TO HAVE YOU SUMMARILY EXECUTED FOR ESPIONAGE.
I VISITED ALL OF THE BOLTHOLES AND SECRET BASES THAT WE USED DURING THE WAR, BUT I SHOULD HAVE KNOWN THAT YOU WOULD HAVE KEPT UP THE TOWER OF LONDON BASE.
WHY WASN'T I CONTACTED? SURELY YOUR AGENCY AND THE B.P.R.D. COULD HAVE BEEN SHARING RESOURCES AND EXPERTISE ALL THIS TIME?

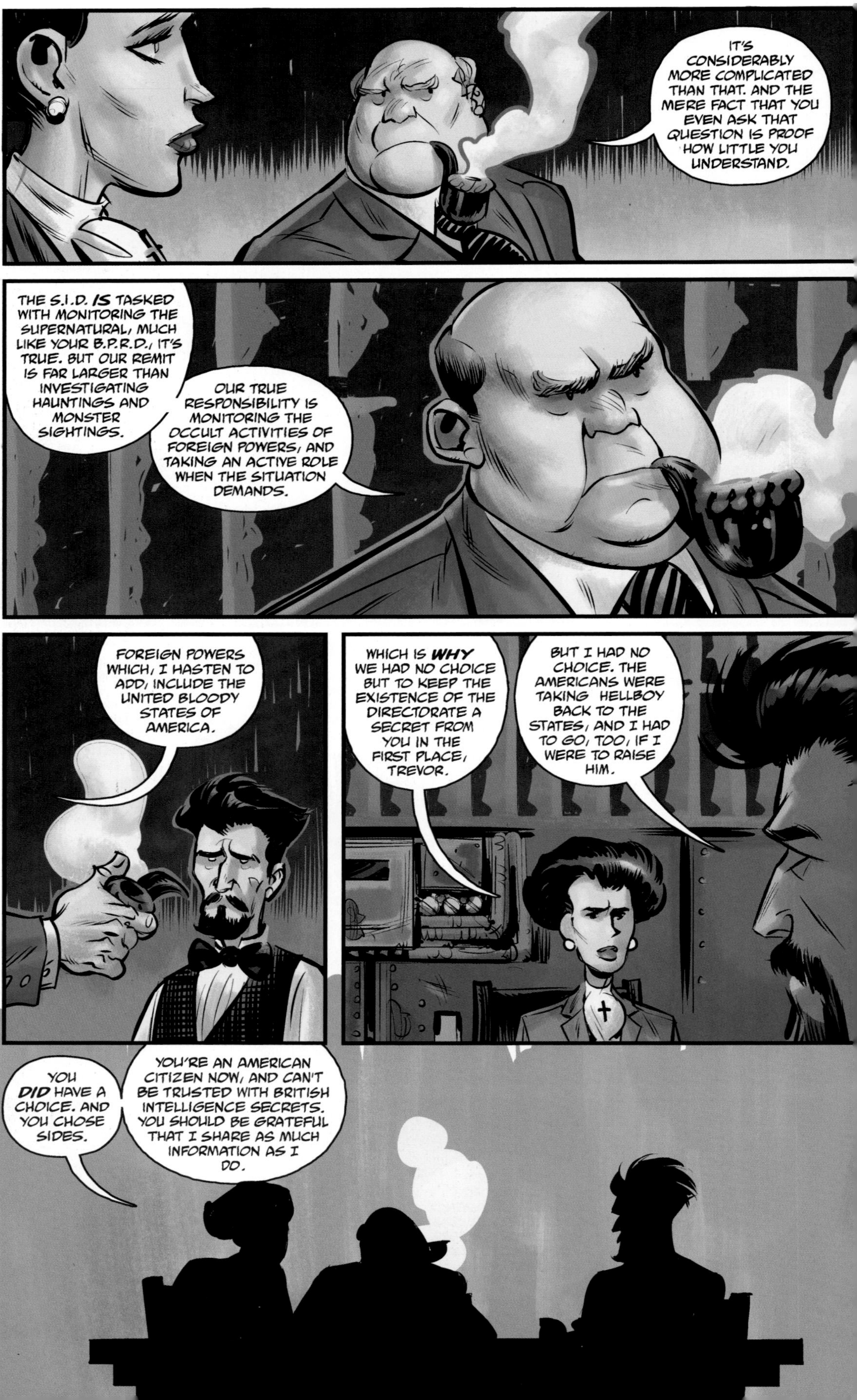
IT'S CONSIDERABLY MORE COMPLICATED THAN THAT. AND THE MERE FACT THAT YOU EVEN ASK THAT QUESTION IS PROOF HOW LITTLE YOU UNDERSTAND.
THE S.I.D. IS TASKED WITH MONITORING THE SUPERNATURAL, MUCH LIKE YOUR B.P.R.D., IT'S TRUE. BUT OUR REMIT IS FAR LARGER THAN INVESTIGATING HAUNTINGS AND MONSTER SIGHTINGS.
OUR TRUE RESPONSIBILITY IS MONITORING THE OCCULT ACTIVITIES OF FOREIGN POWERS, AND TAKING AN ACTIVE ROLE WHEN THE SITUATION DEMANDS.
FOREIGN POWERS WHICH, I HASTEN TO ADD, INCLUDE THE UNITED BLOODY STATES OF AMERICA.
WHICH IS WHY WE HAD NO CHOICE BUT TO KEEP THE EXISTENCE OF THE DIRECTORATE A SECRET FROM YOU IN THE FIRST PLACE, TREVOR.
BUT I HAD NO CHOICE. THE AMERICANS WERE TAKING HELLBOY BACK TO THE STATES, AND I HAD TO GO, TOO, IF I WERE TO RAISE HIM.
YOU DID HAVE A CHOICE. AND YOU CHOSE SIDES.
YOU'RE AN AMERICAN CITIZEN NOW, AND CAN'T BE TRUSTED WITH BRITISH INTELLIGENCE SECRETS. YOU SHOULD BE GRATEFUL THAT I SHARE AS MUCH INFORMATION AS I DO.

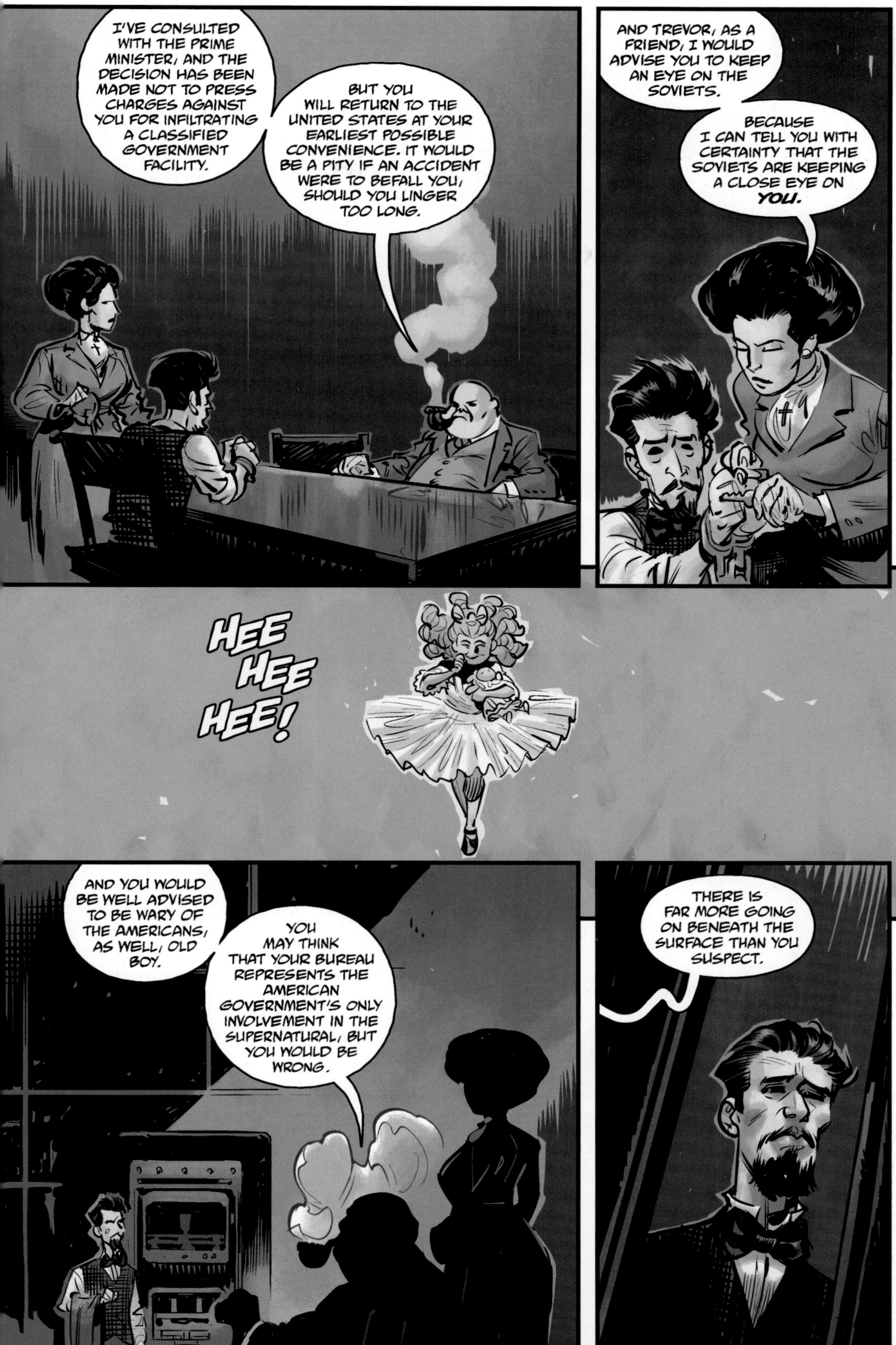

I'VE CONSULTED WITH THE PRIME MINISTER, AND THE DECISION HAS BEEN MADE NOT TO PRESS CHARGES AGAINST YOU FOR INFILTRATING A CLASSIFIED GOVERNMENT FACILITY.
BUT YOU WILL RETURN TO THE UNITED STATES AT YOUR EARLIEST POSSIBLE CONVENIENCE. IT WOULD BE A PITY IF AN ACCIDENT WERE TO BEFALL YOU, SHOULD YOU LINGER TOO LONG.
AND TREVOR, AS A FRIEND, I WOULD ADVISE YOU TO KEEP AN EYE ON THE SOVIETS.
BECAUSE I CAN TELL YOU WITH CERTAINTY THAT THE SOVIETS ARE KEEPING A CLOSE EYE ON **YOU.**
HEE HEE HEE!
AND YOU WOULD BE WELL ADVISED TO BE WARY OF THE AMERICANS, AS WELL, OLD BOY.
YOU MAY THINK THAT YOUR BUREAU REPRESENTS THE AMERICAN GOVERNMENT'S ONLY INVOLVEMENT IN THE SUPERNATURAL, BUT YOU WOULD BE WRONG.
THERE IS FAR MORE GOING ON BENEATH THE SURFACE THAN YOU SUSPECT.

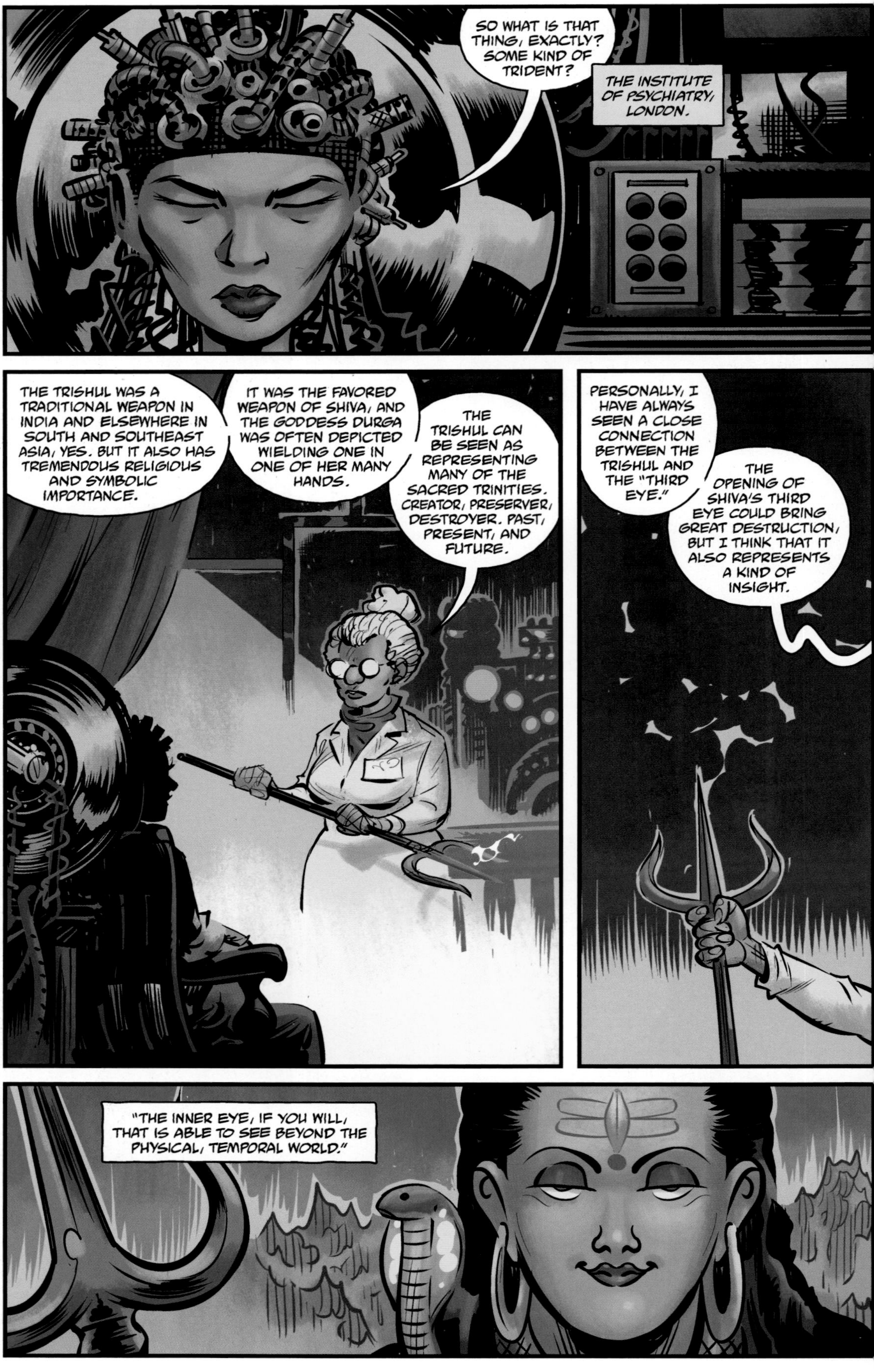
SO WHAT IS THAT THING, EXACTLY? SOME KIND OF TRIDENT?
THE INSTITUTE OF PSYCHIATRY, LONDON.
THE TRISHUL WAS A TRADITIONAL WEAPON IN INDIA AND ELSEWHERE IN SOUTH AND SOUTHEAST ASIA, YES. BUT IT ALSO HAS TREMENDOUS RELIGIOUS AND SYMBOLIC IMPORTANCE.
IT WAS THE FAVORED WEAPON OF SHIVA, AND THE GODDESS DURGA WAS OFTEN DEPICTED WIELDING ONE IN ONE OF HER MANY HANDS.
THE TRISHUL CAN BE SEEN AS REPRESENTING MANY OF THE SACRED TRINITIES. CREATOR, PRESERVER, DESTROYER. PAST, PRESENT, AND FUTURE.
PERSONALLY, I HAVE ALWAYS SEEN A CLOSE CONNECTION BETWEEN THE TRISHUL AND THE "THIRD EYE."
THE OPENING OF SHIVA'S THIRD EYE COULD BRING GREAT DESTRUCTION, BUT I THINK THAT IT ALSO REPRESENTS A KIND OF INSIGHT.
"THE INNER EYE, IF YOU WILL, THAT IS ABLE TO SEE BEYOND THE PHYSICAL, TEMPORAL WORLD."

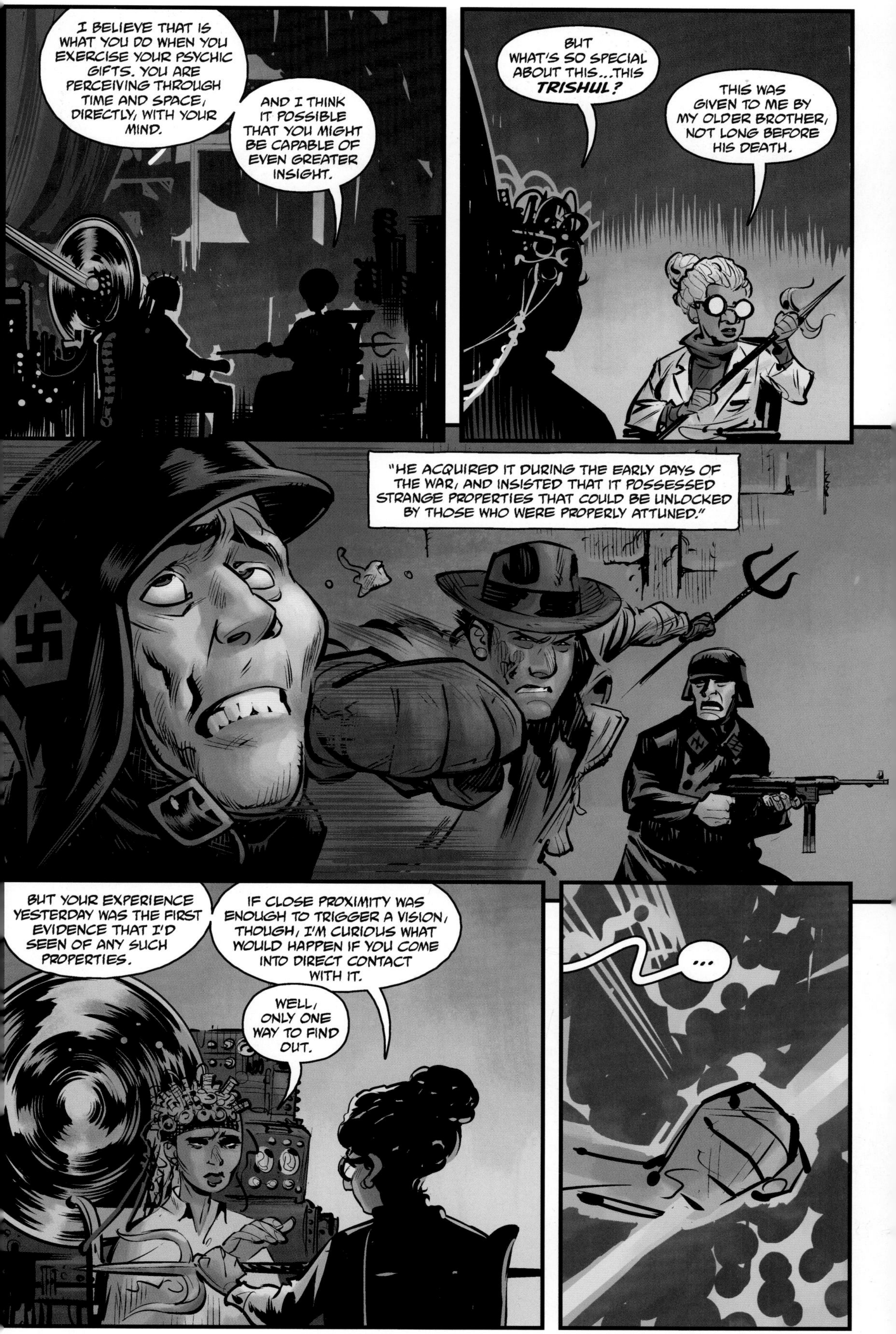
I BELIEVE THAT IS WHAT YOU DO WHEN YOU EXERCISE YOUR PSYCHIC GIFTS. YOU ARE PERCEIVING THROUGH TIME AND SPACE, DIRECTLY, WITH YOUR MIND.
AND I THINK IT POSSIBLE THAT YOU MIGHT BE CAPABLE OF EVEN GREATER INSIGHT.
BUT WHAT'S SO SPECIAL ABOUT THIS...THIS *TRISHUL?*
THIS WAS GIVEN TO ME BY MY OLDER BROTHER, NOT LONG BEFORE HIS DEATH.
"HE ACQUIRED IT DURING THE EARLY DAYS OF THE WAR, AND INSISTED THAT IT POSSESSED STRANGE PROPERTIES THAT COULD BE UNLOCKED BY THOSE WHO WERE PROPERLY ATTUNED."
BUT YOUR EXPERIENCE YESTERDAY WAS THE FIRST EVIDENCE THAT I'D SEEN OF ANY SUCH PROPERTIES.
IF CLOSE PROXIMITY WAS ENOUGH TO TRIGGER A VISION, THOUGH, I'M CURIOUS WHAT WOULD HAPPEN IF YOU COME INTO DIRECT CONTACT WITH IT.
WELL, ONLY ONE WAY TO FIND OUT.
...

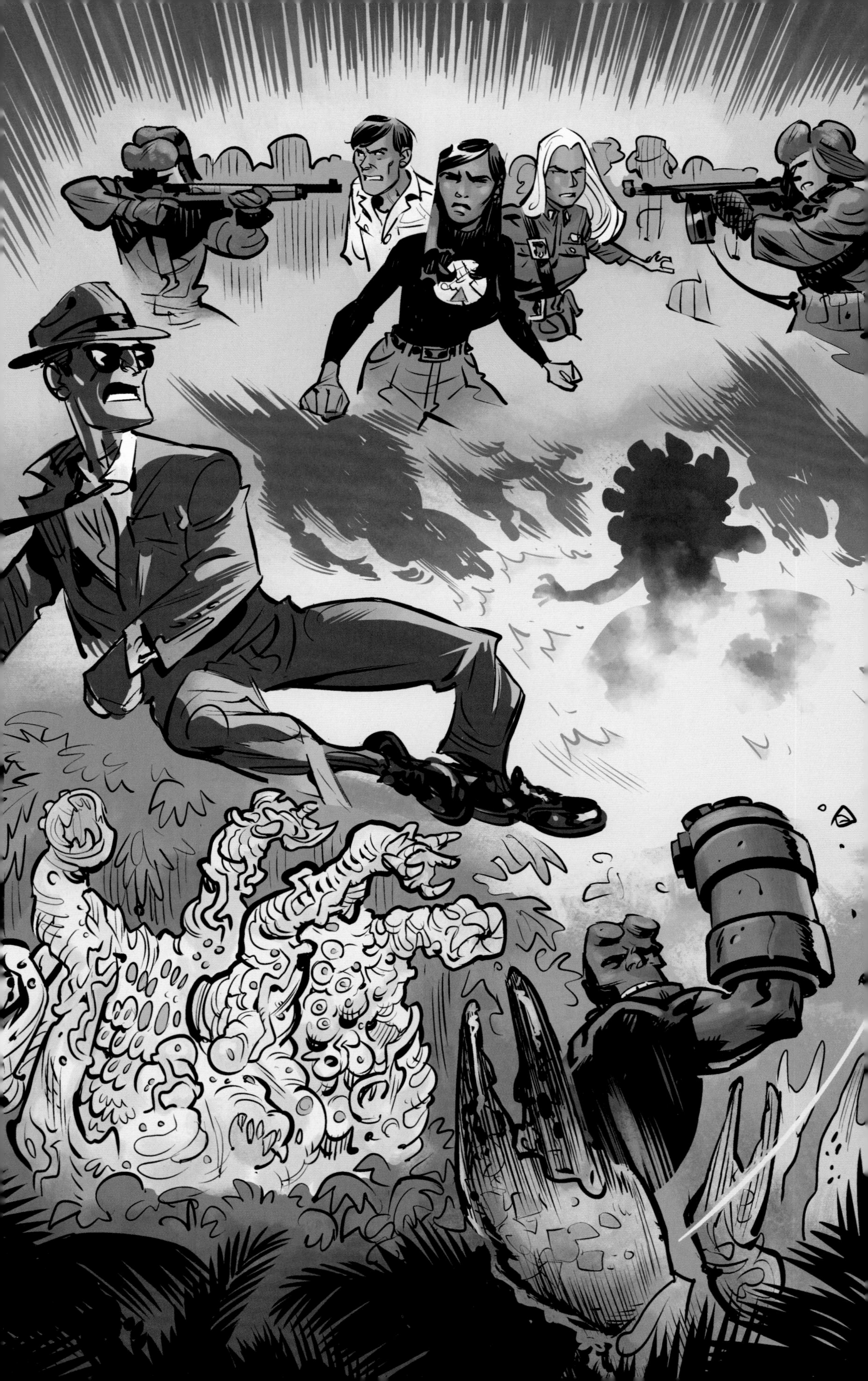

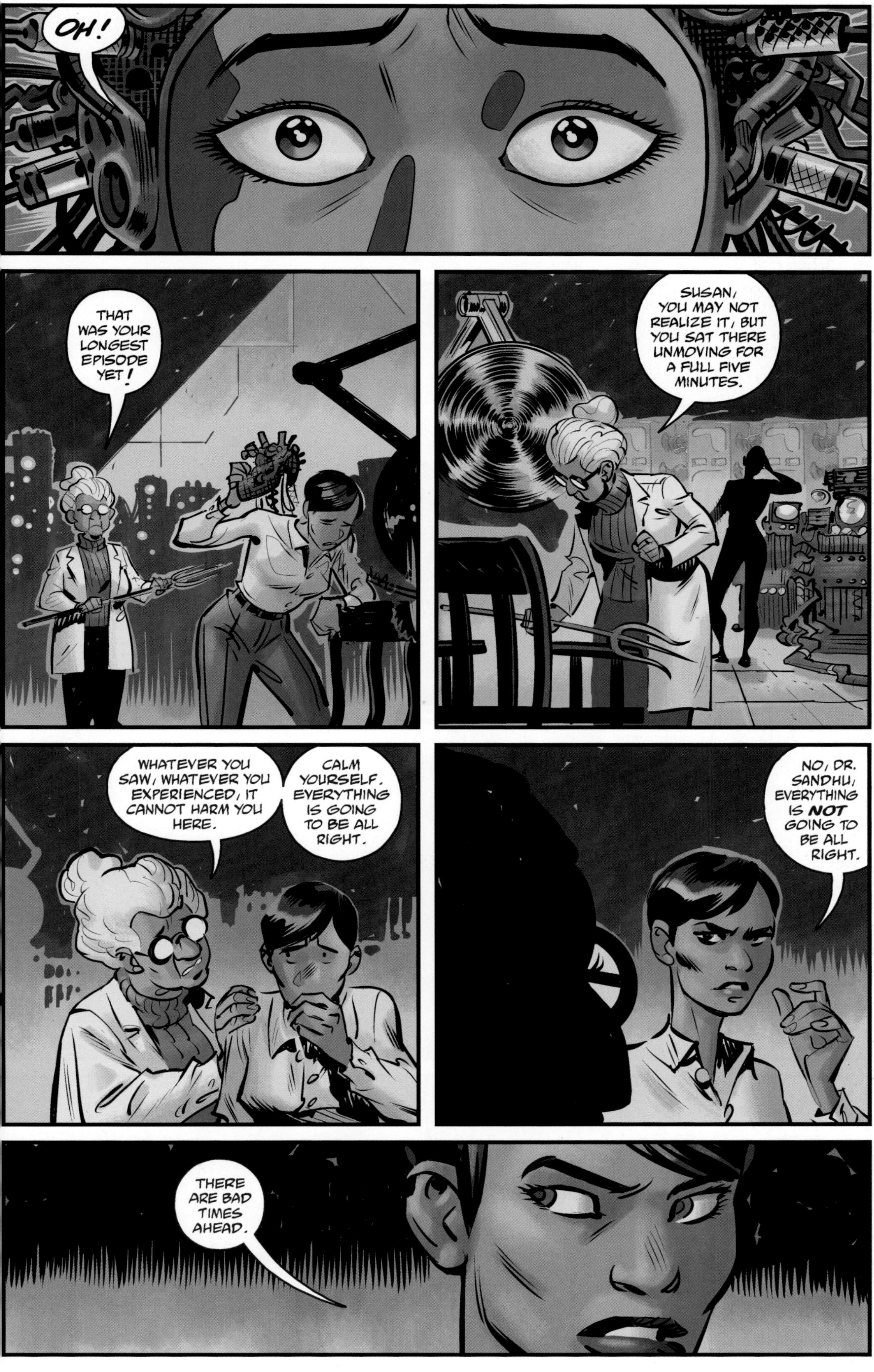
OH!
THAT WAS YOUR LONGEST EPISODE YET!
SUSAN, YOU MAY NOT REALIZE IT, BUT YOU SAT THERE UNMOVING FOR A FULL FIVE MINUTES.
WHATEVER YOU SAW, WHATEVER YOU EXPERIENCED, IT CANNOT HARM YOU HERE.
CALM YOURSELF. EVERYTHING IS GOING TO BE ALL RIGHT.
NO, DR. SANDHU, EVERYTHING IS **NOT** GOING TO BE ALL RIGHT.
THERE ARE BAD TIMES AHEAD.

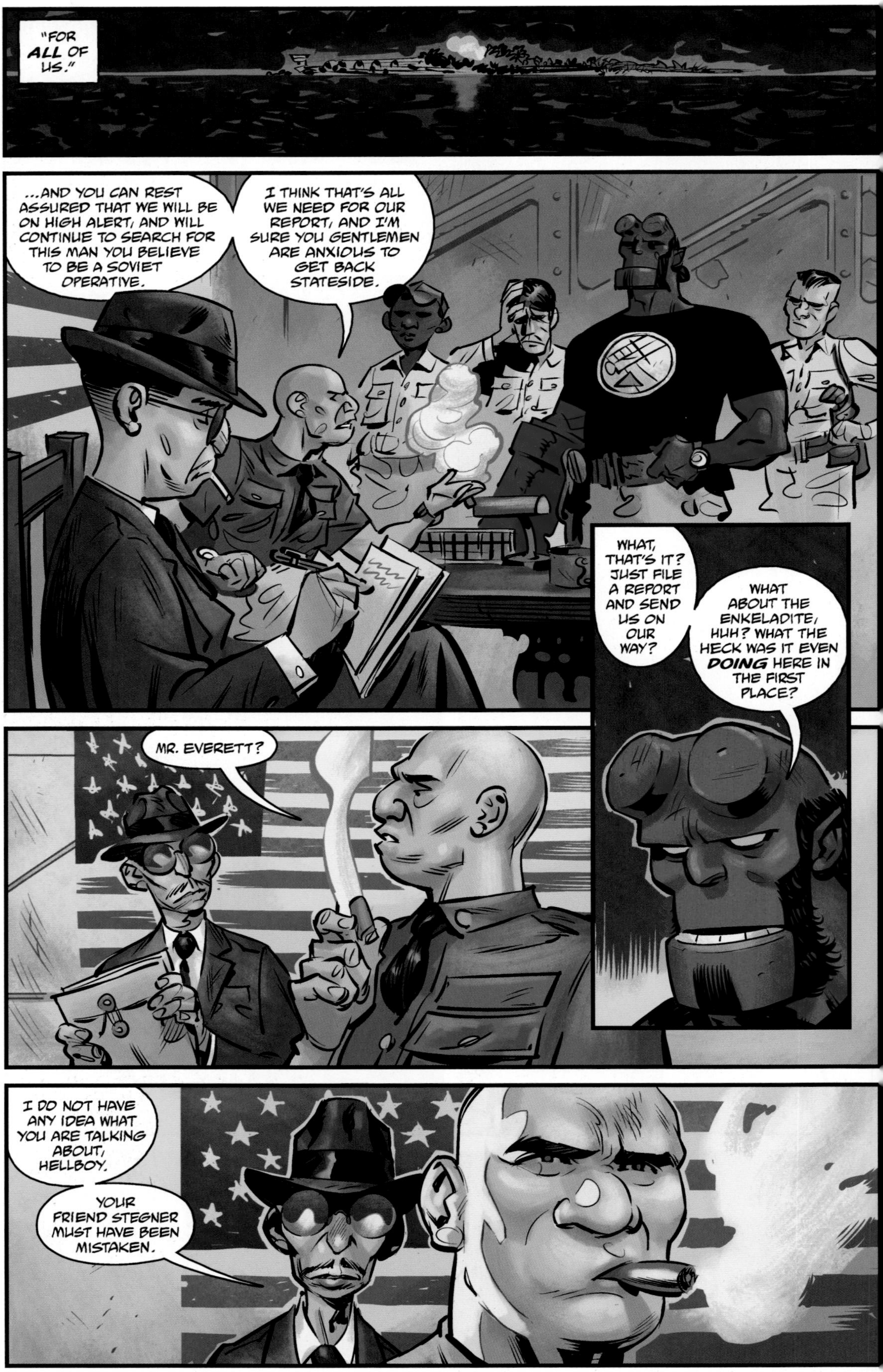
"FOR ALL OF US."
...AND YOU CAN REST ASSURED THAT WE WILL BE ON HIGH ALERT, AND WILL CONTINUE TO SEARCH FOR THIS MAN YOU BELIEVE TO BE A SOVIET OPERATIVE.
I THINK THAT'S ALL WE NEED FOR OUR REPORT, AND I'M SURE YOU GENTLEMEN ARE ANXIOUS TO GET BACK STATESIDE.
WHAT, THAT'S IT? JUST FILE A REPORT AND SEND US ON OUR WAY?
WHAT ABOUT THE ENKELADITE, HUH? WHAT THE HECK WAS IT EVEN DOING HERE IN THE FIRST PLACE?
MR. EVERETT?
I DO NOT HAVE ANY IDEA WHAT YOU ARE TALKING ABOUT, HELLBOY.
YOUR FRIEND STEGNER MUST HAVE BEEN MISTAKEN.

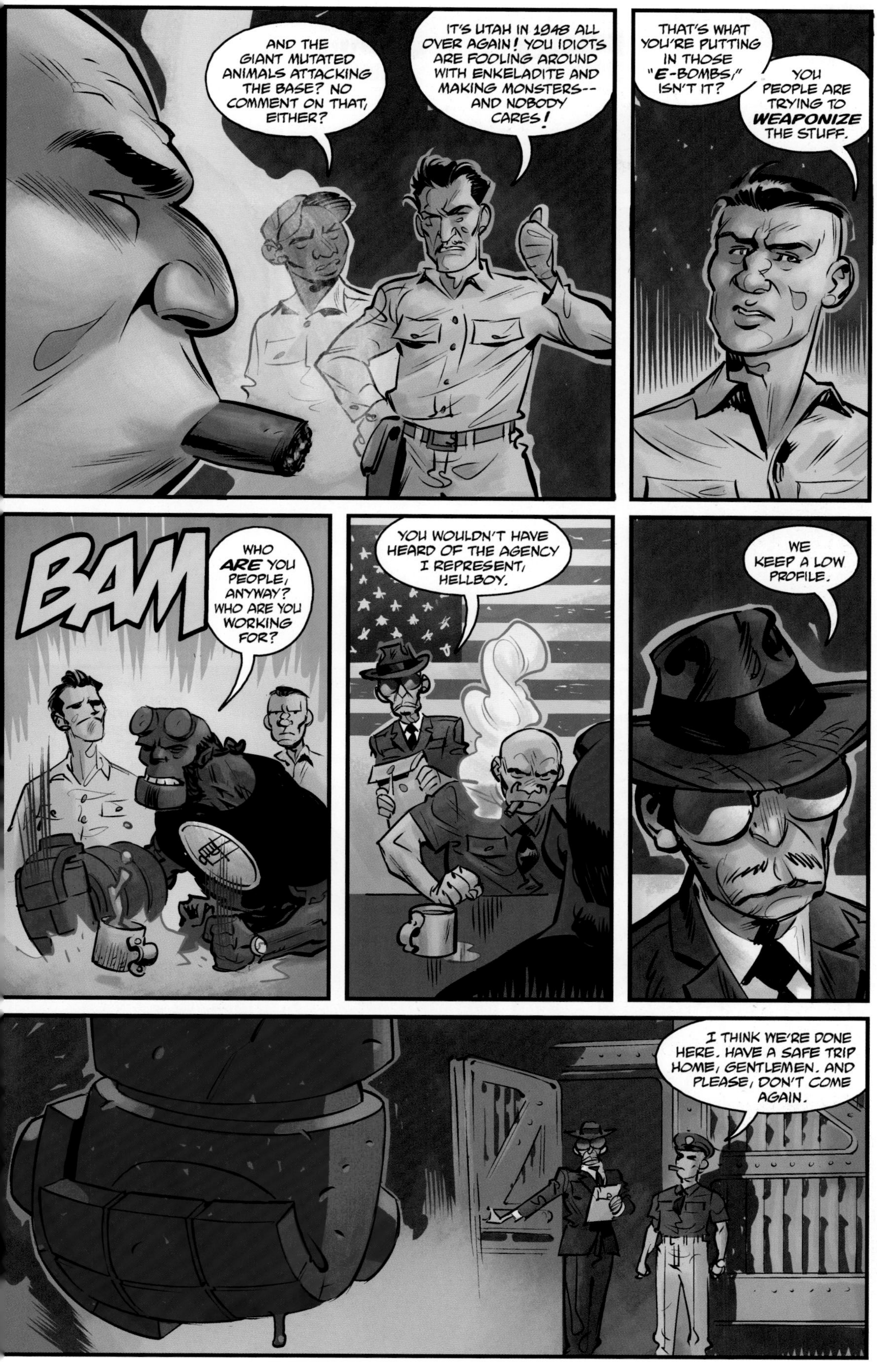
AND THE GIANT MUTATED ANIMALS ATTACKING THE BASE? NO COMMENT ON THAT, EITHER?
IT'S UTAH IN 1948 ALL OVER AGAIN! YOU IDIOTS ARE FOOLING AROUND WITH ENKELADITE AND MAKING MONSTERS-- AND NOBODY CARES!
THAT'S WHAT YOU'RE PUTTING IN THOSE "E-BOMBS," ISN'T IT?
YOU PEOPLE ARE TRYING TO WEAPONIZE THE STUFF.
BAM
WHO ARE YOU PEOPLE, ANYWAY? WHO ARE YOU WORKING FOR?
YOU WOULDN'T HAVE HEARD OF THE AGENCY I REPRESENT, HELLBOY.
WE KEEP A LOW PROFILE.
I THINK WE'RE DONE HERE. HAVE A SAFE TRIP HOME, GENTLEMEN. AND PLEASE, DON'T COME AGAIN.

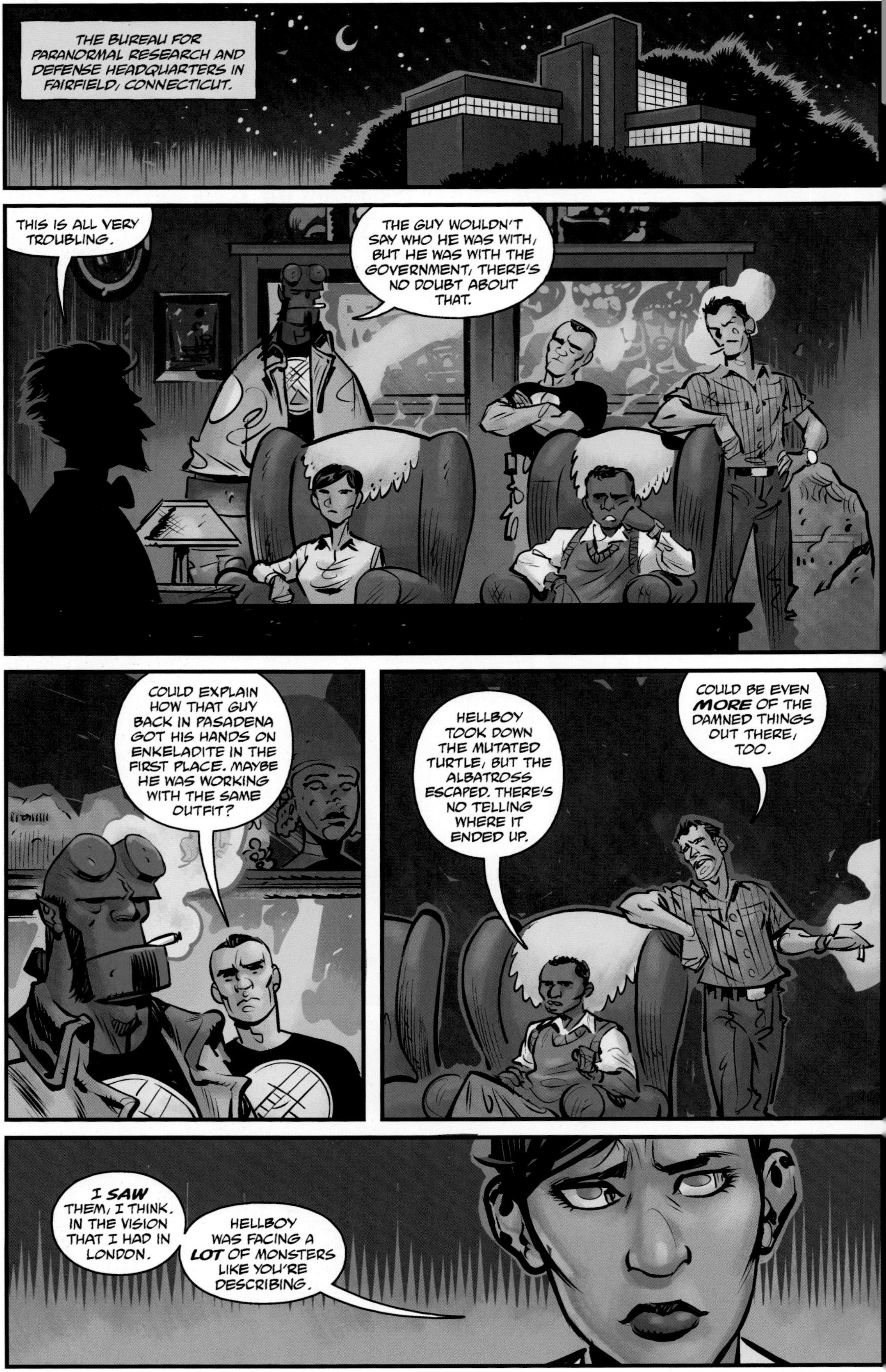
THE BUREAU FOR PARANORMAL RESEARCH AND DEFENSE HEADQUARTERS IN FAIRFIELD, CONNECTICUT.
THIS IS ALL VERY TROUBLING.
THE GUY WOULDN'T SAY WHO HE WAS WITH, BUT HE WAS WITH THE GOVERNMENT, THERE'S NO DOUBT ABOUT THAT.
COULD EXPLAIN HOW THAT GUY BACK IN PASADENA GOT HIS HANDS ON ENKELADITE IN THE FIRST PLACE. MAYBE HE WAS WORKING WITH THE SAME OUTFIT?
HELLBOY TOOK DOWN THE MUTATED TURTLE, BUT THE ALBATROSS ESCAPED. THERE'S NO TELLING WHERE IT ENDED UP.
COULD BE EVEN MORE OF THE DAMNED THINGS OUT THERE, TOO.
I SAW THEM, I THINK. IN THE VISION THAT I HAD IN LONDON.
HELLBOY WAS FACING A LOT OF MONSTERS LIKE YOU'RE DESCRIBING.

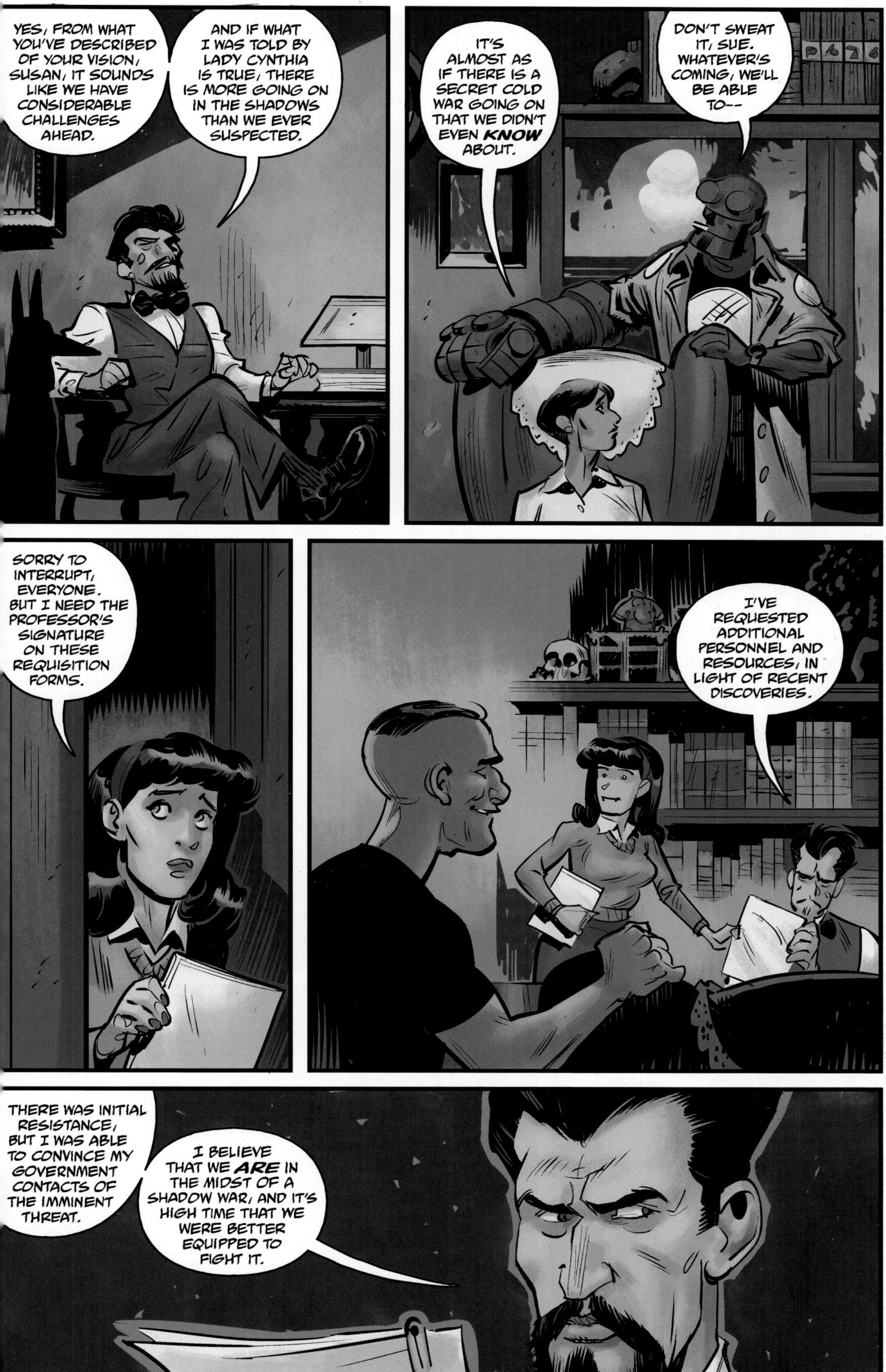
YES, FROM WHAT YOU'VE DESCRIBED OF YOUR VISION, SUSAN, IT SOUNDS LIKE WE HAVE CONSIDERABLE CHALLENGES AHEAD.
AND IF WHAT I WAS TOLD BY LADY CYNTHIA IS TRUE, THERE IS MORE GOING ON IN THE SHADOWS THAN WE EVER SUSPECTED.
IT'S ALMOST AS IF THERE IS A SECRET COLD WAR GOING ON THAT WE DIDN'T EVEN KNOW ABOUT.
DON'T SWEAT IT, SUE. WHATEVER'S COMING, WE'LL BE ABLE TO--
SORRY TO INTERRUPT, EVERYONE. BUT I NEED THE PROFESSOR'S SIGNATURE ON THESE REQUISITION FORMS.
I'VE REQUESTED ADDITIONAL PERSONNEL AND RESOURCES, IN LIGHT OF RECENT DISCOVERIES.
THERE WAS INITIAL RESISTANCE, BUT I WAS ABLE TO CONVINCE MY GOVERNMENT CONTACTS OF THE IMMINENT THREAT.
I BELIEVE THAT WE ARE IN THE MIDST OF A SHADOW WAR, AND IT'S HIGH TIME THAT WE WERE BETTER EQUIPPED TO FIGHT IT.

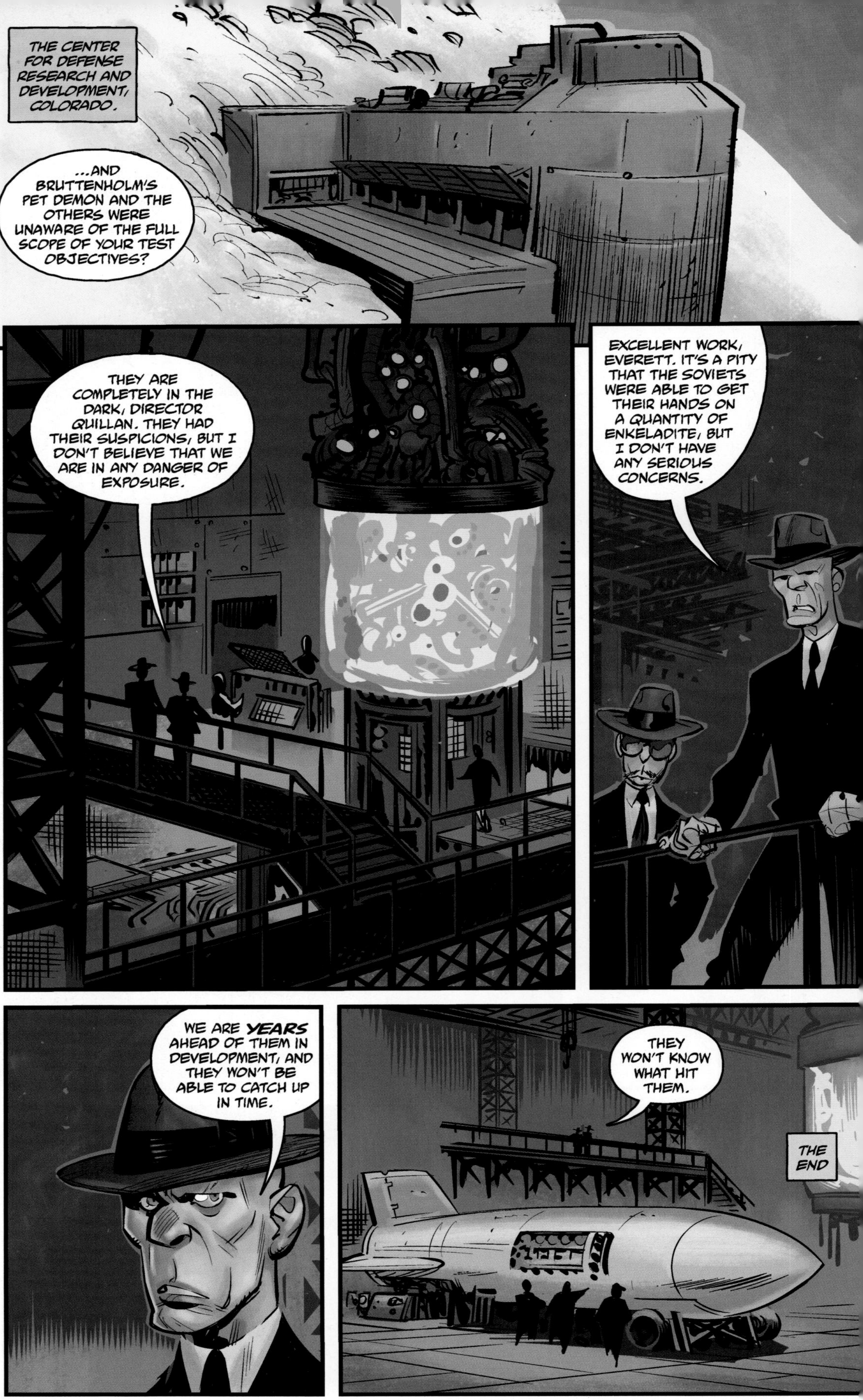
THE CENTER FOR DEFENSE RESEARCH AND DEVELOPMENT, COLORADO.
...AND BRUTTENHOLM'S PET DEMON AND THE OTHERS WERE UNAWARE OF THE FULL SCOPE OF YOUR TEST OBJECTIVES?
THEY ARE COMPLETELY IN THE DARK, DIRECTOR QUILLAN. THEY HAD THEIR SUSPICIONS, BUT I DON'T BELIEVE THAT WE ARE IN ANY DANGER OF EXPOSURE.
EXCELLENT WORK, EVERETT. IT'S A PITY THAT THE SOVIETS WERE ABLE TO GET THEIR HANDS ON A QUANTITY OF ENKELADITE, BUT I DON'T HAVE ANY SERIOUS CONCERNS.
WE ARE YEARS AHEAD OF THEM IN DEVELOPMENT, AND THEY WON'T BE ABLE TO CATCH UP IN TIME.
THEY WON'T KNOW WHAT HIT THEM.
THE END

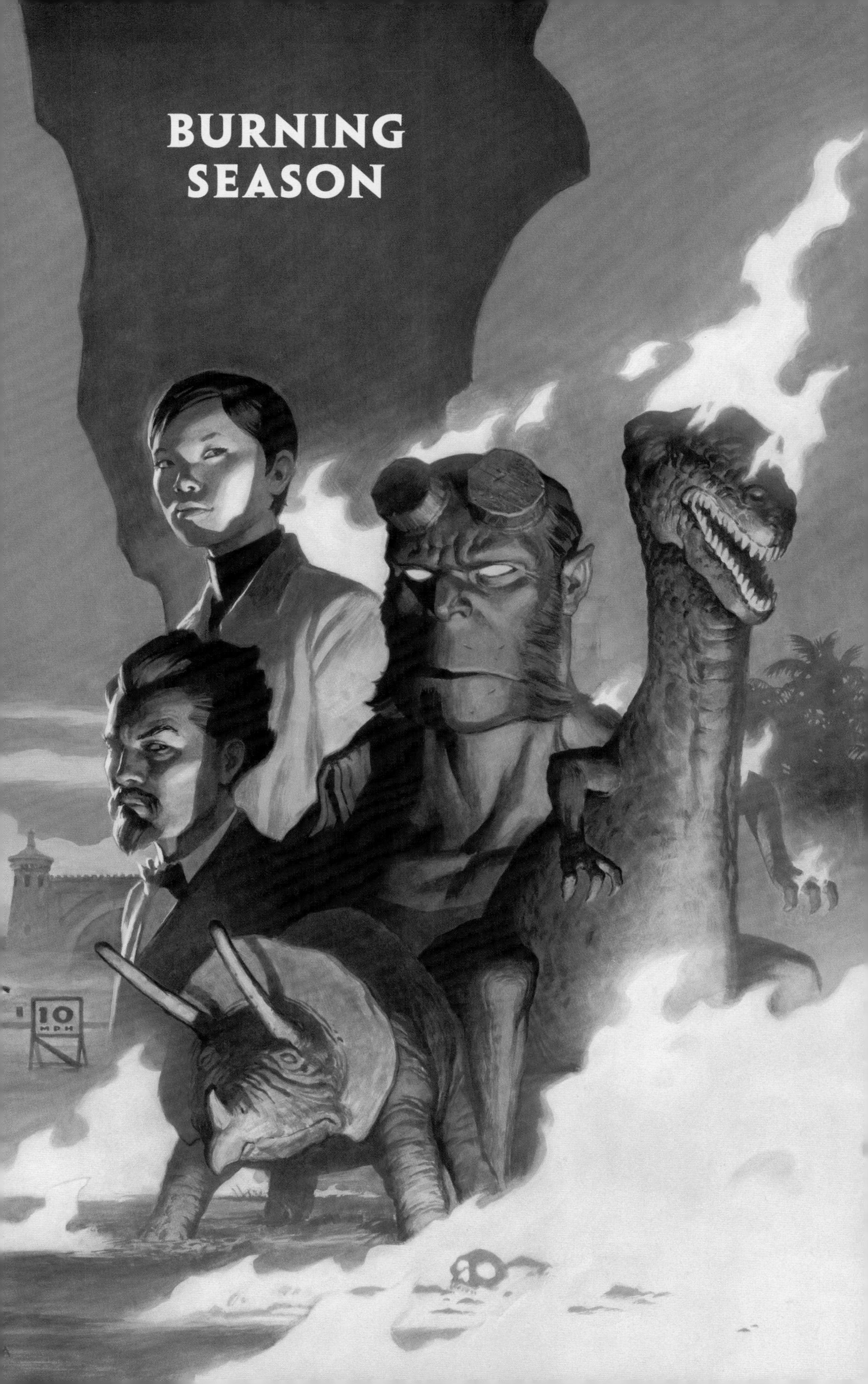
BURNING
SEASON
10
MPH

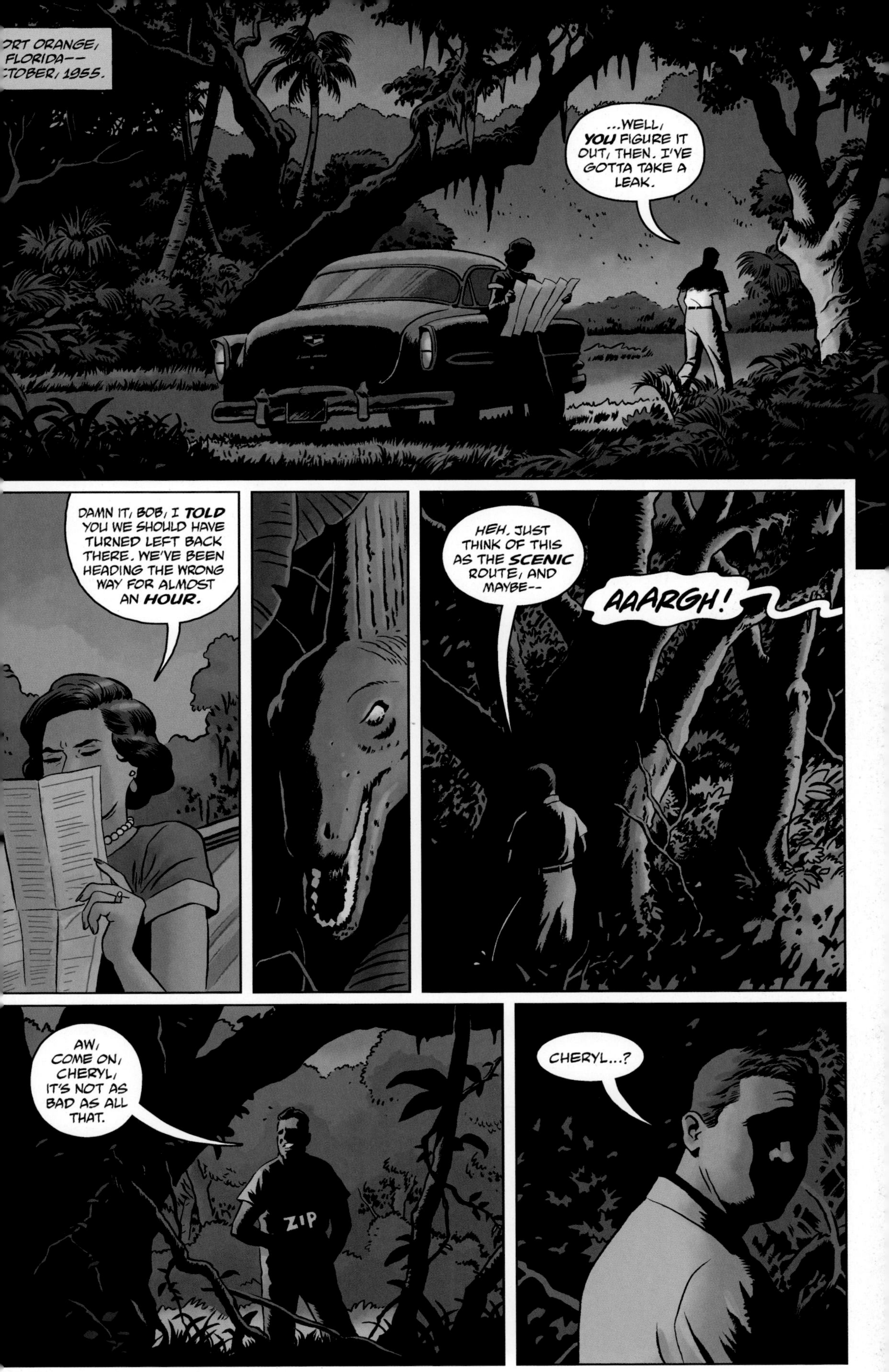
ORT ORANGE, FLORIDA-- CTOBER, 1955.
...WELL, YOU FIGURE IT OUT, THEN. I'VE GOTTA TAKE A LEAK.
DAMN IT, BOB, I TOLD YOU WE SHOULD HAVE TURNED LEFT BACK THERE. WE'VE BEEN HEADING THE WRONG WAY FOR ALMOST AN HOUR.
HEH. JUST THINK OF THIS AS THE SCENIC ROUTE, AND MAYBE--
AAARGH!
AW, COME ON, CHERYL, IT'S NOT AS BAD AS ALL THAT.
ZIP
CHERYL...?

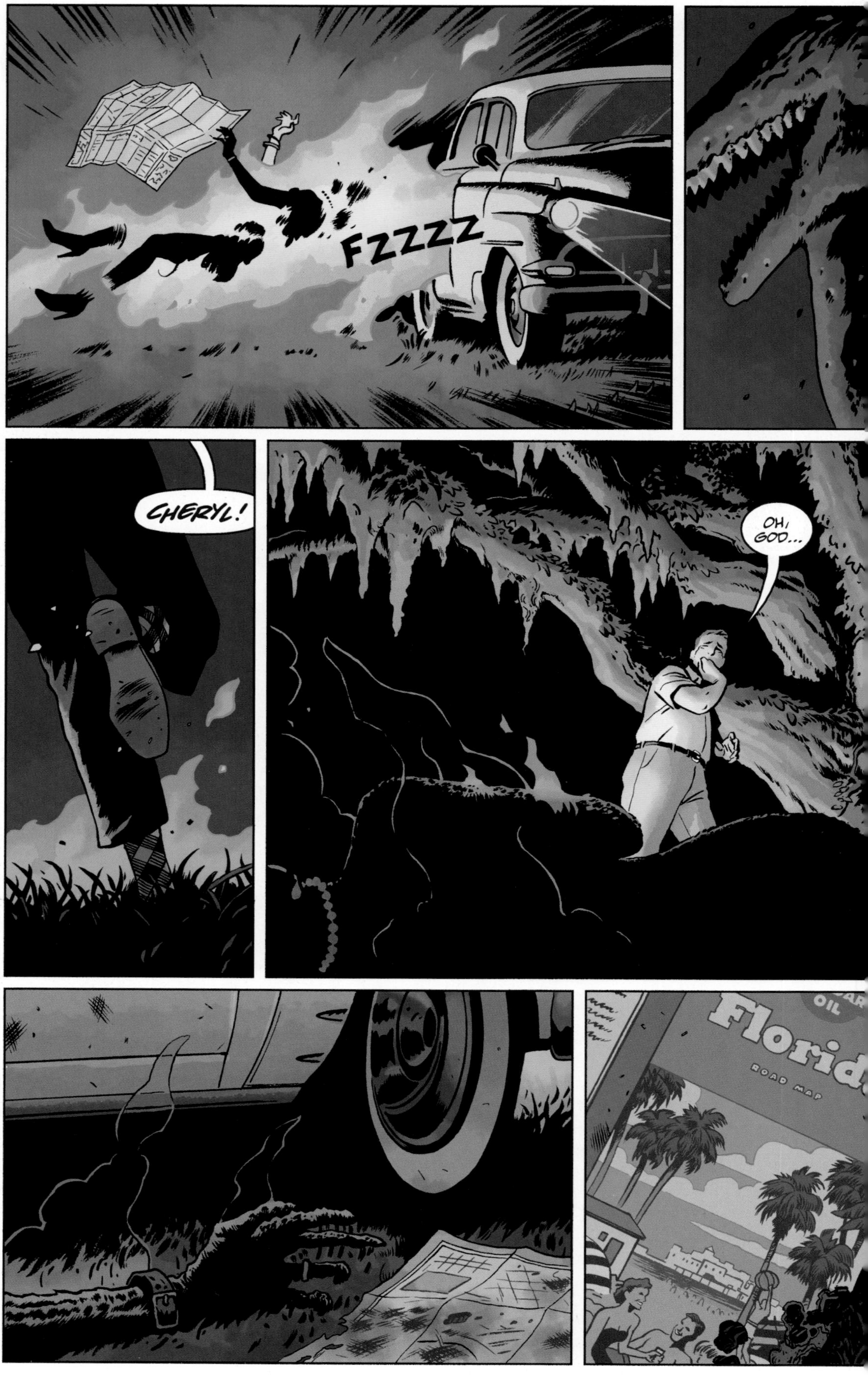
FZZZZ
CHERYL!
OH, GOD...
Florida
ROAD MAP
OIL

...AND THAT'S ABOUT ALL I KNOW, FOLKS. THE POOR GAL JUST BURNED TO A CRISP, RIGHT IN FRONT OF HER HUSBAND'S EYES.

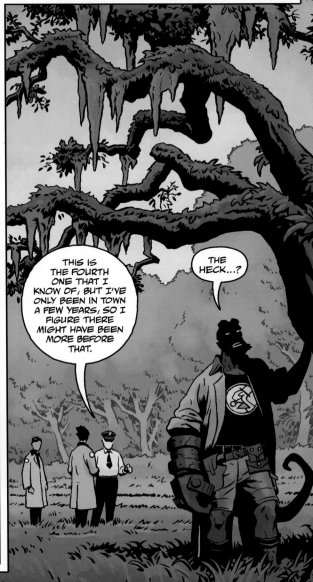

BUT THIS IS NOT THE FIRST SUCH CASE IN THE AREA, IS IT, SHERIFF?

IT WAS BROUGHT TO MY ATTENTION THAT THERE HAVE BEEN A NUMBER OF OTHER SIMILAR UNEXPLAINED DEATHS BY FIRE IN RECENT YEARS.

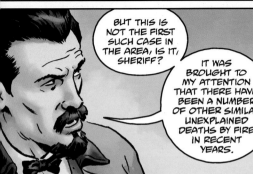

WELL, SIR, THERE'VE BEEN MORE THAN A FEW, I'LL ADMIT. AND ALL OF 'EM IN AND AROUND THESE HERE WOODS.

THIS IS THE FOURTH ONE THAT I KNOW OF, BUT I'VE ONLY BEEN IN TOWN A FEW YEARS, SO I FIGURE THERE MIGHT HAVE BEEN MORE BEFORE THAT.

THE HECK...?

A LOCAL FELLA HAD THOSE BUILT A FEW YEARS BACK. THERE'S A WHOLE MESS OF THEM AROUND.

HE HAD A SCHEME TO TURN THIS SPOT INTO A TOURIST ATTRACTION.

SET UP A LITTLE TRAIN THAT RAN AROUND THE GROUNDS, PUT IN SOME HISTORICAL EXHIBITS, EVEN GOT HIMSELF A BABOON.

DIDN'T TAKE, THOUGH. CLOSED UP SHOP JUST A FEW YEARS LATER.

SEMINOLE VILLAGE

My name is BONGO
OFFICIAL GREETER

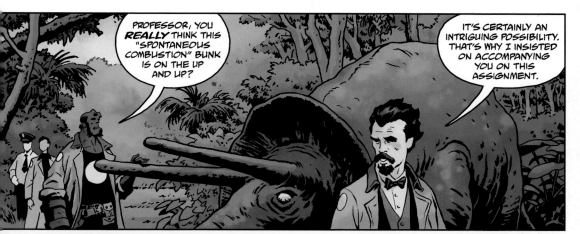

PROFESSOR, YOU *REALLY* THINK THIS "SPONTANEOUS COMBUSTION" BUNK IS ON THE UP AND UP?

IT'S CERTAINLY AN INTRIGUING POSSIBILITY. THAT'S WHY I INSISTED ON ACCOMPANYING YOU ON THIS ASSIGNMENT.

"THE NOTION OF SPONTANEOUS HUMAN COMBUSTION DATES BACK TO THE EIGHTEENTH CENTURY, BUT THERE ARE LEGENDS GOING BACK CENTURIES WITH SIMILAR FEATURES.

"AND WHILE IN MEDIEVAL TIMES SUCH DEATHS WERE ATTRIBUTED TO DEMONIC INFLUENCE, MORE RECENTLY SOME HAVE COME TO BELIEVE THAT THERE IS A MEDICAL CAUSE."

SO IS IT SUPERNATURAL? OR SIMPLY A SCIENTIFIC PROCESS THAT REMAINS AS YET UNEXPLAINED? EITHER WAY, IT SEEMS CLEAR THAT *SOMETHING* IS BEHIND IT.

I DON'T KNOW, SOUNDS PRETTY FISHY.

WE'RE NOT ALONE HERE...

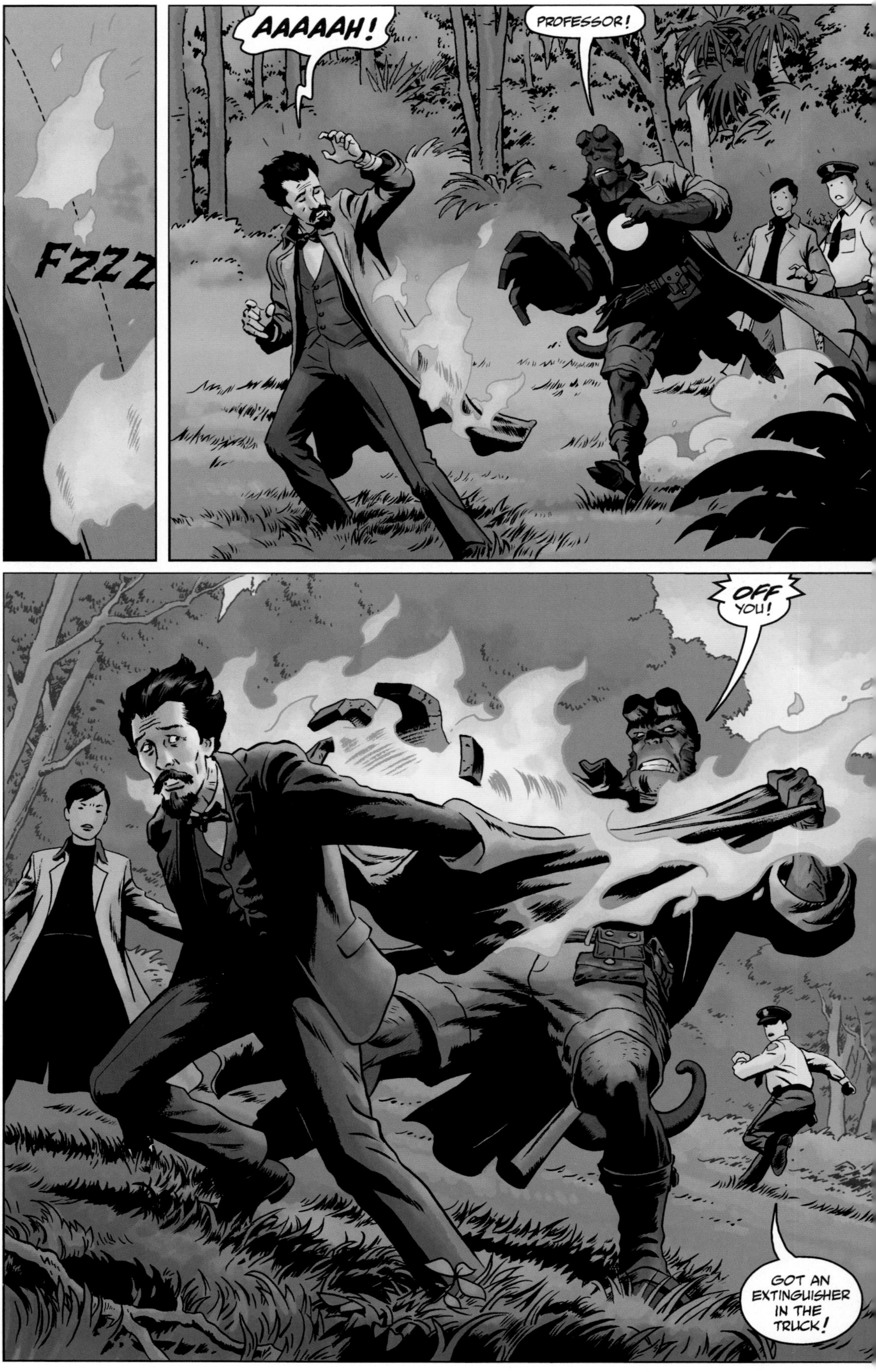
FZZZ
AAAAAH!
PROFESSOR!
OFF YOU!
GOT AN EXTINGUISHER IN THE TRUCK!

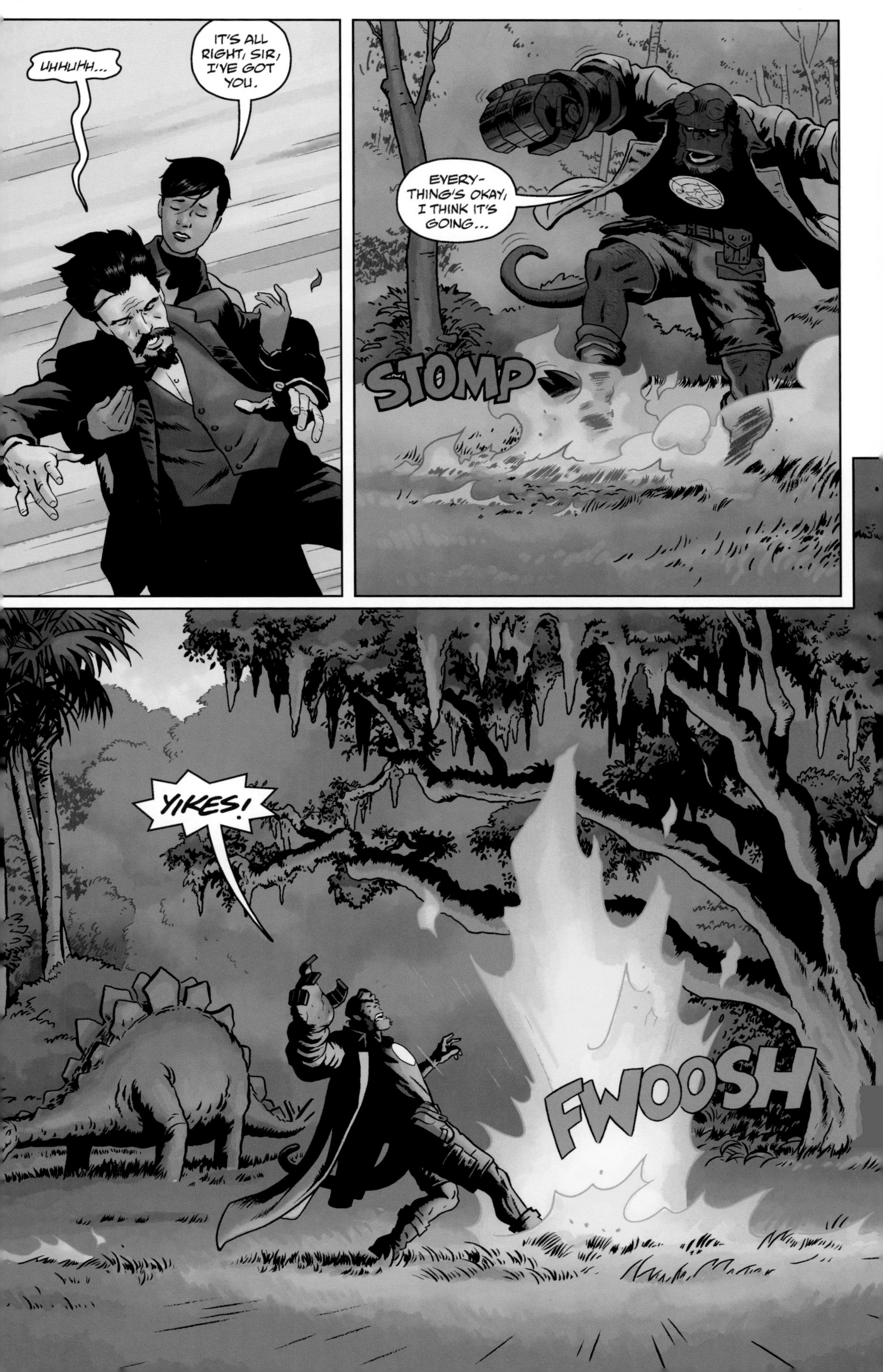
UHHUHH...
IT'S ALL RIGHT, SIR, I'VE GOT YOU.
EVERY-THING'S OKAY, I THINK IT'S GOING...
STOMP
YIKES!
FWOOSH

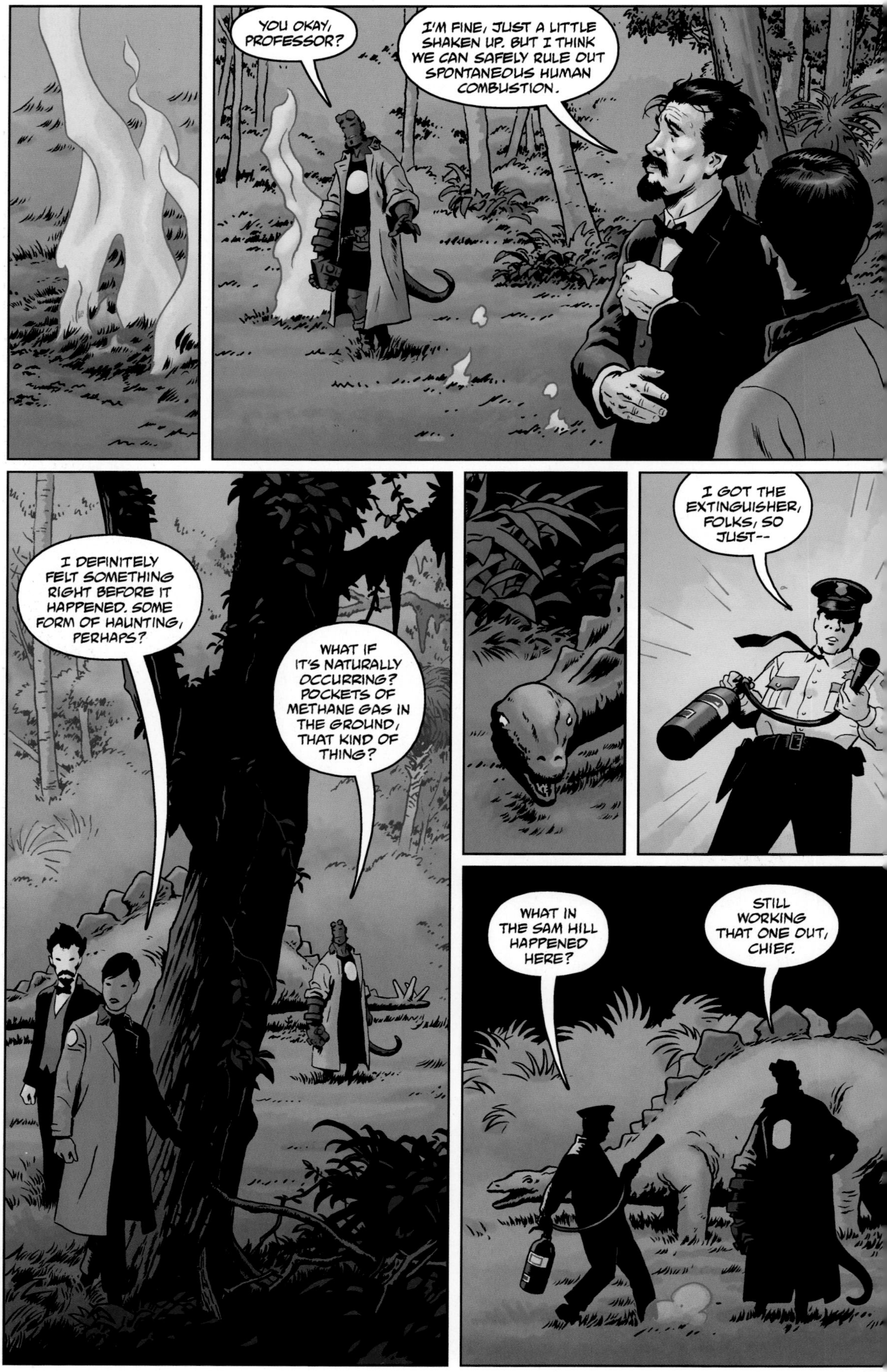
YOU OKAY, PROFESSOR?
I'M FINE, JUST A LITTLE SHAKEN UP. BUT I THINK WE CAN SAFELY RULE OUT SPONTANEOUS HUMAN COMBUSTION.
I DEFINITELY FELT SOMETHING RIGHT BEFORE IT HAPPENED. SOME FORM OF HAUNTING, PERHAPS?
WHAT IF IT'S NATURALLY OCCURRING? POCKETS OF METHANE GAS IN THE GROUND, THAT KIND OF THING?
I GOT THE EXTINGUISHER, FOLKS, SO JUST--
WHAT IN THE SAM HILL HAPPENED HERE?
STILL WORKING THAT ONE OUT, CHIEF.

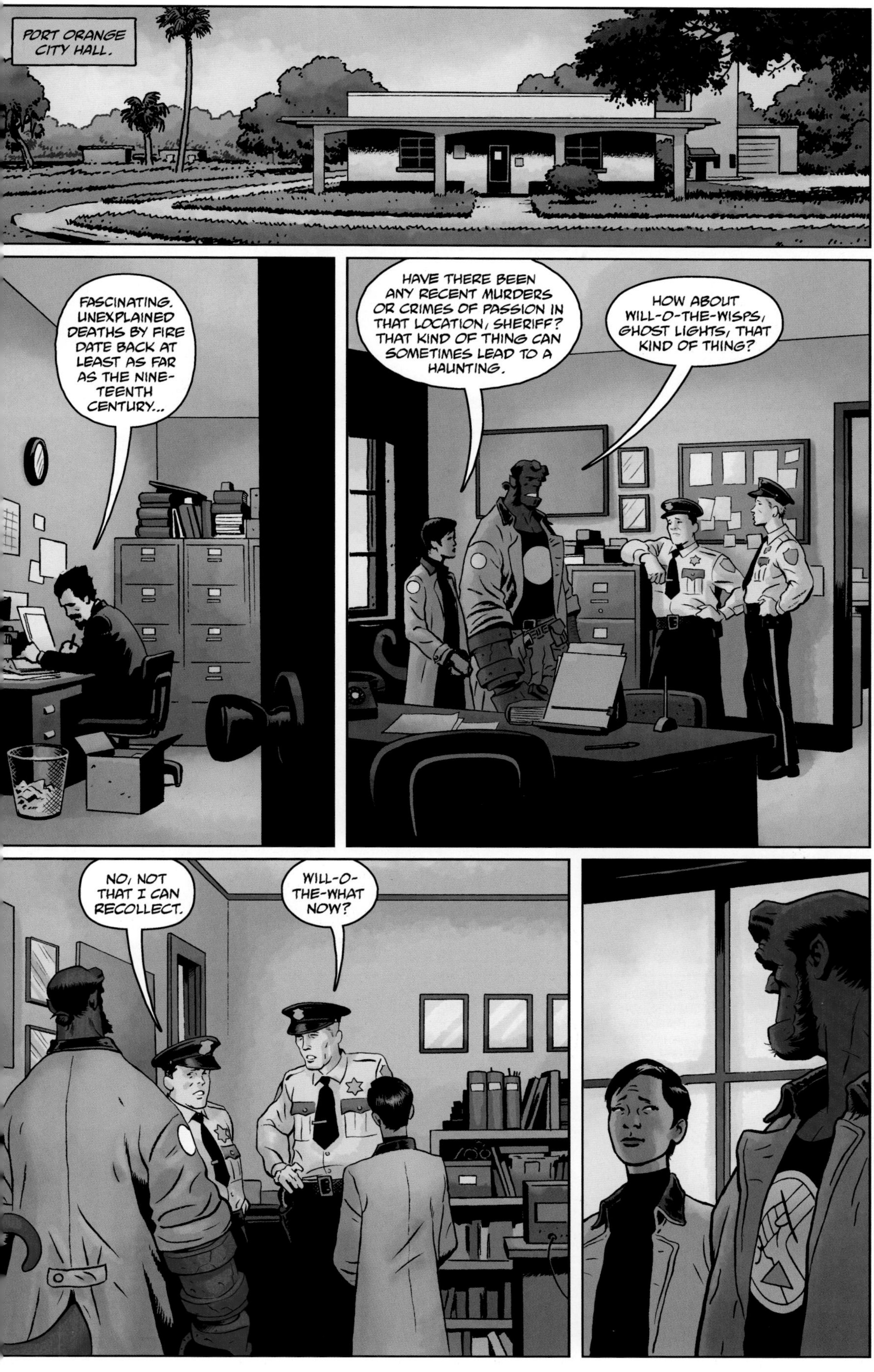
PORT ORANGE CITY HALL.
FASCINATING. UNEXPLAINED DEATHS BY FIRE DATE BACK AT LEAST AS FAR AS THE NINETEENTH CENTURY...
HAVE THERE BEEN ANY RECENT MURDERS OR CRIMES OF PASSION IN THAT LOCATION, SHERIFF? THAT KIND OF THING CAN SOMETIMES LEAD TO A HAUNTING.
HOW ABOUT WILL-O-THE-WISPS, GHOST LIGHTS, THAT KIND OF THING?
NO, NOT THAT I CAN RECOLLECT.
WILL-O-THE-WHAT NOW?

I HOPE YOU HAD MORE LUCK THAN WE DID, PROFESSOR.

FIND ANYTHING THAT MIGHT ACCOUNT FOR A HAUNTING?

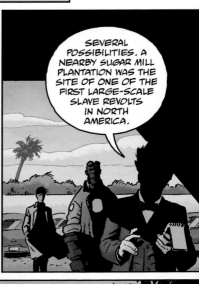

SEVERAL POSSIBILITIES. A NEARBY SUGAR MILL PLANTATION WAS THE SITE OF ONE OF THE FIRST LARGE-SCALE SLAVE REVOLTS IN NORTH AMERICA.

ESCAPED SLAVES JOINED WITH THE REMNANTS OF NATIVE TRIBES THAT HAD BEEN DECIMATED BY ENCOUNTERS WITH EUROPEANS AND AMERICANS, AND BECAME THE "SEMINOLE."

"THE SEMINOLE THEMSELVES WERE DRIVEN OUT BY U.S. TROOPS, FORCED TO EMBARK ON THE 'TRAIL OF TEARS' TO MAKE ROOM FOR WHITE SETTLERS.

"ONE CAN ONLY IMAGIN[E] THAT AN UNQUIET SPIR[IT] MIGHT HAVE LINGERE[D] AFTERWARDS. BUT TH[E] INCITING INCIDENT MIGHT REACH EVEN FURTHER BACK."

THE ORIGINAL INHABITANTS OF THE REGION, THE TIMUCUA, MAY HAVE BEEN THE FIRST NORTH AMERICAN INDIANS TO ENCOUNTER SPANISH EXPLORERS WHEN PONCE DE LEÓN ARRIVED IN 1513.

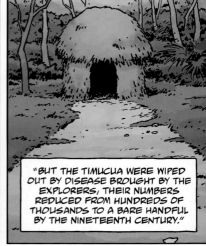

"BUT THE TIMUCUA WERE WIPED OUT BY DISEASE BROUGHT BY THE EXPLORERS, THEIR NUMBERS REDUCED FROM HUNDREDS OF THOUSANDS TO A BARE HANDFUL BY THE NINETEENTH CENTURY."

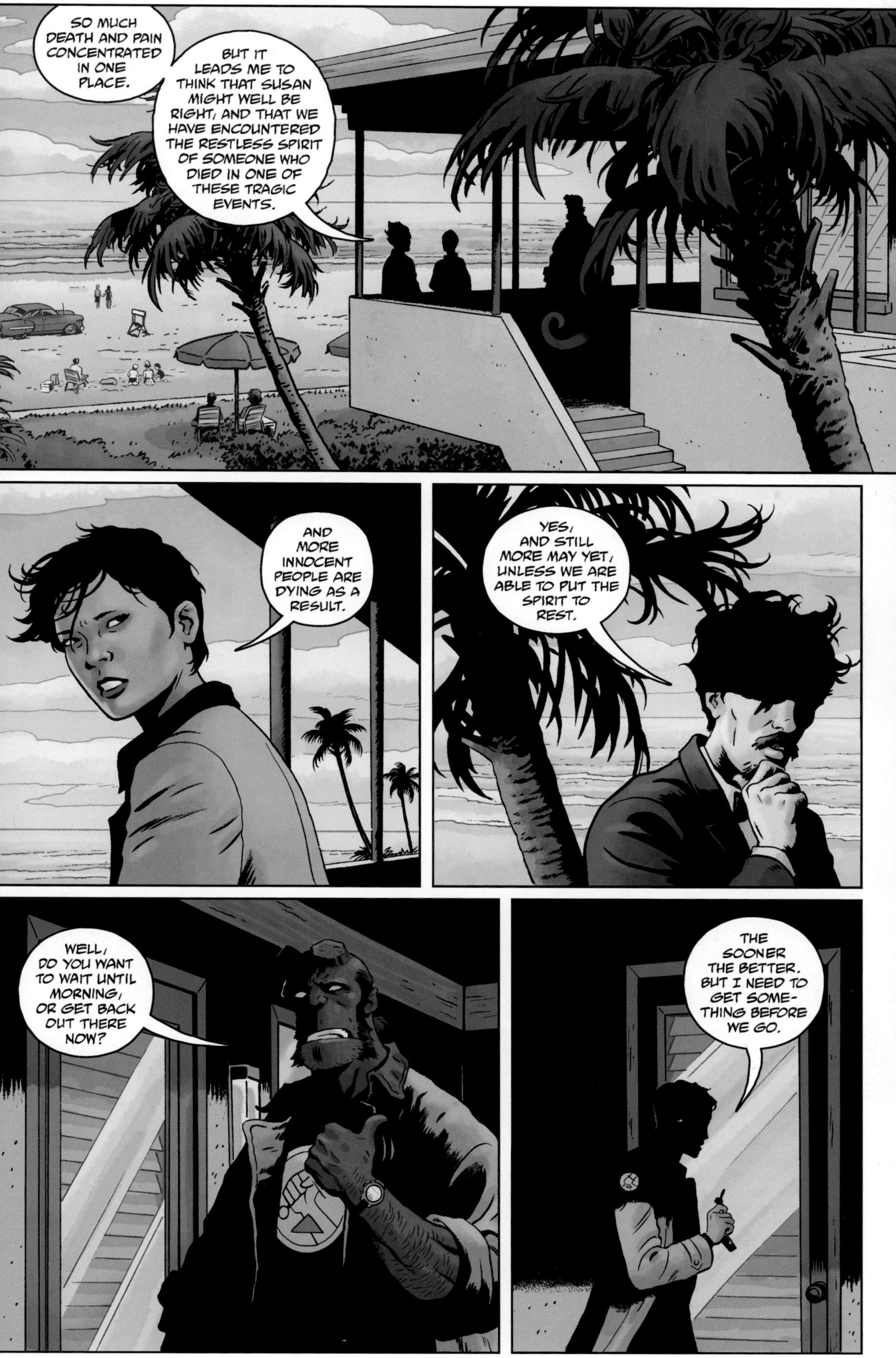
SO MUCH DEATH AND PAIN CONCENTRATED IN ONE PLACE.
BUT IT LEADS ME TO THINK THAT SUSAN MIGHT WELL BE RIGHT, AND THAT WE HAVE ENCOUNTERED THE RESTLESS SPIRIT OF SOMEONE WHO DIED IN ONE OF THESE TRAGIC EVENTS.
AND MORE INNOCENT PEOPLE ARE DYING AS A RESULT.
YES, AND STILL MORE MAY YET, UNLESS WE ARE ABLE TO PUT THE SPIRIT TO REST.
WELL, DO YOU WANT TO WAIT UNTIL MORNING, OR GET BACK OUT THERE NOW?
THE SOONER THE BETTER. BUT I NEED TO GET SOME-THING BEFORE WE GO.

THE RUINS OF THE SUGAR MILL, UNLESS I'M MISTAKEN.

THAT DOOHICKEY OF YOURS REALLY HELP? WITH YOUR VISIONS, I MEAN?

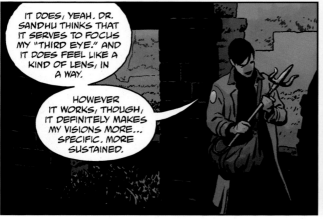

IT DOES, YEAH. DR. SANDHU THINKS THAT IT SERVES TO FOCUS MY "THIRD EYE." AND IT DOES FEEL LIKE A KIND OF LENS, IN A WAY.

HOWEVER IT WORKS, THOUGH, IT DEFINITELY MAKES MY VISIONS MORE... SPECIFIC. MORE SUSTAINED.

AND THE LONGER THE VISIONS LAST, THE EASIER IT IS TO UNDERSTAND THEIR CONTEXT.

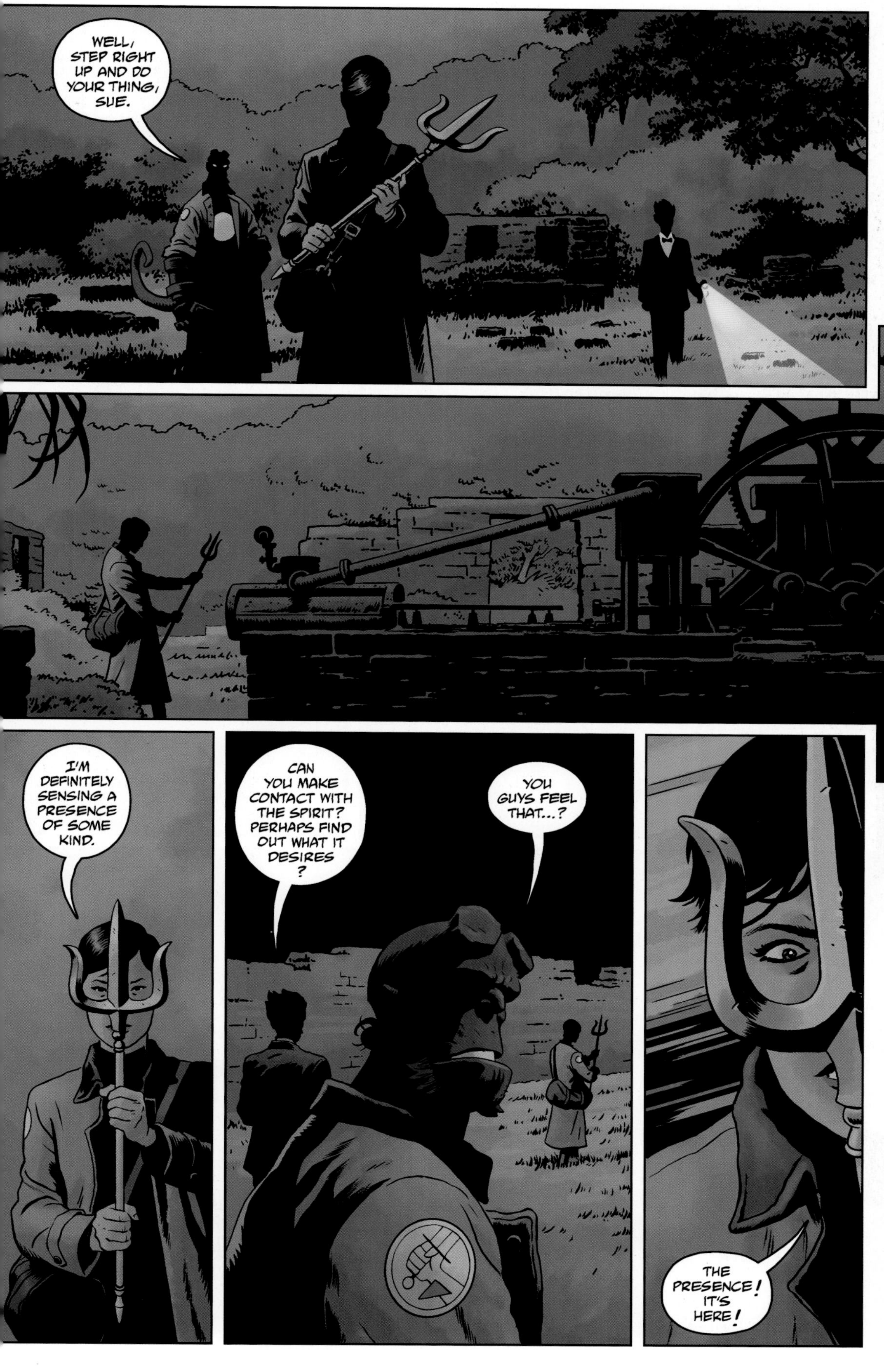
WELL, STEP RIGHT UP AND DO YOUR THING, SUE.
I'M DEFINITELY SENSING A PRESENCE OF SOME KIND.
CAN YOU MAKE CONTACT WITH THE SPIRIT? PERHAPS FIND OUT WHAT IT DESIRES?
YOU GUYS FEEL THAT...?
THE PRESENCE! IT'S HERE!

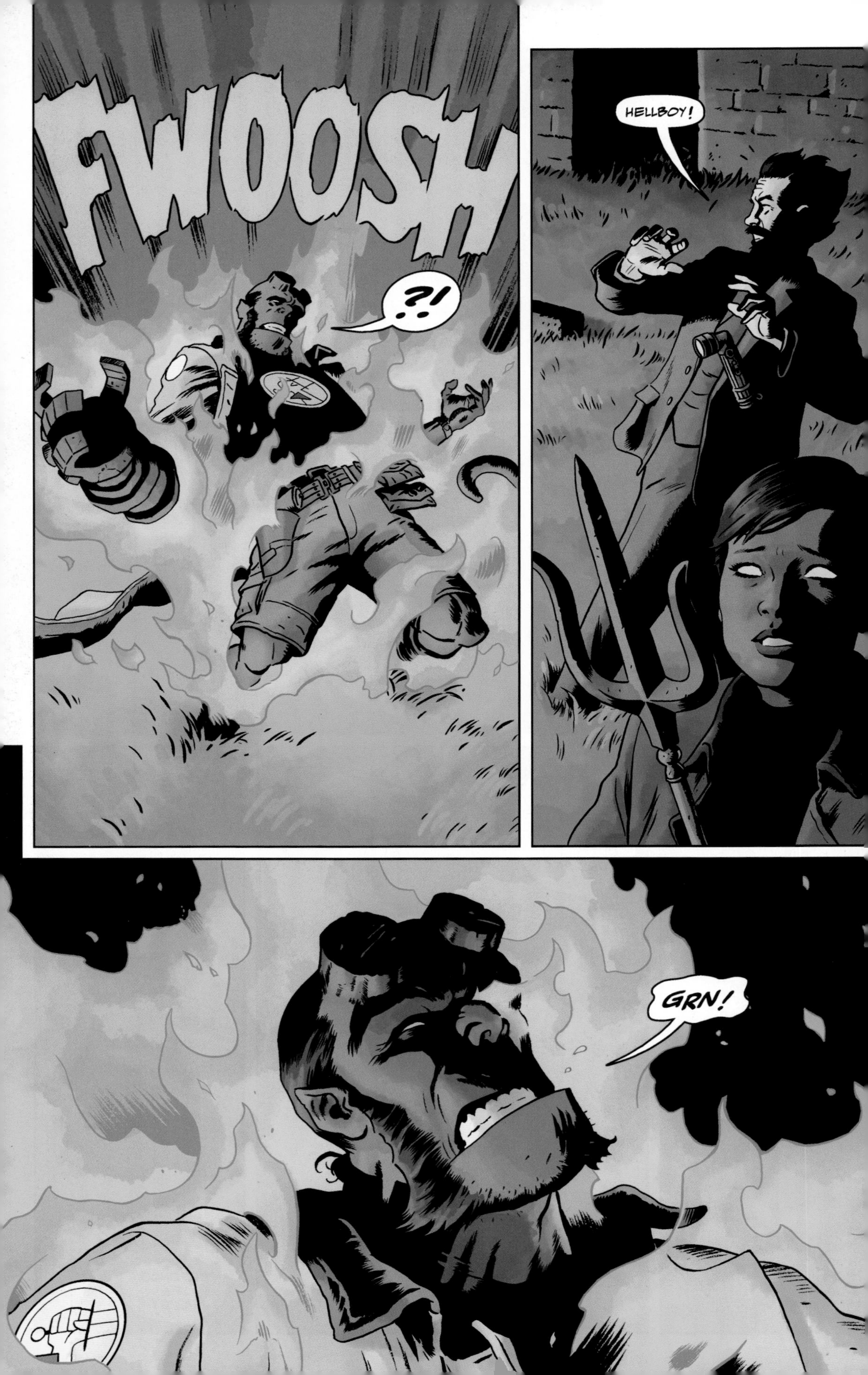
FWOOSH
?!
HELLBOY!
GRN!

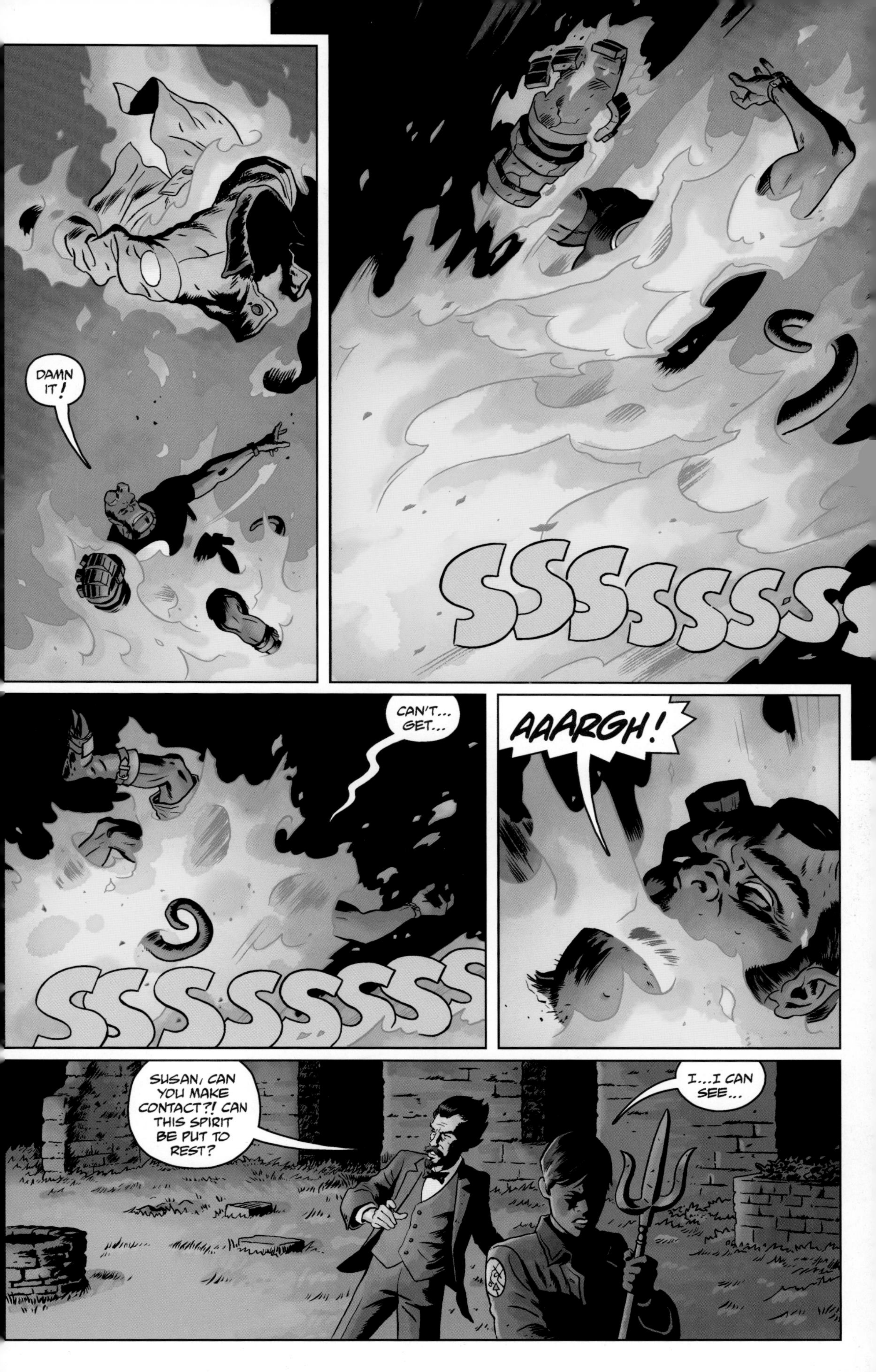
DAMN IT!
SSSSSSSS
CAN'T... GET...
SSSSSSSS
AAARGH!
SUSAN, CAN YOU MAKE CONTACT?! CAN THIS SPIRIT BE PUT TO REST?
I...I CAN SEE...

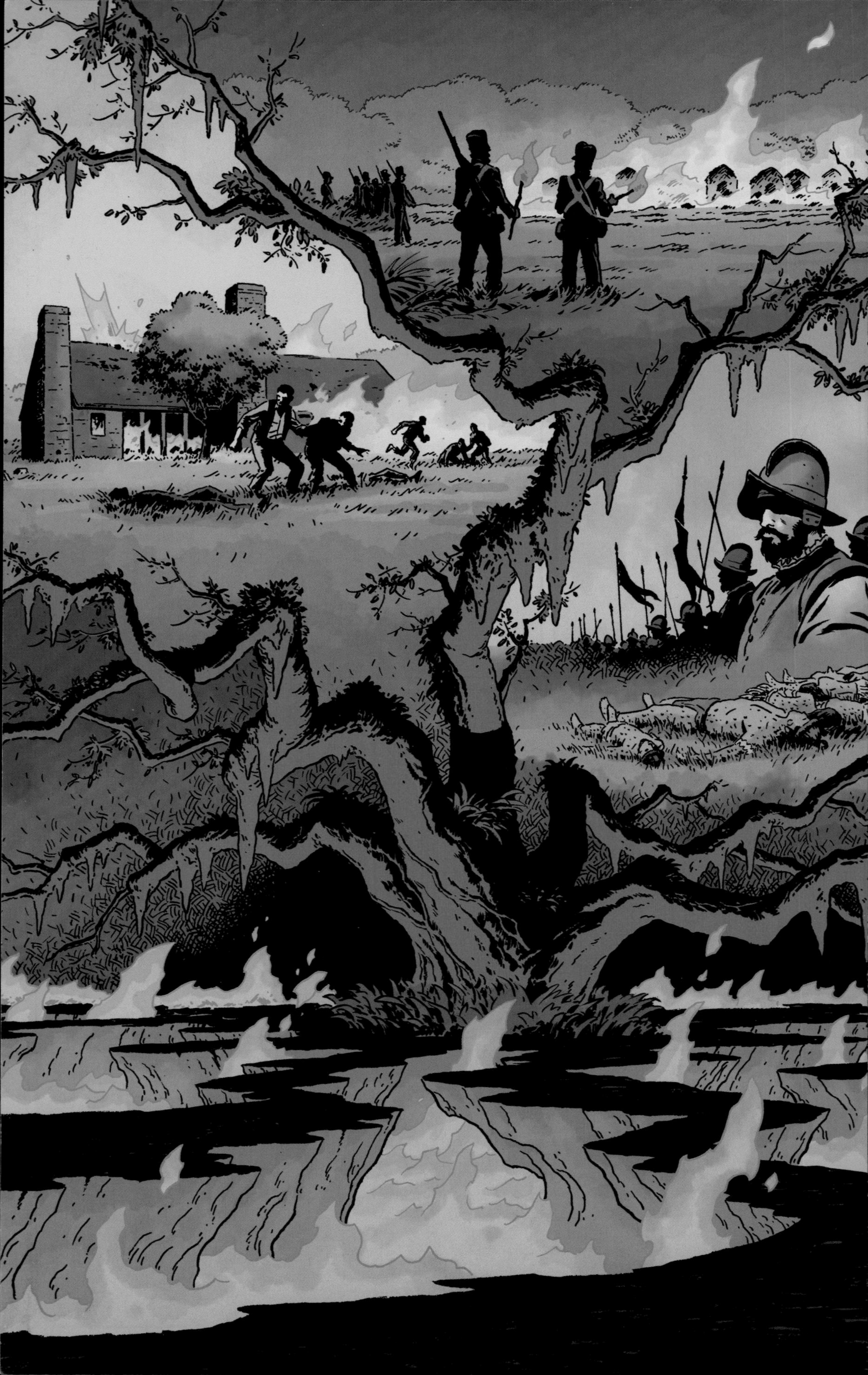

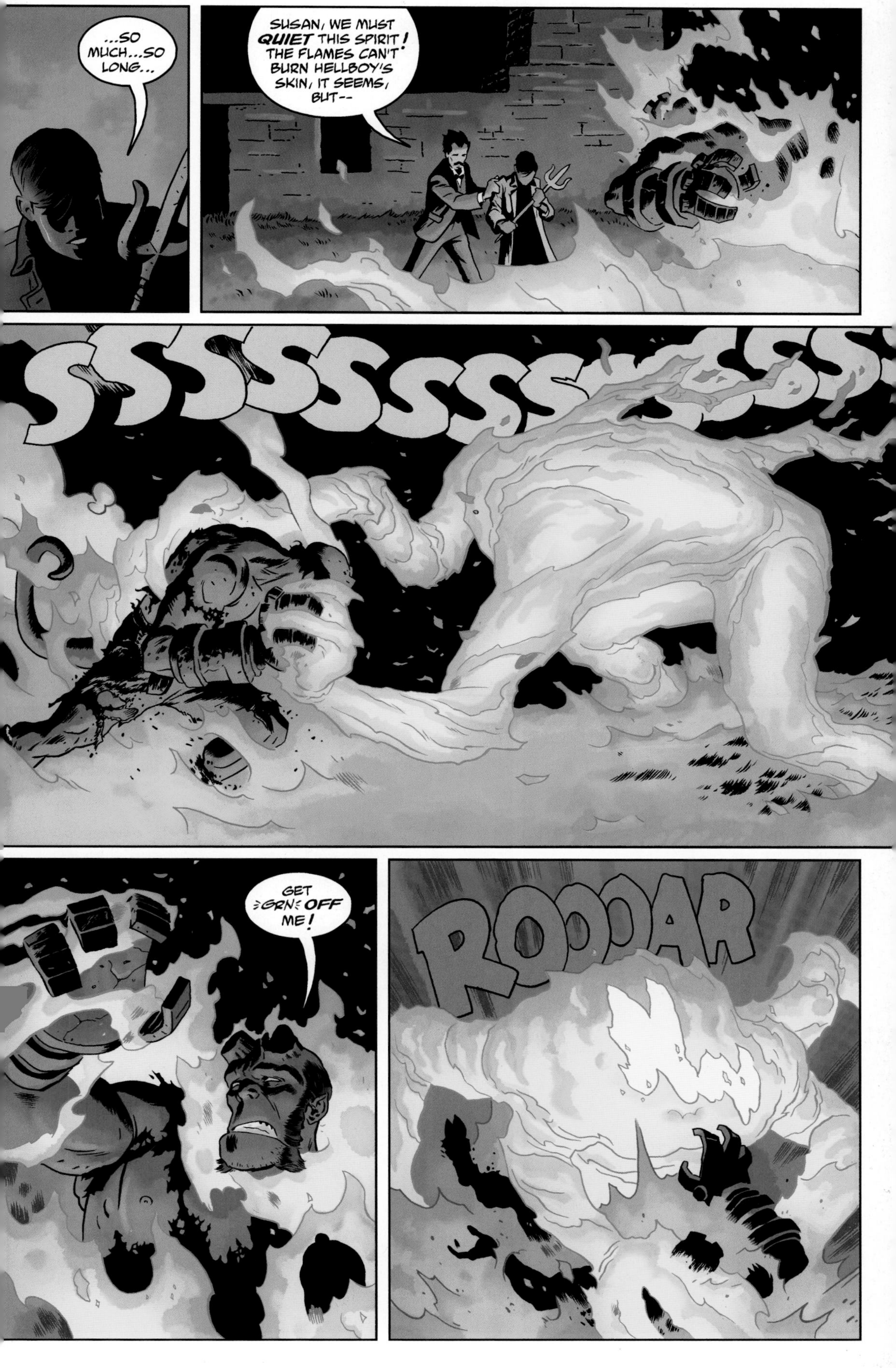
...SO MUCH...SO LONG...
SUSAN, WE MUST QUIET THIS SPIRIT! THE FLAMES CAN'T BURN HELLBOY'S SKIN, IT SEEMS, BUT--
SSSSSSSSSSSS
GET GRN OFF ME!
ROOOAR

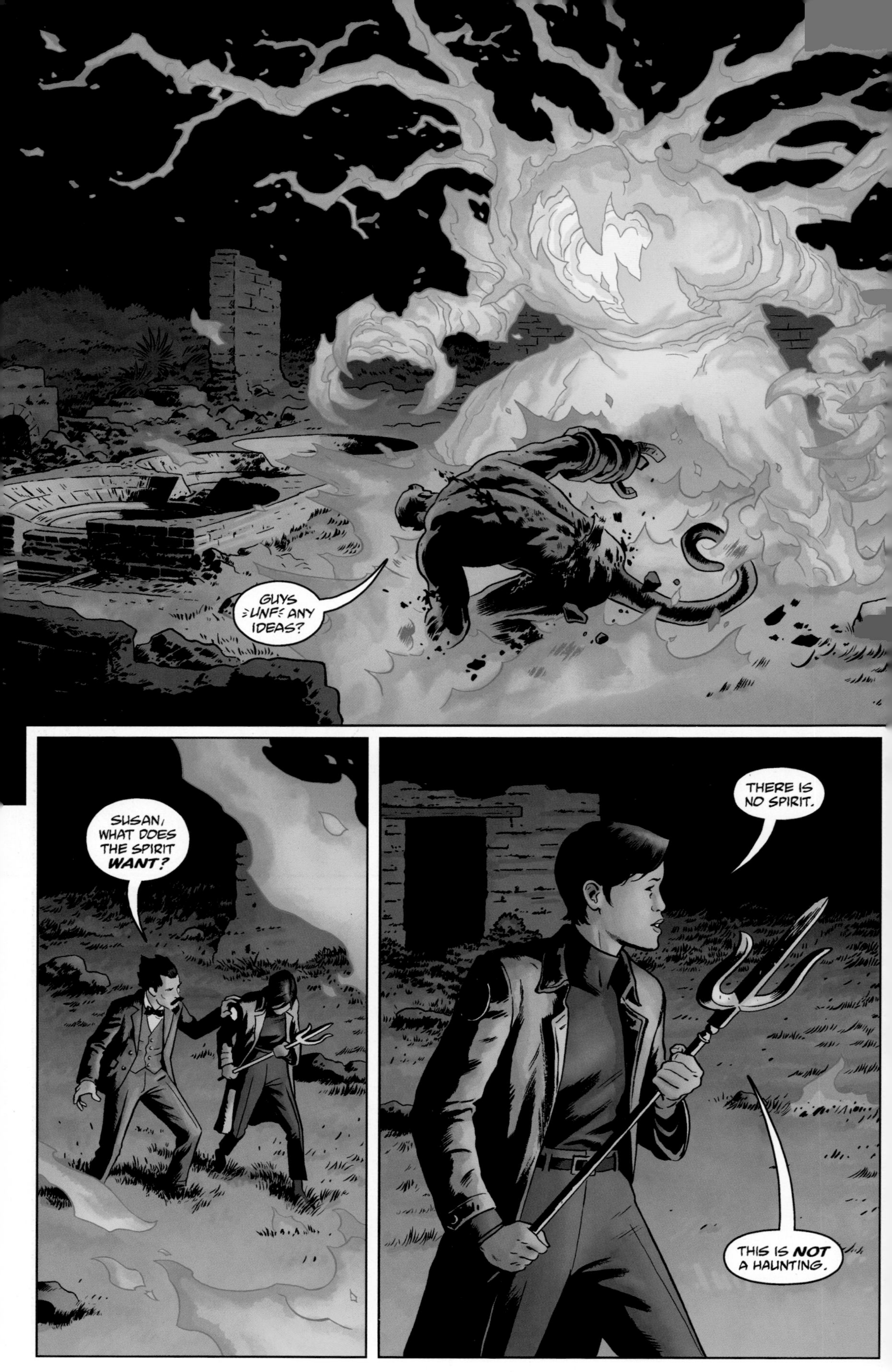
GUYS UNF ANY IDEAS?
SUSAN, WHAT DOES THE SPIRIT WANT?
THERE IS NO SPIRIT.
THIS IS NOT A HAUNTING.

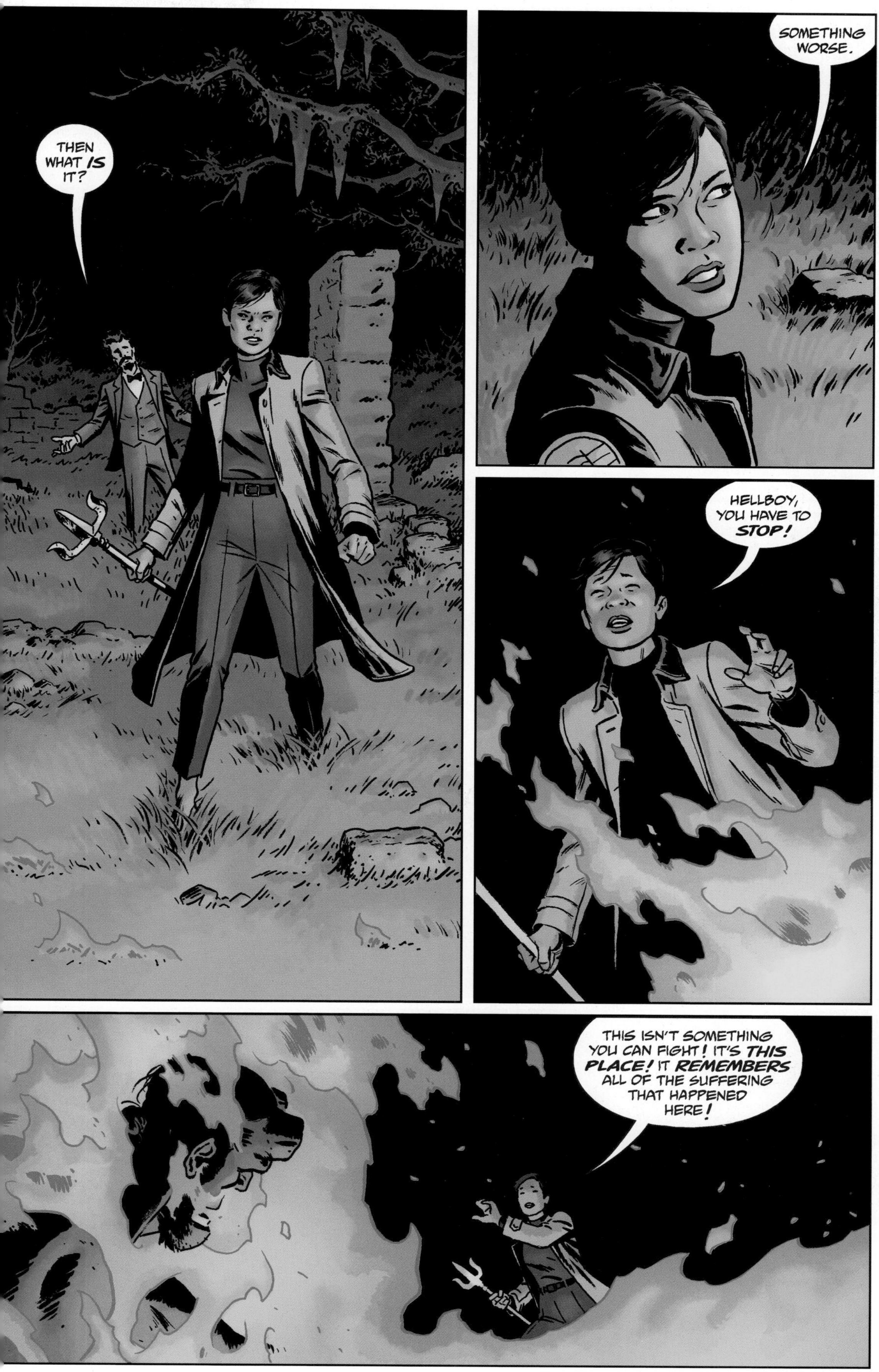
THEN WHAT IS IT?
SOMETHING WORSE.
HELLBOY, YOU HAVE TO STOP!
THIS ISN'T SOMETHING YOU CAN FIGHT! IT'S THIS PLACE! IT REMEMBERS ALL OF THE SUFFERING THAT HAPPENED HERE!

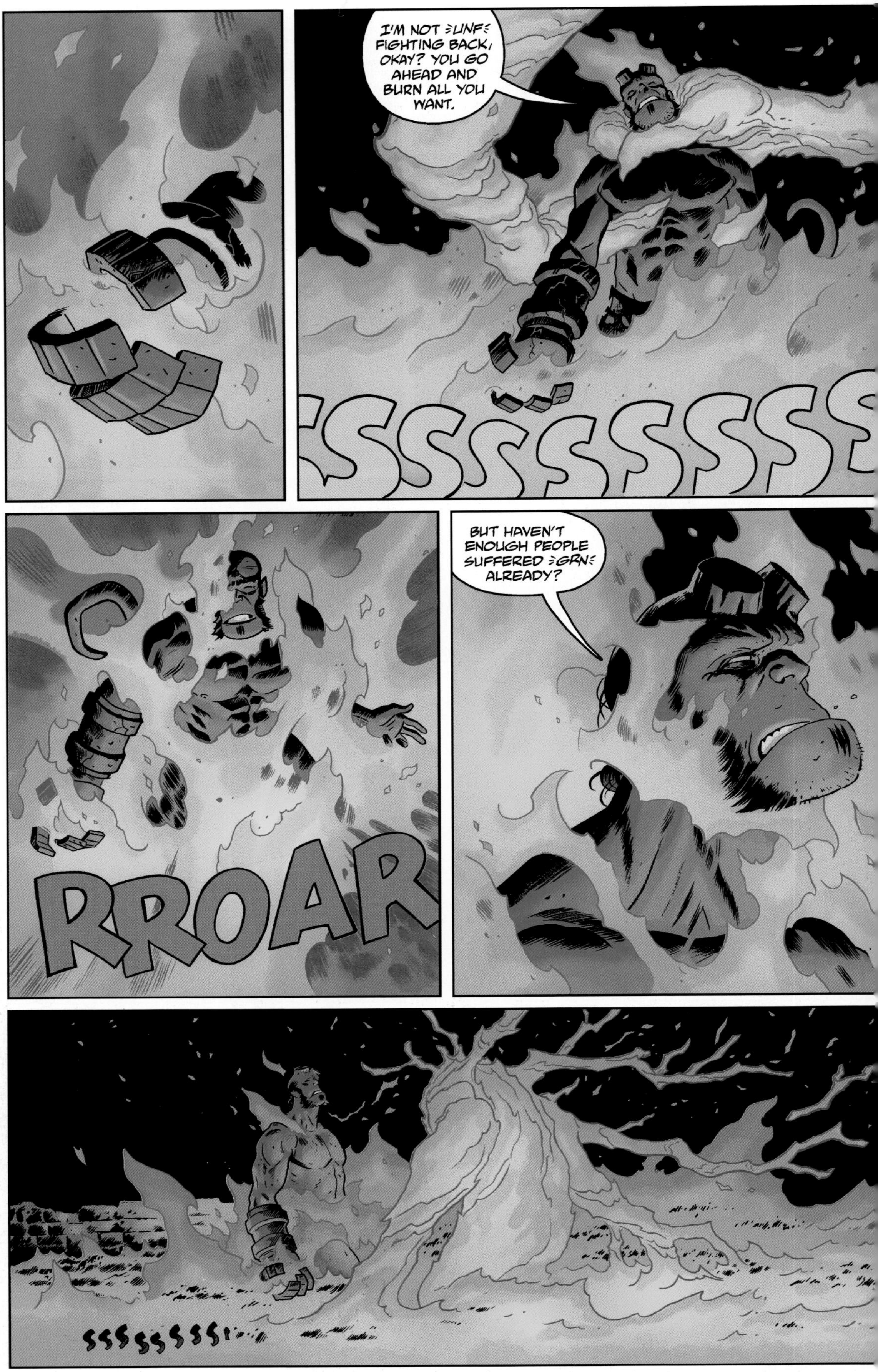
I'M NOT ⋞UNF⋟ FIGHTING BACK, OKAY? YOU GO AHEAD AND BURN ALL YOU WANT.
SSSSSSSSSS
RROAR
BUT HAVEN'T ENOUGH PEOPLE SUFFERED ⋞GRN⋟ ALREADY?
SSSSSSSSS

I GET IT.

YOU'RE ANGRY.

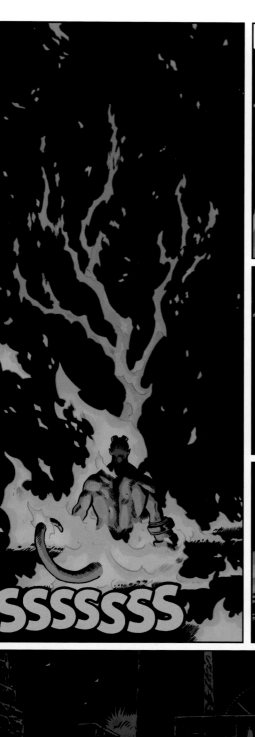

SSSSSSS

S. SSSSSS

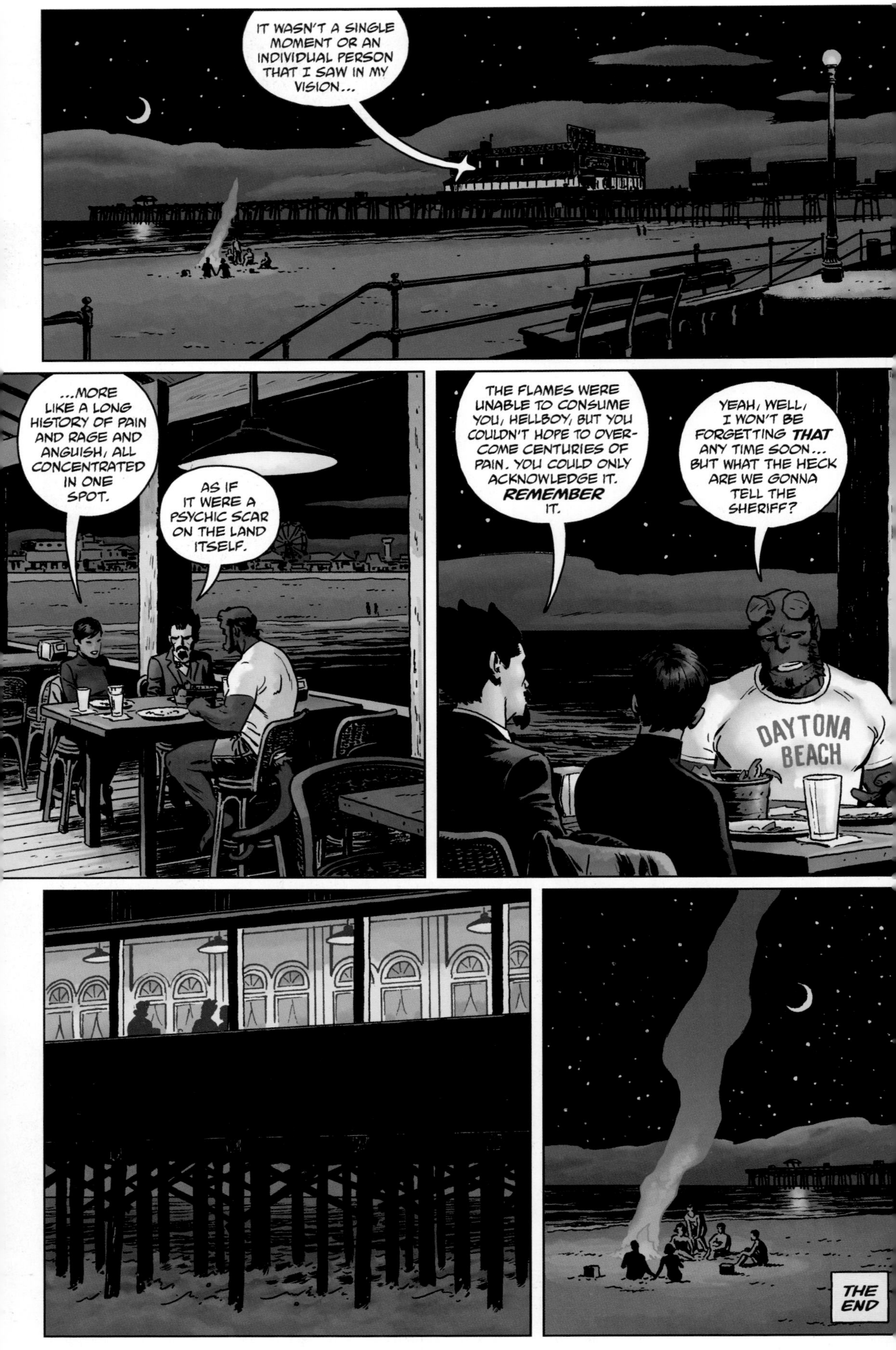
IT WASN'T A SINGLE MOMENT OR AN INDIVIDUAL PERSON THAT I SAW IN MY VISION...
...MORE LIKE A LONG HISTORY OF PAIN AND RAGE AND ANGUISH, ALL CONCENTRATED IN ONE SPOT.
AS IF IT WERE A PSYCHIC SCAR ON THE LAND ITSELF.
THE FLAMES WERE UNABLE TO CONSUME YOU, HELLBOY, BUT YOU COULDN'T HOPE TO OVER-COME CENTURIES OF PAIN. YOU COULD ONLY ACKNOWLEDGE IT. REMEMBER IT.
YEAH, WELL, I WON'T BE FORGETTING THAT ANY TIME SOON... BUT WHAT THE HECK ARE WE GONNA TELL THE SHERIFF?
DAYTONA BEACH
THE END

HELLBOY™ AND THE B.P.R.D. 1955

SKETCHBOOK

Notes by the artists.

Shawn Martinbrough: Being a longtime fan of both Mignola and his "Big Red Guy," I jumped at the chance to draw a *Hellboy* story. However, I must confess it was a bit tricky making the switch from drawing my series "Thief of Thieves" to the story "Secret Nature." For "Thief" I'd become comfortable creating a slick but very grounded world of Ian Fleming type characters in plush international settings. For this *Hellboy* story written by Chris and Mike, I would start with open pastures and a racist redneck and end up with a weird demon haunting a cabin in the woods.

I loved it.

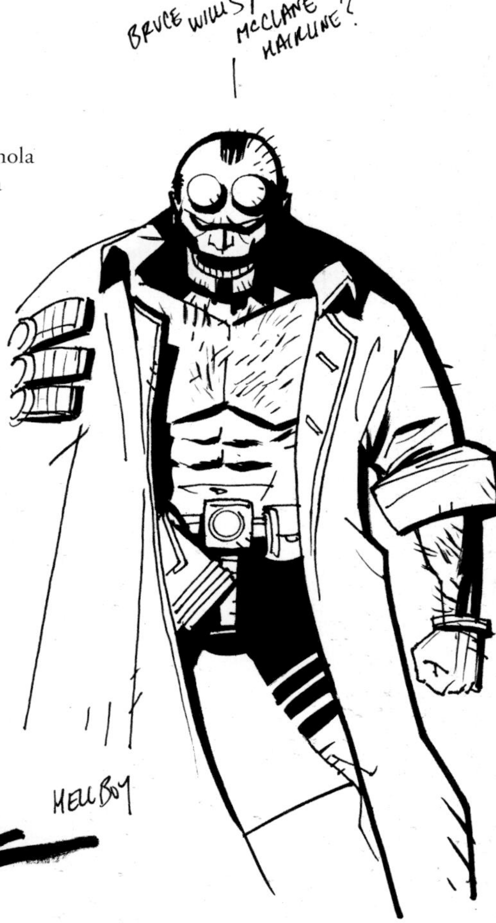
BRUCE WILLIS/
McCLANE HAIRLINE?
HELLBOY

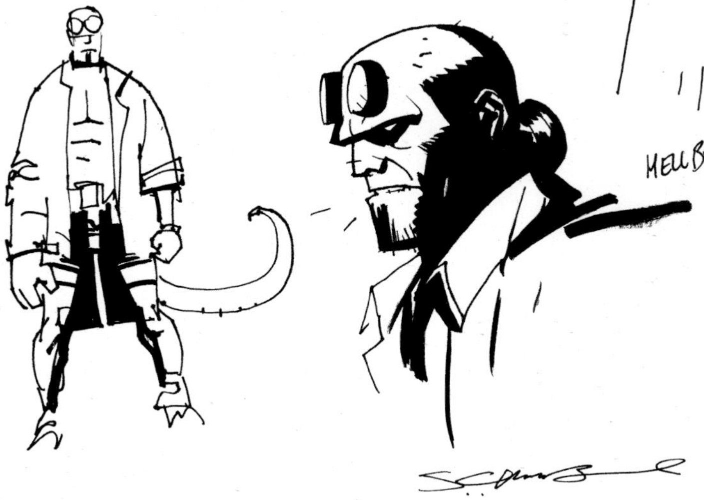

These are my initial Hellboy sketches. I didn't quite have a my "aha" moment on coming close to nailing the character until I started drawing the final pages. Capturing that jawline and only being able to draw the bottom set of teeth are not as easy as it might sound.

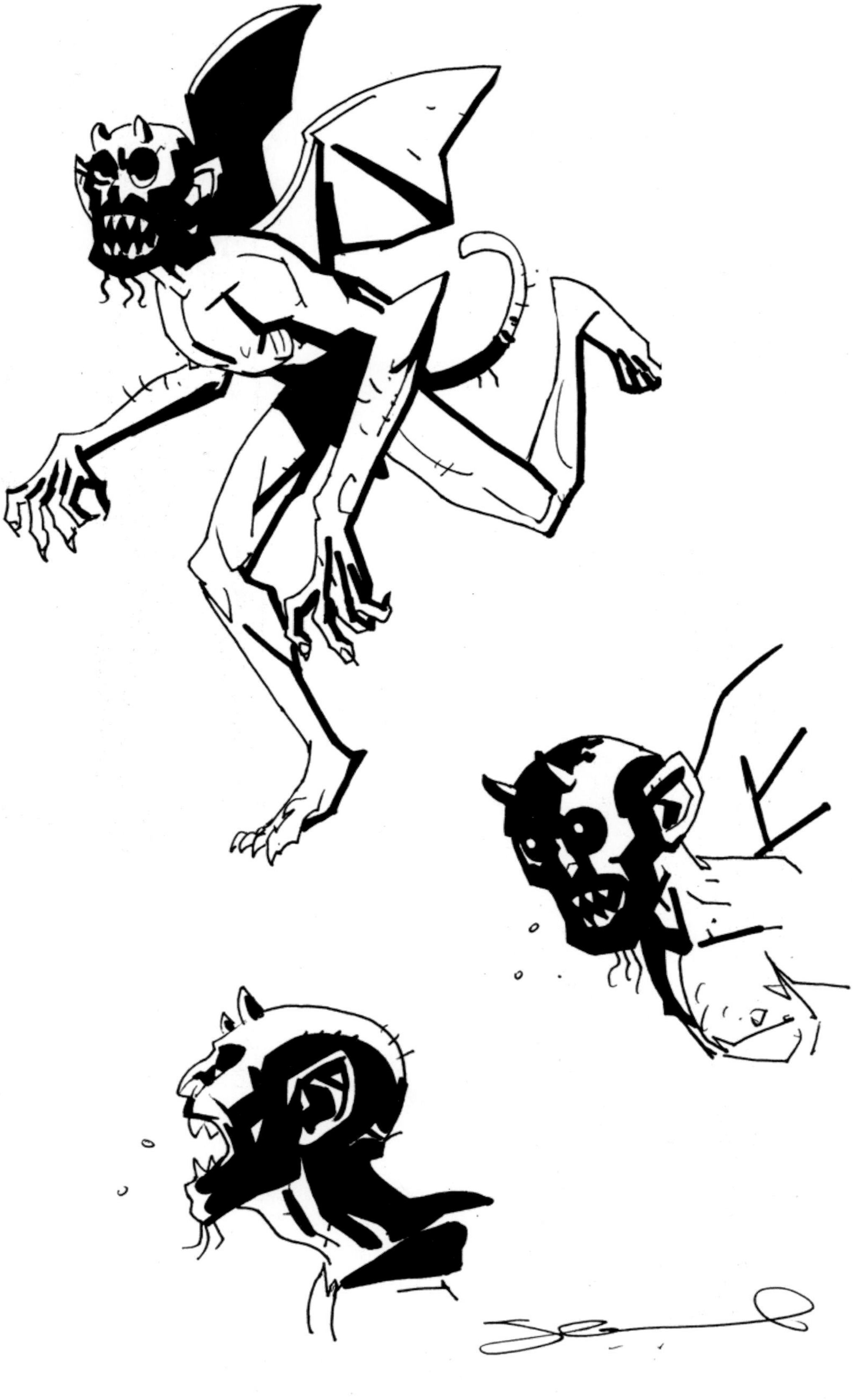

But I did need a bit of a creative push in the beginning. Fortunately, it came in the form of editor Scott Allie who really encouraged me to fully embrace the wonderful weirdness of the B.P.R.D. universe.

These are my initial sketches of the main baddie demon which are based on Mike's original design. I had fun exaggerating the demon's proportions. Giving him elongated arms, legs, and a set of private parts that mostly seem to stay in shadow.

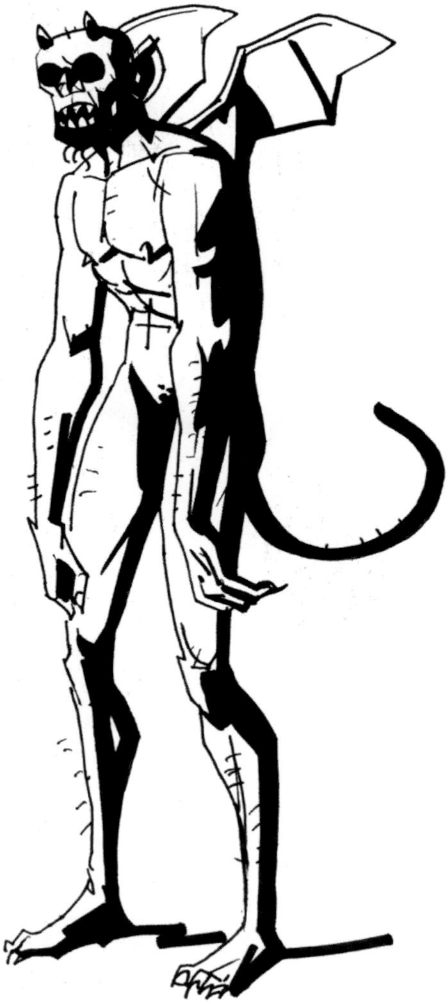

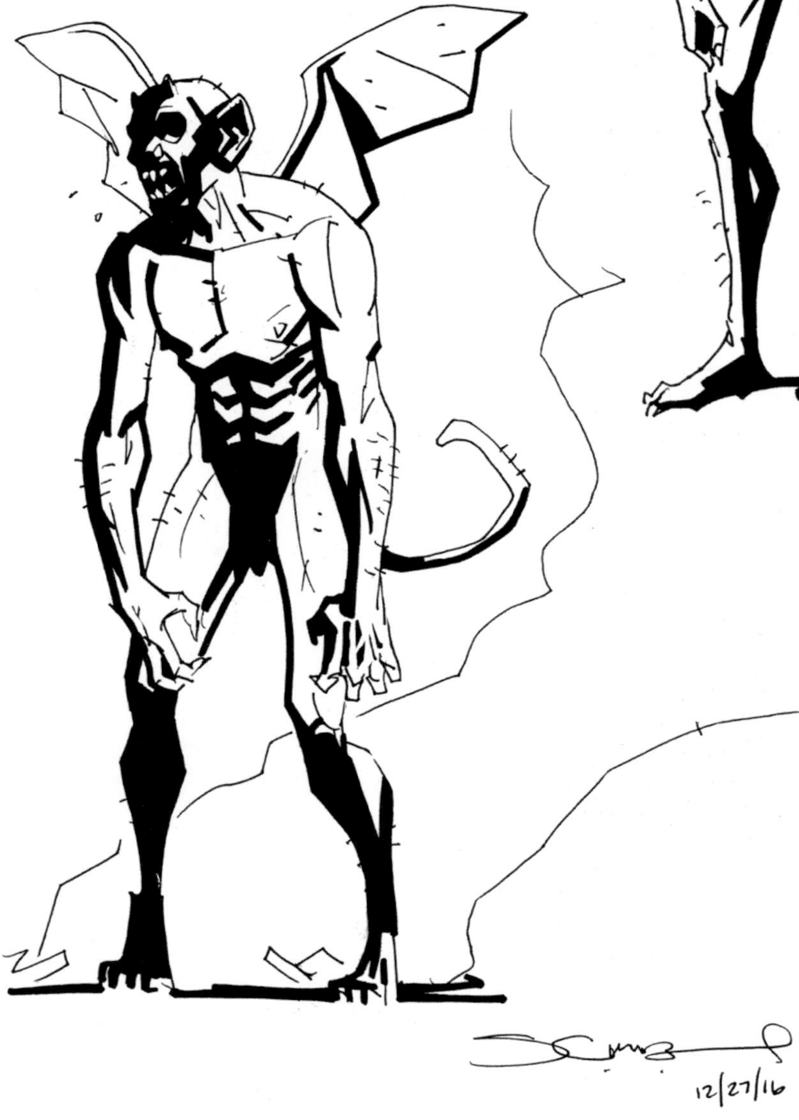
12/27/16

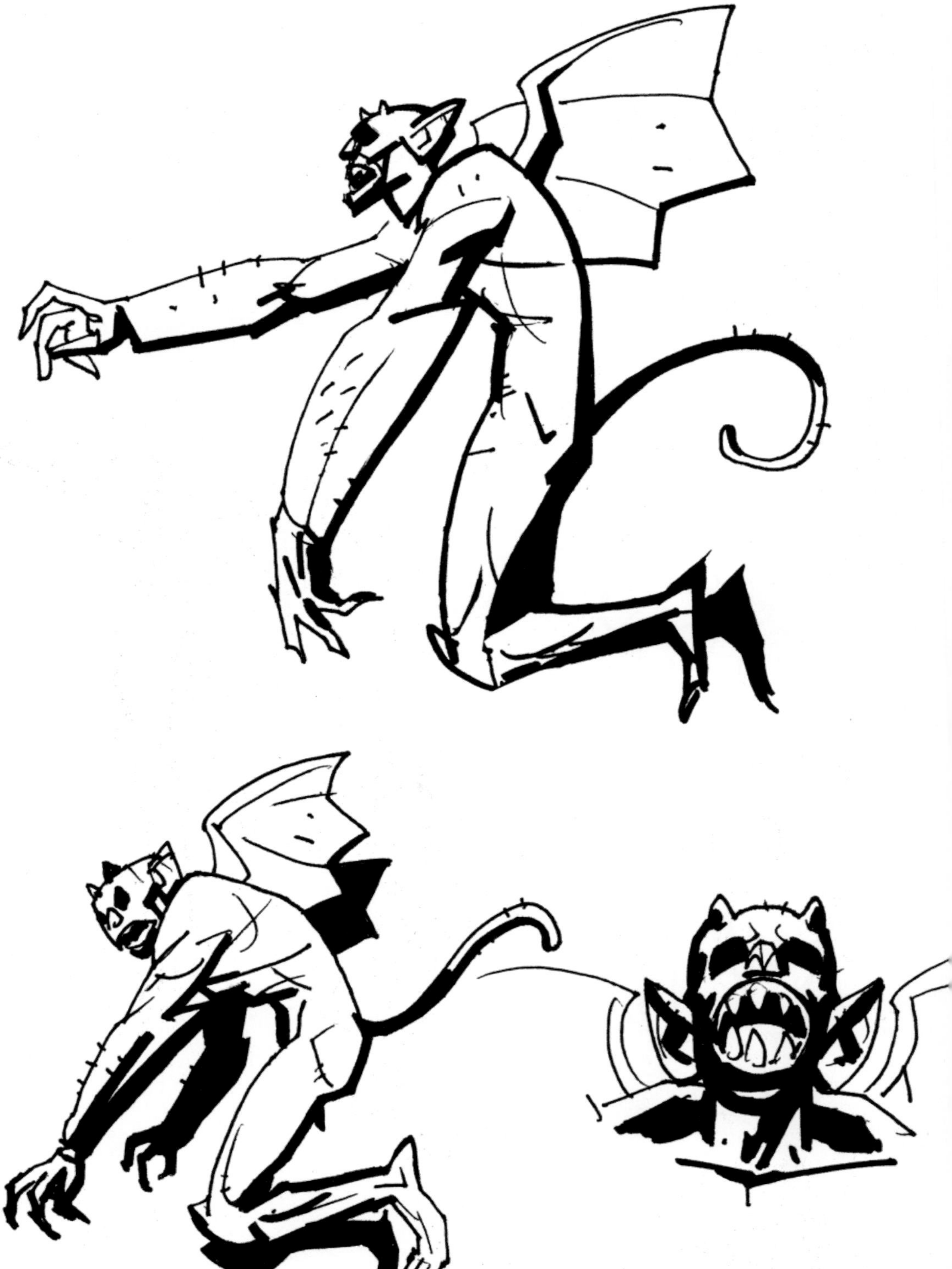

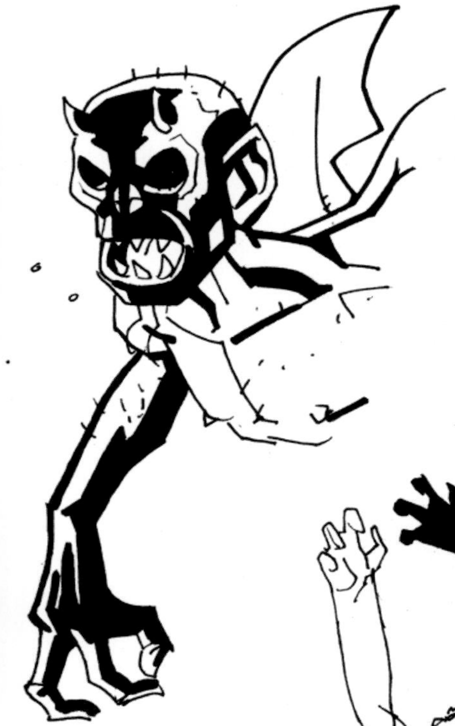

Reinforcing a feral vibe for the demon was also a way to visually distinguish his character. He's constantly spitting or drooling when interacting with Woody and Hellboy.

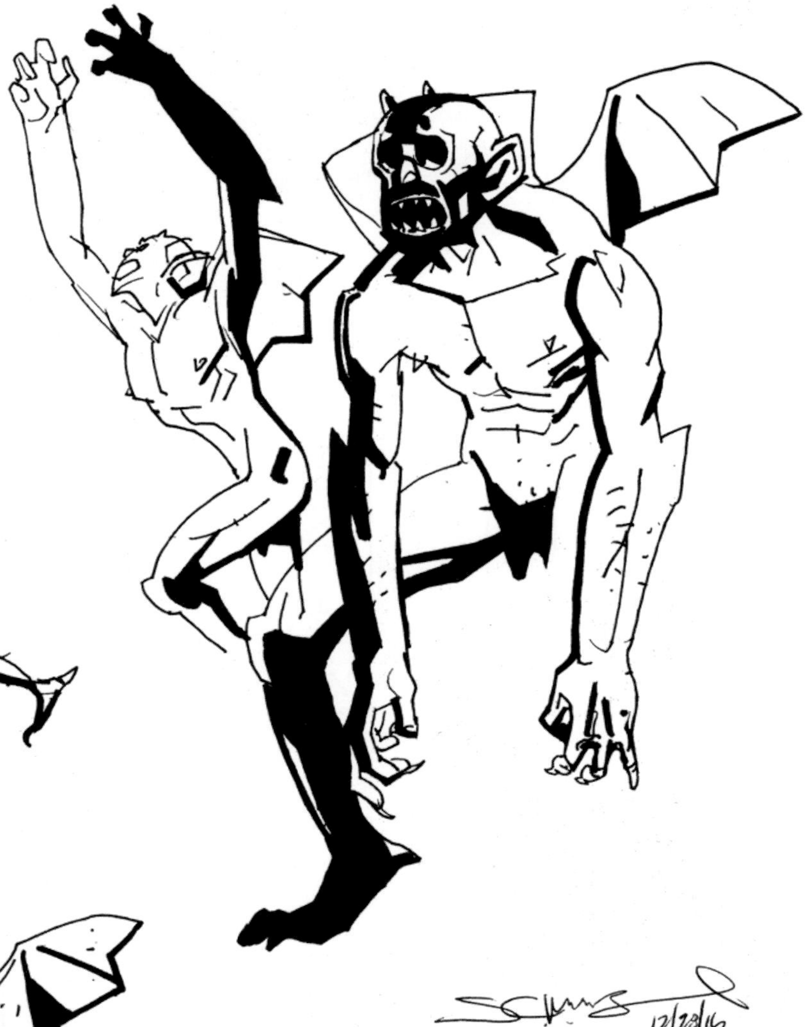

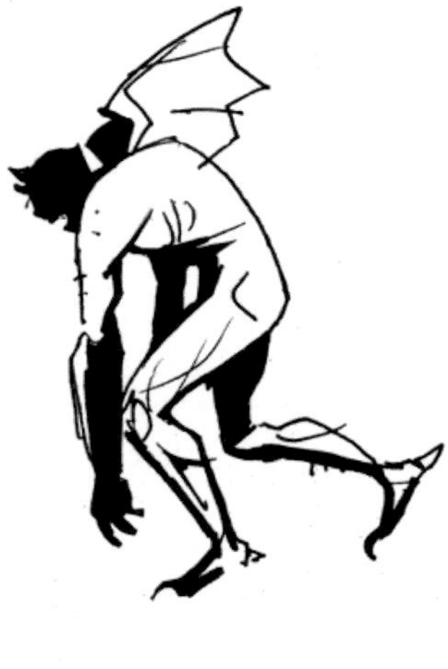

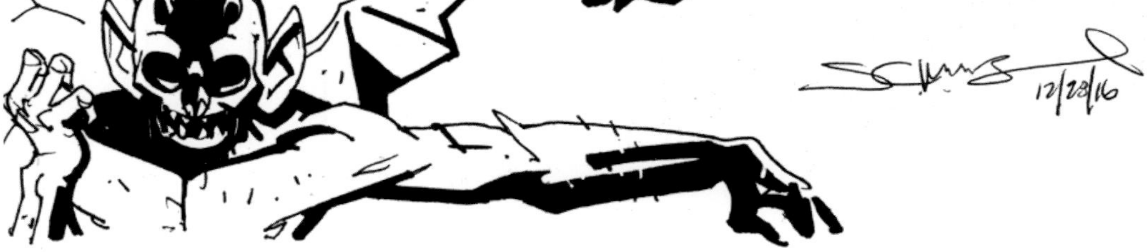
12/28/16

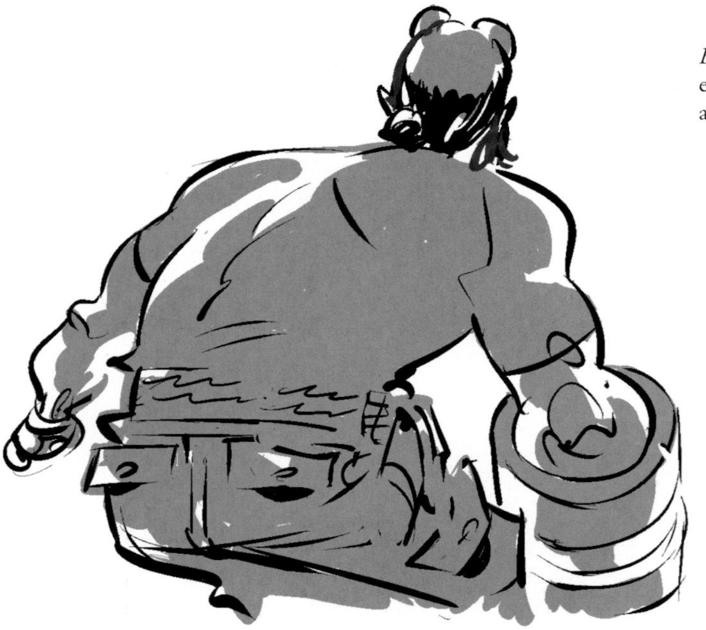

Brian Churilla: I like to break down an entire issue onto a cheat sheet like this; it's a great point of reference to have handy.

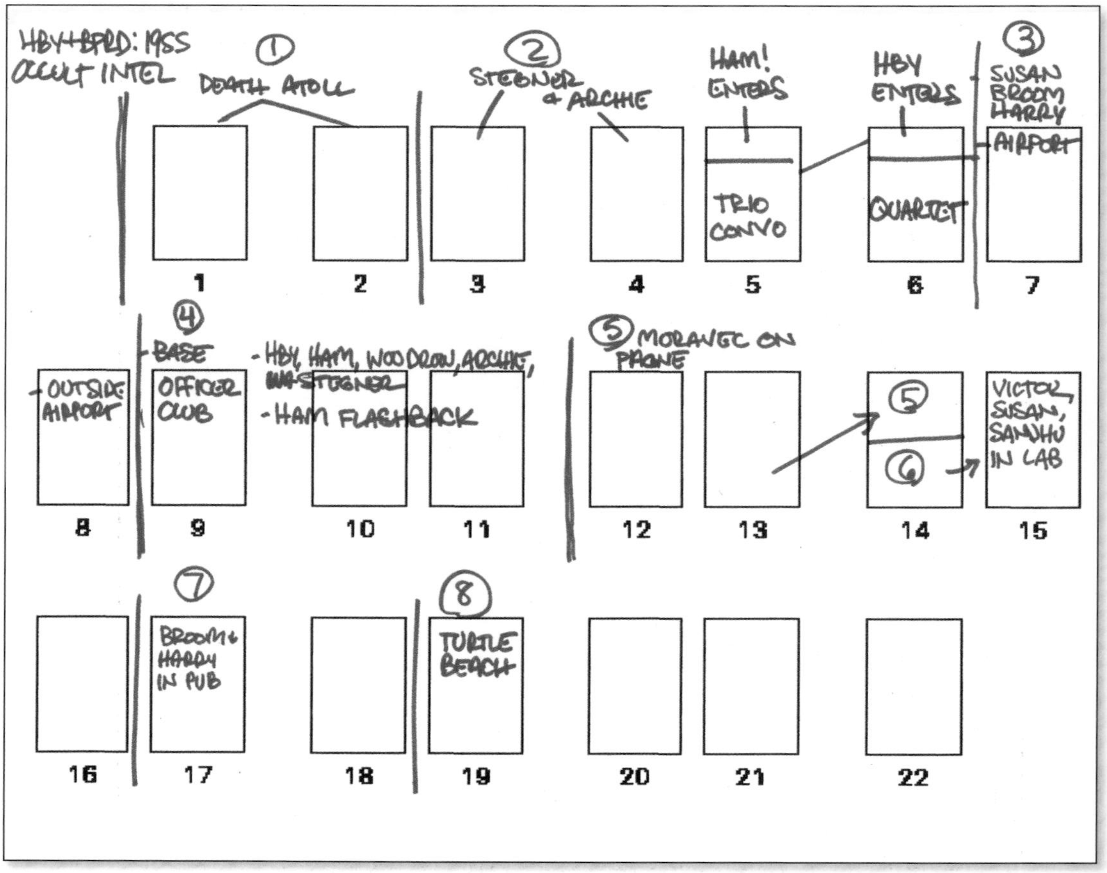

HBY+BPRD: 1955
OCCULT INTEL
1 DEATH ATOLL
2 STEGNER & ARCHIE
HAM! ENTERS
HBY ENTERS
3 SUSAN BROOM HARRY
AIRPORT
TRIO CONVO
QUARTET
1 2 3 4 5 6 7
OUTSIDE AIRPORT
4 BASE
OFFICER CLUB
- HBY, HAM, WOODROW, ARCHIE, STEGNER
- HAM FLASHBACK
5 MORAVEC ON PHONE
5
6
VICTOR, SUSAN, SANDHU IN LAB
8 9 10 11 12 13 14 15
7
BROOM & HARRY IN PUB
8
TURTLE BEACH
16 17 18 19 20 21 22

My layouts often include quick character designs in the margins. More important characters get the full treatment, however.

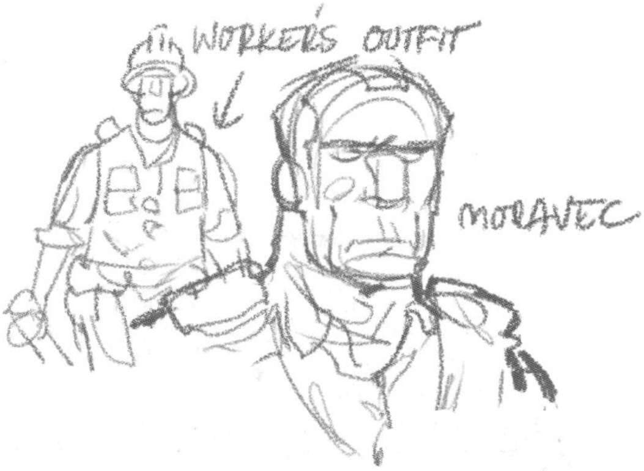
WORKERS OUTFIT
MORAVEC

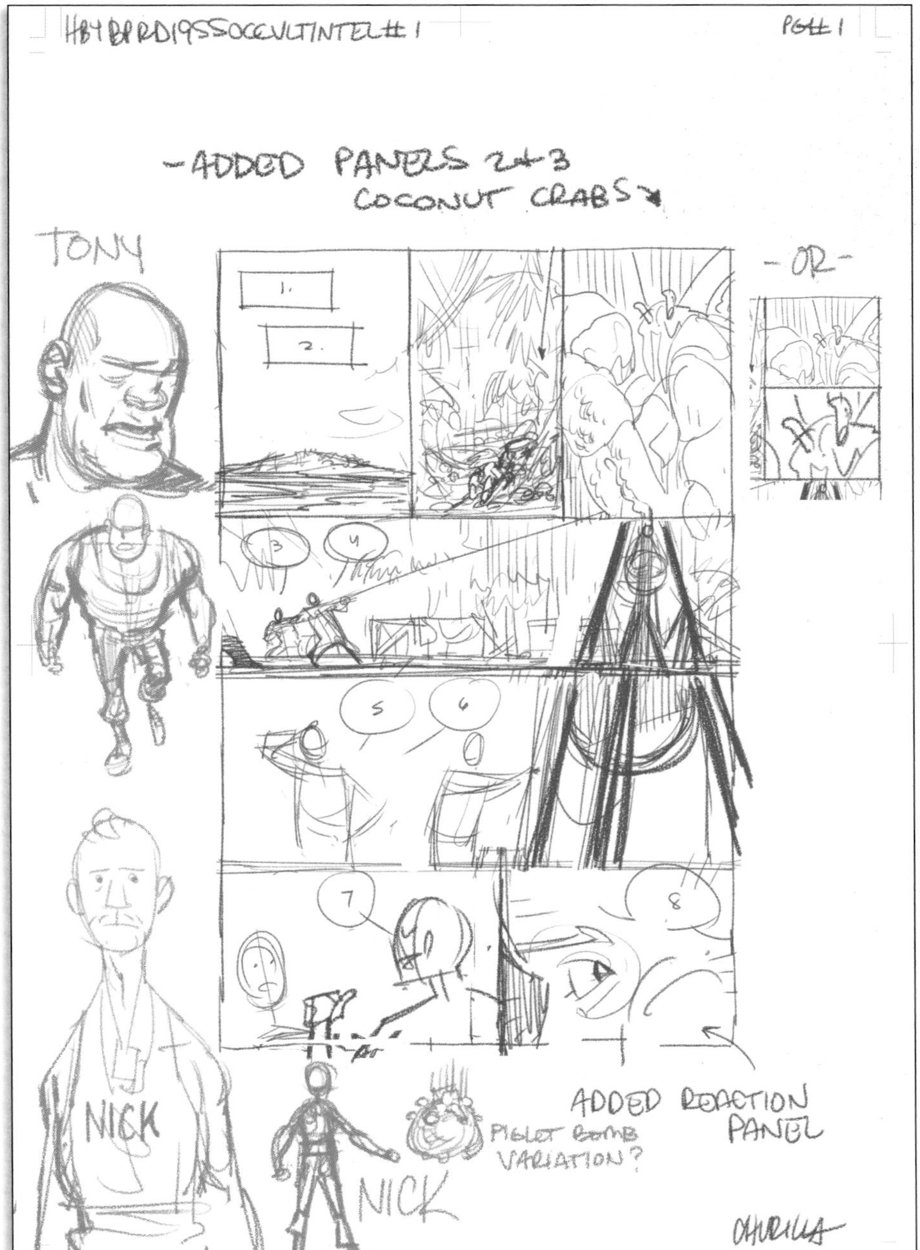
HB4BPRD1955OCCULTINTEL#1
PG#1
-ADDED PANELS 2+3
COCONUT CRABS
TONY
-OR-
1.
2.
3
4
5
6
7
8
NICK
ADDED REACTION PANEL
PIGLET BOMB VARIATION?
NICK

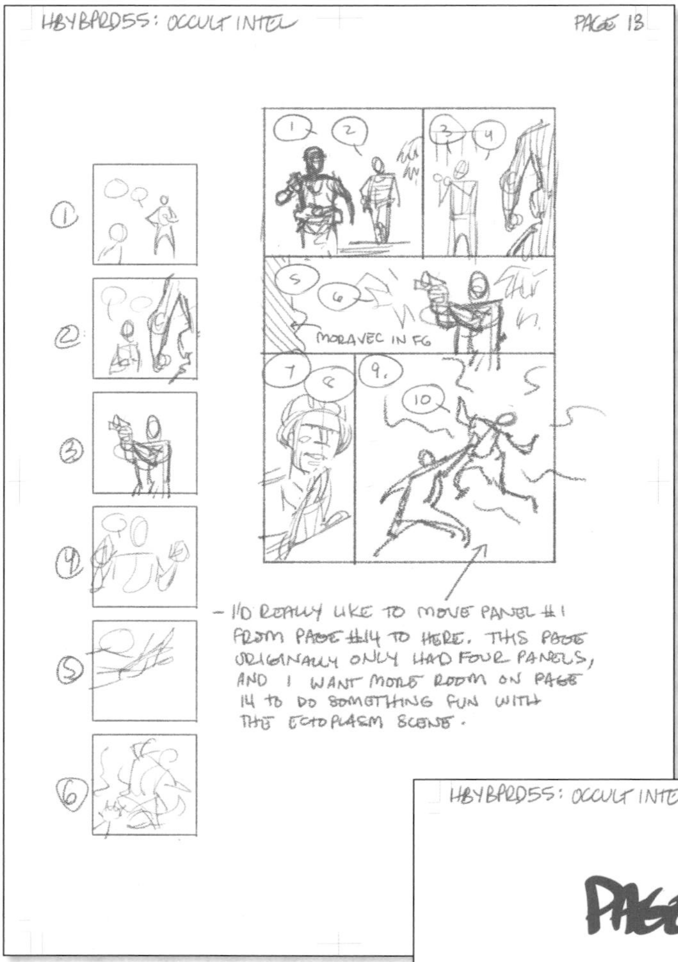
HBYBPRD55: OCCULT INTEL
PAGE 13
MORAVEC IN FG
- I'D REALLY LIKE TO MOVE PANEL #1 FROM PAGE #14 TO HERE. THIS PAGE ORIGINALLY ONLY HAD FOUR PANELS, AND I WANT MORE ROOM ON PAGE 14 TO DO SOMETHING FUN WITH THE ECTOPLASM SCENE.

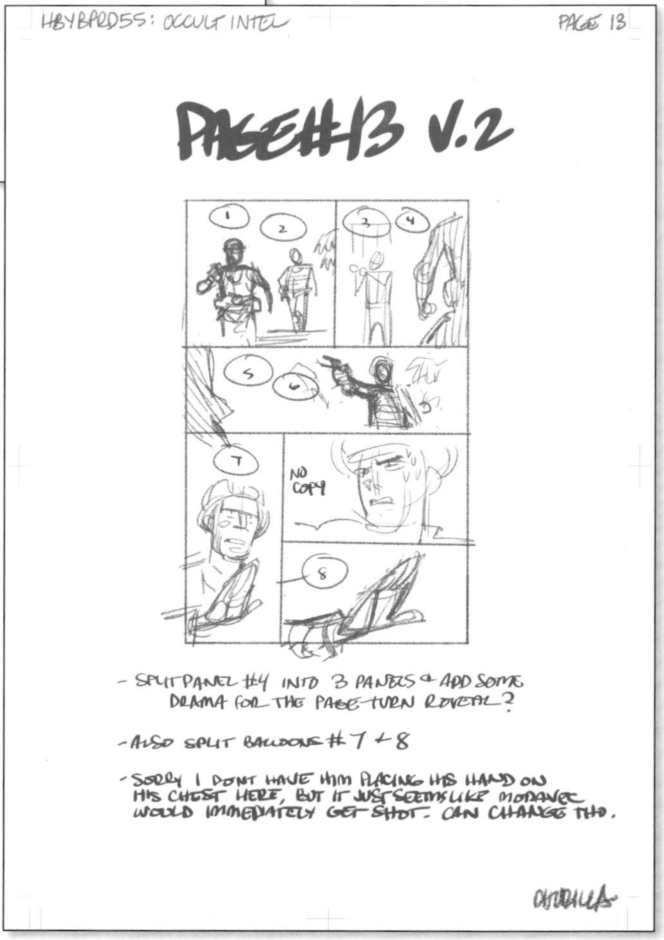
HBYBPRD55: OCCULT INTEL
PAGE 13
PAGE#13 V.2
NO COPY
- SPLIT PANEL #4 INTO 3 PANELS & ADD SOME DRAMA FOR THE PAGE-TURN REVEAL?
- ALSO SPLIT BALLOONS #7 + 8
- SORRY I DONT HAVE HIM PLACING HIS HAND ON HIS CHEST HERE, BUT IT JUST SEEMS LIKE MORAVEC WOULD IMMEDIATELY GET SHOT. CAN CHANGE THO.

Here's a gander at pages that required some editing. You can see the progression from initial layout to edited layout. I got to write two jokes in *Ghost Moon* and *Occult Intelligence*. See if you can spot them!

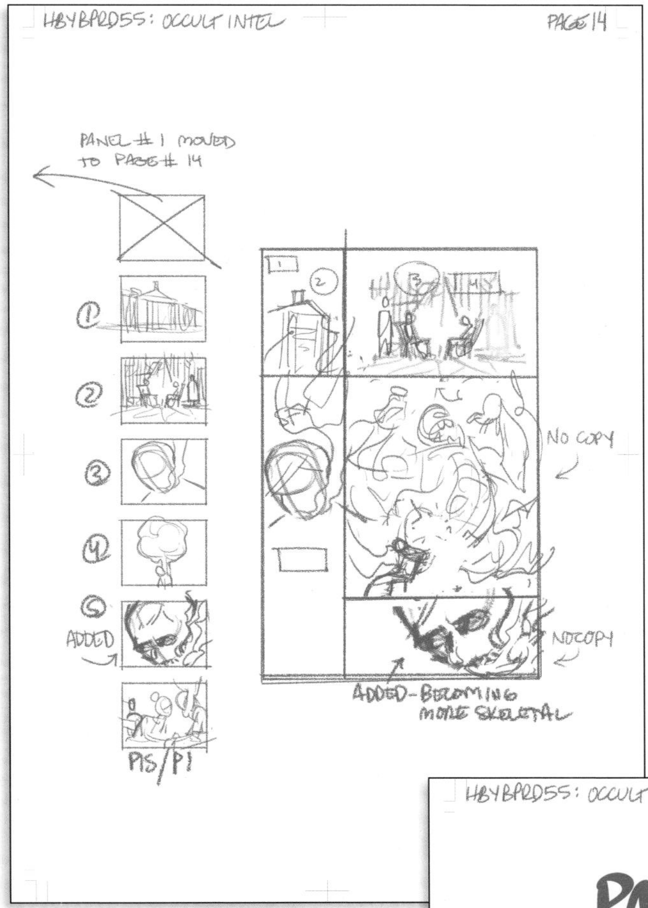
HBYBPRD55: OCCULT INTEL
PAGE 14
PANEL #1 MOVED TO PAGE # 14
ADDED
NO COPY
NO COPY
ADDED-BECOMING MORE SKELETAL
P15/P1

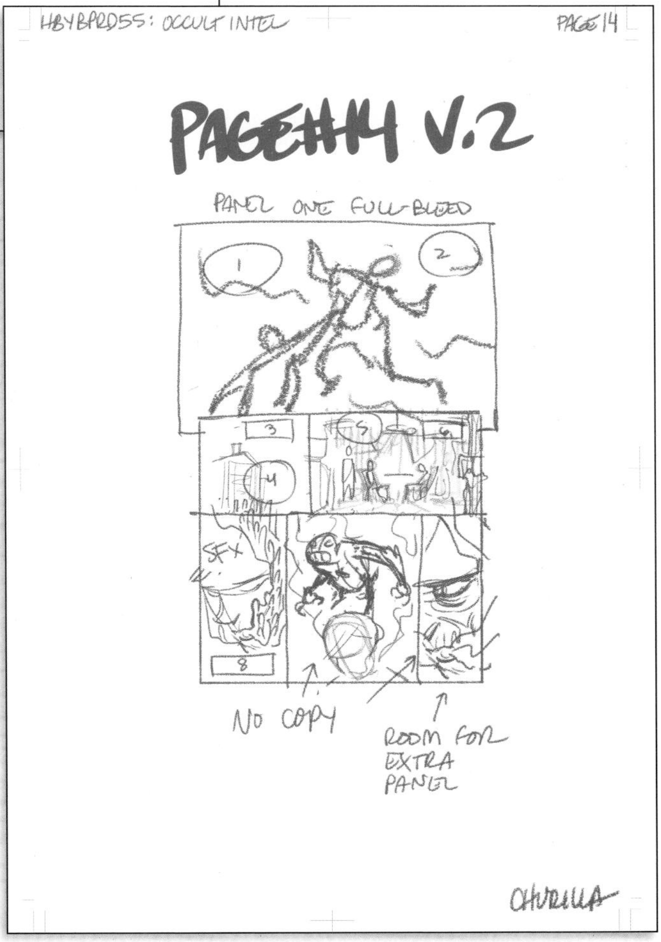
HBYBPRD55: OCCULT INTEL
PAGE 14
PAGE #14 V.2
PANEL ONE FULL-BLEED
SFX
NO COPY
ROOM FOR EXTRA PANEL
CHURILLA

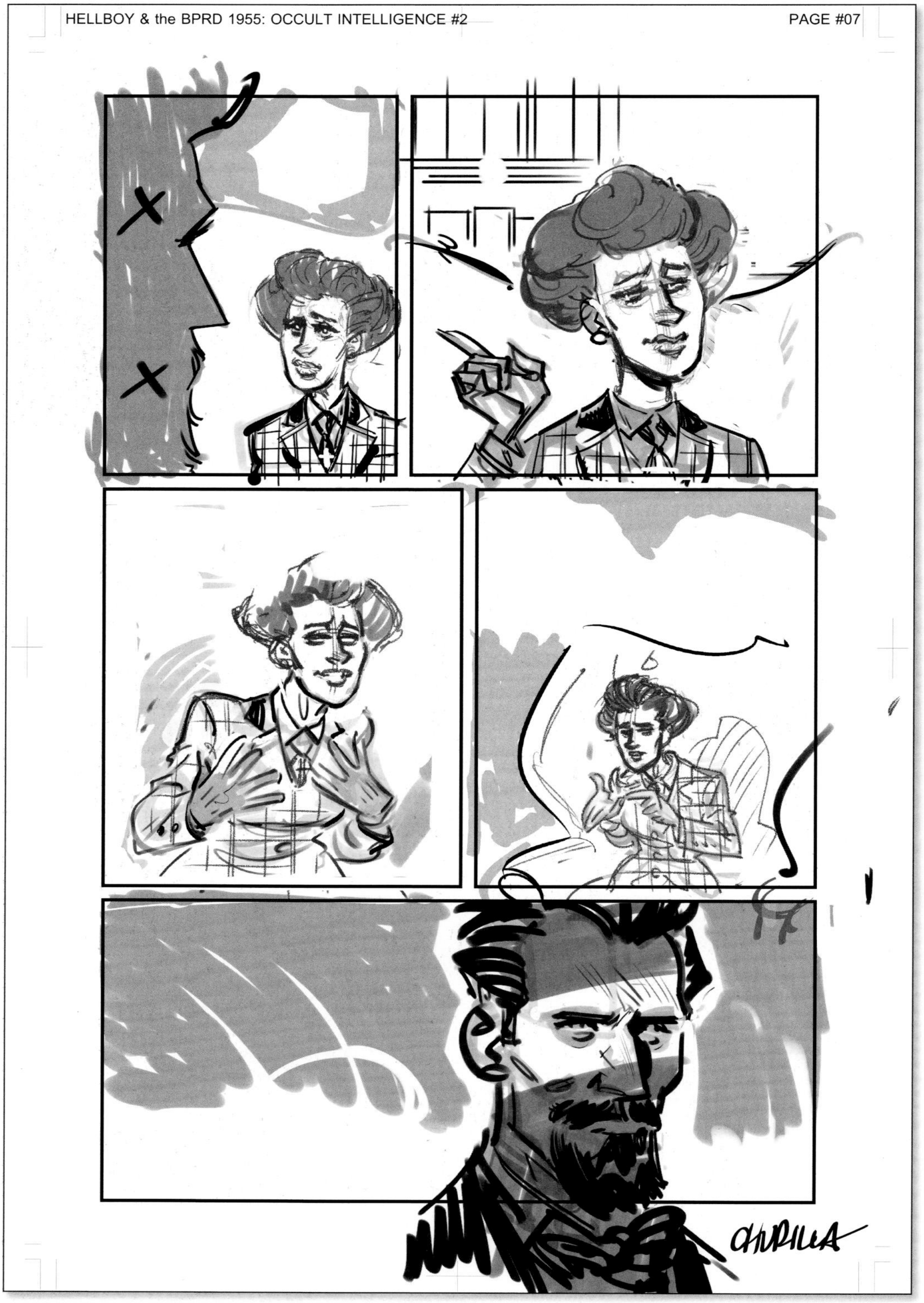
HELLBOY & the BPRD 1955: OCCULT INTELLIGENCE #2
PAGE #07

I'm no master of atmosphere like Mignola, but I try, Here's what my "pencils" look like!

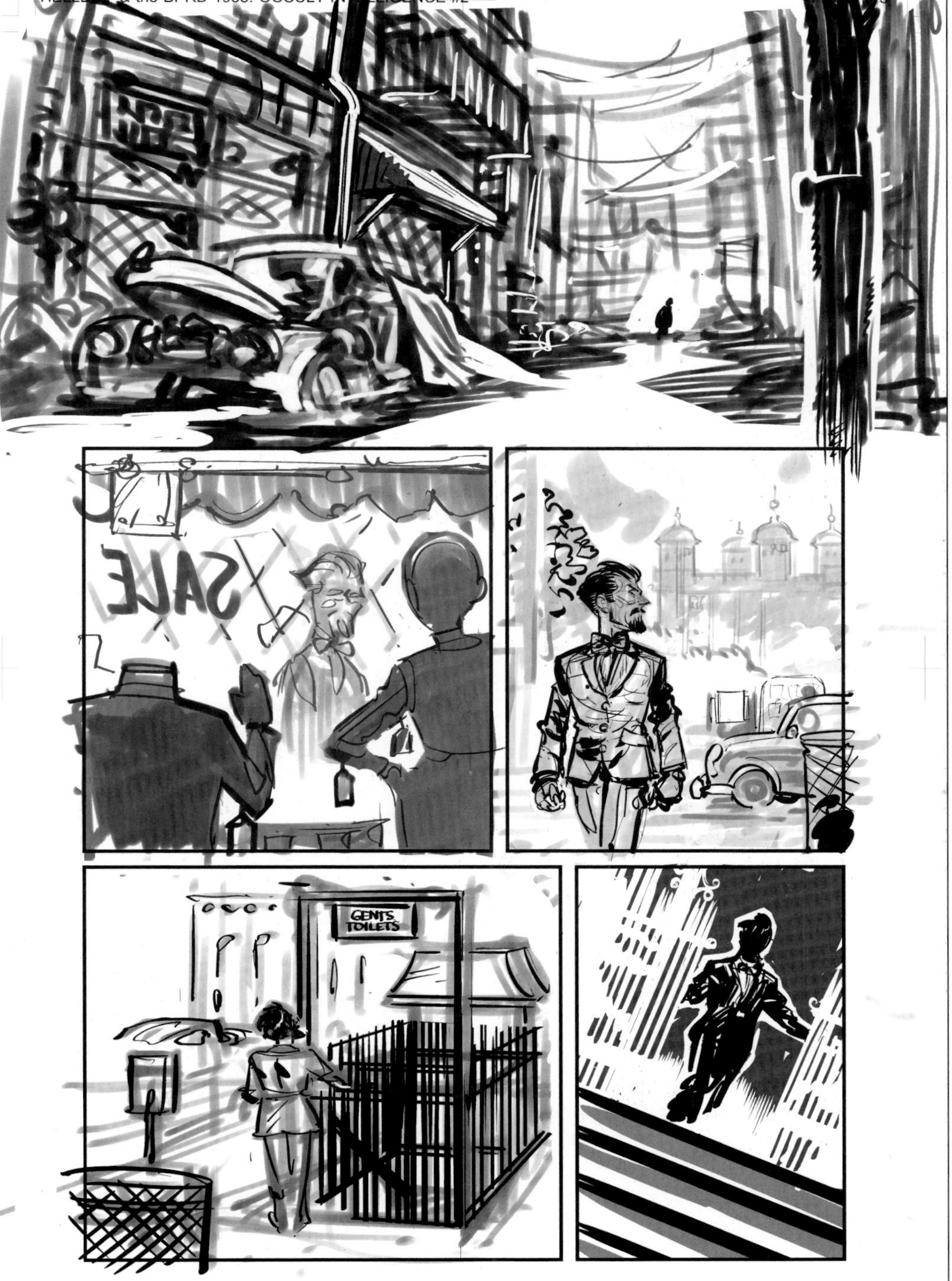
SALE
GENTS TOILETS

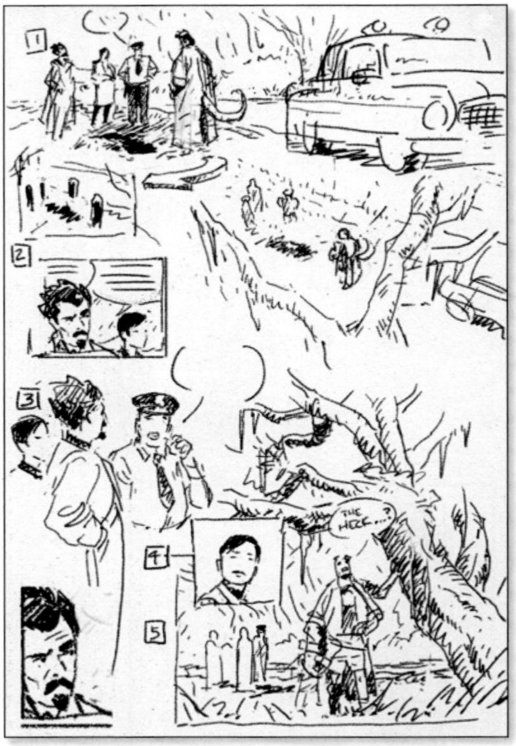
THE HECK...?

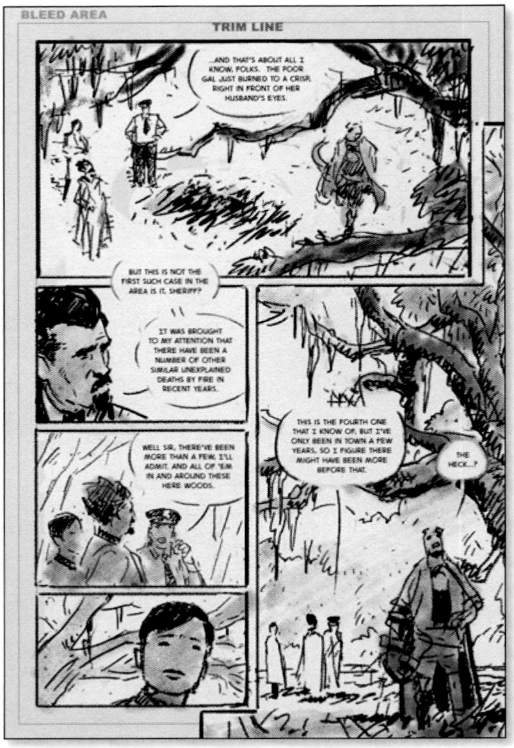
BLEED AREA
TRIM LINE
...AND THAT'S ABOUT ALL I KNOW, FOLKS. THE POOR GAL JUST BURNED TO A CRISP, RIGHT IN FRONT OF HER HUSBAND'S EYES.
BUT THIS IS NOT THE FIRST SUCH CASE IN THE AREA IS IT, SHERIFF?
IT WAS BROUGHT TO MY ATTENTION THAT THERE HAVE BEEN A NUMBER OF OTHER SIMILAR UNEXPLAINED DEATHS BY FIRE IN RECENT YEARS.
WELL SIR, THERE'VE BEEN MORE THAN A FEW, I'LL ADMIT, AND ALL OF 'EM IN AND AROUND THESE HERE WOODS.
THIS IS THE FOURTH ONE THAT I KNOW OF, BUT I'VE ONLY BEEN IN TOWN A FEW YEARS, SO I FIGURE THERE MIGHT HAVE BEEN MORE BEFORE THAT.
THE HECK...?

Paolo Rivera: I plan my pages in a Photoshop document that is split into roughly four sections. The first is a screenshot of the script so I always have easy access. The second is a quarter page of first impression sketches, numbered according to panel. Next is reference, if needed. That could be photos, but more often than not, it's images from previous pages, issues, or character studies. The last section is a detailed layout (with word balloons) for approval. This process can take anywhere from 2.5-6 hours, depending on what's on the page.

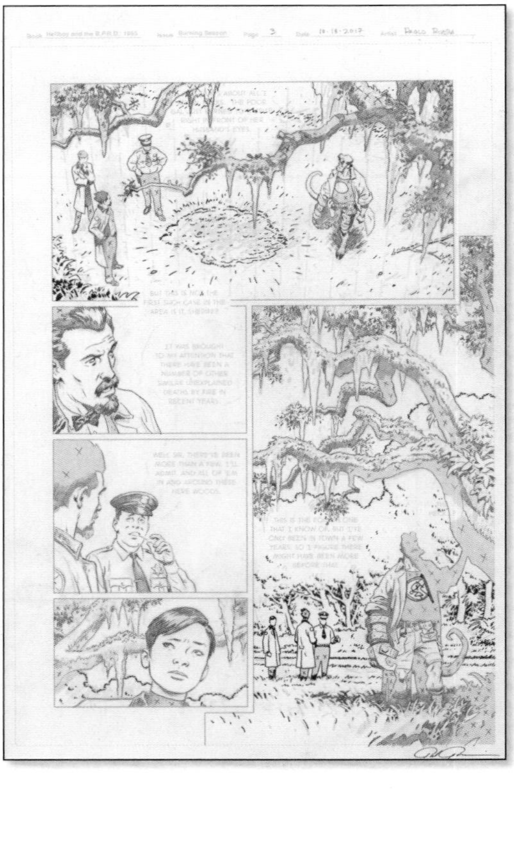

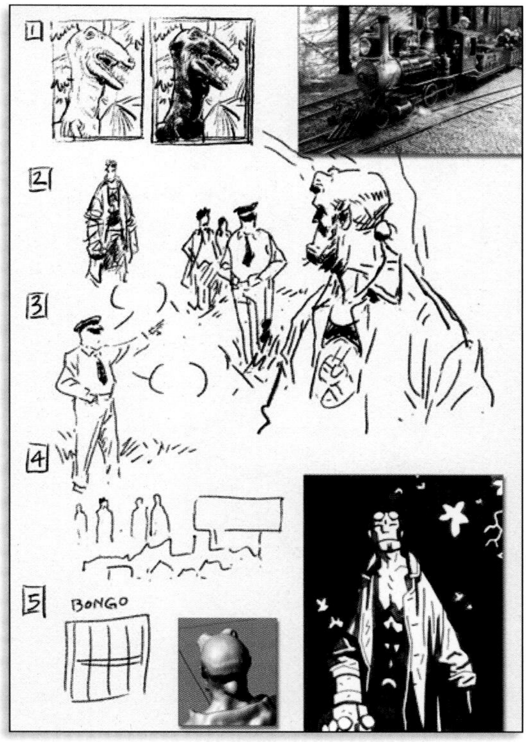
1
2
3
4
5
BONGO

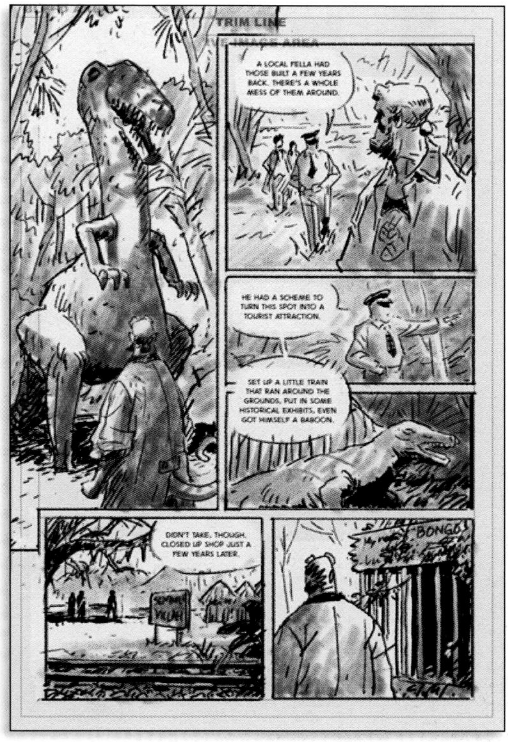
TRIM LINE
A LOCAL FELLA HAD THOSE BUILT A FEW YEARS BACK. THERE'S A WHOLE MESS OF THEM AROUND.
HE HAD A SCHEME TO TURN THIS SPOT INTO A TOURIST ATTRACTION.
SET UP A LITTLE TRAIN THAT RAN AROUND THE GROUNDS, PUT IN SOME HISTORICAL EXHIBITS, EVEN GOT HIMSELF A BABOON.
DIDN'T TAKE, THOUGH. CLOSED UP SHOP JUST A FEW YEARS LATER.
BONGO

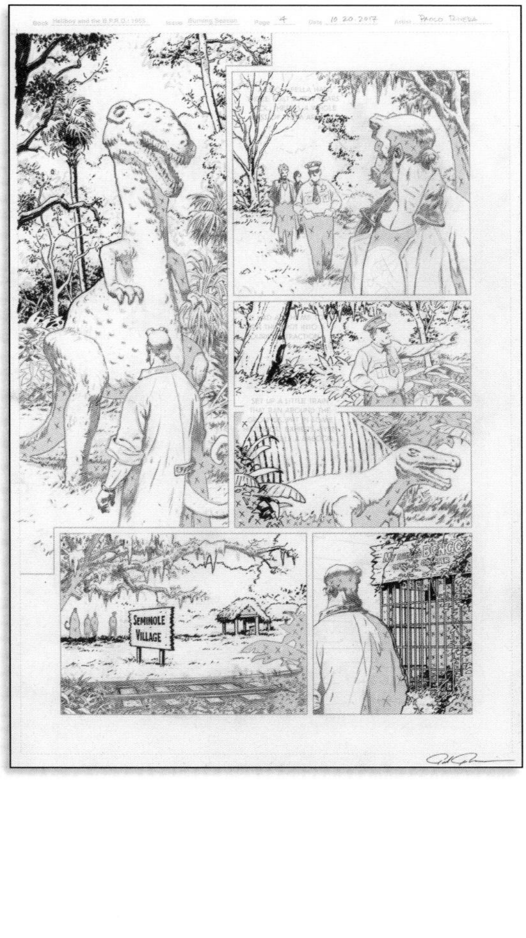
SEMINOLE VILLAGE
BONGO

My dad, Joe Rivera, has inked almost all of my work since 2011. I tried to save him some time on this issue by inking some areas (mostly foliage) but he insisted on doing everything. He prints out my pencils in blue-line and inks over them, so we usually have two originals for each page.

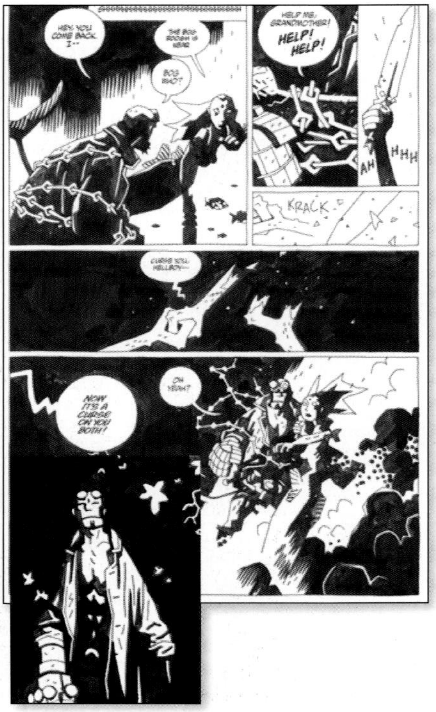
HEY, YOU COME BACK. I--
HELP ME, GRANDMOTHER! HELP! HELP!
AHHHH
KRACK
CURSE YOU, HELLBOY--
NOW IT'S A CURSE ON YOU BOTH!
OH YEAH?

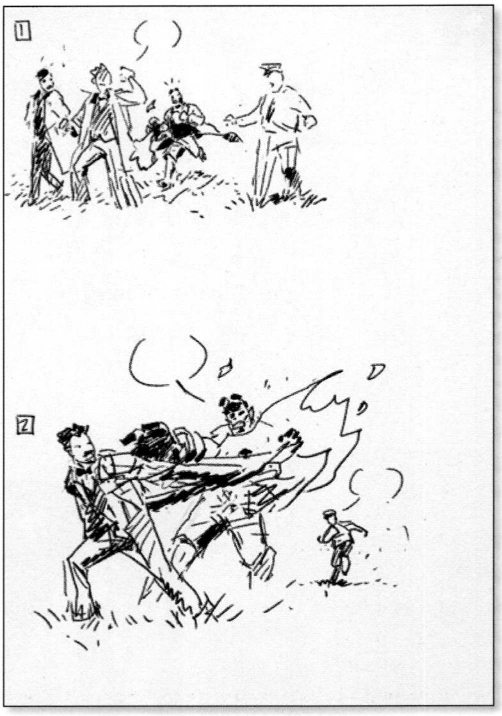
1
2

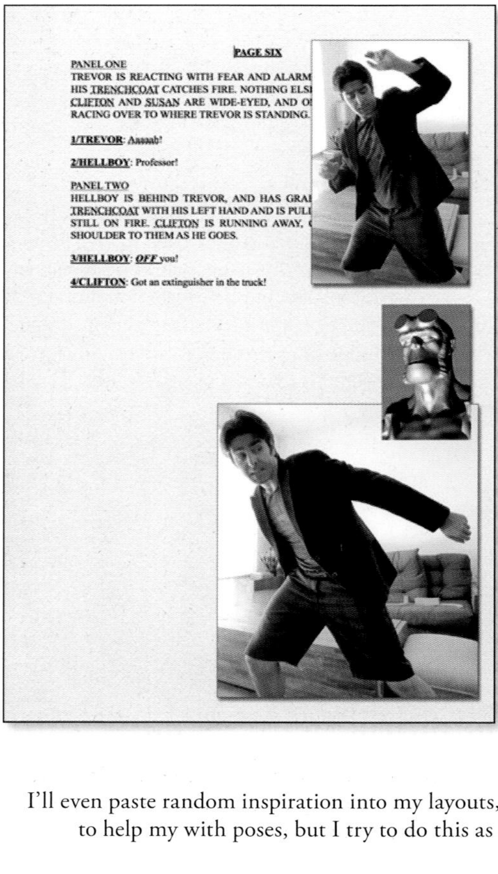
PAGE SIX
PANEL ONE
TREVOR IS REACTING WITH FEAR AND ALARM
HIS TRENCHCOAT CATCHES FIRE. NOTHING ELS
CLIFTON AND SUSAN ARE WIDE-EYED, AND O
RACING OVER TO WHERE TREVOR IS STANDING.
1/TREVOR: Aaaaah!
2/HELLBOY: Professor!
PANEL TWO
HELLBOY IS BEHIND TREVOR, AND HAS GRA
TRENCHCOAT WITH HIS LEFT HAND AND IS PUL
STILL ON FIRE. CLIFTON IS RUNNING AWAY,
SHOULDER TO THEM AS HE GOES.
3/HELLBOY: OFF you!
4/CLIFTON: Got an extinguisher in the truck!

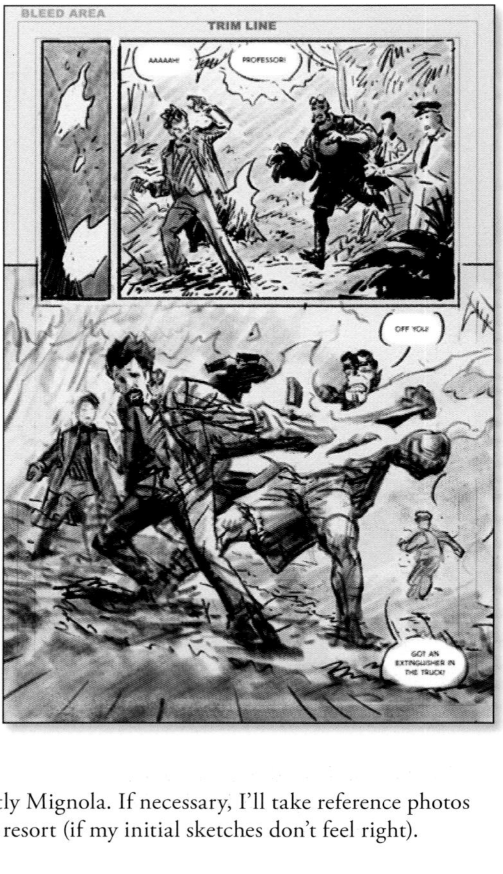
BLEED AREA
TRIM LINE
AAAAAH!
PROFESSOR!
OFF YOU!
GOT AN EXTINGUISHER IN THE TRUCK!

I'll even paste random inspiration into my layouts, mostly Mignola. If necessary, I'll take reference photos to help my with poses, but I try to do this as a last resort (if my initial sketches don't feel right).

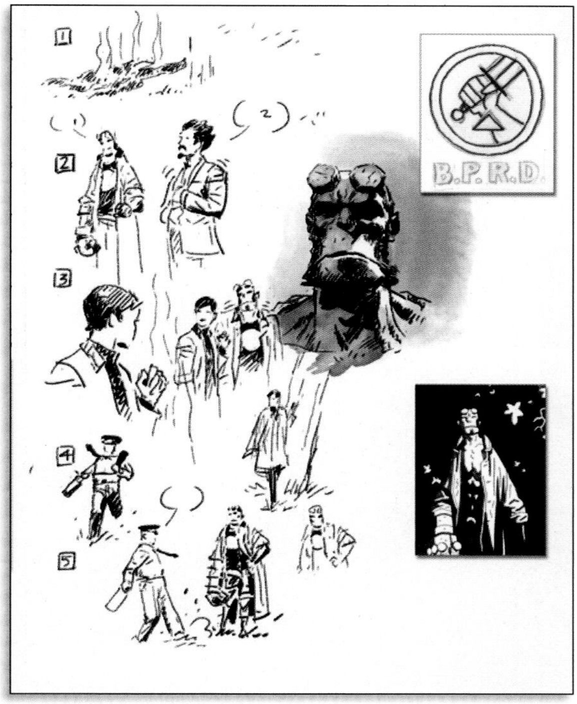

B.P.R.D.

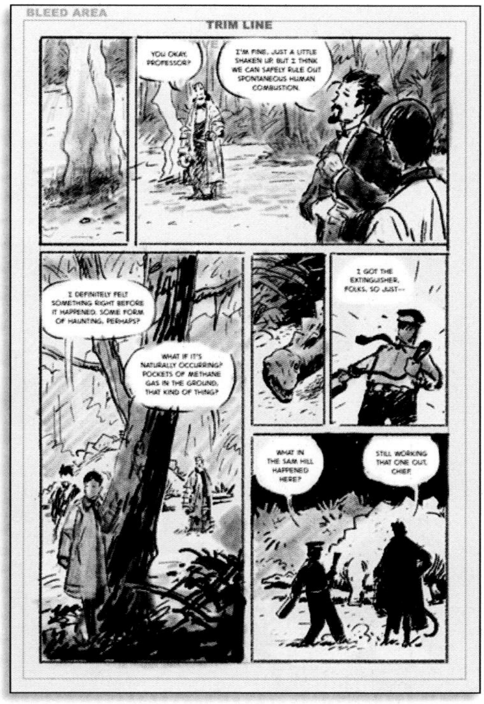

BLEED AREA
TRIM LINE
YOU OKAY, PROFESSOR?
I'M FINE, JUST A LITTLE SHAKEN UP. BUT I THINK WE CAN SAFELY RULE OUT SPONTANEOUS HUMAN COMBUSTION.
I DEFINITELY FELT SOMETHING RIGHT BEFORE IT HAPPENED. SOME FORM OF HAUNTING, PERHAPS?
WHAT IF IT'S NATURALLY OCCURRING? POCKETS OF METHANE GAS IN THE GROUND. THAT KIND OF THING?
I GOT THE EXTINGUISHER, FOLKS, SO JUST--
WHAT IN THE SAM HILL HAPPENED HERE?
STILL WORKING THAT ONE OUT, CHIEF.

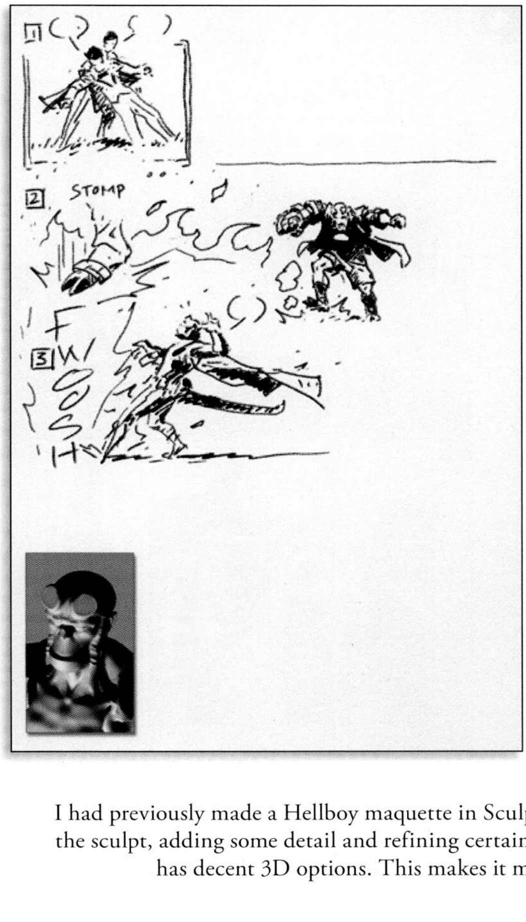

STOMP

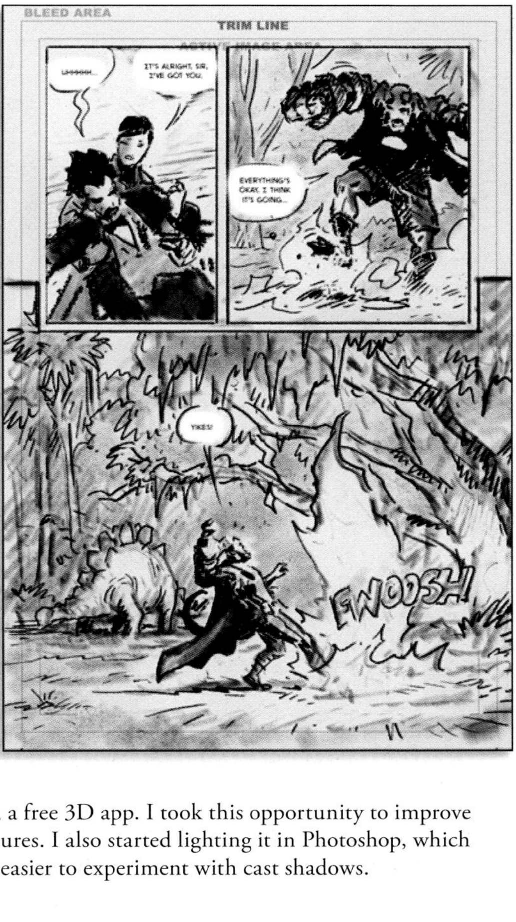

BLEED AREA
TRIM LINE
UHHHHH...
IT'S ALRIGHT, SIR, I'VE GOT YOU.
EVERYTHING'S OKAY, I THINK IT'S GOING...
YIKES!
FWOOSH!

I had previously made a Hellboy maquette in Sculptris, a free 3D app. I took this opportunity to improve the sculpt, adding some detail and refining certain features. I also started lighting it in Photoshop, which has decent 3D options. This makes it much easier to experiment with cast shadows.

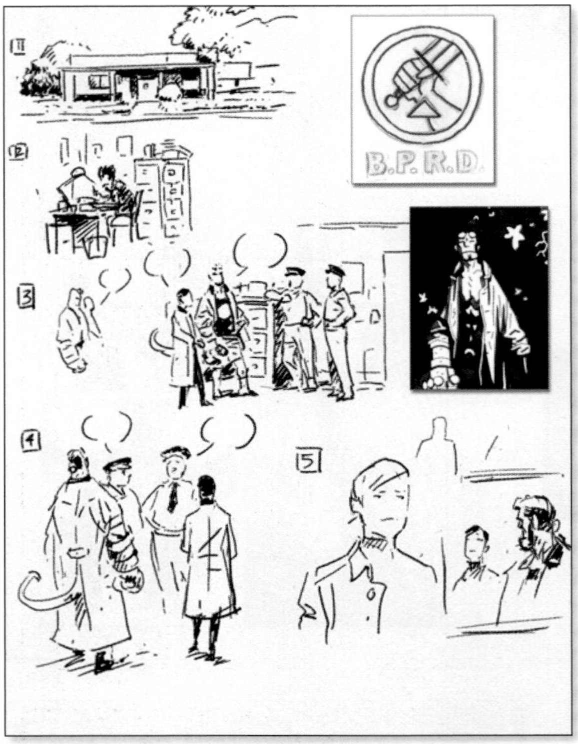
B.P.R.D.

Even though these are drawn digitally, they are pretty convincing as traditional sketches. That's thanks to Kyle T. Webster's brushes, which are now part of the standard Photoshop arsenal. Furthermore, I like adding a layer of simulated grain to give my eyes something to lock on to besides pure, white light. You can't see it here, but I also use a transparent yellow layer (a blue-light filter) to help reduce the eye strain of staring at a screen all day long.

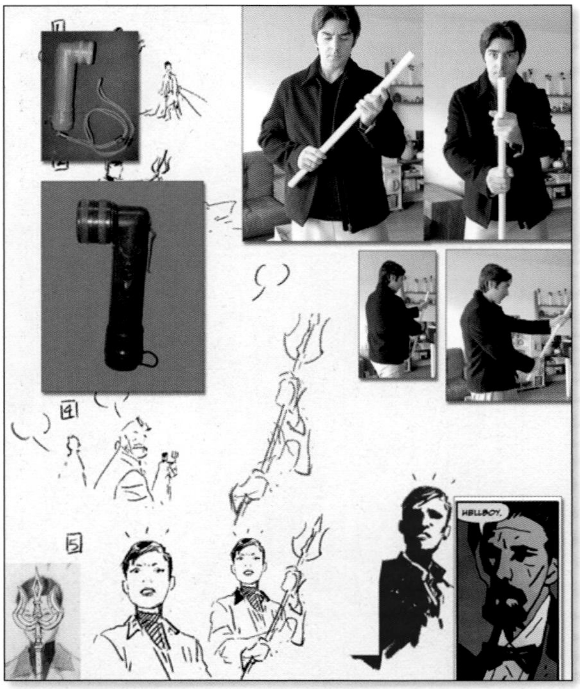
HELLBOY.

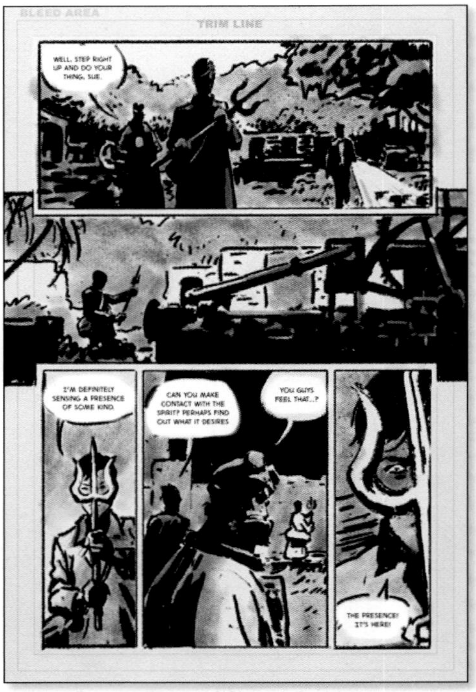
BLEED AREA
TRIM LINE
WELL, STEP RIGHT UP AND DO YOUR THING, SUE.
I'M DEFINITELY SENSING A PRESENCE OF SOME KIND.
CAN YOU MAKE CONTACT WITH THE SPIRIT? PERHAPS FIND OUT WHAT IT DESIRES
YOU GUYS FEEL THAT...?
THE PRESENCE! IT'S HERE!

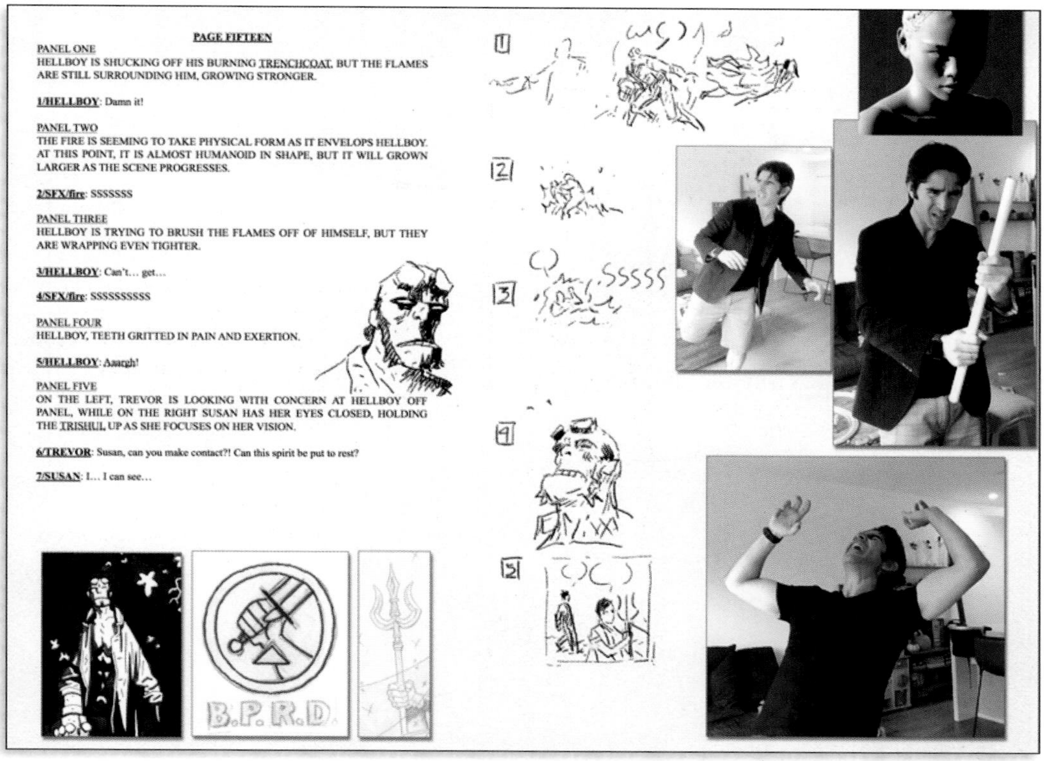

PAGE FIFTEEN

PANEL ONE
HELLBOY IS SHUCKING OFF HIS BURNING TRENCHCOAT, BUT THE FLAMES ARE STILL SURROUNDING HIM, GROWING STRONGER.

1/HELLBOY: Damn it!

PANEL TWO
THE FIRE IS SEEMING TO TAKE PHYSICAL FORM AS IT ENVELOPS HELLBOY. AT THIS POINT, IT IS ALMOST HUMANOID IN SHAPE, BUT IT WILL GROWN LARGER AS THE SCENE PROGRESSES.

2/SFX/fire: SSSSSSS

PANEL THREE
HELLBOY IS TRYING TO BRUSH THE FLAMES OFF OF HIMSELF, BUT THEY ARE WRAPPING EVEN TIGHTER.

3/HELLBOY: Can't… get…

4/SFX/fire: SSSSSSSSS

PANEL FOUR
HELLBOY, TEETH GRITTED IN PAIN AND EXERTION.

5/HELLBOY: Aaargh!

PANEL FIVE
ON THE LEFT, TREVOR IS LOOKING WITH CONCERN AT HELLBOY OFF PANEL, WHILE ON THE RIGHT SUSAN HAS HER EYES CLOSED, HOLDING THE TRISHUL UP AS SHE FOCUSES ON HER VISION.

6/TREVOR: Susan, can you make contact?! Can this spirit be put to rest?

7/SUSAN: I… I can see…

B.P.R.D.

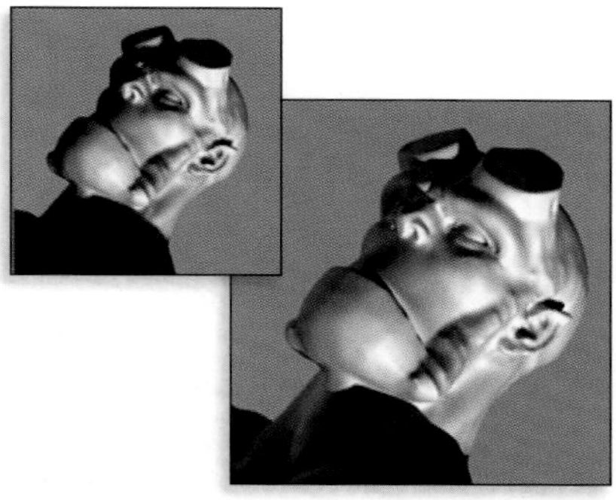

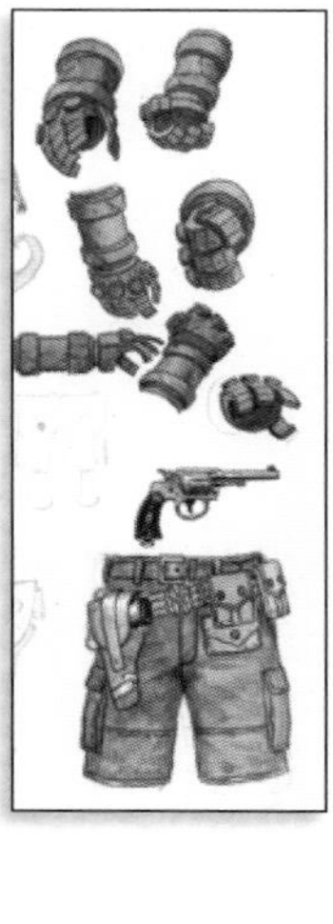

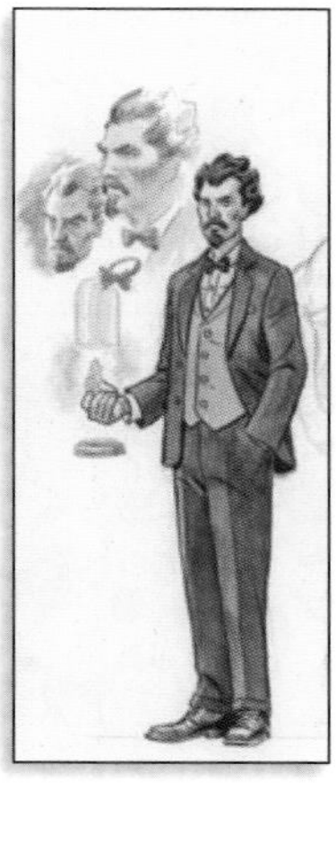

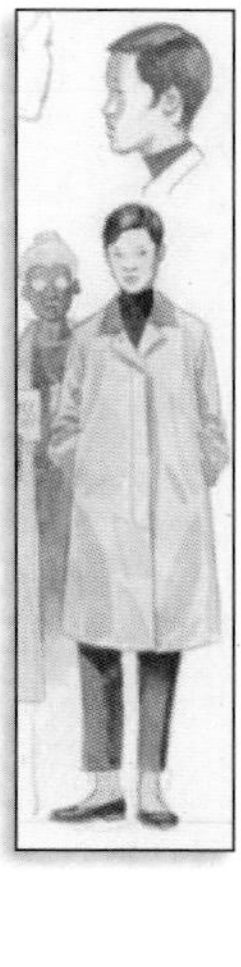

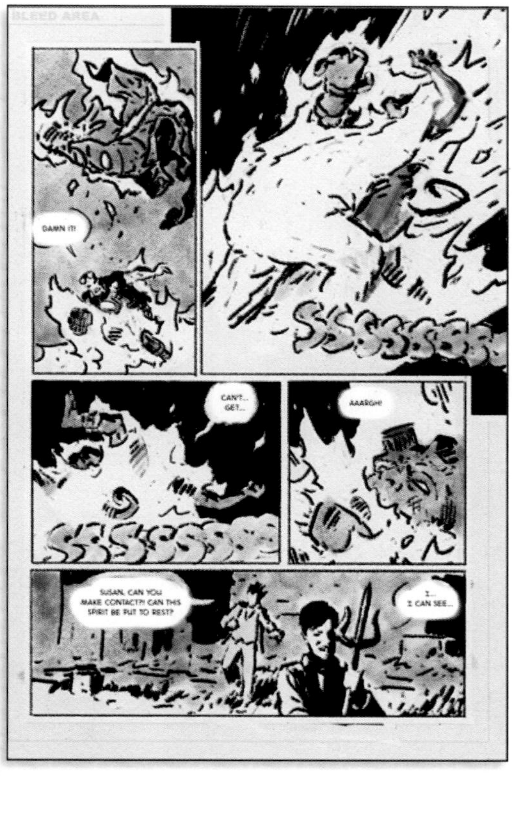
BLEED AREA
DAMN IT!
CAN'T... GET...
AAARGH!
SUSAN, CAN YOU MAKE CONTACT?! CAN THIS SPIRIT BE PUT TO REST?
I... I CAN SEE...

You might recognize some of these character studies from my last Hellboy adventure. In comic book time (and real life) only two years have passed. I have more gray hair, but they look pretty much the same.

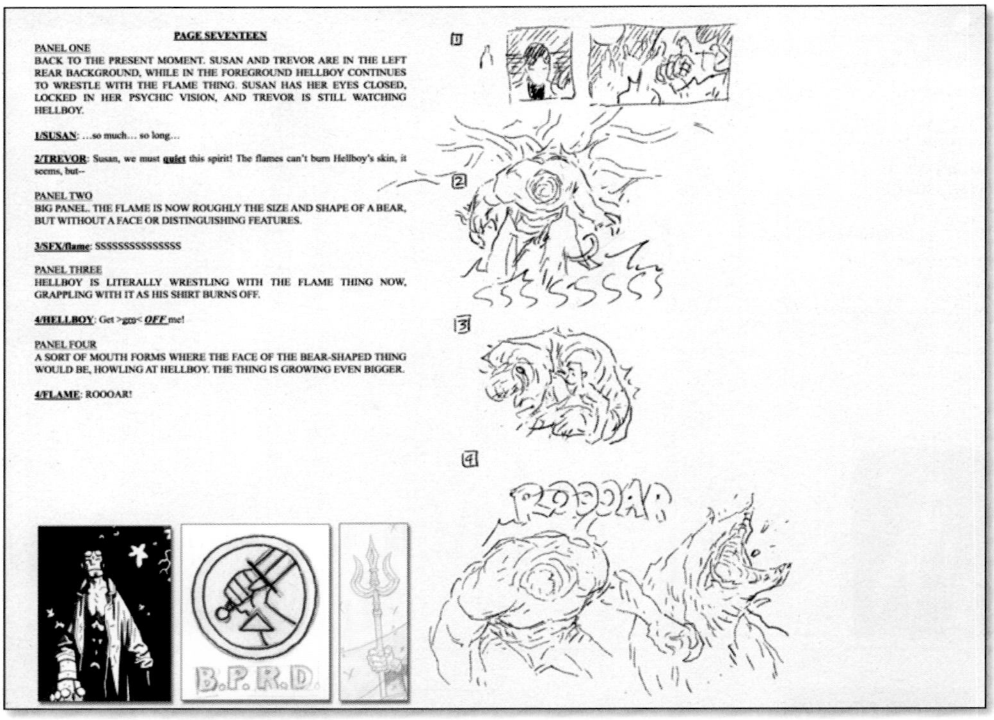

PAGE SEVENTEEN

PANEL ONE
BACK TO THE PRESENT MOMENT. SUSAN AND TREVOR ARE IN THE LEFT REAR BACKGROUND, WHILE IN THE FOREGROUND HELLBOY CONTINUES TO WRESTLE WITH THE FLAME THING. SUSAN HAS HER EYES CLOSED, LOCKED IN HER PSYCHIC VISION, AND TREVOR IS STILL WATCHING HELLBOY.

1/SUSAN: …so much… so long…

2/TREVOR: Susan, we must **quiet** this spirit! The flames can't burn Hellboy's skin, it seems, but--

PANEL TWO
BIG PANEL. THE FLAME IS NOW ROUGHLY THE SIZE AND SHAPE OF A BEAR, BUT WITHOUT A FACE OR DISTINGUISHING FEATURES.

3/SFX/flame: SSSSSSSSSSSSSS

PANEL THREE
HELLBOY IS LITERALLY WRESTLING WITH THE FLAME THING NOW, GRAPPLING WITH IT AS HIS SHIRT BURNS OFF.

4/HELLBOY: Get >grr< ***OFF*** me!

PANEL FOUR
A SORT OF MOUTH FORMS WHERE THE FACE OF THE BEAR-SHAPED THING WOULD BE, HOWLING AT HELLBOY. THE THING IS GROWING EVEN BIGGER.

4/FLAME: ROOOAR!

B.P.R.D.

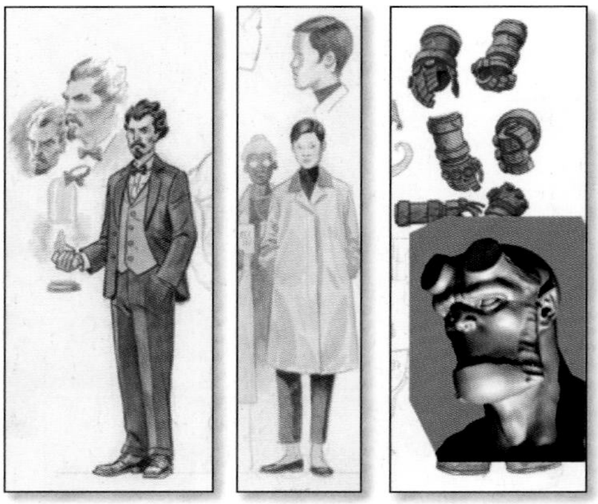

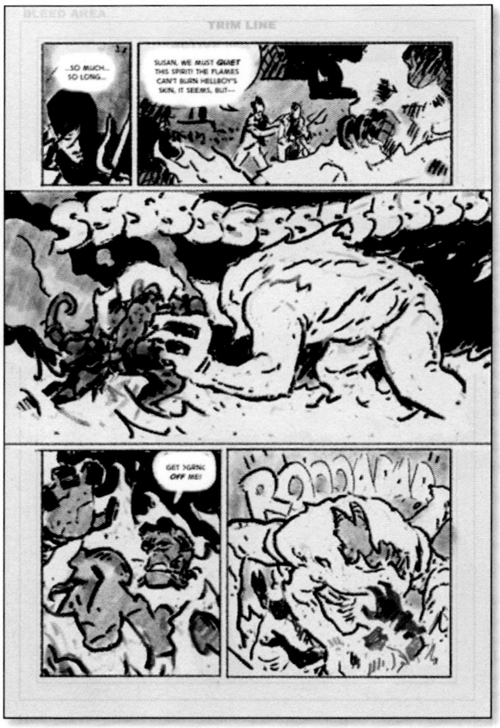
BLEED AREA
TRIM LINE
…SO MUCH… SO LONG…
SUSAN, WE MUST QUIET THIS SPIRIT! THE FLAMES CAN'T BURN HELLBOY'S SKIN, IT SEEMS, BUT—

If I have to design a new character, but am unsure of the look, I just start drawing. Chances are I'll have a much better idea by the time the layouts are finished. It helps to see them in action, and you can always fill in the details during the pencil stage.

SSSSSSSS

1
SSSSS
2
RROAR
3
4
SSSSSSSSSS

I could draw Hellboy burning all day.
And I did.

TRIM LINE
I'M NOT >UNF< FIGHTING BACK, OKAY? YOU GO AHEAD AND BURN ALL YOU WANT.
SSSSSSSSSS
RROAR
BUT HAVEN'T ENOUGH PEOPLE SUFFERED >GRNK< ALREADY?
SSSSSSSS

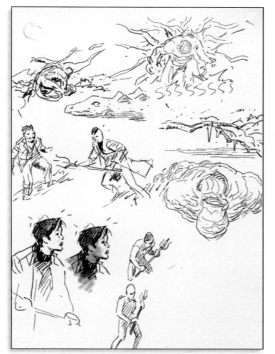

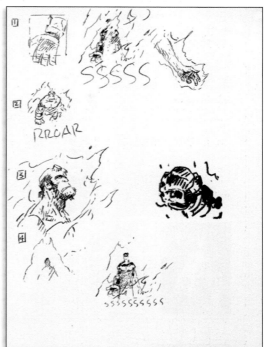

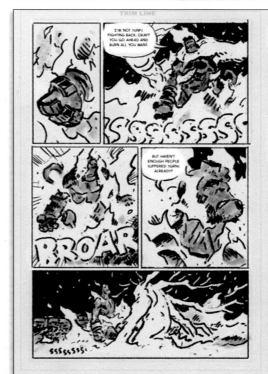

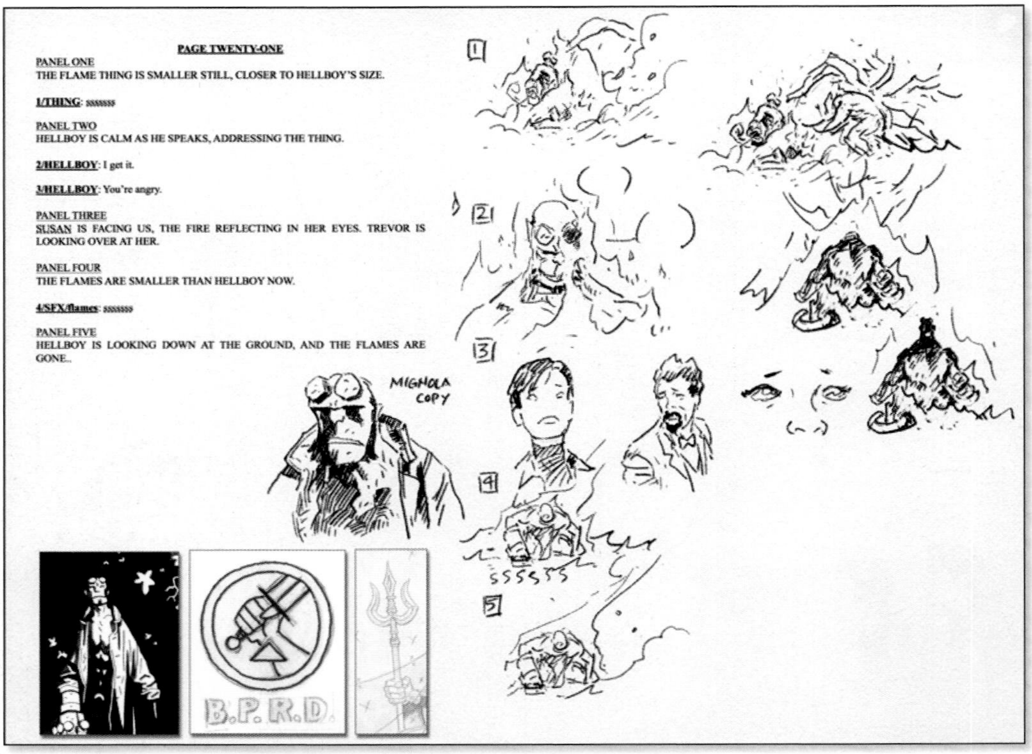
PAGE TWENTY-ONE
PANEL ONE
THE FLAME THING IS SMALLER STILL, CLOSER TO HELLBOY'S SIZE.

1/THING: ssssssss

PANEL TWO
HELLBOY IS CALM AS HE SPEAKS, ADDRESSING THE THING.

2/HELLBOY: I get it.

3/HELLBOY: You're angry.

PANEL THREE
SUSAN IS FACING US, THE FIRE REFLECTING IN HER EYES. TREVOR IS LOOKING OVER AT HER.

PANEL FOUR
THE FLAMES ARE SMALLER THAN HELLBOY NOW.

4/SFX/flames: ssssssss

PANEL FIVE
HELLBOY IS LOOKING DOWN AT THE GROUND, AND THE FLAMES ARE GONE..

1
2
3
MIGNOLA COPY
4
SSSSSS
5
B.P.R.D.

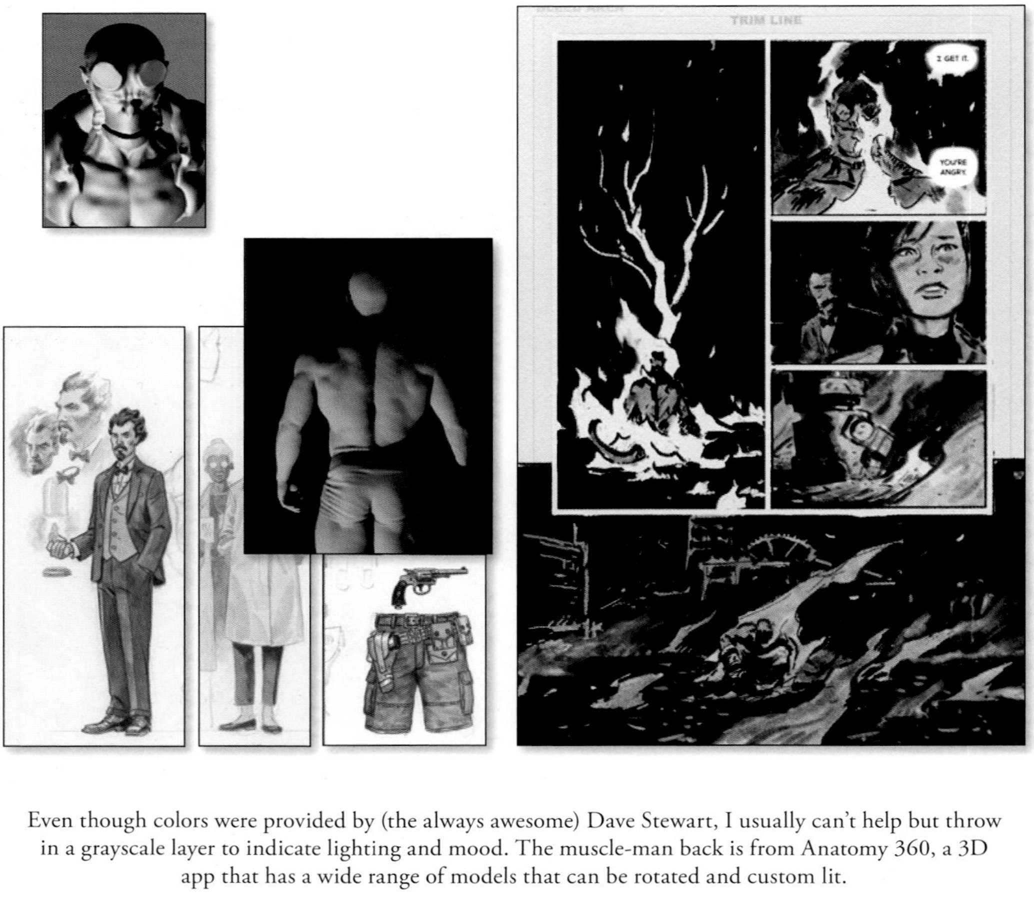
TRIM LINE
I GET IT.
YOU'RE ANGRY.

Even though colors were provided by (the always awesome) Dave Stewart, I usually can't help but throw in a grayscale layer to indicate lighting and mood. The muscle-man back is from Anatomy 360, a 3D app that has a wide range of models that can be rotated and custom lit.

These cover layouts are drawn digitally. I keep them purposefully small so I'm not tempted to add any detail. I loved drawing the mutated turtle so much that I sculpted a digital maquette as reference for the trade cover.

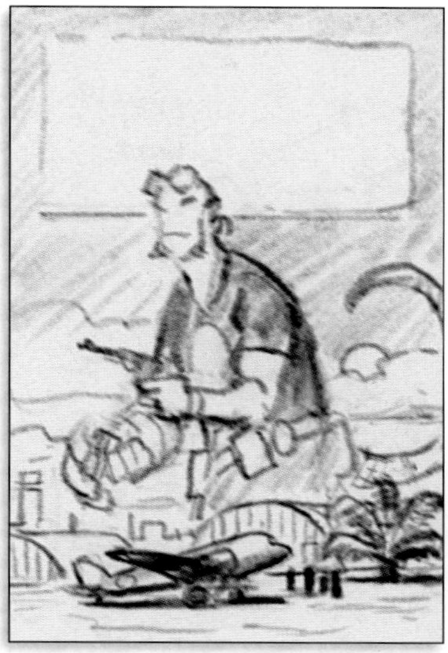

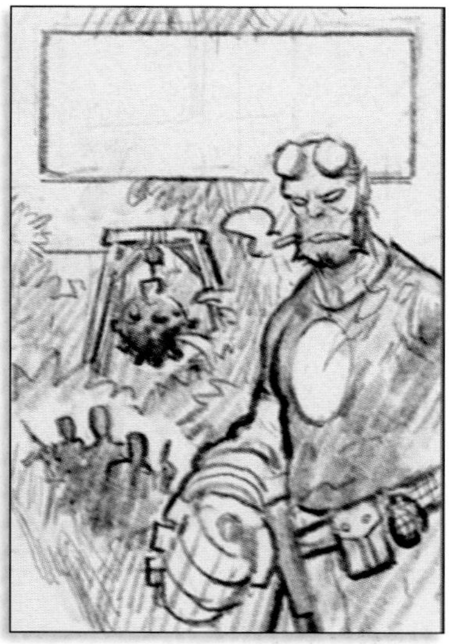

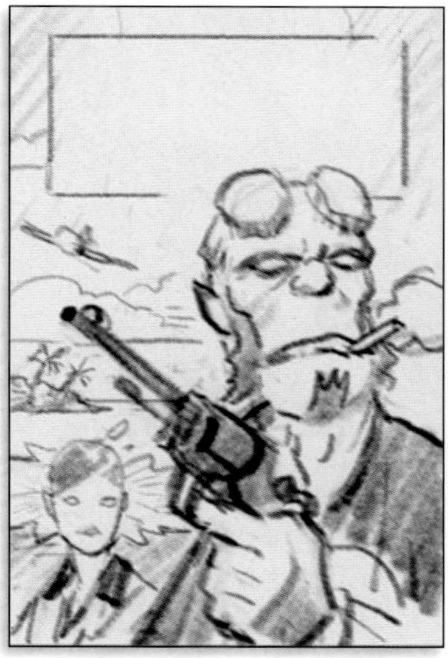

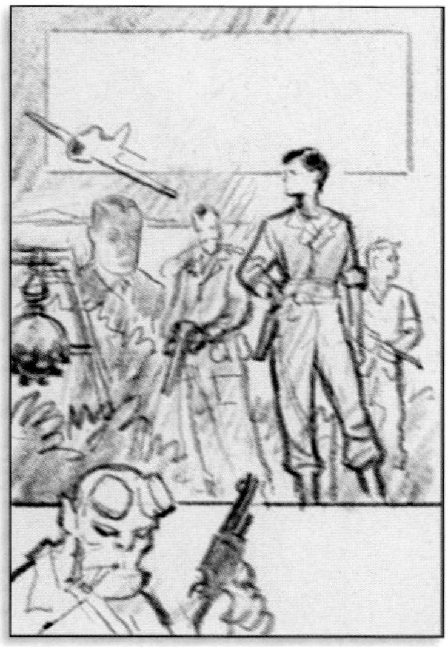

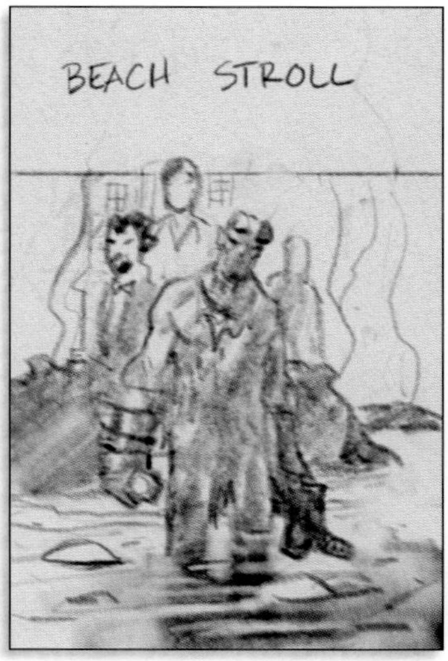
BEACH STROLL

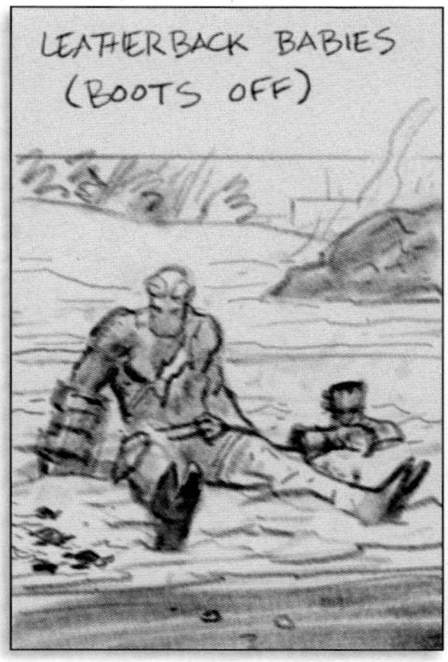
LEATHERBACK BABIES
(BOOTS OFF)

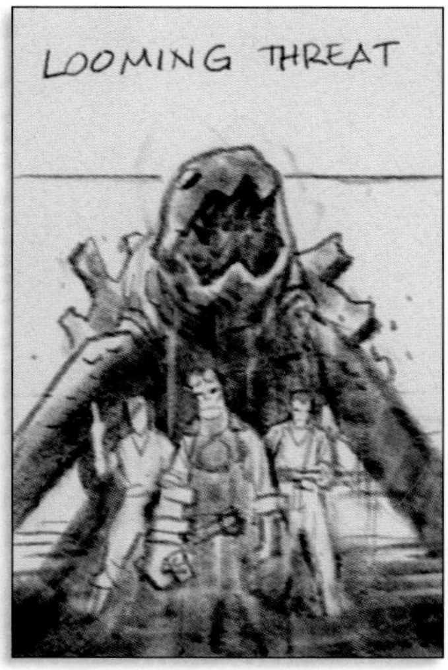
LOOMING THREAT

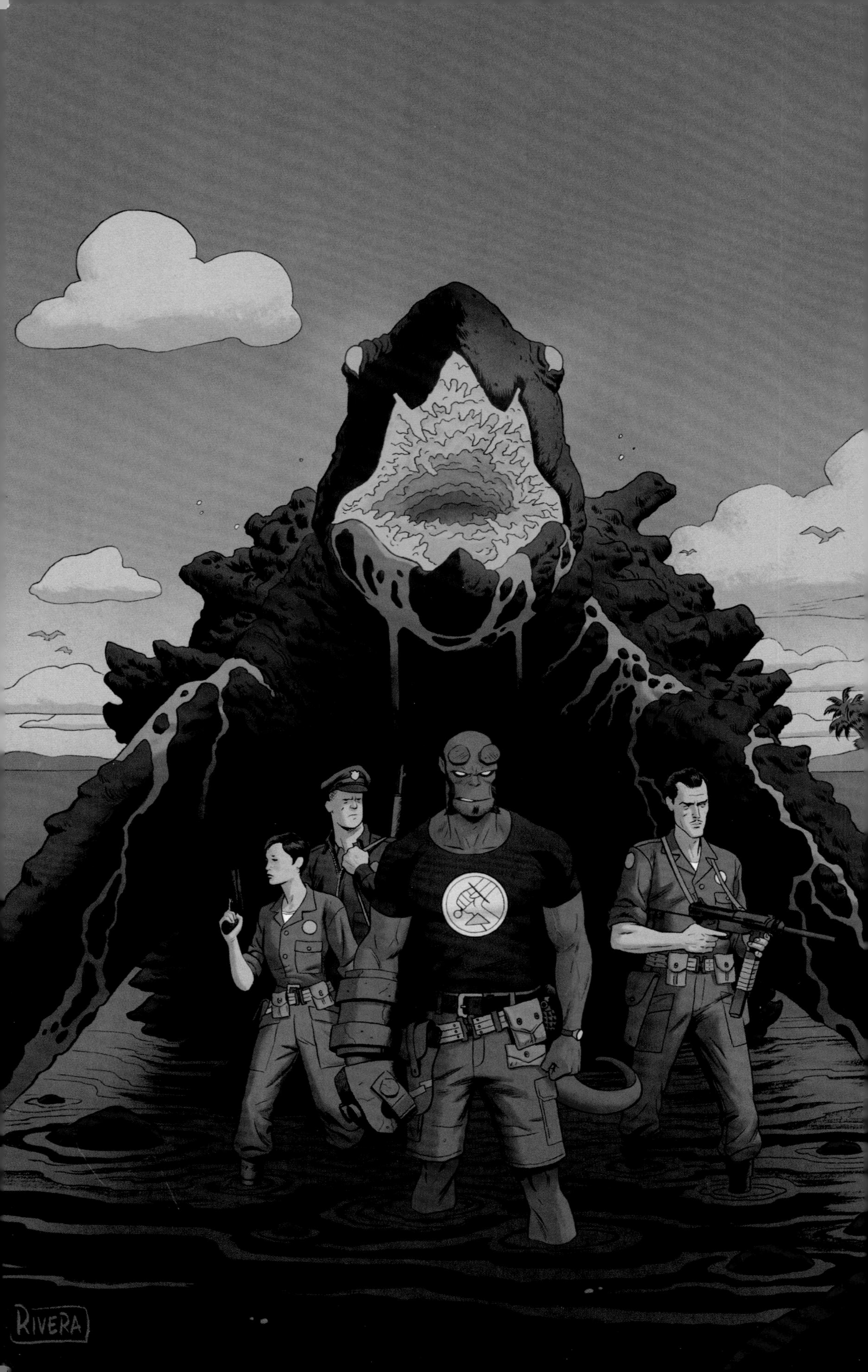
RIVERA

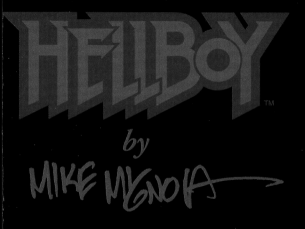

HELLBOY™

by MIKE MIGNOLA

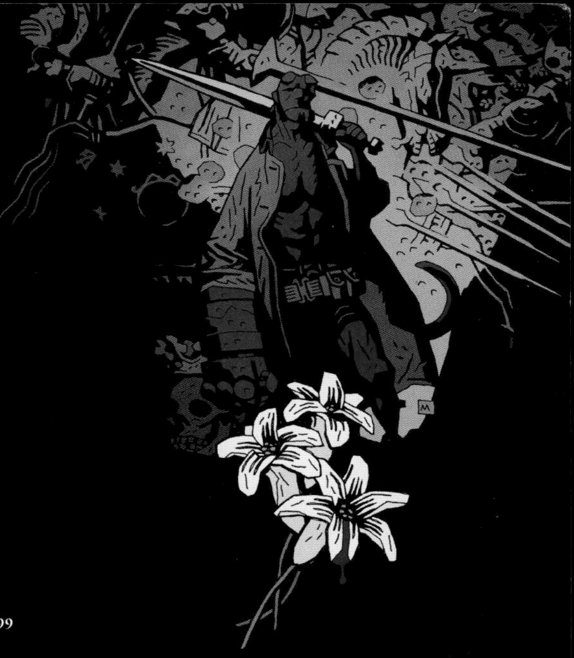

HELLBOY LIBRARY EDITION

VOLUME 1:
Seed of Destruction
and Wake the Devil
ISBN 978-1-59307-910-9 | $49.99

VOLUME 2:
The Chained Coffin
and The Right Hand of Doom
ISBN 978-1-59307-989-5 | $49.99

VOLUME 3:
Conqueror Worm
and Strange Places
ISBN 978-1-59582-352-6 | $49.99

VOLUME 4:
The Crooked Man and
The Troll Witch
with Richard Corben and others
ISBN 978-1-59582-658-9 | $49.99

VOLUME 5:
Darkness Calls and The Wild Hunt
with Duncan Fegredo
ISBN 978-1-59582-886-6 | $49.99

VOLUME 6:
The Storm and the Fury
and The Bride of Hell
with Duncan Fegredo, Richard Corben,
Kevin Nowlan, and Scott Hampton
ISBN 978-1-61655-133-9 | $49.99

HELLBOY IN HELL
ISBN 978-1-50670-363-3 | $49.99

THE RIGHT HAND
OF DOOM
ISBN 978-1-59307-093-9 | $17.99

CONQUEROR WORM
ISBN 978-1-59307-092-2 | $17.99

STRANGE PLACES
ISBN 978-1-59307-475-3 | $17.99

THE TROLL WITCH
AND OTHERS
with Richard Corben and others
ISBN 978-1-59307-860-7 | $17.99

HELLBOY OMNIBUS
VOLUME 1:
Seed of Destruction
with John Byrne
ISBN 978-1-50670-666-5 | $24.99

DARKNESS CALLS
with Duncan Fegredo
ISBN 978-1-59307-896-6 | $19.99

THE WILD HUNT
with Duncan Fegredo
ISBN 978-1-59582-431-8 | $19.99

THE CROOKED MAN AND OTHERS
with Richard Corben
ISBN 978-1-59582-477-6 | $19.99

THE BRIDE OF HELL AND OTHERS
with Richard Corben, Kevin Nowlan, and
Scott Hampton
ISBN 978-1-59582-740-1 | $19.99

THE STORM AND THE FURY
with Duncan Fegredo
ISBN 978-1-59582-827-9 | $19.99

INTO THE SILENT SEA
with Gary Gianni
ISBN 978-1-50670-143-1 | $14.99

HELLBOY IN MEXICO
with Richard Corben, Fábio Moon,
Gabriel Bá, and others
ISBN 978-1-61655-897-0 | $19.99

HELLBOY: THE FIRST 20 YEARS
ISBN 978-1-61655-353-1 | $19.99

GARY GIANNI'S MONSTERMEN
AND OTHER SCARY STORIES
by Gary Gianni
ISBN 978-1-59582-829-3 | $24.99

HELLBOY: WEIRD TALES
ISBN 978-1-61655-510-8 | $24.99

HELLBOY: MASKS AND MONSTERS
with James Robinson and Scott Benefiel
ISBN 978-1-59582-567-4 | $17.99

HELLBOY: AN ASSORTMENT
OF HORRORS
ISBN 978-1-50670-343-5 | $14.99

HELLBOY: THE COMPLETE
SHORT STORIES VOLUME 1
with John Byrne, Corben, Fegredo,
and others
ISBN 978-1-50670-664-1 | $24.99

HELLBOY AND THE B.P.R.D.: 1952
with John Arcudi and Alex Maleev
ISBN 978-1-61655-660-0 | $19.99

HELLBOY AND THE B.P.R.D.: 1953
with Chris Roberson, Ben Stenbeck,
Paolo Rivera, and Joe Rivera
ISBN 978-1-61655-967-0 | $19.99

HELLBOY AND THE B.P.R.D.: 1954
with Roberson, Corben, Churilla, and others
ISBN 978-1-50670-207-0 | $19.99

HELLBOY AND THE B.P.R.D.: 1955
with Roberson, Churilla, Rivera,
and Shawn Martinbrough
ISBN 978-1-50670-531-6 | $19.99

THE HELLBOY 100 PROJECT
TPB: ISBN 978-1-61655-932-8 | $12.99
HC: ISBN 978-1-61655-933-5 | $24.99

NOVELS

HELLBOY: EMERALD HELL
by Tom Piccirilli
ISBN 978-1-59582-141-6 | $12.99

HELLBOY: THE ALL-SEEING EYE
by Mark Morris
ISBN 978-1-59582-142-3 | $12.99

HELLBOY: THE FIRE WOLVES
by Tim Lebbon
ISBN 978-1-59582-204-8 | $12.99

HELLBOY: THE ICE WOLVES
by Mark Chadbourn
ISBN 978-1-59582-205-5 | $12.99

AVAILABLE AT YOUR LOCAL COMICS SHOP OR BOOKSTORE! • To find a comics shop in your area, visit comicshoplocator.com.
For more information or to order direct visit DarkHorse.com or call 1-800-862-0052 Mon.–Fri. 9 AM to 5 PM Pacific Time.
Prices and availability subject to change without notice.

DarkHorse.com

Also by MIKE MIGNOLA

B.P.R.D. PLAGUE OF FROGS
VOLUME 1
with John Arcudi, Guy Davis, and others
TPB: ISBN 978-1-59582-675-6 | $19.99

VOLUME 2
ISBN 978-1-59582-676-3 | $24.99

VOLUME 3
ISBN 978-1-61655-622-8 | $24.99

VOLUME 4
ISBN 978-1-61655-641-9 | $24.99

1946–1948
with Joshua Dysart, Paul Azaceta, Fábio Moon,
Gabriel Bá, Max Fiumara, and Arcudi
ISBN 978-1-61655-646-4 | $34.99

BEING HUMAN
with Scott Allie, Arcudi, Davis, and others
ISBN 978-1-59582-756-2 | $17.99

VAMPIRE
with Moon and Bá
ISBN 978-1-61655-196-4 | $19.99

B.P.R.D. HELL ON EARTH
VOLUME 1
with Allie, Arcudi, Davis, Tyler Crook,
and others
ISBN 978-1-50670-360-2 | $34.99

VOLUME 2
ISBN 978-1-50670-388-6 | $34.99

A COLD DAY IN HELL
with Arcudi, Peter Snejbjerg, and
Laurence Campbell
ISBN 978-1-61655-199-5 | $19.99

THE REIGN OF THE BLACK FLAME
with Arcudi and Harren
ISBN 978-1-61655-471-2 | $19.99

THE DEVIL'S WINGS
with Arcudi, Campbell,
Joe Querio, and Crook
ISBN 978-1-61655-617-4 | $19.99

LAKE OF FIRE
with Arcudi and Crook
ISBN 978-1-61655-402-6 | $19.99

FLESH AND STONE
with Arcudi and Harren
ISBN 978-1-61655-762-1 | $19.99

METAMORPHOSIS
with Arcudi, Snejbjerg,
and Julián Totino Tedesco
ISBN 978-1-61655-794-2 | $19.99

END OF DAYS
with Arcudi and Campbell
ISBN 978-1-61655-910-6 | $19.99

THE EXORCIST
with Cameron Stewart, Chris Roberson,
and Mike Norton
ISBN 978-1-50670-011-3 | $19.99

COMETH THE HOUR
with Arcudi and Campbell
ISBN 978-1-50670-131-8 | $19.99

ABE SAPIEN
THE DROWNING
with Jason Shawn Alexander
ISBN 978-1-59582-185-0 | $17.99

THE DEVIL DOES NOT JEST
AND OTHER STORIES
with Arcudi, Harren, and others
ISBN 978-1-59582-925-2 | $17.99

DARK AND TERRIBLE
VOLUME 1
with Allie, S. Fiumara, and M. Fiumara
ISBN 978-1-50670-538-5 | $34.99

VOLUME 2
ISBN 978-1-50670-385-5 | $34.99

LOST LIVES
AND OTHER STORIES
with Allie, Arcudi, Michael Avon Oeming,
and others
ISBN 978-1-50670-220-9 | $19.99

LOBSTER JOHNSON
THE IRON PROMETHEUS
with Arcudi, Tonci Zonjic, and others
ISBN 978-1-59307-975-8 | $17.99

THE BURNING HAND
ISBN 978-1-61655-031-8 | $17.99

SATAN SMELLS A RAT
ISBN 978-1-61655-203-9 | $18.99

GET THE LOBSTER
ISBN 978-1-61655-505-4 | $19.99

THE PIRATE'S GHOST AND METAL
MONSTERS OF MIDTOWN
ISBN 978-1-50670-206-3 | $19.99

A CHAIN FORGED IN LIFE
ISBN 978-1-50670-178-3 | $19.99

WITCHFINDER
IN THE SERVICE OF ANGELS
with Ben Stenbeck
ISBN 978-1-59582-483-7 | $17.99

LOST AND GONE FOREVER
with Arcudi and John Severin
ISBN 978-1-59582-794-4 | $17.99

THE MYSTERIES OF UNLAND
with Kim Newman, Maura McHugh,
and Crook
ISBN 978-1-61655-630-3 | $19.99

CITY OF THE DEAD
with Roberson and Stenbeck
ISBN 978-1-50670-166-0 | $19.99

RISE OF THE BLACK FLAME
with Roberson and Christopher Mitten
ISBN 978-1-50670-155-4 | $19.99

**THE VISITOR: HOW AND
WHY HE STAYED**
with Roberson, Paul Grist,
and Bill Crabtree
ISBN 978-1-50670-345-9 | $19.99

**FRANKENSTEIN
UNDERGROUND**
with Stenbeck
ISBN 978-1-61655-782-9 | $19.99

**JOE GOLEM: OCCULT
DETECTIVE—**
THE RAT CATCHER & THE SUNKEN DEAD
with Christopher Golden and Patric Reynolds
ISBN 978-1-61655-964-9 | $24.99

BALTIMORE
THE PLAGUE SHIPS
with Golden, Stenbeck, and Peter Bergting
ISBN 978-1-59582-677-0 | $24.99

THE CURSE BELLS
ISBN 978-1-59582-674-9 | $24.99

A PASSING STRANGER
AND OTHER STORIES
ISBN 978-1-61655-182-7 | $24.99

CHAPEL OF BONES
ISBN 978-1-61655-328-9 | $24.99

THE APOSTLE AND THE WITCH OF HARJU
ISBN 978-1-61655-618-1 | $24.99

THE CULT OF THE RED KING
ISBN 978-1-61655-821-5 | $24.99

EMPTY GRAVES
ISBN 978-1-50670-042-7 | $24.99

THE RED KINGDOM
ISBN 978-1-50670-197-4 | $24.99

NOVELS
LOBSTER JOHNSON: THE SATAN FACTORY
with Thomas E. Sniegoski
ISBN 978-1-59582-203-1 | $12.95

JOE GOLEM AND THE DROWNING CITY
with Golden
ISBN 978-1-59582-971-9 | $99.99

BALTIMORE; OR, THE STEADFAST
TIN SOLDIER & THE VAMPIRE
with Golden
ISBN 978-1-61655-803-1 | $12.99

AVAILABLE AT YOUR LOCAL COMICS SHOP OR BOOKSTORE! • To find a comics shop in your area, visit comicshoplocator.com.
For more information or to order direct visit DarkHorse.com or call 1-800-862-0052 Mon.–Fri. 9 AM to 5 PM Pacific Time.
Prices and availability subject to change without notice.